LeAnne Howe

Shell Shaker

aunt lute books | San Francisco

First Edition

Aunt Lute Books
P.O. Box 410687
San Francisco, CA 94141

Front cover art: Jaune Quick-to-See Smith, *War Shirt, 1992,* Oil and mixed media collage on canvas diptych, 60 x 84 in. Museum purchase; funds provided by Tamar and Emil Weiss and prior gifts of Roland B. Swart, 1993.27 A-B The Montclair Art Museum, Montclair, New Jersey.

Back cover art: Mickey Howley (photographer and co-creator), Brad Cushman (owner and co-creator), "The Big Peanutmobile."

Cover and text design and typography: Kajun Design

Senior Editor: Joan Pinkvoss
Managing Editor: Shay Brawn
Production: Gina Gemello, Shahara Godfrey, Marielle Gomez, Tasha Marks, Tamara Martínez, Laura Reizman, Golda Sargento

This book was funded in part by grants from the LEF Foundation, the California Arts Council, and the National Endowment for the Arts.

Library of Congress Cataloging-in-Publication Data

Howe, LeAnne.
    Shell shaker / by LeAnne Howe.—1st ed.
        p. cm.
    ISBN 1-879960-61-3
        1. United States—History—Colonial period, ca. 1600-1775—Fiction. 2. Choctaw Indians—Fiction. 3. Organized crime—Fiction. 4. Casinos—fiction. I. Title.

PS3608.O95 S48 2001
813'.6—dc21

2001046250

Printed in the United States of America
10 9 8 7 6

For Joseph, Randall, Chelsey, Alyssa, and April,
And especially for Jim Wilson,
with love

Portions of this book appeared in slightly altered form in the following publications:

"Blood Sacrifice," *Through The Eye Of The Deer,* Aunt Lute Books, 1999.
"Shell Shakers" *Story,* F & W Publications, Volume 44.3.
"Danse de l'amour, Danse de mort," *Earth Song, Sky Spirit: An Anthology of Native American Writers,* Doubleday & Co., 1992.
"Dance of the Dead," *Looking Glass,* San Diego University Press, 1991.
"The Bone Picker," *Fiction International #20,* 1991.

Songs lyrics that appear in the chapter "Funerals By Delores" are from Arrah Wanna, An Irish Indian Matrimonial Venture. Music by Theodore Morse, words by Jack Drislane, published by F. B. Haviland Publishing Company, 1906.

Acknowledgments

For the generous support while researching and writing this book, I want to thank the National Endowment for the Humanities; Smithsonian Institution's Native American Community Scholar Program at the National Museum of American History, Washington D.C.; MacDowell Colony; Ragdale Foundation; Atlantic Center for the Arts; and D'Arcy McNickle Center for American Indian History, Newberry Library, Chicago, Illinois.

Sincere thanks go to my editor, Joan Pinkvoss, and Gina Gemello and all the staff at Aunt Lute Books for their patience with me and for their meticulous efforts in bringing *Shell Shaker* to life.

For their encouragement while I was an MFA candidate at Vermont College of Norwich University, I am indebted to: Christopher Noel, Mary Grimm, Ellen Lesser, Pamela Painter, Doug Glover, and Lois Rosenthal, editor of *Story*, who published an early chapter of the novel.

I am thankful for the friends who've supported me over the years and never lost faith in my ability to finish the book: Lisa Kepple, Mary BlackBonnet, Jeanne Claire van Ryzin, Dean Rader, Spencer Smith, Wendy Botham, Alan Velie, Robert Clinton, Linda Farve, Gwen and Brantley Willis, Carol Miller, Jean M. O'Brien, Carla McDonald, Brenda Child, Patricia K. Galloway, Helen Tanner, Harvey Markowitz, Rayna Green, Theda Perdue, Mike Green (and all the members of the NEH Summer Seminar in Lexington, Kentucky, in 1991), Professor Ray McCullars, and the late Professor Clinton Keeler, who said, "you can write." A very special thanks to professor, author, and friend Geary Hobson, and to my dear friends the late Roxy Gordon and Judy Gordon of Wowapi Press, who published my first collection of short stories in 1985.

I say yakoke, yakoke, many thanks, to my beloved relatives, those who are related by blood, and those who are related the Indian way: Izola Hoeh and the late Richard Hoeh; Kevin Lynch; the late Christine Poyor; Billy Poynor; Gayle Goomda; Kathy Poynor; Justin Data and the late Scott Morrison; and for Iva Zenorda Cecil, who taught me to tell stories. For my extended Sioux family: Susan Power; Susan Power Sr.; Ken Bordeaux, family, friend, and mentor; and Craig Howe.

And finally, for Bruce Fry, who still believed in me after I lost a million dollars.

1 | Blood Sacrifice

YANÀBI TOWN, EASTERN DISTRICT OF THE CHOCTAWS
SEPTEMBER 22, 1738
AUTUMNAL EQUINOX

A no ma Chahta sia hoke oke. Call me Shakbatina, a Shell Shaker. I am an *Inholahta* woman, born into the tradition of our grandmother, the first Shell Shaker of our people. We are the peacemakers for the Choctaws.

The story of the *Inholahta* begins a long time ago when Grandmother was very young. The town where she lived was far away and near a river. Food was plentiful. Even Grandmother's cabin was dripping with beans. Made of green canes and lashed together with vines that had crawled out of the earth, her cabin continually sprouted new growth.

In the middle of the town's square grounds, where all the celebrations occurred, everything was wide open. Like a party. Every day the men sang with a drum in the square grounds while the women tended their children and drank from gourds filled with sweet peach juice. Life was a series of games and dances. The town champion of *toli,* the stickball game, was our grandfather. His name was Tuscalusa, Black Warrior, and he was a great leader, robust and dynamic. After the stickball games, which took many days and nights to play out, Tuscalusa would dance with only one woman, our grandmother. They were so beautiful together. Their skin was smooth, and their teeth were white and straight. They sounded alike, so potent their voices could call the lightning. We are watery versions of them.

There was once a road, an ancient trade route that began in the east. Like the wind gathering, receding, returning, it went through hundreds of towns until it reached the middle of the square grounds where Grandfather played stickball. Down this road came a terrible story. It said:

> A dangerous enemy has arrived on our shores with weapons of fire. He is camped a few days away in the town of Talisi. He will devour your family. Soon he will be on the move again. He's a very different kind of Osano, bloodsucker, he always hungers for more.

When Tuscalusa heard this, he and his warriors began to make plans to save the people from the invader. Because he was a well-known stick-ball player, he would be the one to lead the enemy into a trap. He realized he would probably have to die in order to lure the *Osano* away.

It was then our grandmother did an extraordinary thing. She built a fire and she strapped the empty shells of turtles around each ankle. She didn't sing aloud because she was afraid the children would hear sorrow in her voice, so she only moved her lips in silent prayers. For four days and nights she never stopped dancing around the fire, extolling the heroics of the man she loved. Amazingly, the fire did not go out. *Miko Luak,* fire's spirit, was so spellbound by her story that he would not leave for fear of missing important details of Tuscalusa's courage.

On the fourth night, Grandmother's ankles were swollen and bloody where the shells and leather twine had cut into them. The ground around the fire was red with her blood, but still she danced, and it was then *Miko Luak* took pity on her. He carried her prayers up to *Itilauichi,* the Autumnal Equinox, who listened with compassion. *Itilauichi* learned that Grandmother had begun her ceremony on his special day of the year.

"What you have endured confirms that you are sincere," he said. "Through your sacrifice of blood you have proven yourself worthy. The things you desire for the people will be given." Then he gave her this song and told her to sing it when she needed his help.

> Itilauichi, *Autumnal Equinox, on your day when I sing this song you will make things even.*

After learning that *Itilauichi* had given his word to Grandmother, our ancestors prepared for what was coming. The next twelve days were spent in ceremony. Tuscalusa and his stickball players drank black drink and prayed around the fire. Grandmother taught her sisters the Snake Dance and how to imitate the movements of a coiling and uncoiling snake, a sign of power. She also showed the women how to tie on the turtle shells without cutting their legs.

On the thirteenth day all ceremonies stopped. It was time for good-byes. Tuscalusa put a tiny black stone in our grandmother's mouth and told her to swallow it. He said it represented his spirit. She presented him with a *kasmo*, a feathered shawl with locks of her hair woven through it. She told him the *kasmo* represented her spirit and if he wore it they would never be parted. That was what Itilauichi had promised her.

The next morning, Tuscalusa wrapped the *kasmo* around his shoulders and left to meet the invader, Hispano de Soto. His plan was to pretend to be captured by the enemy. Tuscalusa allowed himself to be put in chains, and he bowed his head like a pitiful child. De Soto, the most greedy *Osano*, was unable to reason that Tuscalusa was leading him into a trap. He believed our grandfather was a coward who had surrendered without a fight. Unbeknownst to de Soto, the man standing before him was only a shell. All that Grandfather had been, his essence, was held inside of Grandmother for safekeeping. It was part of their sacred plan.

For seven more days in the month of *Hash Bissa,* October, Hispano de Soto marched Grandfather to the town of Mabila. All along the way, Grandfather's *iksa,* group, surrendered to the *Hispanos.* But the Mabilians, our clever cousins, were in on the plan to drive de Soto out of the region and they entertained the invaders with a bountiful feast. Tuscalusa and his stickball players waited for the signal to begin fighting. At the appointed time Grandfather's shell reunited with his body, and the battle began. The stickball players fought bravely against the foreigners. The *Hispanos* attacked the walls of the Mabilian fort, cutting them down and setting fire to the houses within. The whole town was burned. Unspeakable acts were then committed by *Hispano Osano.* They fell into a barbaric blood lust and cut off the heads and hands of the stickball players, and the Mabilians. Later, the *Hispanos* displayed them wherever they went as souvenirs of their courage.

Grandmother instantly knew something was wrong. The stone churned in her stomach and she vomited it into her hands. It had changed color from black to gray and had holes in it like a skull, and she knew Tuscalusa was dead. Instead of crying for her husband, which was her duty, she gathered her six younger sisters and made a powerful speech. She said Tuscalusa and his *iksa* brothers gave their lives so the women and children would not become the slaves of foreigners. She told her sisters they would mourn their husbands after they were safely away from the invaders.

All agreed. The women put away their sorrow until the time was right and they could properly mourn for the dead. Our grandmother sang the song *Itilauichi* taught her—and that's when it happened. A moment opened. A flurry of color took flight. Lips opened in awe, then transformed into multicolored beaks and wings. Voices thinned out, and tangled in throats that turned into other voices. A song of birds. Grandmother and her sisters soared over the heads of the *Hispanos* and dropped excrement on them. Then they flew away. For many days and nights, people from other clans said that they saw a flock of strange birds crisscrossing the *Ahepatanichi*, the river that caused all life to rise up. When these variegated creatures reached our present homelands, their wings fell off. The sisters went back to living according to customs. They built our seven original Choctaw towns. Yanàbi Town is one of them.

After living through the horrors of warfare, Grandmother decided she would become a peacemaker. She taught her sisters the art of negotiation and how to find solutions to disputes. She became well-known as a leader who spoke for peace and the fair exchange of goods between towns.

When Grandmother's life came to an end many years later, *Itilauichi* kept his promise to her. She was strapped on her burial scaffold and released by the bone-picking ceremony to join Tuscalusa. Together they reside high on Holy Spirits Bluff. Sometimes they appear as eagles, or the kettling hawks suspended in the sky. Other times they are the mated swans we see along the rivers and bayous. They have never left us. Because Grandmother shed blood for the people's survival, our women continue to honor *Itilauichi* by shaking shells.

I am a Shell Shaker. I know when it is time to return to the earth. Today, I will tear myself from the arms of my family and stand in for my first daughter, Anoleta, who has been wrongly accused of the murder of a Chickasaw woman from the Red Fox village. I will sacrifice myself, knowing that peace will follow between our two tribes.

I study the expressions of the Inholahta gathered in my yard. They seem cold, and indifferent to the fact that the Red Fox people are waiting outside of our town to conduct my execution. Everyone knows what must happen now; my death will avert war between the Choctaws and the Chickasaws. I can see uncertainty spreading across Anoleta's face like an affliction. She is my first daughter and bears all the responsibility of heading our clan after I am executed. Her thick hair is matted and hangs in clumps down her back. Already Anoleta mourns me, although my deathblow has not been struck. A few might want to blame her for what is going to happen so I must keep talking until all the *Inholahta* people agree to support my decision. They must also publicly say that Anoleta is innocent of killing the Chickasaw woman. This will guarantee that in the future she will be thought of as an honorable leader.

In a way, I am responsible for the disaster at the Red Fox village. I had sent Anoleta to them as an emissary of our town. I was still recovering from the *Inkilish okla* disease that had killed so many of our people. She was to exchange vegetable seeds and bowls filled with special healing plants for flints. Then something strange happened. A woman accused Anoleta of stealing the affections of her husband. Both women had known for a long time they were married to the same man, so I don't understand her actions. It is not unusual for warriors to marry women from different towns as long as they can provide meat for both families. But when the woman from the Red Fox village was found dead the next morning, the people said Anoleta was the killer. I did not know at the time this incident would affect my family for generations to come.

I wait for a public reply from the *Inholahta*. Why are they so hesitant? I have talked with everyone over the past month. I have explained repeatedly why my death will assuage the Red Fox clan and the Chickasaws. Don't they want to avoid bloodshed? When I can stand their silence no longer, I begin to chant loudly:

> *Hatak okla hut okchaya bilia hoh-illi bila,* the people are ever living, ever dying, ever alive!
> *Hatak okla hut okchaya bilia hoh-illi bila,* the people are ever living, ever dying, ever alive!

Finally, one old aunt, too old to stand, returns my chant from her seat at our council fire.

> *Hatak okla hut okchaya bilia hoh-illi bila.*

Then another woman and her brother join in until all of my clan, some seventy people, begin chanting:

> *Hatak okla hut okchaya bilia hoh-illi bila.*
> *Hatak okla hut okchaya bilia hoh-illi bila.*

Hatak okla hut okchaya bilia hoh-illi bila.
Hatak okla hut okchaya bilia hoh-illi bila.

"Very well," I say. "We are ever living, ever dying—you agree. If that is so, you must support me and honor the traditions of the first Shell Shaker, the oldest of seven sisters, our savior and creator, Grandmother of Birds."

I fold my arms and again wait patiently for a relative to stand up and praise my strategies for saving Anoleta and averting war. They must declare my daughter's innocence and vow to protect her. But they sit silent as owls. I sniff the gray stone I hold in my hand, the one that belonged to Grandmother of Birds. It smells of sediment and potato roots and other things I carry in my satchel. After the bone-picking ceremony all my possessions will be divided among my daughters. My essence will be mingled with theirs. As it should be.

A small boy bawls, and runs to me crying, *"Alleh, alleh, alleh."* A child's cry. Someone has taken his toy bow. When I pick him up in my arms to hug him, he pulls back and looks inquisitively at the hole in my eyebrow and the scar rivulets on my cheek. I gaze back at him. I want him to remember what the *Inkilish okla* disease has done to me.

Finally I speak again. "Are we not the *Inholahta,* the ones who walk the thinking path? Do you agree that sacrificing myself to make peace with the Red Fox clan and the Chickasaws is a good decision?"

The child looks away from my face and follows the crowd with interest as they murmur softly to each other. Again I wait for someone to respond. I search the crowd, anticipating the words that should be spoken. I wonder how Onatima, my mother's mother, managed to wait for months in total silence when she was unhappy with the speeches the men were making in councils.

I still remember the day when she stopped speaking to me, too. I'd offended her by stealing vermilion to paint my face. Onatima would not acknowledge me for weeks afterwards. That day had begun with an unusual event. A warrior was making a ceremony to his enemy in the center of Yanàbi Town. I was curious and wanted to watch, while the other children were frightened and ran away. Even though I was young, I had known warriors who'd been dragged off by marauding bands of *Inkilish okla.* I wanted to see what would happen to me if I were captured by our enemy, so I watched and waited.

The warrior, Ilapintabi, Kills It Himself, jammed the head of his victim onto a post, then thrust his sharp blade into the soft flesh of the neck, fastening it to the wood. Then he painted his own face red. Tied hawk feathers in his hair. Danced and sang in a defiant gravel voice:

Head man of the horseflies, you cannot stop what's coming. My face is painted so you cannot see me. I ravage, ravage, ravage. There I went along and you saw my tracks. Head man of the horseflies, my face is painted so you cannot see me. You saw my tracks and cried. Too late. Head man of the horseflies you cannot stop what is coming.

Ilapintabi's cries washed over me like a soothing rain. To me, he'd become a magnificent bird. His hawk feathers kettled in the air just above his head, like amputated glory whirling in the wind. After his song I was cleansed of fear.

I remained with Ilapintabi until my mother wrestled me away to help gather food for our meal. I hurriedly collected corn, beans, and squash from our fields, then raced back to the center of town. Ilapintabi was still there, but the head of the killed was gone. Disappointed that I'd missed the last part of his ceremony, I walked within inches of Ilapintabi. He was now covered head to toe in white chalk, signifying that he'd made peace with his adversary. He sat totally still and did not move when I touched his face.

So that was *na tohbi,* the something white. I'd overheard the elders discussing it many times, but until that moment I had never understood what they meant. Ilapintabi had slipped out of his body and into *na tohbi.*

In my eagerness to join him, I'd run back to Onatima's cabin and stolen a small pot of vermilion and a knife. With a stick I dabbed the red paint all over my face. I held my small palms out to *Hashtali,* whose eye is the Sun. My feet moved in a circle and I stretched my arms like a soaring bird.

Just as I charged back to show Ilapintabi, Onatima grabbed me off the path to town. Her mouth dropped wide as a scoop when she saw the knife clutched in my hand like a weapon and my face painted for war. She plucked the knife from my hands and mumbled ancient prayers. Her maternal belly sagged and heaved as she searched for the vermilion. I scrambled to find it, but it was lost. Mortified, I ran out of the yard and threw myself into the cold river and cried as I washed the red stains from my face and body.

After a month of endless silences, when it seemed to me that my shadow shrank to a tiny reflection of itself, Onatima finally spoke to me.

"Come and sit by the fire, *alla tek,* my girl. Let's have a smoke and gossip about our cousins, the Crawfish People. Have I told you why they call us the Long Hairs?"

My spirit revived. Being asked to gossip with the old woman was a sign I could again sit at her campfire. I believed the incident was forgotten, but I was wrong.

When Onatima lay dying many years later, I offered her water, and she refused me. "Never steal from your family, we lose confidence in you and won't drink from your hands. Red is the color for warriors. What a terrible fate for a granddaughter of peacemakers."

A wave of shame filled me so thoroughly that I cut a lock of my hair to show my disgrace. This was the lesson I would not forget, one that I taught my daughters. Never steal from your family. Never wear the vermilion unless you plan to kill or seek revenge.

I am living in a very different time from Onatima. Wars are more prevalent. The *alikchi,* our doctors, can't cure the diseases of the invaders. The epidemic that ate my skin still tortures me. Patience is a thing I can no longer afford. At last I shout, "Do you accept my daughter's innocence?"

"*Yummak osh alhpesa,*" replies one of the women. "That is it."

When I hear this I am relieved. "Then you also accept my decision to take my daughter's place in the blood sacrifice."

"*Yummak osh alhpesa.* The *Inholahta* people honor your decision and we take Anoleta into our hearts," she answers.

"On this day I will follow our Choctaw ancestors to our Mother Mound at Nanih Waiya. When released by the bone-picking, I will grow and sprout up like green corn. From the mound I will watch over our people. Do not cry for me, I am a fast grower." Then my relatives repeat their pledge to me four more times.

I am scarcely aware of what I am doing after that. I turn to my brother, Nitakechi, and ask him to invite the Red Fox people to eat with us. It is proper for them to join us in a feast, a final gesture of reconciliation. In a short while he comes back with a large delegation of hungry Red Fox people. He motions for the men to move to one side of the yard, and the women to the other. He brings a large pot of corn and deer meat soup, and our guests use their hands like greedy spoons to fill their mouths.

I watch my brother closely as happy Red Fox people, wearing their finest regalia, shove their way toward him expecting more food. A young Red Fox boy begs for more and Nitakechi dutifully walks to the fire to fetch more meat. I hold my breath when I see how his hands tremble; his eyes have the menacing look of *hatak apa*, a cannibal. I know they are testing him, trying to see if he really wants to make peace. When he returns with a haunch of deer, our eyes meet briefly and I hear him say to the pushy boy, "Yes, feed your hunger. Next time you will feed me." Then he walks away on the verge of tears. I know why. He wanted to kill that child. For *Inholahta* elders this is heresy.

I admit I do not understand the Red Fox clan of the Chickasaws, even though we are cousins. We share hunting lands and we understand each other's language. But unlike us, the Red Fox people are envious and selfish. I think this explains why the victim hated my daughter. When she saw how beautiful Anoleta was, she must have flown into a rage.

I am told that the Red Fox woman ran at my girl like a rabid animal shouting, *"isht ahollo,"* witch, and throwing handfuls of rotting turkey heads at my girl. Jealousy must have consumed her. I can think of no other reason. Soon four other Red Fox women captured Anoleta. They held her down and cut handfuls of her long hair. Then they chased her out of their yard and pushed her into the swamp. Anoleta had to flee through the murky waters and high grass until she reached a town within our district. The next morning, the jealous Red Fox woman was found lying on the floor of her cabin in a grisly mess. Her legs were spread wide apart and bloody. Her face was frozen in a sexed smile, as if delighted to death by the worker ants eating her. Cradled in the crook of her arm was her shriveled heart, torn from her body.

At the time, I thought it was delicious justice. After all, they'd cut Anoleta's hair and thrown her to the alligators. But the method of murder was not our way. Yanàbi Town people always aim for the head. Not the heart. The Red Fox people were outraged and whipped themselves into a frenzy. They claimed Anoleta had committed the murder in a fit of revenge. They demanded blood for blood. In preparation for war, the Red Fox dispatched one hundred warriors and elders to seek the support of the Alibamu Conchatys.

The Alibamu Conchatys are the cousins of both the Choctaws and Chickasaws, and they often judge the disputes between squabbling tribes. An old woman who remembered our family sent a runner to Yanàbi Town to warn us that the Red Fox were crying for war. They were famous whiners. The Red Fox never missed an opportunity to turn misfortune into providence. Think of all the food they save by eating out of others' hands.

The night we received the news Nitakechi lit the pipes in the council. He said the Chickasaw woman from the Red Fox village was dead because the *Inkilish okla* wanted our land.

How could this be? Women were the land. *Intek aliha,* the sisterhood, controlled the rich fertile fields that sustained the people. Killing a woman for land would be like killing the future. "Why would the Red Fox allow such a thing to happen?" I asked.

"Because they are under the influence of the *Inkilish okla,* who map their lands with the graves of women. They have convinced the greedy Red Fox clan that Anoleta is a killer. If we go to war against Red Fox clan, the rest of the Chickasaws will join in the fight against us. Then the *Inkilish okla* will devour everyone's land after we're all dead. The *Inkilish okla* are somehow responsible for this woman's death, I believe it," said my brother. "If the Red Fox people weren't so busy making brats they'd see it, too."

I knew my brother was speaking the truth. The *Inkilish okla* were evil. They had traded me disease for our corn. It was in their blankets, the ones I brought back to Yanàbi Town. The disease destroyed many of our people and knapped my body like a piece of flint. Since then, I'd often dreamed of hanging *Inkilish okla* intestines in the trees so everyone could see their shit.

"Kill them. Kill them all, *Inkilish okla* and Red Fox alike," I said. "As for me, I will speak to my friend Bienville and ask him to join us in wiping out the Chickasaws."

Nitakechi smoked a long time before answering me. He was embarrassed that I'd shown my true feelings, which was very improper for an *Inholahta* woman.

"No," he said. "It is better to negotiate. If we merely defeat the Red Fox we will end up feeding them the rest of their lives. And ours."

Seven days later, Yanàbi Town sent two hundred and fifty men from the *Imoklasha iksa* to the Alibamu Conchatys' town. Our warriors stained their feet and legs red, and set fire to bundles of cane. They challenged the Red Fox to come out of the protective bosom of the Alibamu Conchatys and die like men. We had to show our strength so that everyone, Red Fox and Alibamu Conchatys alike, would want to negotiate. But I was told the Red Fox laughed and laughed when they saw the warriors from Yanàbi Town. Who knows the humor of the Red Fox? Probably they laughed because, like dogs, they'd shitted themselves in fear.

The Alibamu Conchatys elders agreed to judge the conflict. I knew what this would mean. Feeding hundreds of mouths was a daunting task. I was told that even the council of leaders had to hunt so there would be enough meat to feed everyone. I could almost see the grandmothers and the nursing women with sick babies stirring pots of *pashofa* night and day, holding off bellies hungry for war. Everyone would remember this time as the costly season.

My brother, sent as a representative of the *Inholahta*, was up against a flamboyant talker at the councils. A Red Fox woman had covered her face in blue paint as a sign that she was telling the truth. She had monopolized all meetings. She repeated her claims that Anoleta had killed her friend.

Nitakechi had mistakenly believed that his audience could be swayed by logic. He explained that Anoleta was not a witch, and that she knew nothing about conjuring the hearts out of people. He admitted that she might have improperly bragged about her husband, calling him the *Imataha Chitto,* the greatest giver, the one who would one day unite the tribes. My brother explained that Anoleta was not a killer, nor was she jealous of the Red Fox woman. He used all the methods of peacemaking that had been passed down from Grandmother of Birds. He tried to explain that this incident was another plan of the foreigners to divide and conquer us. "The foreigners will never be strong enough to destroy us. We will do it for them." He talked and cajoled the council for four weeks, until his voice grew hoarse.

A long time had passed before my brother returned from the Alibamu Conchatys. His face had the awful appearance of someone who had not slept for many days. He tried not to show his pain. I didn't listen carefully to what he said. Just distant thinking. I already knew what he was going to say. The Alibamu Conchatys believed my daughter must be the killer because she and the Red Fox woman were both wives of the renegade warrior, Red Shoes. The warrior we'd once taken into our hearts had grown into a giant *Osano* in the tradition of Hispano de Soto. Red Shoes always hungered for more. Often he would spy on our towns for the *Inkilish okla* in return for trade goods and weapons. How had he hidden his true self for so long; that was a question I repeatedly asked myself.

Several days before my brother's return, my husband, Koi Chitto, had come to my cabin to present me with a gift. A porcupine skin. He had obtained it when he hunted with the Alibamu Conchatys and Red Fox warriors while the negotiations were going on to save our daughter. He reminded me that when our ancestors lived further north they believed the porcupine was another symbol of the sun. He said that in the moonlight the animal's quills seemed to radiate light, a sign that one thing can hold the essence of another. Then he left. I realized why he had told me that story. It was his way of saying that nothing is ever lost.

I had prepared the skin and stitched the stories of our Seven Grandmothers into a sash that I wrapped around me. I felt like it was my protection against what was coming. I told all this to Nitakechi the day he brought the news. We smoked tobacco and for the longest time talked of our family. Of small things. The color of sky, the taste of this year's berries, the sweet smell of green corn in spring. We also spoke at length about who the *Imataha Chitto* might be. I teased him by saying that the *Imataha Chitto* was most likely a woman. "Probably the woman in your dreams. I think it is time you found her and became her husband." He laughed, saying only, "You are right."

I reassured Nitakechi that my decision to exchange my life for Anoleta's life was final, and I exacted his promise that he would prepare my body for the burial scaffold after the execution. When evening came my brother said he would remember this day the rest of his life. He took a look around my cabin and said it's always been like this between us. I said yes it has. And it will be after my death.

After carting the last basket of smoked meat to the Red Fox women in my yard, I lug pots of cool water from the ox-bow pond for them to wash their hands in. This is my final lesson to my daughters. How to make *Inholahta* hospitality. In this case how to host gangs. Finally I go to find a comfortable seat away from everyone. I want to be alone with my thoughts.

I find a pale wild onion pushing up through the dirt. Narrow and bent. It is the last of its kind this season. I am down to my own one self too, so I pull it up and bite into it. Pungent and tough, the onion kisses my tongue. The taste curls my lips into a smile.

I turn toward the cypress trees. I watch the light cap them in blazing reds and yellows. The forest breathes heavily around me. At sunset the bluebirds chitter in the tops of the trees. People and things I've forgotten come rushing back to me. Grandmothers planting corn, making pots, cutting cane for baskets, scraping hides, reciting morning prayers, singing sleep to tired children. I long to have lived to see my own grandchildren, but this is not meant to be.

I brush the dirt off my hands. It seems to me that an entirely different woman danced beneath these trees with my husband Koi Chitto so many years ago. In those days my hair streamed down my back and made a cape over my arms. Now it is thin and stringy like a starving dog's. The effects of the disease.

The night we met, I wore a short deerskin dress fastened around my breasts that left my buttocks partially exposed. At the time it was fashionable for young girls to flaunt themselves that way. I felt beautiful when I stepped onto the dance grounds. There were so many dancers that night. I had to strain to hear the singers above the hundreds of dancers. When Koi Chitto walked across my mother's yard and led me in the Pleasure Dance, I quit listening to the song and thought about him as a potential husband.

I'd noticed him two seasons before, but decided he wasn't much. Too bony. He was already making children with an older woman from Yashoo Town. I thought he wasn't a good enough hunter to support two families. But that night I changed my mind. He seemed mysterious and strange. He held my hands so tightly during the last dance that the juice of his palms crawled up my arms and entered my mouth like a sweet vapor. Swallowing, I'd tasted love.

Koi Chitto was a warrior from *Imoklasha*, the war clan. Since there were no rules against multiple marriages, I moved him into my mother's house. Within a season my belly swelled in contentment. Anoleta was born, followed by Neshoba, and Haya. The next twenty years he lived and hunted around our territory, providing meat and hides for us. It seems Koi Chitto tethered my heart to his skinny bones and there I remain.

I stretch my legs. They still ache from the *Inkilish okla* disease. When all the sick and dying were placed in sweat tents I prayed to the disease to kill me. Prayed that my relatives would abandon me. Prayed to the fire to smother me. After I recovered I asked Neshoba to put Koi Chitto's things outside the door of my cabin. He picked them up and never returned to my bed. He understood that I couldn't bear to have him look at the disease under my skirt. Until the catastrophe at the Red Fox village I hadn't known why I lived and others died. Now it is clear to me.

I am to be the first warrior killed in battle against the Red Fox. Red Shoes and the *Inkilish okla* must be planning to attack our town.

Suddenly, I realize that there is so little time left. I have so much to do. When I reach my cabin Haya is crying gulping sobs. I pull her to me and tell her that she can close her eyes if she wants, or Neshoba will take her away before it happens.

"You can't go, Mother," she says in a pleading voice. "I will take Anoleta's place in the blood revenge. *Chishke apela*... help me Mother, nothing good will come of me after you are gone."

I blame myself for Haya's nervousness. Before I had realized I was making another baby, I'd eaten too much rabbit. Too much rabbit makes a child twitch. It can't be helped now. All these rules for making babies—too much deer and you bring a child who runs away; too much big cat and you bring a child who turns assassin. I hope my girls remember all the rules.

I put my head on Haya's shoulder. We have been through this before. All the reasons have been discussed. I try to comfort her. I tell her that she must understand she cannot stop what is coming. "If I do what you ask, what will your uncle or your father think of me?" I say. "I gave you life, now I must go first. Anoleta and Neshoba and your aunts will look after you. You will never be alone."

I motion for my second daughter Neshoba to come. "Quick, quickly, while I still have strength." When she reaches us, I give Grandmother's stone to Neshoba. "Take Haya into the forest," I say, "and do not to return until night has come." Then I kneel down and cradle my baby. Although Haya is no longer an infant, I still think of her that way because she is my youngest. I push the hair out of her eyes and kiss her again, inhaling her innocent breath. Then I give her to Neshoba. Haya begins to weep, but her sister takes her by the hand and I watch them disappear through a canebrake. I want to run after them, touch them one more time—but I don't dare. I might yield. What I am, my essence, will live inside my daughters.

Next, I speak softly with Anoleta. I tell her to use all the skills I have taught her. "Ask our friend, Jean Baptiste Bienville, to fight Red Shoes and the *Inkilish okla*. Bienville hates them as much as we do." I hold her for the longest time and she promises to fulfill her obligations. Finally, I enter my cabin to remove my sticky work dress and prepare myself. I massage the swell of pockmarks on my sagging breasts. My arms are full of flesh and heavy as porous wood. The epidemic has chewed me to pieces. After today, I will be through with pain. I pull on my white deer-skin dress and fasten the black and white porcupine sash across my shoulder like a shield.

I rub my fingers over the threads and feel strangely calm. At last I understand why Onatima was so angry at me all those years ago. I was born into the peace clan, but in my heart I've always chosen a weapon. It is the reason I was attracted to the warrior Ilapintabi, and tried to imitate his war dance. The reason why my first instincts were to wipe out the *Inkilish okla* for bringing us a disease. Why I now seek revenge.

I decide that as a final gesture I will show the people my true self. After all, I am a descendant of two powerful ancestors, Grandmother of Birds and Tuscalusa. I dig around in my basket and find a pot of vermilion. Plunging two fingers in the paint, I mark my cheeks and spread the vermilion over my chin and down my neck the old-fashioned way Ilapintabi once stained his face. When I finish I whoop *tushka panya*, a warrior's death cry. Then I hiss the words, "Grandmother, do you see me? I will make the peace for you, but in my heart I want a war!"

When I walk out of my cabin some of the *Inholahta* women put on a face of stone to hide their surprise. Others look down and squint at their hands, but clearly they understand. Dressed in white with my face painted red, I have split myself in two. My message to my people is that we must fight to survive.

Next, I address the Red Fox clan in my yard. Out of the corner of my eye I see Koi Chitto standing next to my brother. So, he could not stay away. Like a warrior controlling my fear, I sing my last song.

Head man of the horseflies, my face is painted so you cannot see me. You'll see my tracks and cry. Too late. Head man of the horseflies, my face is painted so you cannot see me. Too late, head man, you cannot stop what is coming.

The Choctaws of Yanàbi Town erupt in laughter at my insulting song. No one from the Red Fox village smiles. I look at Koi Chitto and he beams with affection. Nods his approval, and I continue.

Head man of the horseflies, my face is painted so you cannot see me. I am the Shell Shaker, a descendant of Grandmother of Birds and Tuscalusa. The actions I take honor them both. I am standing in for my first daughter, Anoleta, to make the peace. Itilauichi, Autumnal Equinox, on your day when I sing this song you will make things even.

The Red Fox politely accept my death in exchange for Anoleta's life and agree that there will be no war between the Choctaws and Chickasaws. In the presence of my family and all the people gathered in my yard, I stretch out on a log, face down, close my eyes, and pray for courage.

As is the custom, a relative of the Red Fox victim carries out the execution. A one-eyed elder named Imayatabe steps forward slowly with his war club. For the longest time I hear him speak gentle words to the people, asking that the path be wiped clean between our two tribes.

Then there is silence.

I suck in my breath. I feel an icy hot explosion in my head. Deafening. Blood gurgles from my mouth. My hands spring to my head involuntarily, blood is seeping out of my head and flecks of bone are strewn through my hair. My arms jerk wildly, like a wounded bird trying to fly away, as the old man hits me again. I sense movement all around. Maybe Koi Chitto angrily knocks the man away? I feel my body twitch, perhaps someone turns me over. I can no longer see, my head is unraveling.

In that last moment, I have the burning desire to live and cling to the body. It is lean and compact... Koi Chitto... *Hah!*... he is here. I can feel him saying, give it up. I gasp for air and have no fear.

I feel myself growing younger in this place. I grieve for my daughters when I hear their rhythmic wailings. I grieve for the red-raw faces, teeth, eyes, cheeks, and black-haired people. I grieve for the Seven Grandmothers dancing in the distance as they shrink to almost nothing, then reappear as a flock of multicolored birds, just beyond my reach.

An unknown language floats around me. Each word is in Old Code that I must decipher. Suddenly there are streaks of white and the delicious scent of tobacco fills the air as the spirit of an animal appears. Big Mother Porcupine walks into view and takes me by the hand. I open my mouth to speak but my thoughts escape into the wind.

2 | The Will To Power

Durant, Oklahoma
Sunday, September 22, 1991
Autumnal Equinox

Auda Billy sits on the side of her twin bed in the small upstairs bedroom of the house where she was born. At four A.M., the house is warm as wool and peopled with aunts and uncles, rabbits, ghosts of rabbits, and other relatives.

The house was built over a century ago on the edge of the town, the area now known as Old Durant. Old Durant stopped narrating to the Choctaws after the whites took over the town in 1907. Statehood for Oklahoma. The spirits moved away, shed their skin that bound land and people together. Now they've returned, pulling stars down from the sky, causing a fifty-mile-long prairie fire. From the Mineral Bayou Bridge in Durant to the outskirts of Hugo, Oklahoma, all the land along Highway 70 is seared black like a piece of burnt toast.

It's a sign. They've come back to pick a fight.

Auda's family knows nothing of the red fires that rage across the town, barely missing them. They can't hear the tormented cries of the farmers and merchants who are watching their properties go up in flames. They don't know about the Bokchito minister who chokes to death on smoke and soot, trying to save his church named "Radiance Is Accomplished." They've been rocked to sleep along with all the other Indians by the powerful medicine of *Itilauichi*. It happens that way sometimes. When the earth shifts, and day and night are in perfect balance, Indians have all the luck.

But Auda doesn't feel lucky. After working all day Saturday, she rushed home and locked herself in her bedroom. At midnight she showered. Two hours later she showered, again. At four A.M. she's given up her ceaseless to-ing and fro-ing. Her chronic hunger for water. She isn't sick. She isn't mad. Dazed, she eats the room with her stare until the furniture, her clothes, even the cool silver and turquoise dots of her bedroom wallpaper are consumed. She's been waiting for something to happen. At last it does. Out of the nothingness a spirit emerges. A Shell Shaker appears for Auda.

Shoosh! Shoosh! Shoosh! Shoosh!

Auda watches the spirit woman with turtle shells strapped to her ankles. She's big-breasted and wears a deerskin dress, bloodied at the neck and hem. Smoke rises from the turtle shells and forms a constellation on the ceiling. Auda knows the dance. Every spring she shakes shells with other Indian women in Southeastern Oklahoma. Although most women now recycle evaporated milk cans in place of turtle shells, the dance still spiritually reconnects the earth and Indian people during Green Corn time. But this Shell Shaker's song is different, it stirs an older memory coming to life inside her.

Shoosh! Shoosh! Shoosh! Shoosh!

Auda sees herself with hundreds of Shell Shakers around an ancient fire. A small woman with a scar on her cheek, whom she believes to be her younger sister, is next to her. She laughs and gossips with her sister between dances. Suddenly they grab the hands of a warrior making mud pies on top of the Nanih Waiya. They lead the warrior around the fire like a prize, smiling and cajoling, but, finally, they push him into the blistering flames.

When she blinks, her room returns to normal, a comfort zone where she can retreat from the present. In the bookcase she stores her dissertation copies, history books, family pictures, and a powder blue phonograph stacked with Motown's Greatest Hits singles, all 45s. She's even kept the black velvet painting of Elvis she bought at a state fair. Her bed still wears the quilt her aunts, Delores and Dovie Love, made for her. They cross-stitched the usual Choctaw designs: the eye of friendship, the sunburst, and the coiled snake that represents the power of the people to subdue their enemies. All memories she wants to cherish.

Auda's hands tremble as she smoothes her tangled wet hair. She coughs and realizes the entire room is filled with smoke. She opens the window. The sky is waking up gray. She sees her uncle Isaac in the backyard talking with a group of Indian men about last night's fire. So the whole world is smoky? Good, she doesn't want to be in this alone.

She crawls into bed. It's six A.M., Sunday morning. She clings to her pillow and almost sleeps. Outside, an ambulance drowns out the men's conversation. She tries to focus on what the Shell Shaker said, but instead hears a child's voice crying inside her, *"Chishke apel....*Mother help me." At last, she does remember yesterday—his bulging eyes, his knife at her throat, and her own legs kicking up a storm.

"Get your ass in my office," he bellowed, "and don't leave anything out on your desk."

Auda walked into the room. He slammed the door behind her and pushed her face against the wall. He stood behind her, pressing his body into hers, whispering in her ear.

"Why didn't you wear the dress I told you to? I'm not trying to talk you into anything. You'll do what I say or else."

Auda tried to turn her head but he held her too tightly. She could only look at him out of the corner of her eye. With his right hand he pulled a knife from his pocket, opened it with his thumb, and held it beside her face. He pushed the blade against her cheek and jabbed his tongue in her ear, then greedily sucked a red welt on her neck.

She squealed in pain.

"Hush, I'm not hurting you. I'm marking you, the way you once marked me," he said, nicking her cheek. Then he put the knife away and casually prowled around her body.

Auda kicked his shins. He clapped her left temple so hard that her head swam. She smelled his sweat oozing on her blouse. When he unzipped his pants and brought out a swollen penis, Auda breathed in the sick scent of dread.

The man ran off at the mouth, talked of tight dresses, of shooting off his gun, of pussy. He smacked his lips as if he were munching on some-thing.

Auda bit the insides of her cheeks. To her he looked more like a *Osano,* horsefly, than a human being. She remembered what her uncle told her. Some warriors, he said, become *Osano.* They pass through many changes before learning how to use their killing mouths. Better watch out, he added, they carnage their own when the competition for food is desperate. As the man mashed her into the wall, all she could think of was how to gather her power. She thought of her mother, prayed to be more like her. Called the light. At once a thin web of white entered the room, a protective membrane kneaded together by her mother's mothers, descended over her and she slipped out of her body. She surrendered nothing to Redford McAlester, seventh Chief of the Oklahoma Choctaws.

Auda sits up in bed and wipes the tears from her face. She looks at the photograph next to her bed. It's of Redford McAlester when he was twenty-one. He's caught in mid-laugh, as if someone has poked him in the ribs. He's in New Hampshire at his graduation from Dartmouth. His dark lashes curl up around stone-cut cheeks. He is tall and thin for a Choctaw—six feet, three inches. He reminds her of the Choctaw Lighthorsemen from the nineteenth century. Gaunt and mean, but in a good way.

She studies his picture. Only now does she understand. That's how he liked to portray himself, poor, with a poor Indian's good luck. It's a story she's heard him tell often. Someone noticed his intelligence. Sent him away to college to learn white man's ways. Then on to Harvard Law School. He came back, changed for the better. It's the photograph that comes closest to the way he never was. Ridiculous, she thinks, looking back on his past.

Redford McAlester was campaigning for chief when she met him in 1983. At first, he told her, he'd missed Washington, D.C.—clerking for an Indian law firm, meeting U.S. senators and high-powered businessmen. The parties. She listened. Redford McAlester was his mother's cake and candy boy. His words. When she asked him to explain, he said that his late mother had wanted him to become a Southern Baptist preacher, but also follow the traditions of his ancestors. "So when I'd go to church, I'd get cake; at Stomp Dances, candy," he said, grinning. "It only made me fat as a kid." That made her even more suspicious. But after he lectured to the Choctaws that night, and said he would give all of his time and energy to reuniting the people in Oklahoma and Mississippi, she realized that he was wholly Choctaw. He told the Choctaw people that they owed it to themselves to elect a chief who would fight the federal government for Choctaw sovereignty. He told them that the threads of American history were interwoven in Choctaw history, not the other way around. All this he explained in the fluid language of their people, and it made her proud. Slowly she came to believe that she'd found a leader, someone to believe in.

Choctaw women don't cultivate desire. Either it is in the men who arouse them, or not. Either it is there at first glance, or it will never be. It was like that for Auda. From that first night she believed there would never be anyone else but Redford McAlester. To her, his slick black hair glistened like a halo. She resigned from her job as assistant professor of history at Southeastern Oklahoma State University to manage his campaign. This wasn't unusual; Billy women were leaders in the community. She was following a family tradition.

Cautiously, her mother agreed to support him for chief, but had long since renounced her support. Both her sisters, Adair and Tema, flew to Oklahoma at different times to meet McAlester. Adair even introduced him at a luncheon of the Choctaw women's society, the *Intek Aliha*. He was a hit.

At times, though, Auda knew he tried too hard to impress the people. He began transliterating from Nietzsche's *The Will To Power.* "Feelings About Choctaw Values Are Always Behind the Times." The words sounded precisely right when he spoke them, although her uncle Isaac complained he couldn't make any sense of what McAlester was saying. That's when she decided to write all his campaign speeches. He agreed. "If we're going to become partners, I should get used to speaking your words." He winked, and pressed his lips against hers. He had a sensual mouth, his lips were more purple than dark red. He used them softly that day to feel his way down her neck and lingered there long enough to savor her pulse, measure the sweat and blood she would willingly give to his campaign. She memorized him too, the scent of his dark brown skin, the suit coat that perpetually smelled of dry-cleaning fluids mingled with the fresh tobacco he carried in his pockets. How could she know that what he wanted to seem, he seemed. She wanted him to become hers, and he did. For a time.

She worked frantically to ensure he would be elected. First, she convinced women from the other large families to support him. If you want to get elected in Choctaw Country, you must have the women on your side. And in the end, it was the women—the Choctaw grandmothers, the young mothers, even the little girls—who collectively breathed Redford McAlester into existence as a warrior chief. He won easily. After he appointed Auda to the position of Assistant Chief, the women of the tribe treated him like a child. Gave him everything he wanted at the monthly council meetings. Fed his hunger for power with their support. Whites call these "political victories," but it is so much more in Indian politics.

Over the years the dirty tricks of his administration—the lies, the double-dealing with corrupt outsiders—had consumed them all. Sometimes his political enemies died. Other times they moved out of the community. In some instances he had them "de-tribed." Their voter registration cards were revoked, and the official letter from the tribe bluntly read: "No longer enrolled." It all looked perfectly normal from the outside, but, in 1991, McAlester's body was gorged with bad medicine. Beautiful became obese. Even his assistants greeted him by asking, *"Chi niah katimi?"* "How's your fat?"

Her mouth is open against the pillow. She lies, as still as she can, feeling only her nostrils flare. How could she have been so blind? The national news media may have crowned McAlester the "Casino Chief," the one responsible for bringing his tribe into the twentieth century, but she was responsible for creating his image within the tribe. She sent flowers, in his name, to tribal employees on their birthdays. She sent baskets of food, always in his name, to families who were down on their luck. But over the years, McAlester became harder to handle. Sometimes he'd even refused to attend the funerals of elders unless she could promise him that a newspaper photographer was covering the event. It continued that way until finally she'd given up. Abandoned all hope, like she'd abandoned her struggles to correct history. McAlester was not, nor ever would be, *Imataha Chitto,* the greatest giver.

Always when she imagines the two of them together, she returns to their first year in office. The long car trips together on the Talimena Drive in the mountains of Southeastern Oklahoma. Their afternoon picnics. These are also the memories she will keep, when everything seemed to be just right, and they believed in the same things.

The road is again in her eye. The night he won the election they drove to the victory party at the Old Chief's House in Swink, Oklahoma. He pulled her next to him in the front seat of the car and said he wanted her more than he wanted to become chief. "We will never be parted, I promise." When they arrived in Swink, the house was filled with friends and families. Mostly hers. Since his parents and the rest of his relatives were dead, he had only a couple friends from NARF, the Native American Rights Fund, in Washington. Members of the Durant Chamber of Commerce, former university colleagues, state legislators and dozens of Choctaw families were there for her. Everything was out in the open. He announced that he was going to appoint her assistant chief and gave her seven white long-stemmed roses. He looked at her very quickly, but enough for his eyes to pass a message. It was as though he'd said he wanted her in front of their supporters. That strong. She cradled the roses in her arms like a baby. He told the crowd that the roses represented the Seven Grandmothers, and the seven ancient towns in Mississippi. She lowered her eyes while he spoke so no one could see how much she wanted this.

Auda breathes in the smoke, and every tendon in her body pulls taut. She feels pain. Her hands clench the quilt, and slowly she goes over what happened. Strained muscles contort her face as the obscene vision returns. A fat chief, his mouth like a zero, hunched her against a dark paneled wall. When his chubby red face popped, he spurted a million doomed Choctaws onto the back of her blue skirt before they slid onto the carpet.

"Wipe yourself off!" McAlester struggled to his desk and grabbed a clean handkerchief from the drawer. "Now get out of here," he ordered. "One of these days I'll give it to you again, but not until you beg me."

He brushed off his pants.

"*Ofi tek.*" Bitch. Quickly, he straightened his Harvard tie. He pulled a hand mirror out of his desk to check himself, then performed like a Saturday Night Live comedian into a make-believe camera. "Does your engine need an oil and lube? Well, folks, come on down to the Choctaw Nation headquarters in Durant, and this red chief will give you the kind of oil and lube that only a full-blooded Indian can perform. Discounts for cash and family groups."

Sweat rolled down his forehead and he glared at her. "I didn't hurt you. There was a time when you couldn't wait to be alone with me." He put the mirror down and laughed. "If you wanna keep your job, you better learn to turn the other cheek."

"What have you become?" she whispered.

"Everything," he answered, dryly. "You needed to be shown who's Chief around here. Remember, I'm the one who appointed you assistant chief. But the keyword here is *assistant*. You think you know so much about our people just because you wrote one lousy history book!"

"That isn't why you did this to me," she hissed. She saw McAlester battling something inside himself, but he gave up and allowed the beast to look out of his eyes.

"Let me tell you what I did do for you. I used the *Inkilish okla* and *Filanchi okla* against each other, which saved our people from being colonized. Because of what I did, the councils of Natchez, Alibamu, Chahtas, Talapoosas, and Abihkas would sing my praises as I entered their towns. I am *Imataha Chitto*, the greatest leader this nation has ever had!" He was screaming, and Auda realized he had slipped into madness.

"ALL I'VE EVER ASKED IS THAT YOU SHOW ME SOME GODDAMN RESPECT AND WEAR THE GODDAMN DRESS I BOUGHT FOR YOU!"

She took another clean handkerchief from his desk drawer and cleaned her skirt. She saw him for what he was, a true *Osano*, what Choctaws abhorred most. A predator of his own people. Her mother had been right all along.

Abruptly his mood lifted. He inhaled deeply, like an athlete bracing for a long race, then he picked up the telephone and began speaking in a sweet measured voice. "Get me the finance manager, please, ma'am." He listened patiently to the voice on the other end of the telephone.

"I know it's a beautiful Saturday afternoon, ma'am, but great leaders never rest," he said softly. "I keep the money coming in so the Choctaw Nation can hire wonderful folks like yourself. Your Chief works for you, remember that."

McAlester drummed his fingers on the desk while he waited for Carl Tonica to answer. "Sorry to bother you at home, but I want to send the assistant chief to Ireland with the rest of the Choctaw delegation. That potato famine anniversary has turned into one interest-bearing media account we can't let go of. I'm so thankful the old chiefs donated seven hundred dollars to the starving Irish in 1847, I could kiss all their graves." McAlester held his hand over the receiver and whispered, "You do want to go to Ireland with me, don't you?"

Images of bayonets and axes paraded in Auda's brain. The feathers of a buzzard squeezed out a bullet that fired into Redford McAlester's head. Her tears, like a hail of gallstones, battered his body into a bloody mess while her voice remained placid.

"Sure, why wouldn't I?"

McAlester turned his attention back to the phone. "Carl, put a wet towel on your head. The more tribal we appear, the more the Irish love us. The more the Irish love us, the more we're able to move our money in and out of their banks. Besides, Auda is one beautiful woman in a traditional Choctaw dress. She'll turn heads."

Like a man on amphetamines, the Chief laughed at his own obscenities, but stopped abruptly. "Call Ireland on Monday, I've already got the ten million. James Joyce knows what to do." He paused. "Hell man, the

Feds are the least of our worries. By the time the Genovese family figures out their money is missing, I'll have it worked out."

McAlester lit a cigarette and puffed white rings of smoke into the air, and this time when he spoke his tone was ironic. "How much money did you pocket last year, Carl?" Silence.

"I hope you've saved it—maybe it's time you retired since you're so goddamn squeamish." He leaned back in his office chair with an air of casual amusement, as Carl Tonica was most likely begging to keep his job. "It's all in the game, Carl. Stop worrying, I'm not going to cut you out of your share."

He hung up and turned to Auda. "It's settled, you're going to Ireland and we're going to reenact the Great Irish Potato Famine of 1847. Then you and I will reenact the Trail of Tears for the Irish and cry at all the international photo-ops. We'll be like—" He stopped in mid-sentence and seemed to remember himself. "Carl will have travel vouchers for you on Monday. Go home now. I want this warfare between us to end."

"I do too," she said in a tired voice. Auda walked out of his office, but fell down in the hallway. When she pulled herself up, she believed that no one had seen or heard a thing.

From somewhere in the bedroom, delirium takes a breath. A voice like an alarm spits out her name.

Auda Billy, do you hear? Do you understand? We have returned. You can use any fire. Use them all. There are woods stripped and burned for you. There are dead leaves to feed the flames. There are words burning inside the wood. Amid the fires and more fires, amid woods and rivers, amid wind there are voices. The copper-gilt medals of the foreigners have lost their luster forever. Inside this turmoil we have slept. This day we branch our antlers and dress. Your time has come. Black time becomes red.

Auda switches off the alarm. Seven forty-five. She looks in the mirror. The small cut on her cheek has crusted over with dried blood. Cover it up. You've got to hurry. A few gray hairs have sprouted overnight. After yanking them from her head, she stores them in a box on her dresser and combs her long black hair. Carefully she perfumes her legs and inner thighs and pulls on a new pair of pantyhose. Finally, she opens her closet and confronts the dress he bought her. A short tight chemise, its fresh blood color emanates a menacing quality. And like everything McAlester buys, it's imported. She rubs the Spandex and silk material between her fingers. She reads the manufacturer's label. *"Prodotta in Italia."* She remembers how the pack of short stocky men looked the day they arrived in Durant. They seemed to smell of New York City contracts and formaldehyde solution. Something akin to poison. Choctaw secretaries, council members, and custodians all stepped aside for the strangers in dark Armani suits who traveled in controlled chaos. The men cut an emotional swath through the Choctaw Nation, planning how they would develop the vacant Choctaw land outside of Durant into a magnificent casino palace and hotel complex. After construction began they all left, except one.

Vico D'Amato represented Shamrock Resorts, the management company that was financing the Casino of the Sun and its adjacent four-story hotel. Auda considered D'Amato a study in monotony. Except for the ruby solitaire on his little finger that he twisted when he was nervous, he always wore gray—suits, ties, socks, even his loafers. He had thinning hair and Auda guessed he was around fifty-five.

D'Amato said that his family hated the Feds as much as the Indians did. Every afternoon at the same time she'd find D'Amato with his feet propped up on McAlester's desk, talking confidently with a highball glass in his hand. Once he asked her to strike a pose. "Miss Billy, you ever been in the movies?" he asked. "With your beautiful hair and eyes you could pass for Sicilian."

"You know Vic, the way you talk you could be reciting the Lord's Prayer, and it would still sound vulgar," McAlester chortled. "Auda, tell Vic to get his feet off my desk and go back to his own office."

The two men became close. They both loved spaghetti westerns for their violent, yet philosophical message. They even promised each other that they would set up a movie studio in Southeastern Oklahoma, not so much to make money, but to have something to do after they retired.

In the beginning, Auda tried to warn McAlester about getting involved with D'Amato's employers. "You're gambling with the Choctaw people's tribal sovereignty. We can't borrow millions of dollars from these people, Red, they're the Mafia!"

He twinkled at her that day, as if placating a two-year-old. "Let me worry about that, honey. I'm not going to lose control of the tribe, I promise."

Why hadn't she been able to see it then? He was already transforming himself into what the foreigners wanted: a front man.

We're whirling our tongues like hatchets, do you hear? Auda, do you understand? You can use any fire.

Hurriedly, Auda returns to the mirror, her mouth half-open. She accentuates the almond shape of her eyes, modifies the arch of her brows to hide her angry face. Powders her cheeks with scarlet blush. Gobs on red lipstick. Puts on the dress and is spellbound by her reflection. There, she thinks, transformation complete. No longer woman, but warrior.

Sliding into a pair of red stiletto pumps, Auda pushes seven silver bracelets up her wrist and struts out of the room. She doesn't know why the Shell Shaker revealed her past to her. Or whose voice called her name. But she understands the future. She can use any fire. She will use them all. She is Auda the Redeemer. Red is the Choctaw color for war.

Auda races downstairs to the back porch and digs in her briefcase for the keys to her Jeep. There's commotion everywhere. Television reporters are interviewing the neighbors about last night's prairie fire, the autumnal equinox, the meteorites. A soot-covered fire truck roars around the corner with another in tow. She looks at her pet rabbit. Jean Baptiste, her prize French Angora, is dancing in his cage as if trying to delay her from what she is going to do. She rushes back into the house, retrieves a bit of apple and shoves it through the wires. No use forgetting loved ones. She sees her mother across the street, steeped in the smoky air like an apparition. When she was a little girl she believed her mother was the woman in the creation story who lived on top of mountains and ate from the lips of the volcano.

Auda catches her mother's gaze before she leaves. It is unwavering, it steels her. She thinks about the Irish as she speeds along the magnolia-lined streets of her hometown. Belfast is probably not so different from Durant. She turns into the tribal headquarters parking lot. At last her history is mute.

At nine A.M. a gunshot echoes through the Choctaw Nation headquarters. Auda feels her chin quivering like an old lady's. She sees the bullet hit its mark. Watches the .45 caliber pistol fall to the floor as if in slow motion. Then nothing.

She regains consciousness as a Bryan County sheriff's deputy is breaking down the door of the chief's office. Auda hears him scream. Together they look at McAlester. He's leaning back in his chair, his boxer shorts and suit pants down around his ankles, parading his flabbiness. There is blue-black hair and bloody bone splattered on the wall behind him. Most of the back of his head is gone, but his cheeks are blotted with the imprint of red lips.

The deputy rushes outside the office to a crowd of tribal employees who nervously wait. She can almost see his queasy expression as he reports the news.

"It was a cruel joke," she hears him say. "She shot him with his pants down."

By nine-fifteen buzzards wait in the sky. When the tribal police arrive, the Choctaw sergeant is so angry he punches Auda in the mouth.

Some time later, Auda comes to in a jail cell. She doesn't know where she is, or how much time has passed. Her lips and jaw ache, and there's blood all over her dress. Just as she tries to sit up on the cot, Susan Billy is being escorted into her cell by a Bryan County sheriff's deputy.

"I hope you understand," says the deputy to her mother, "that the sheriff doesn't let just anyone visit the prisoners."

Susan Billy thanks him, and he locks them both inside the cell and walks away.

"I tried to do what the spirit wanted," whispers Auda, not even sure any sound emerges. Her mother sits down on the cot and gives her a look that says, "say no more." She gently grasps Auda's hands, examining each finger, one by one, as if she's never seen them before. Auda thinks their hands resemble the splayed brittle twigs of an oak tree. Daughter kindling, mother limbs.

Finally the sheriff, a big hulking man named Carter Diggs, enters the cell and towers over them. He nods politely at her mother, but orders Auda to stand up. "Auda Billy, I'm charging you with the murder of forty-four-year-old Choctaw Chief, Redford McAlester. Although there are no fingerprints on the weapon found at the murder scene and no powder burns on your hands, I believe you are guilty as charged. Besides," he says, looking directly at her mother, "considering the mood at tribal police headquarters, I think I'm doing you a favor by booking you here."

Auda nods that she understands. The sheriff reads her her rights then leaves. A Choctaw policewoman from the tribal headquarters and a deputy enter the cell to guard her. Then her mother, who has been silent all this time, stands up and says calmly, "I killed Chief Redford

McAlester. It was my gun and I shot him in the head... *Osano abi bolle li tok.*"

"What was that last remark?" asks the deputy. The Choctaw police-woman translates in a voice filled with disbelief. "The old one said she killed the Casino Chief."

3 | Intek Aliha, The Sisterhood

"**S**o you see, I have seven, and twenty-four? Thirty-one hours to live. Here's your lark, Torvald." The theater goes black. The auditorium at the Dallas Theatre rocks with applause, the gold curtain falls, and Tema Billy knows she has nailed her performance as Nora Helmer in *A Doll's House.* Throughout the first and second acts, her performance was icy and focused. She verily stalked the stage in order to give Nora Helmer a sense of foreboding. Tema feels impending doom, but dismisses it as her transformation into character; next, she will build Nora's edginess into a powerful storm that frees her from the suffocating Torvald Helmer.

When Tema tried out for the role, the director told her he was impressed with her passionate interpretation of Nora Helmer. After she had gotten the part, he asked her why she thought she played Nora with such clarity. She replied that Torvald Helmer's relationship with Nora was very much like federal government's paternalism of American Indians. "Somewhere inside Nora, she's always known that she was destined to leave her husband, in the same way that we Indians know we will one day break free of the federal government." The director seemed surprised, and said that he hadn't known that she was Native American. He thought she was Italian.

She waits for her cue in Act Three and busies herself by tying and untying the long black shawl over her costume. Several yards away the stage manager beckons her from the left-hand prompt corner. He points to the set door that is unexpectedly sticking as the actors enter and exit the stage. She motions to him that she knows about it.

Tema is delighted to be so close to home, only an hour from Durant, Oklahoma. She took the job at the Dallas Theatre so that her son, Hoppy, could be near her family. She'd always meant to return to Choctaw Country to live, but somehow found excuses not to. Tema left Oklahoma in the spring of 1972, the year she turned eighteen and announced to her mother she was leaving Durant forever. She enrolled in Okmulgee Tech to become a plumber and pipe fitter for six dollars an hour. That was big money for an Indian woman. At Okmulgee the next fall, her friend Jon Grounds, a Euchee from Sapulpa, joined an American Indian dance company and she followed him to New York. Although they never married, their son, Hopaii Iskitini, Little Prophet, was born the following year. Over the years Hopaii, nicknamed Hoppy, had lived up to the name. Sometimes it seemed he really could see the future. When he was five, he asked her at breakfast one morning if Daddy was going away for a while. By the end of the day it was true. Jon returned to Sapulpa and to his mother's house to learn the traditions of his people. Occasionally he sends for Hoppy to participate in Euchee ceremonies, but her son remains wholly Choctaw.

After Jon left, Tema decided to stay in New York City. She liked the variety of working at different jobs, something she'd never have if she returned to the small town of Durant. Some days she was a waitress in a famous restaurant, other times she drove a truck for a green grocer on Staten Island. Eventually she went with a girlfriend to try out for an acting job, an extra in the soaps. She knew nothing about acting, but the woman at the casting call liked the way she looked. "You can pass for anything," she had said.

Over the years Tema won bit roles playing Italians, Greeks, Spanish dancers, and an occasional Polynesian. In the evenings, she continued working as a waitress. When she won the coveted role in *The Conference of the Birds*, she began to develop her strengths as an actress—her bearing, vocal power, and magnetism onstage. The experience changed her. She discovered that she liked being someone else. No, Durant wasn't for her. Even if she'd never become an actress, she wasn't about to go home and run the tribe. Her mother had always expected Auda to be politically active, but not Tema.

"Thank God, Mother got her wish," she mutters, under her breath.

A friendly stagehand touches her on the sleeve and startles her. He points to the door; now it's her turn to wave at him. "I see it," she mouths.

Her husband Borden Beane, who plays Torvald Helmer, nods that he also knows the door is sticking. Their cue comes and Borden gives the door a shove. It unexpectedly shuts behind him. Tema pushes hard on the door, but it's jammed and she's left offstage.

Borden ad-libs and calls to her through the door, "Nora, my little lark, stop acting a fool."

Tema throws her weight on the door; it opens and she trips over the sill, tumbling face-first onto the stage. For a second, the fall stuns her. She raises her head and looks at the audience, then up at Borden who is enough of a pro to issue her his hand.

"My dear, you are such a little sparrow, always trying to amuse me."

From somewhere in the theater, Tema hears the words that freeze her to the floor. *"Hatak abi."* Mankiller. A bodiless voice calls to her in Choctaw and the sound resonates in her ears. She can't move.

"Hatak abi." Mankiller.

The audience begins to fidget. Three hundred people in the theater and Borden expect her to get up.

"Hatak abi."

Terror. She stares blankly into white footlights that grow brighter and brighter at the lip of the stage. That hissing, gurgling voice—she hears it winding among the seats like a great invisible python ready to gorge itself on her body. Just then something reaches out of the gloom and grabs her by the neck. She jumps up and yelps and mills her arms until the thing goes away.

She snaps back into character and screams her lines. "No, no, no, I can't stand it anymore, I've got to get out of here!"

Borden looks surprised, as if to say, not only are you changing your lines, but we rehearsed the scene so differently. "But Nora dear—" he replies.

Tema feels her performance coming under control and she resolves to finish Act Three. If she makes it through one curtain call, she'll break her contract and drive to Oklahoma tonight. Her mother will know what to do.

"Oh, I beg you, please, Torvald. From the bottom of my heart, *please—* only an hour more!"

"Your hands killed Red Shoes!" the voice says, in Choctaw.

Tema clutches her ears and realizes that the danger is coming from the front row. Her mind races. The backstage door is jammed. The wing of the stage is her only escape, but she must remain calm. Sweat pours out of her body. Tema feels her heart pounding—and then it hits her. How dare this thing stalk her! She has done nothing wrong. She leans toward the audience and whispers, her voice as dry as matches, "*Wishia cha...go away.*" Probably no one else notices. Like magic, the voice retreats.

She returns to playing Nora.

Applause thunders from high up in the balcony down to the orchestra seating, and the stage goes dark. One curtain call later, Tema hurries to her dressing room with Borden following close behind.

"Congratulations, darling. Bad luck about your fall, but you made it part of the performance. No one noticed. Tomorrow night will be better."

"I won't be here tomorrow, I'm leaving. Someone hollered '*hatak abi*' at me from the front row. I've got to get out of here and find Hoppy. I know his band is performing at a bar in Deep Elum so maybe if I hurry..."

"Hollered? My, my, my, our home training is rearing its ugly head tonight."

"Borden Beane, damn it, it's not *hahlahed*, it's *hol*-lered, I'm from Oklahoma. We say *hol*-lered," drawls Tema. "So sue me, but I'm getting out of here tonight!"

"Hatak attic?" says Borden, rolling the words on his tongue. "Really, Tema, it's opening night. You fell face-down onstage, but you recovered magnificently. I never heard a thing and I was out there the whole time."

She heads for the bathroom and slams the door with theatrical gusto. She looks at her hands. Are these the hands of a killer, like the voice said? She stretches out her fingers. They are not the well-manicured fingers of her sister Adair, nor are they the small delicate hands of Auda. No, her hands are wide and hard, like ping-pong paddles. They look as if they belong to a weight lifter. She purposefully camouflages them while performing. She'd once read that Fred Astaire thought his hands were too large to belong to a dancer, so he kept them cupped or hidden in his clothes when on camera. While preparing for her role as Nora, she watched a dozen Fred Astaire movies to learn how he made his hands seem so insignificant.

Am I capable of murder, she wonders? She makes a fist and punches the air like a boxer. What did the voice mean? She's unable to explain it to herself, much less to Borden. Until they met in a show in London, Borden's whole life revolved around the Royal Shakespeare Theatre.

Why shouldn't he think she's imagining things? The only ghosts he's ever seen have been onstage.

After a few minutes she comes out of the bathroom and sits in a chair at the dressing table. Borden drags a chair beside her. He peels off his eyebrows and hair piece, then reaches for a bottle of sparkling raspberry juice and pours them both a drink.

"Let me say again that I never heard 'hatak whatever,'" he says in perfect diction that annoys the hell out of her. "Maybe one of the men snoring in the front row burped and you misunderstood."

"They weren't asleep. They were a good audience."

"Asleep is the wrong word," he quips. "They were dead drunk. During my exit line, I heard a veritable chorus of honkers."

Tema sets the glass down and wonders why white men turn everything into a debate. "The first time I heard the voice was in Act Two, but I thought I was imagining things. Then I heard it again and again."

"What does 'hatak abbey' mean?"

Tema knows her husband. Each time he purposefully mispronounces the Choctaw words, she considers punching him, but doesn't. "Borden, you're totally oblivious to anything that isn't directly related to your performance. Something is after me, don't you understand? I'm afraid. As soon I get back to our apartment, I'm calling my mother to see if anything is wrong."

"*Yes, do that. Try to calm yourself and collect your thoughts again, my little sparrow.*"

"Songbird," corrects Tema. "If you're going to quote lines from the script at least get them right. Really you *are* Torvald sometimes."

"Songbird," he repeats. "Don't say that. I am not like Torvald Helmer, and I'm trying to help."

"In your own way maybe, but not like I—" Before she can get the words out of her mouth, Borden springs from his chair. Moments later, he comes back into the room brandishing a carpenter's hammer.

"I'll pummel anyone who dares slander the mighty Choctaws by calling them loathsome names I can't pronounce."

Tema puts both elbows on her knees. She wants to confront Borden's lack of sensitivity, but instead laughs at his antics. He must think she's playing a game. In so many ways they are complete opposites. She's so much older than he is, even though they're both thirty-seven. All his life he's plowed his energy into acting. Until lately, she's never thought of acting as a permanent career. She likes uncertainty, it's her spiritual birthmark. But Borden is different. He's truly English to his bone marrow, with a family tree as long as hers. He trained at the Royal Academy and brings a methodical approach to the craft, while she relies on intuition, a gut feeling.

She smiles and looks at Borden standing there with a hammer held high in the air. It's his long legs she loves. Paler than milk, they like to dance to music that ends in intercourse. Then without thinking she stands up and pulls him close, and puts her hands on his buttocks.

"Yes, do that while we're having a row," says Borden. "This is sexual stimulation edged with anger. I can take it."

Tema then pulls his mouth to hers, talking softly to his lips. "Nora is a role that is the total opposite of me. She always thought that she should be a wife. Until you came along I never, ever, considered marriage."

"I know, darling," he says, closing his eyes.

"But then I said, 'Wait a minute, I may never get the opportunity to play a part that is so different from me, and that's what acting is all about.' Even though I've denied it, I want to become a serious actress, not an Indian Barbie doll. Nora Helmer may be Ibsen's skylark, but she's my feathered Indian woman soaring above the stage like a bird of prey."

"Darling, you *can* fly," says Borden, slightly aroused.

Tema kisses him. She doesn't like to admit how much she truly needs him, especially when she's feeling so vulnerable. When he pulls her close enough to feel his arousal, her cheeks redden, and she pushes him away. "But even as much as I want this role, I have to leave tonight," she says, abruptly. "Try and understand."

It's Borden's turn to blush and he turns his back on her. "Bloody hell, Tema," he says, quickly adjusting his pants. "I don't understand."

"I'm afraid."

"Of what?"

"Of bad spirits, for one thing."

Staring down at the floor, she says, "there was something ominous in the audience tonight. The voice said I was Red Shoes' killer, or something like that. I've got to go home and find out what is wrong. When the danger passes I'll join you in New York, or anywhere else you want. I'll be the best ethnic extra the world has ever known—I'll play Cubans, or Latinos, or Lebanese. Besides, everything's so retro in Dallas anyway. I think we've ruined our careers by coming here.

Borden explodes. "Oh, let's please remember what we're fighting about! Coming to Dallas was your idea. We were deliriously happy living in London, where I made a good living, I might add. I took this job in 'Big D,' as you called it, so we could work together. So Hoppy could spend time with your family. Just look at how I've changed my life in order to be with you. You don't take me seriously, either. I've long suspected that it's because I'm English, and your family hates me. *And no one in the blasted theater called you a 'hatak ape.'*"

"The words are *hatak abi* and it means mankiller."

"Rubbish," retorts Borden. "You are not a killer."

"Don't you see, the Choctaw words have been spoken aloud. They said my hands are the hands that killed Red Shoes."

Borden falls silent; after a while he says in a low voice, "No, I don't understand that kind of irrational thinking. In essence you're saying that speech determines actions. Like God saying, 'let there be light,' and the lights come on."

"Yes, that's the way it works."

"Darling, we are actors, the universal peacemakers. Acting is the reflection of events that can teach us the folly of humanity, or its greatness. That's what Shakespeare and Goethe remind us over and over. Tonight, your Nora took control of the stage and transformed us. That's what a brilliant performance does. If more people came to the theater and understood Shakespeare and Goethe, there would be no more wars, or killing, or suffering."

"The English have had Shakespeare for five hundred years and it didn't stop you from colonizing the world," she says softly.

"Okay, bad example, but you know what I mean. You've said as much yourself. Tonight the stage door jammed, you forgot your lines, now you're unhappy with yourself, that's why you want to run away."

"IT made the door jam on me."

"This is intolerable." He sighs aloud.

There is a long silence and finally he says, "Tema, I'll gladly go back to New York when our contract ends. Don't think I want to stay here, I'm completely fed up with snoring audiences and people who say 'all y'all.'" He sinks down into a chair. "And with fighting you."

"This is not a fight. This is a vigorous discussion," says Tema.

"No, we're fighting. This is what married folk do," he says, "they fight —excuse me, 'discuss vigorously'—when they're mad at each other."

The dressing room seems to gather shadows. Tema thinks of her mother and father. As far as she knows, they never argued. There were the occasional hard looks at strangers when something bad happened, but never at each other. When her father, Presley War Maker, died, Tema was in Mrs. Phelps' third grade class holding a Dick and Jane reader. She can still see Adair being escorted in by the principal and blurting out to the class that their father had had an explosion in the brain. That's how children relate things. They'd seen anger smoldering in their father's eyes; they believed it finally exploded. Later she would learn to say "aneurysm" in the brain, not explosion. Though explosion was probably the more correct explanation.

"Tema, I want to understand you and your culture, " says Borden. "You are right, I don't know anything about Choctaw beliefs, but you don't give me much of a chance to learn, do you?" He walks over to her. "I will stand beside you on any stage, or stand against any ghost who tries to harm you."

"I want us to be together, always, and," she adds, "to respect each other's beliefs."

"Then let's go home and get some rest. And make up."

"Borden, I need you to believe what I'm telling you."

"My darling, you are not a killer, and no one can make you a killer. For once, admit that you're exhausted and maybe you imagined this. We were good tonight, especially you," he whispers, looking directly into her eyes.

Tema feels an odd sensation, as if she's hearing an echo. She scoops her hands heavenward, and performs one of Nora's lines.

"And think of it, soon the spring will come and the big blue sky! Perhaps we shall be able to take a little trip—perhaps I shall see the sea again! Oh, it's a wonderful thing to be alive and be happy!"

Borden kisses her hand. "You don't know much about the English, either. We'll fight to the death to protect those we love."

Tema puts her hand across his mouth. *"Shu-sh-h-h!* Don't speak about death. Let's go home, I *am* really tired."

She quickly changes into a pair of blue jeans, and a black leather tee. She punks up her short brown hair with butch wax, then opens the drawer of her vanity and picks up her Swiss Army knife, inserts it in her left boot.

"Good lord," he says, shaking his head.

She puts her hand inside of his and vows that, for once, she will listen to Borden. Perhaps she is overly tired. Imagining voices. But as they walk across the darkened stage, she feels an eeriness lingering around her. "The past haunts us all," she says to Borden, "I've always known that."

The next morning Tema hears her son pounding on the bedroom door of their Dallas apartment. "Mother, Borden, get up!"

"What's the matter?" she asks, pulling on a robe and rushing to the door.

"This fax came from Uncle Isaac, it was sitting in the machine all night. Mother, why don't you ever check these things?" he says, waving the paper in front of her.

Tema realizes for the first time that, at eighteen, her son's eyes are exactly like those of his grandfather Presley War Maker. Intense and black, Hoppy's eyebrows knit together as if he's always expecting danger.

"Hoppy, why is your hair emerald green?" she asks, taking the fax from him.

"Mom, please...forget about my hair. Just read this."

On Sunday, September 22, someone killed Redford McAlester and the police believe it was your sister. Your mother is also being held in the county jail for the murder. I'm calling the Billy clan together and I need you to come home. Uncle Isaac.

Tema fingers the sheet of paper, re-reads the words one by one, as if they were written in Braille. Then it hits her: September 22, her mother's birthday. What could Auda have been thinking?

Tema grieves for her sister and for her sister's mixed-up alliances. The last time she saw McAlester he'd grown so fat she hardly recognized him. She and Borden and Hoppy had just returned from London. They'd planned to stay in Durant for a couple of weeks, but the tension between Auda and her mother was so electric, they only stayed a brief two nights. When McAlester came by for a visit, he made sure she knew it was obligatory. He talked about himself in third person, almost as if he were two people. "Never let a chief cut your hair," he had said to her, then he laughed until he coughed. Later, Tema asked her mother what he meant. Susan Billy had practically hissed when she said it was a *Osano's* way of saying he'd had someone killed.

"You're kidding, of course," she had replied.

"It's been done—just ask your sister," her mother said. "We've got to get rid of him."

Tema reads the fax one last time. Surely, this is not what her mother had in mind. She hands it to Borden, who has been talking to Hoppy. He reads the short message quickly and looks up at her. "No wonder you couldn't reach them by phone last night," he says. "You were right, I was wrong. Of course you must go. I'll call the understudy and square things here with the rest of the company."

She looks at Borden and suddenly a sense of forboding comes over her. "I don't know how long I'll be gone."

NEW ORLEANS, LOUISIANA
MONDAY, SEPTEMBER 23, 1991

Adair Billy shuffles down the dormant halls of LaHarve and Hennepin in a pair of lime green flip-flops, wearing a worn-out sweat suit. She carries a cup of chicory coffee and the *Times-Picayune*. It's early, 5:30 A.M. In two hours, the prosperous securities investment firm will be hopping with anticipation of the stock market's activity.

Adair's co-workers say they can set their clocks by her Monday through Friday ritual. She arrives at work, 5:15 A.M. Makes coffee. Picks up her messages. Checks last night's buy or sell orders for accuracy. Changes out of her flip-flops into shoes. By 7:00, she's read the local paper, the *Wall Street Journal, Reuters News Service,* and other industry reports, and is prepared to comment on where the market will open.

She likes being predictable. People know what to expect from her—what makes her angry, what she wants. Her clients trust her to manipulate profits for them based on tax advantages. Marriages. Divorces. Retirement. She either talks them into investing a wad of money into the S&P 500, or cautions them against being too greedy.

"You've been in the market long enough to know you've been handed a bonanza."

"This is no time to gamble. Invest in stocks slowly."

"Cash in some chips now, especially since you're over sixty and can sell without tax consequences."

"Balance is everything."

At thirty-eight, Adair Billy has the world in her pocketbook. Baby brokers, the first-year boys at LaHarve and Hennepin, call her the "Wall Street Shaman." When men at parties rush to her side with lighters and pencil-thin cigarettes, she understands what they want. They hope she'll impart some new market strategy to them, offered up in exchange for flattery and attention. Occasionally she sleeps with them. The bedroom questions are always the same. "What funds do you find extremely attractive?" "In my situation would you hold or sell?" "Do you have confidence in the economy to hold off recession long enough to…*blah, blah, blah?*"

She joined the firm in New Orleans after finishing her M.B.A. at Southern Methodist University in 1977. The securities business suited her—as the middle daughter in the family, she is in some ways the most independent. Good training for a broker. She cut her teeth selling municipals. In 1983, she began buying large blocks of junk bonds from a California firm and selling them to institutional clients. At that time the bonds were earning much higher yields than treasuries. Her strategy was the old cliché "risk versus reward." Junk bonds were risky because if a corporation defaulted on its debt, the bonds were worthless.

Adair made her reputation in 1985 when she abruptly pulled all her clients out of the junk market even though the default rates were low. When the story broke that the Securities and Exchange Commission was investigating junk bond king Michael Milken and stock manipulator Ivan F. Boesky for insider trading, junk bonds plummeted. Her clients made hefty profits, while those who'd stayed with Milken and Boesky lost their shirts. Because Wall Street is very superstitious, people believed she had the ability to predict the future. They assumed it was her Native upbringing. In this case, they were right. A voice woke her up in the middle of the night and said, "Milken and Boesky are underwater." While she knew they weren't literally drowning, she understood the warning. Move as far away from them as possible. When the scandals broke, she played it cool and allowed her firm to tout her as an industry guru. If people wanted to think she was prophetic, that she had Indian spiritual powers, so be it. Just as long as she didn't become like so many others on Wall Street. Predatory.

Besides, she does hear voices. The hard part is determining whether or not they are talking to her.

Sunrise.

It invariably happens in the same way, but Adair takes a moment each morning to watch. From her eleventh-floor office it gives halo and weight to objects. Buildings and rooftops vibrate as light skims over them. It was bred into her that the first seconds of sunlight carry messages from *Hashtali* to her people.

Across the city is the ancient river, the Mississippi. Being at the earth's edge is where Adair feels most alive. She can't imagine living anywhere else but New Orleans, where so much Choctaw history occurred. Yet there remains no trace of her people. Amazingly, nothing.

The town was laid out in the elbow of the river, an outpost of the Old World, in 1718. She imagines how the shifting power struggles influenced its birth. First there were the Indians who pushed flat boats down river to trade, then came the French with their sailing corvettes, followed by the Spanish, whose ships sank when they tried to penetrate the mouth of the Mississippi. Waves of immigrants from all over the world would come later.

During the humid summer months she sometimes takes the six-minute walk from her office on Poydras Street to the French Quarter, where the air reeks of rum mingled with the blunt smells of the Mississippi. Two-and-a-half centuries ago, New Orleans probably looked very much as it does now, the streets full of beggars and traders. The homeless of Europe.

Frequently she visits the area where Jean Baptiste Le Moyne Sieur de Bienville, the founder of New Orleans, made his residence. She's read all the local articles written about him in the *Times-Picayune* that appear during Mardi Gras. He was born in Canada in 1680, Jean Baptiste Le Moyne, the twelfth child of Charles Le Moyne, the Sieur de Longueuil of Quebec. At age eleven Jean Baptiste was invested with the title of "Sieur de Bienville." He followed his older brothers into the navy, Pierre d'Iberville and De Serigny, who were proving to the world that the Canadians were indomitable *coureurs de bois*. At seventeen, Bienville was made a *garde-marin*, midshipman, and served with his brother d'Iberville in military exploits against the English at Hudson Bay in 1697. After the war, d'Iberville brought Bienville south to establish a colony in the Lower Mississippi Valley. In 1699, the two brothers set foot on what is now Ocean Springs, Mississippi, near Biloxi. This became France's toe-hold in Louisiana.

A local librarian told Adair that Bienville had the finest house in the French Quarter. His residence would have been bounded by the Customs House, Chartes, Decatur, and Bienville Streets. It was a two-story with an attic and six large doors on the first floor, all opening to the outside wraparound porch. A hotel really. In her mind she sees the house. It is well-built, with upright joists filled with mortar between the interstices. The exterior would have been whitewashed with slack lime, the interior wainscoted. In the upstairs there were large windows but because there wasn't enough glass, the frames were enclosed with very thin linen, admitting as much light as glass.

Bienville built the large house to entertain Choctaws. That much is acknowledged, even by white historians. It was a calculated move on his part; by hosting Choctaws for several weeks every March, the French governor was insuring the safety of his colony. Choctaws would protect the French against the English, and other tribes in the region. Her people traded their muscle for French commodities: hatchets, knives, cooking pots, vermilion face paint, fine Belgium wool, and the ever-popular French musket.

Adair tells herself she's following a tradition established by her ancestors. After all, Indians were the first commodity traders of the New World. She does much the same by providing a communications network that brings people together who want to exchange one thing for another: pork bellies, cotton futures, computer company shares, technology stocks, or U.S. treasuries. Maybe she's her ancestors toehold in New Orleans, the one to re-establish a Choctaw power base. Yet to even think about herself in those terms goes against her home training. "Never think too much of yourself." "If you have a special gift, others must be the ones to point this out." Her mother's words repeated so often they burned into her subconscious. To shake off her arrogance, Adair studies the accomplishments of her ancestors.

In 1700, Choctaw commodity traders could hand off a portion of their shares of French goods to other tribes eager to get in on the action. Their trading partners would swap the goods, and the system reproduced itself all over the Lower Mississippi Valley. French goods were low risk, high liquidity. If the Choctaws got mixed up in a war, they could rely on their trading partners for support. Just like England and America do today.

Market sense, that's what her people had long before there was a Wall Street with its "low risk, high liquidity" jargon. *Mabilia,* Mobile, was the trade jargon of her people. It's Choctaw for slick.

Adair takes a long drag from a cigarette, then notes the clock on her desk. Time to get dressed before trading begins. She walks over to her office bureau and pulls out a black suit and matching men's oxfords, carefully removing a dry-cleaning tag from her gunmetal gray blouse.

She slips one leg into the straight-legged pants, then the other. Men always notice a beautiful woman, so she began dressing like a man. It was her way of making them trust her. As she buttons her jacket, she wonders why historians, including her sister, focused on Indian warfare, instead of Indian commerce.

In 1982, she'd flown back to Oklahoma to hear Auda lecture on Choctaw history, shortly after Auda's book was published. The Oklahoma Historical Society had touted Auda as the first Choctaw academic to write on the tribe's early interactions with the French. Adair had hoped the lecture would focus on the Choctaw's legacy of commerce, but it wasn't to be. When the hands shot up around the auditorium for questions, Adair was startled. She'd forgotten how angry whites can become when their own history is used against them.

"I thought only the Cherokees walked the Trail of Tears."

"The Choctaws were the first tribe to be removed from our ancient homelands. Our people walked all the way from the Lower Mississippi Valley to Oklahoma with very little to eat or drink. The road to the promised land was terrible. Dead horses and their dead riders littered the way. Dead women lay in the road with babies dried to their breasts, tranquil, as if napping. A sacred compost for scavengers."

"So how many died?"

"Four thousand."

"Excuse me?"

"Four thousand Choctaws."

"The total number of Indians?"

"Thousands."

"Ouch. But how do you know that for sure?"

"Andrew Jackson's government took a census before and after."

"Census takers make mistakes."

"Yes, ma'am, exactly right, it could have been more."

"Or less, especially since we know how scarcely populated America was before contact."

" ... "

"You seem irritated..."

" ... "

"American Indians didn't invent the wheel. Let's face facts, they hadn't a written language, nor a concept of money."

"It has nothing to do with how densely populated a country is, otherwise India would be the most highly developed nation on earth."

Adair raised her hand to take issue with the woman's last comment, but Auda ignored her.

"I'll tell you a story," her sister began. "Off and on during the early years of the eighteenth century, the French-supporting Choctaws fought the English-supporting Chickasaws. Each tribe adopted a foreign tribe. It's similar to the peculiar way white Americans adopt foreign children today. They want to give the child a better life. The parent cares for, and protects, the child. This is no doubt love but, ultimately, they want to make the foreign child 'American,' a persona of the parent. During the eighteenth century, hundreds and hundreds of Indians died in the effort to acculturate their foreign adoptees. Some years the Chickasaw and Choctaws only burned each other's corn. Other times, they seized each other's pack trains. Winter raids took place when the ground was covered with dry leaves and Choctaw warriors had to have enough patience to remove them one by one with their toes. There is a battlefield, I can show you, where more than a thousand Choctaw, Chickasaw, English, and French died.

"When our enemies began killing our beloved men, it was the Choctaw women who whirled their tongues like hatchets and took up the fight that day. They pulled red water and fire from their menstruating bodies and smeared it across their chests. Even the seasoned English soldiers who carried muskets and powder horns dropped their weapons and ran back into the swamps. They couldn't fight bullet-proof blood."

Auda paused solemnly. "The earth still gives up little mementos from this battle, a fragment of ax blade, pottery shards, splinters of flint from a war club. It was our women who chased down the traitors within our midst, but for what? To protect disagreeable foreigners, the new Americans, who would one day have the gall to explain our history to us."

Auda looked directly at her interrogator. "I only have one question for you. How would you know whether America was sparsely populated at contact, unless that was the propaganda you'd been taught in the colonizer's schools?"

There was an audible gasp at that last remark. Adair winced. Even she knew it was considered poor form to insult a paying audience. Auda should have stopped long before the menstrual blood story. White women have never known what to do with their blood. She could see them turning the image over in their minds trying to figure out what it all meant.

Until that evening, Adair hadn't realized how much of a cultural agitator her sister had become. When Auda compared the removal of all American Indians in the Southeast to the removal of Palestinians from their homes in Jerusalem, the audience hissed. A staff member from the Oklahoma Historical Society quickly stepped onstage to try to rescue the situation. He thanked Auda for her talk and announced that copies of her book could be purchased in the lobby. The applause was paltry. No appeal could have helped.

Adair could tell the staff member was Indian, but what tribe was anyone's guess; there are sixty-six Indian Nations in Oklahoma. He guided Auda to the reception in the foyer; everyone was wearing forced smiles. For a long while, Adair studied the two Indians, her sister and the man. They were surrounded by New Agers, academics, and Oklahoma City's business elite. She liked the looks of the Indian, the way he presented himself to crowd of Historical Society patrons, proud but not haughty. He had serious, pleasant eyes that occasionally glanced in her direction. His broad smile and long brown hair pulled into a ponytail meant, to her, that he felt secure enough to mingle easily with whites while still keeping certain Indian traditions. At last she acknowledged him with a friendly look, then she untied the red scarf knotted at her neck and stepped outside to take in some fresh air.

When it happens for the first time, it's like discovering you've been speaking with a borrowed tongue. You think the words are yours but, in fact, they're someone else's. Long before humans learned to clothe their feelings in words, love was a rhythm that two people shared. Once in sync, it was not ever necessary to ever speak of it. Rarely do Indians say "love" to a partner the way whites do. It is a rhythm they feel continuously, unto death.

She stepped back inside the building and found him leaning casually against a wall, observing her sister in an argument with another woman. Although he was keeping his face as impassive as possible, he seemed to be thoroughly enjoying the show her sister was providing. What could have happened in the last twenty minutes? She pushed her way through the crowd. The atmosphere was hot with tension. What was her sister thinking? Didn't Auda realize that she'd already made most of the Oklahomans uncomfortable, talking about women's periods and blood revenge?

"Miss Billy, let her alone," said a voice from the crowd.

"Thank you," replied the woman, "I hope all of you will bear witness to this outrage."

Auda was not only holding her book, but a large plastic cup of whiskey. Adair's color rose; why did the stereotype have to be Indians and alcohol? Why couldn't it be Indians and race cars, or Indians and chocolate wafers?

"Adair, not a moment too soon," said Auda, steadying herself. "I've been seized."

"How much of that have you had?" whispered Adair, pointing to her drink.

"Couldn't say, I started before my lecture," thundered Auda. "But if she thinks I'm one of those perverse William Faulkner Indians, a mute character of the Southern literati, she has another think coming." She turned back to the woman in question. "Listen ma'am, my sister here is a fighter, and she won't take guff off you like I will."

Auda's adversary was boxy like a Cadillac, in her mid-sixties, and upholstered cover to cover in fine imported leather. She wore a large diamond ring that refracted light around the room, making Auda say cruel things about Tinker Bell being raised from the dead.

"C'mon," whispered Adair, "let's get out of here."

The woman inhaled herself to a full five feet tall. "It's the Marxists what's started it," she said to the others. "American professors were never like this until the Marxists took over education. A respectable woman can't even defend her own heritage. Imagine her comparing Israel's struggles against the Palestinians to the fascists."

"Good grief. Let that poor woman alone, Auda. She's probably somebody's grandmother," said Adair.

"I am," said the woman. "I got four grandchildren in Brooklyn, all studying summers on a kibbutz in Israel. Plus I got another grandchild who is a Seneca Indian and lives on the reservation. Lady, we're a multicultural family, so you better watch out who you're calling a whining Zionist!"

The crowd was turning into something of a mob. Adair was about the drag her sister out of the lobby when he intervened again. "Excuse me, Miss Billy, but you're wanted on the phone."

Up close, Adair remembers thinking that his skin looked as if it had been polished by layers of chestnut varnish. Much later that evening, she would learn that he worked part-time at the Historical Society. The rest of the week he was occupied in law school. When he offered Auda his arm he looked completely relaxed, as if he had nothing better to do than to escort her wherever she wanted to go.

"If you insist," Auda said politely. Then loudly to those gathered around, "But Adair and I were just about to hold an auction and relinquish a memento from our childhood, our family's allotment deed."

"Oh God, Auda shut up. You're a terrible drunk, a shot or two of Jack Daniels and you turn into a complete toad."

"Four terrible toads," said Auda, proudly. As they reached the exit, she turned and shouted theatrically, "Elvis has left the building!"

Together they walked her sister down the street to her hotel. Auda chattered like a child, associating one thing with another. She noted the weather, then recited a list of Choctaw words for tornado, hurricane, and volcano. She blabbed about her new boyfriend Red, "the future of our tribe." She told the clerk at the front desk that Adair had been voted the girl most likely to become a professional boxer by her high school classmates.

"Her nickname was 'Living War Club,'" Auda reported proudly. When the clerk ignored her, she whispered, "If I ever have to lecture to another audience like that one again... I wish our ancestors would march into the room and shoot them all with a bazooka." Thankfully by the time the elevator opened on the seventh floor, Auda's battery was running low and she passed out in her hotel suite.

Adair asked him to wait while she got her sister settled. She came back out and extended her hand. "I don't know how to thank you, Mr...,"

"Gore Battiste."

Adair took back her hand, but not before she'd registered the smell of his hair, his unbuttoned jacket, his loosened tie. "My sister is a brilliant woman, but tonight she wasn't herself."

She decided against making any more excuses for Auda, she didn't know him well enough to have to explain. Gore merely smiled, but there was something very sly about the way he looked at her, as if he knew what was going through her mind. She suggested that they have dinner and he agreed. The two of them had a quick meal in the hotel's restaurant. Afterwards they went up to her room.

She stepped in close and put her arms around his neck. When she kissed him, he did the only thing he could and still call himself a red-blooded Indian. He kissed back.

"I want to do this the right way, but I don't have time," he said. "I wish I did, but you live in New Orleans. I live in law school."

She didn't answer, but led him to bed. Later she would say she had forgotten his name, but remembered how his skin submerged into hers.

Of course she was lying, she knew his name, although her inclination was to forget it. She remembered everything about Gore Battiste: his crooked little smile, what high school in Tulsa he graduated from, how he liked to have his feet rubbed.

Adair notes the time, 6:45 A.M. She walks into the ladies' room at LaHarve and Hennepin, looks in the mirror, and says loudly, "Forget him. It's been nine years, he's not going to call."

A year or so after the one-night stand with Gore Battiste, she had decided to cultivate a new image, different from the one he would remember of her. She couldn't stand the thought of running into him again and looking the same, like nothing had changed for her—after him. She cut her long hair into a short bob like Louise Brooks, the silent film star of the twenties who said, "If I bore you it will be with a knife." She took to wearing men's loafers. Smoking Cuban cigars, expensive contraband she acquires from the N'awlins Blue Bloods, some of whom call her a "bachelorette," code for "we're not sure whether she's a lesbian or not." She knows they could care less. This is New Orleans, after all. As long as she makes money for them, she could be a serial killer and they would turn a blind eye.

Adair tells herself that having a routine and the solitude of wealth makes her feel secure—not chasing after some Alabama Conchatys lawyer with a last name that sounds uncannily like "Baptiste."

Another thing. She discovered that night that she wasn't the only one in the family with a temper. Recently she'd come to think of Auda as a timid little academic poring over books. All true, but there was another side to Auda that she kept hidden. Even Gore remarked that night that Auda had the makings of a true leader. "Too bad she feels so unworthy."

Adair returns to the comfort of her leather chair. She still has a few minutes before the market opens at eight, so she peruses the paper. The lead story says fall has arrived in New Orleans, chilling the gulf city with record low temperatures of seventy degrees. She chuckles at what N'awlins people call "chilly." She scans the rest of the headlines and a small news item jumps out. "Teen Savagely Killed by Pet Python." She puts down her coffee and pulls a pair of antique gold-plated scissors from her desk drawer. She methodically cuts the gruesome report out of the newspaper, and whistles as she reads how a New Orleans teenager was strangled by his eleven-foot-long pet python, Pocahontas. "Well, no wonder," she says aloud.

According to the New Orleans police, the eighty-pound snake was quite aggressive. When they found seventeen-year-old Jean Forgeron dead in the basement of his home, his body was covered with bites. An autopsy revealed that he'd been suffocated. Pythons suffocate their prey before swallowing it whole, although police said there was no indication the snake had tried to swallow the boy.

"She was hissing and playing with her kill," said police sergeant Adrien Duchesne. "The snake had to be shot before we could retrieve the body," he said. The paper went on to quote the boy's bereaved father: "Pocahontas was such a sleek little thing when we bought her. We didn't know that someday she would grow into a killer."

Adair pulls out her file marked "personal" and thumbs through her clippings. The past couple of weeks the newspaper has been lousy with uncommon deaths: "Tourist Eaten by Alligator in Florida." "Man Killed at Same Train Crossing after Surviving Similar Crash in 1929." "Dog Shoots Master." That was a particularly interesting case to her. It happened during a hunting outing when a spaniel stepped on the trigger of a shotgun and blasted his owner in both legs. The man bled to death before he could be taken from the field to a hospital.

She doesn't know why, but she's fascinated with the macabre. Saving the newspaper clippings has become a hobby. She keeps another folder of clippings on Redford McAlester. She fingers through a few. From 1989. "McAlester Cuts Ribbon at Opening of Casino of the Sun." "Casino Gives Away Millions, Monthly!" "Casino Chief McAlester Announces Wholesale Indian Store." Then 1990. "Casino Funds Elderly Housing Project." If you just read the headlines, the Choctaws seem pretty prosperous, but then why are her mother and so many of the elders working to undo McAlester? For months there have been rumors on Wall Street about a tribe laying off large sums of money in foreign bank accounts. She tried talking to Auda about it, but her sister clammed up. Adair thinks she's figured it out, but she's patient. She'll wait for more information before she makes a move against her sister's lover.

Just as she's about to put away the file she hears a peculiar sound coming from outside her office door, like something heavy being dragged across carpet. Then a muffled pop goes off like a toy gun. *Pow! Pow! Pow!*

A sound from her childhood. She remembers hunting in the library of the Billy house. The sway of fringe as she tracked a large invisible bear behind her mother's portières. Something made her stop as if her heart had failed. A glint of gunmetal, and the next thing she knew she'd smashed the butt of her toy on the moveable lump running along floorboards. She ran, yelling to her father, who pulled the bloody thing off the oak floor. After that, the two of them went on hunting parties, raiding the basement in search of bigger invaders. He called her *"Pichahli."* Mouse Master. In a soothing voice he said she was the true hunter of the family. That whatever she tracked she would find.

A few weeks later she bragged to her girlfriends in the fourth grade.

All my Barbie dolls have fur coats.

Ah-h-h... where did you get them?

Trapping and skinning rats with my dad.

Ooo-oo... yuk.

The dragging sound grows louder. LaHarve and Hennepin is a stodgy old New Orleans firm. Rarely do they have furniture moved at this time in the morning. She opens the door. Nothing there except a fax envelope taped to her door. She rips it open with her scissors, reads the contents: *McAlester dead. Auda and Susan arrested. Come home. Uncle Isaac.*

She lights another cigarette and inhales deeply. She thinks for a moment about what her strategy should be. The next move. She checks the opening stock quotes and calls her New York trading desk.

"Stanley, sell ten thousand shares of General Electric for me. Yeah," she says in a smoky voice, "I know it's going up but sell it just the same, I need the cash flow. I'll get my assistant to give you my account number." She then calls her secretary and asks him to telephone an Oklahoma attorney named Gore Battiste. "Call the Oklahoma Bar Association if you have to, I'm sure he's listed."

A mixture of dread and arousal invades her. What if he doesn't remember her. What if he's married with nine children. The trick will be to pretend she doesn't care, one way or the other. Besides, she's got to concentrate on what's truly important: her family. She walks back to the window and watches the sky. At last the morning smog lifts off the river like a blanket. Already the sky is turning a sour blue. It reminds her of a story her father told her.

Around daybreak, they fly through the air like sparklers. I've seen them. They muddy up the sky.

Who does?

Bad spirits.

How do they do that?

They fix up themselves, then they fly. Blood drips off them and glitters in the sun like red rain. It's so beautiful you'll want to catch it with your hands, but don't. That's when they can slip inside you. Better watch out, or you'll lose yourself to them.

Adair unlocks the mahogany cabinet next to the window and quickly pours herself a shot of scotch. She feels oddly elated. She raises her glass, gesturing toward the morning sun. "To my sister Auda, who finally killed the bastard."

4 | Choctough

Life is trying on Choctaws in Durant.

Isaac Billy can't work. There's a gate in his head. Just as he feels he's on the verge of a supreme insight, he remembers yesterday and is stymied. Two thousand five hundred acres surrounding his hometown were burned up in a prairie fire in the wee hours of Sunday morning. A short time later his niece, Auda Billy, was found sitting on the floor next to the dead chief, her dress splattered with his blood, the murder weapon beside her. Much to his horror, his sister Susan Billy had confessed to the assassination. Currently, every Choctaw in the county whose last name is Billy is being harassed by police.

Isaac has been accosted too. At eight-thirty this morning a deputy from the sheriff's office presented him with a warrant to search his sister's garage. It seems the town's most treasured sculpture, Durant's Big Peanut, was stolen sometime after midnight. The gray, four-foot long heavy cast-aluminum statue was a gift to the city from a businessman who'd wanted there to be a downtown attraction that honored local peanut growers. The deputy claimed he was ending speculation by members of the Peanut Growers' Club that the sacred nut was hidden in the Billy garage. Of course, he found nothing, but the deputy told Isaac that he'd also issued an APB on the Choctaw student who'd turned a perfectly good 1976 Delta 88 into Durant's Big Peanutmobile.

"Last summer, during the Fourth of July Parade, everyone thought those plaster casts of our peanut were pretty funny—glued on the car like wings. But with the peanut gone missing...well, no one's laughing now, Mr. Billy."

"Maybe you need to find your sense of humor, Vernon," Isaac replied.

"Be careful, sir, murder and mayhem are no laughing matter. College students, especially artists, are always troublemakers. I figure he probably knows who stole the peanut. Or perhaps he took it himself. Remember this: whoever steals art generally turns killer."

Isaac just stared in disbelief. He'd known Vernon Klinkenbaird since he moved into town with his parents in 1980. The young deputy couldn't be much over twenty-one. "I'm due back at the county office," he said, adjusting his weapon, then himself, before speeding away in an unmarked car.

"Odd," he mutters now, remembering the incident. Isaac looks at the gray haze in the sky and thinks it's sinking. He blames all this on the heavy satellites roving the world announcing every fifteen minutes that yesterday his sister confessed to murdering Choctaw Chief Redford McAlester. As he crosses the street to his newspaper office a Winnebago almost runs him over. The woman behind the wheel slams on the brakes and jumps out of the vehicle. She runs toward him wearing a short tight skirt, waving a microphone like a baton. "You're Isaac Billy, are you not?" she demands.

A foreigner. Isaac stares at the woman whose hair is the color of sweet potatoes.

"I'm so sorry, sir. I'm not accustomed to driving on the wrong side of the road," she says, giggling. She tells him she's a reporter for CNN and wants to get a feed for the BBC.

Typical Brit, he thinks. Feeding off the misery of Indians has always been their greatest joy. As she chatters on he decides he's being interviewed by the Duchess of York. She's perky. Smartly dressed. She has small white teeth, and is kind of chubby the way he likes younger women. Yup, she's Fergie, all right. He'd read somewhere that she's writing children's books. Things must be getting tough in England if the Duchess of York has had to start freelancing.

Isaac is amazed that the English are paying any attention to the Choctaws. He understands why the Irish are interested in them. They have something in common: colonialism and potatoes. Choctaws never liked the English. Isaac believes they've always preferred *Les Français*. Better food. Even Dixon DuRant, the town's founder, was half Choctaw, half French.

"Mr. Billy, just look into the camera and I'll give you the lead-in," commands the pretty Duchess.

He clears his throat and prepares to respond.

"Sunday afternoon of the autumnal equinox, a holy day as far as Choctaws are concerned, seventy-year-old Susan Billy confessed to the murder of Redford McAlester, Chief of the Choctaw Nation of Oklahoma, the fourth largest tribe by population in the United States. I'm talking with Isaac Billy, brother of the assassin. Sir, would it be fair to say that yesterday's savage-style assassination was an ancient Choctaw ritual, a kind of *coup d'état*, so to speak, so your family can gain control of your tribe?"

Just like always when he doesn't want to respond, Isaac feigns ignorance and performs like a John Wayne Indian, something he learned at boarding school. With a stubby gnarled forefinger he tilts his 10X Stetson back on his forehead. Looks down at the ground kind of uncertain-like. Kicks it like he's sorry, and pidgin speaks, "Me—no—Inkilish." Pausing innocently, then, *"Chishke ut chi pisa okpulo aiahni mut alla nakni in na fohka foka Chichi tok,"* which roughly means "your mother thought you were ugly, so she made you dress like a boy." Isaac wishes he hadn't said that, but knows she can't understand Choctaw. When she fires another question, pronouncing her proper British very loudly and slowly as if he's deaf, Isaac decides she is a royal fool.

"Was–there–a–love–triangle–between–Chief–Redford–McAlester– Auda–Billy–and–your–sister–Susan–Billy? Is–this–murder–perhaps– the–simple–act–of–rage–by–an–older–woman–jealous–of–her–daughter?" she shouts.

Isaac explodes, but the words come out sounding like a whisper. *"Osano chi samanta Osano!"* He smiles wide for the camera, tips his white cowboy hat and turns his back. Calling someone a horsefly, or bloodsucker, is a terrible insult to a Choctaw. But he sighs deeply. The English are used to being called worse. Yup, much worse.

"Imoshe," the television cameraman says, as he peers from behind his bulky equipment.

Isaac turns around and recognizes a distant relative. Someone who, as a boy, once sat on his lap. Someone who still affectionately addresses him as *"Imoshe,"* a sign of respect, Uncle. Worse still, someone who is freelancing for CNN. Isaac considers the possibility that his "nephew" will give him away to the British. After all, they are filming in front of his newspaper office. The sign on the door plainly advertises, in English, "Isaac Billy, Editor-in-Chief."

"Come on, Miss," urges the Choctaw cameraman. "He doesn't know anything. He's just an addled old man."

Isaac waits in front of his office, sniffing the breeze until the Winnebago belonging to the Duchess of York disappears. He wonders how the English outsmarted Indians. Quickly loading his computer, printer, and office mail into his truck, he heads east. He'll lay low at his ranch outside of Soper, Oklahoma, and reason things out. So what if Redford McAlester is stone dead, Isaac says to himself. McAlester's body was measured for a wooden suit years ago. "Yup, he really was."

Like old-timey radio tubes signaling to outer space, shiny aluminum cans and glass bottles flicker in the sun along Highway 70. They are visible now that the fire burned away the prairie grass. Isaac frowns and his throat tightens, seeing all the trash bunched up along the shoulders of the highway. Car litter makes him angry. Whites say that Indians weren't doing anything with the land; well, certainly nothing like this.

Forty-seven miles out of Durant on Highway 70, the land is still smoking from the blaze. Nervous firefighters remain posted along the farm-to-market roads, patrolling for more fires. The cemetery headstones at Muddy Boggy Creek are covered in soot and look like black tongues sticking out of the ground. As he passes the old church, Radiance Is Accomplished, volunteers sift through the debris. Memories of Yesterday, the junk shop where he occasionally stops and flirts with the owner, is destroyed. But in the Indian town of NeKoosa, the Choctaw Bus Stop, Mom's Choctaw Movie Rental, and the Okie Welding Shoppe have survived. Durant isn't the only city affected, he says to himself.

The words *your sister confessed* keep repeating in Isaac's head. He thinks of things he should have said to Fergie. Indian chiefs aren't the only ones who get savagely done in. There have been others. President Kennedy. Lord Mountbatten. Choctaws aren't the only ones with blood on their hands.

"White people," he mumbles, turning onto Lost Arrow Road, a tiny dirt lane that points north toward his ranch. He's grateful he learned to read and write English so he could earn a living in the white world, even though he still doesn't understand what the missionaries thought they were doing to the Indians at the boarding school. When he was a boy the government boarding schools were notorious for hiring sadists. Whites called them "strict disciplinarians." Or "preachers." From time to time he sees their faces in the dark. A ghost banquet of mottle-eyed strangers trying to nibble their way inside him. His impression the first day of school was that all white teachers were fat. The woman who led them to the kitchen had a mouth like a snout. When that mouth came nattering up close behind him, just like a feral hog, he spit at her and yelled, *"Niah sipokni."* Old Fats. Isaac thinks he was about seven at the time. Susan was eleven and protective of him, so she started a fight with Old Fats, yelling in Choctaw, which was strictly against the rules. They dragged Susan away and Isaac didn't see her again until a week later. It was snowing. They'd just shaved her head. Ice crystals glimmered on her scalp where the barber's straight razor had scraped too closely. Her face was swollen, her eyes like sad almonds, but she was still on her feet. Wrapped proudly in the blanket Nowatima, their great-grandmother, had given her, Susan looked just like a star in heaven.

Yesterday was the same. He stood in his newspaper office and watched helplessly as the television reporter interviewed the Acting Chief, Carl Tonica. Tonica said he'd personally felt for a long time that the entire Billy clan was out to get McAlester so that Auda Billy could become chief. Isaac believed that Tonica was upset, talking nonsense, so he drove to the tribal headquarters. He thought he could reason with the man, explain that this must be a mistake. His niece and his sister could not have murdered Chief McAlester. In the old days, his family were *Inholahta;* everyone knows that peacemakers never take up arms. When he arrived at the parking lot, there were dozens of non-Indians with deer rifles slung over their shoulders, standing around their cars talking quietly among themselves. There were guards at all the entrances of the tribal headquarters. Isaac spotted Hector D'Amato smoking cigarettes among the strangers in front of the building. Hector had only shown up in Choctaw Country last June. He was much younger than Vico. Auda disliked him, even more than his older brother, saying that Hector was the more dangerous of the two. He always wore fancy clothes, and charmed all the ladies at the tribal headquarters with chocolates and flowers on their birthdays. "So he could pump them for tribal secrets," said Auda. She also said that while Vico had bad diction and often spoke like a gangster, Hector had impeccable grammar. Finally she discovered why: Hector and McAlester had been roommates at Dartmouth.

Hector saw Isaac walking toward him and motioned for a tribal policeman to stop him. Isaac was frisked and told not to move. "I'm sorry,

Mr. Billy," he said sincerely, "the tribal headquarters are off-limits to you. Mr. Tonica will explain why."

When the acting chief came outside, Isaac could see that Tonica was truly afraid of Hector. One eye was swollen, and both hands were bruised, as if he'd had a run-in with someone big and mean. Probably one of Hector's hired thugs. As Tonica spoke, he was huffing and belching foul-smelling stomach gas into the air. Poor bastard, thought Isaac, he doesn't know that he's also being poisoned.

"This place is for Choctaws only," said the acting chief. "I'm revoking your Choctaw voter registration cards. All the Billys are prevented from using the Choctaw hospital if, God forbid, something terrible should happen to you. The tribal council also requested—before they were disbanded—that I petition the President of the United States and ask him to repeal your family's "Degree of Indian Blood" cards. In other words, you and your family are de-tribed." Tonica paused, then laughed like a lunatic. "Poof! You Billys are no longer Choctaws."

"This is Sunday, Carl, you didn't get all that done in one day," said Isaac.

"Don't be so sure. I'm in charge now and the Bureau of Indian Affairs will approve whatever I think is best to keep the peace. Things have changed since yesterday when your sister and niece killed our beloved chief."

Hatred boiled in Isaac's throat like lava. How could this ignoramus think that a piece of paper could dissolve Indian blood?

Tonica waved the documents in Isaac's face. "Oh, it's legal, and you're trespassing on Choctaw land. Your family is in for more trouble than you can imagine. Two BIA agents are on their way to search your sister's house and conduct a thorough investigation," he said, looking at Hector D'Amato for approval. "If you know what's good for you, you'll let them in."

Isaac spat in his face. "*Chishke ala aiathto!*" Your mother's vagina.

Tonica understood the insult and leapt at Isaac. The two men tumbled down the steps, punching and hitting each other and Isaac lost his hat and glasses. A tribal cop pulled them apart. "Gentlemen, please," Hector said softly, "we don't want to draw a crowd. It's not good for business."

"You're a dead man, Billy!" Tonica screamed. "*Hatak illi!* The words have been spoken. You're dead."

"Let's finish this right here," snorted Isaac, picking his cowboy hat off the ground. Tonica lunged at him again, but Isaac side-stepped him. The Acting Chief of the Choctaws landed flat on his face. Still pretty quick for a sixty-six year old, thought Isaac. Cutting steers for the past fifty years had taught him that move.

"Get him out of here," yelled Tonica. "I'm going to kill you, Isaac Billy!"

"Just like you killed McAlester!" shouted Isaac, as the tribal cop shoved him off Choctaw land and into the street.

The words were out now in the open. Even those backing Tonica would have to admit they'd heard his death threat. "Carl, you better think twice about starting a civil war—this is the 90s," he said, looking around for his glasses.

"Are these yours?" asked Hector, politely. Isaac reached for the glasses, but Hector dropped them on the pavement and mashed them with his shoe heel. "Whoops," he said smiling, "accidents happen. " Then he walked back inside the building.

Isaac headed for his truck. He dug around in the glove box until he found a pair of old black-framed glasses. Adair called them his "Buddy Hollys." She'd teased him so much the last time she was home that he bought a pair of gold wire rims. Now they looked like they belonged to some caved-in skull.

That's when Isaac started thinking about all that had happened in such a short time: land all burned up; his family behind bars; the fool, Carl Tonica, running the tribe for Italians. He blamed himself for not being more active in tribal politics. Maybe he should have been sitting on the tribal council all these years, but he'd preferred to take refuge at his ranch and talk to his cattle. Hide out. Even last year, when Susan openly accused Redford McAlester at a tribal council meeting of becoming a blood-brother of the Mafia, Isaac didn't take action. Rather, he'd criticized Susan for showing her true feelings in public. "All McAlester's going to do is prevent you from attending any more council meetings," he had said. And he was right.

The following week, McAlester had passed a law barring anyone from speaking at the tribal council meetings, except the chief. All future business of the tribe would be conducted in McAlester's private offices. When Isaac finally decided to call the elders together, Auda had asked him to wait a while longer. She said she was trying to reason with McAlester, to convince him that a chief couldn't make a law that so blatantly violated Choctaw traditions. Isaac had to blame himself for not following his instincts. He could have gathered all the elders together and peacefully removed the *Osano* from office, but he hadn't. For years he'd been shirking his duty, no denying it. Now he will have to make amends for failing his family. But under no circumstances did he believe his sister and his niece killed the chief.

He started the truck and headed toward his sister's. It was the home where so many Billys had lived. He and Susan had been born there, and it's where they returned after boarding school. The stately two-story, red brick house was built in 1888 by Nowatima. She'd gotten the money from Dixon DuRant, the Choctaw-Frenchman who founded Durant. Nowatima wanted a house large enough for all her descendants to live under one roof. When she was forty-three, though never officially married to DuRant, she had her only daughter by him, Laura Billy. Laura helped create Durant's first library—a big controversy among the Billy family, since Choctaws preferred to tell their stories out loud. Laura cultivated a field of sunflowers in order to host a yearly sunflower festival to honor *Hashtali,* although that last piece of information, from what Isaac heard, was withheld from the public. She finally married a fourth cousin, George Billy, and gave birth to Isaac's mother, Callie Billy, on June 22, 1898. He knows the exact date because his mother's birth is listed on the Dawes Rolls, officially documenting them as "Full-bloods." Callie grew up shaking shells on the dance grounds in Southeastern Oklahoma. Met his father, John Miko, at a dance in Tushkahoma. Nowatima told Isaac that Callie had had six stillborn babies before Susan. And then Isaac had come along four years later. He was seven when Callie and John were killed in the car wreck. Things got really bad for Susan and Isaac after that. Since Nowatima was so old, outliving her daughter and granddaughters, the court appointed a white guardian for them, and they were sent to a boarding school for Indian orphans. It wasn't until Susan turned eighteen that they were allowed to leave and return to live with Nowatima.

The house appeared lonely as he pulled into the driveway, but inside it still smelled of homemade bread. The aroma acted like a sweet tonic on Isaac's nerves. Susan must have been standing over the kitchen table with her sleeves rolled up to the elbows, patting dough into round balls, when she decided to confess to murdering McAlester. Isaac surveyed the upstairs to make sure deputy Vernon Klinkenbaird hadn't broken in. As he passed a mirror in the hall, he couldn't help but notice that he was a mess. His khaki shirt was dirty and torn at the pocket from the fight.

Behind his Buddy Hollys, his dark brown eyes seemed lost in wrinkles and time. He combed his salt-and-pepper hair, kept short since his army days. He tucked in his shirt and walked downstairs. He no longer looked anything like he pictured himself. He was an old, dark-red Indian man with a little potbelly, and he sensed that he didn't have too much longer to put things in order.

The huge west windows in the downstairs foyer warmed the wooden floors with sunlight. Toys belonging to neighborhood children were scattered everywhere. The library seemed like the most comforting room. In a way, it was the family museum. A French musket that once belonged to a famous Choctaw warrior rested on the fireplace mantle, and two ancient Choctaw burden baskets sat on a side table. The family's most precious possessions, however, were stored in a small trunk in a corner of the room: a tiny black and white porcupine sash, and some turtle shells. Both were said to have belonged to a powerful ancestor, a Shell Shaker. Isaac looked at the turtle shells, but did not touch them. He was afraid he might drop them. He gently lifted the sash out of the trunk and fingered the delicate hide. The quills from the porcupine had been stitched across the front in various designs, although now they were nearly unrecognizable. When the doorbell rang, he carefully put the sash away before answering.

Two sturdy bodies stood before him with dark coats, fierce heads, and lapping tongues. Doberman pinschers. At first, this strange turn of events reassured him. Dogs can sense the truth of most any situation and, fortunately, they are mute. Isaac pictured them nosing the empty house at a quick gait. He saw them sniffing in his direction, their tall ears pointed and ever alert, the smell of fur and urine about them. One of them barked at him several times. A long moment passed before Isaac realized this was not a dog's bark, but in fact a government agent attempting speech.

"Isaac Billy, we have a warrant to search—,"

"Uh-oh … looks like a trickster's after me."

"Old man, don't cut me off before I'm finished telling you why I'm here. If you try to interfere with an official Bureau of Indian Affairs' investigation you will be prosecuted to the… *ruff, ruff, ruff, ruff.*"

Isaac stared blankly at the two agents. "Sorry boys, I'm a little confused, I thought you were the barking dogs I heard."

One of the agents smiled at Isaac, but addressed his zealous partner. "This old-timer is really a dinosaur of another era."

"Yup," said Isaac, affecting feeble-mindedness.

"C'mon, I don't wanna spend my entire Sunday with some old man," said the other.

Isaac whistled softly and gestured to the BIA men to come in, as if they were really dogs. Neither seemed offended, but the whole house reacted violently, creaking and groaning at the invasion. A foul odor tracked the two men around as they snapped pictures and dug through Auda's drawers, pulling out her underwear and pantyhose and holding them up in the light. "Evidence gathering," the nasty one said. When they split up to widen the search, it was the nasty one Isaac continued to follow.

From Susan Billy's bedroom, the agent decided to take the only surviving picture of her husband, Presley War Maker. What he wanted with a picture of a dead Indian, Isaac couldn't imagine. Susan never let her daughters use his last name, War Maker. Some thought it was because they were never officially married by a white preacher, but that wasn't the reason. His sister maintained it was against her culture. "We are Billys," she had said. "That is final."

Isaac had always thought it was a good thing. Susan was following a very old tradition. In the old days, Choctaw children always traced their kinship through their mother's family. Not their father's. "It's a good way," he muttered. "Women outlive us anyhow."

When the toilet flushed, Isaac knew the government was finally leaving the house. He watched as they headed next door to pester the neighbors. That's when he discovered Auda's pet rabbit, Jean Baptiste, was missing from his cage. Someone must have let him out. He searched along the foundation of the house but finally gave up. Their lives were chaotic, now the missing rabbit. He had to get in touch with his nieces, Tema and Adair, so he drove to his office and faxed them two short notes. Later he would contact his distant relatives in Mississippi, and also Delores Love and her sister Dovie Love, in Poteau, Oklahoma.

And that was yesterday.

Isaac tells himself he has to move on as he drives toward his trailer in Soper. "I haven't missed work since the day I quit the Love Ranch in 1942," he mutters.

Like all other major events in his life, this must revolve around Indian women. The fire, the chief's bloody death, Durant's Big Peanut theft, all these events occurred during the autumnal equinox. Of course, this is *Tek inhashi!* Girls' Month is a time when things break open. Major changes happen during this time. The old is sloughed off and discharged, the new begins. He doesn't understand what it all means, but he's going to find out. If two jailed Billy women are so dangerous that Tonica and the Italians have raised an army of non-Indians to protect them, what will they do when four women come together?

"*Tek inhashi,*" he whispers, as he pulls to a stop in front of his trailer. Tema and Adair will be arriving tonight and he's glad they'll be taking charge of the situation. He wonders where Delores and Dovie are. They should be arriving soon too. When he steps out of the truck, the big yellow dog GeorgeBush runs to greet him. Isaac grabs handfuls of yellow fur and dogtalks with GeorgeBush, telling him about his broken glasses, the doberman pinschers, and all the other terrible things that have happened. He frequently names his favorite animals after U.S. presidents, it jacks up the price. Four years ago he sold Richard Nixon, his prize bull, for fifteen thousand dollars. Not that he will sell GeorgeBush, he just liked the name. He lugs his computer and printer into his trailer and begins heating up some red beans and fried potatoes. He pours a glass of cold buttermilk that he crumbles cornbread into.

Outside, the wind vibrates with the call of bullfrogs, and insects churning the last leaves of autumn into their death canopy. After he's eaten, Isaac boils a cup of white corn in a small amount of water. He takes the plate of corn outside and puts it on a tree stump. He stands facing the evening sunset. Everywhere he went today people stared back in astonishment. He caught whiffs of their conversations. "Shot him in the head." "Red lipstick all over his face." Isaac clears his mind, holds his hands upward and sings in a low voice:

"*Tubbi itid abachi kiah heh. Tubbi itid abachi kiah heh!*"

In an instant the answer comes. He remembers someone who can help, an old lady he met years ago at the stomp grounds. She was a wild-looking thing, with wiry hair down to the middle of her back. She wore awful-looking clothes and scared everyone she came in contact with, including him. She had once showed up at boarding school and talked to Susan. When he asked his sister what the old lady wanted, Susan shrugged and said the old lady only wanted to tell her stories. Isaac can't believe he'd forgotten her; surely she must be over a hundred years old by now. He nods politely to the wind and to the setting sun, then walks back inside the trailer, leaving the food, a gift for the spirits. Everything will be all right now.

In the late evening, he pours himself a cup of coffee and begins opening the mail for his weekly newspaper column. When he first started the paper in 1960 it was called *The Choctaw Swapper.* He began it as a way to advertise his cattle. Several years later, after seeing the Woody Allen movie, he changed the name to *Everything You Ever Wanted to Know About Choctaws, But Were Afraid to Ask.* He introduced an inside column by the same name. He wrote about Choctaw dances, and the best way to cook pashofa, a Choctaw delicacy. He used his mother's recipe as the standard everyone should follow. He wrote a long treatise entitled "The Choctaw Warrior's Shirt: What Is It?" He cited historical articles that Auda had published and made pronouncements on the correct color *real* warriors should wear. This issue sparked a debate of gigantic proportions among his old lady friends. He was soon forced to underwrite a newspaper contest to end the controversy. He judged the contest and reaped the rewards—three shirts of varying shades of red. "Perks" is what he wrote in his income tax file, a term he learned after attending an Indian journalists' conference in Oklahoma City.

Until very recently Isaac's personal income came solely from buying and selling livestock. But when he debuted his latest column, *Advice to the Choctaw Lovelorn,* he began to actually make money on his paper. Indians from all over southeastern Oklahoma wrote to him for advice concerning their love life. And they subscribed. When people began calling him "The Indian Ann Landers," overconfidence swelled him up like a tick. He became careless; he knew it was wrong at the time, but lust had him all charged up. That's what he told Susan when he got tangled in the "Billy media affair," as it had come to be known at Emo Jim's cafe.

Isaac looks up at the column on the wall and thoughtfully re-reads his mistake.

Dear Isaac: I am a chunky but beautiful Choctaw old lady. My husband is the closest thing to a soul mate I have found, but he's eighty now and sex no longer interests him. Until recently I've been saving myself, but sex still interests me. I would like a fling, but have no intention of leaving my soul mate. What should I do?
—Disappointed.

Dear Disappointed: Follow your heart and a healthy five-foot-six-inch tall Choctaw old man. There is someone near your age, someone you can trust, who won't want to break up your happy home. That way you will make everyone contented.

Isaac sighs. He never intended anything serious to come from this liaison. He's known for many years that true love has escaped him, that he might as well make the best of it alone. Besides, he would have gotten away with the affair if he hadn't put his own height in the paper. Of course, Susan knew right away who the woman was. It seemed the woman had told everyone about her problems. When Susan read his column she bawled him out.

"One of these days, you're going to get that big white cowboy hat of yours knocked off your head, old man! I don't care what she's telling you. Her husband is not feeble and he's not blind, either. You'd better put a stop to this before we have to lie about you on your tombstone."

He chuckles. If only Susan were here to scold him now. He chugs cold coffee and opens another letter, marked "Very Personal."

Dear Isaac: I am a Choctaw teenager, age eighteen. My boyfriend is twenty-five, and a Crow. He has asked me to marry him. He wants to take me to Montana. Should I do it? I am scared of leaving my mother and father because I am the youngest of four children.
    —Uncertain in Durant

Dear Uncertain: Choctaws don't marry birds.

He whistles while he types his response. He never got along with Crows. Custer lovers. Just as he is about to put away his typewriter, he stops and thinks about what he's written. Perhaps this Crow fellow is her true love, and he's discouraging her. If only someone had given him good advice about marrying his true love. Isaac tears up his response and writes a new one.

Dear Uncertain: It has long been my feeling that Indians only find true love once. Since you mentioned the age difference, I can say that it should never matter when two people are meant for each other. I have observed that while Crows do not like to fly (but Choctaws can and do), there are many airplanes available to you that come and go between Montana and Oklahoma. If this man is your true love, then don't let anything stand in your way of finding happiness. Life is too short.

At that moment his trailer door swings opens and Hoppy Billy pokes his head in. He is followed by Nick Carney, the artist who created Durant's Big Peanutmobile. Isaac acknowledges Nick, but looks skeptically at his nephew's leprechaun-green colored hair. The short bangs are spiked up in front and look kind of stiff.

"Eendians don't have green hair!" he snorts. "What happened to you? Women paint your hair while you were drunk? They did that to me once. I woke up after an all-nighter and the women had painted my fingernails bright pink. *Ooo-ee-e,* did the fellas give me heck. Come in. It's late, bad spirits are out after dark. Better shut the door... how'd you know where to find me?"

"I knew where I'd find you. Besides a Chickasaw guy at the gas station in Bokchito told me he saw your truck."

"How would he know? Chicks got no medicine. I got medicine. Maybe you got the wrong Isaac. That's me, Isaac medicine man, not Isaac paperboy. Yup, you got the wrong man. " Isaac grins.

His nephew does not crack a smile. For an instant, Isaac sees Presley War Maker reflected in Hoppy's eyes. Yup, Hoppy sure looks a lot like his grandfather.

"Has anyone told you, Uncle Tonto, that you should have been an actor?"

Isaac bursts out laughing.

"How ya doin', Mr. Billy?" says Nick. "I just came along for the ride, and well, ... to ask if I could park my car in back of your trailer. Me and the Big Peanutmobile are on the lam."

"Sure," says Isaac, smiling, "all enemies of the state are welcome." Turning to Hoppy, he asks. "Where's your mother?"

"She went to pick up Aunt Adair at the airport in the City. After that, they were going to meet some Indian lawyer who flew in from Tulsa. Then the plan is to spring the women from prison." Hoppy opens a cabinet door and rummages through the sacks of corn and salt. "Got any fresh coffee, Uncle? Not this dirty dishwater you're drinking."

Isaac dotes on his nephew. Many times he's wished he had a son, but that was not to be. "You two warriors ready to take on the spirits?" asks Isaac.

"That's why we're here. Nick's got to lay low, and someone has been following me around lately, a kind of woolly-headed old woman. Last night I saw her at the bar where we were playing."

Isaac mulls it over. "Could be one in the same. Some call her Divine Sarah. They say she speaks old-code Choctaw, and a whole bunch of languages I don't. She might be over at Talihina Way."

"I'm ready," says Hoppy. "As soon as I have something black and decent to drink."

Isaac points to his blue metal coffeepot on the stove. Hoppy gives him a disgusted look and retrieves a one-pound bag of finely ground espresso and a plastic Melitta filter out of the grocery sack he's brought in. He walks to the sink and pours Isaac's coffee down the drain. Boiling fresh water, he works over the brown powder.

"*Ooo-ee-e,*" laughs Isaac, inhaling the aroma of dark-roasted coffee. "You young warriors sure know how to live."

It is very nearly midnight when Isaac, Hoppy, and Nick drive north toward Talihina, a small town on the edge of the Ouachita National Forest.

"How long until we get to this wild woman's place?" asks Hoppy.

Isaac shrugs. "About an hour and a half. You know, ninety-five percent of the people living in Talihina are Choctaws," he boasts. "Not to change the subject," he says, clearing his throat, "but does your mother know that you've been seeing … *um,* visiting, other Choctaws besides myself on the weekends?"

"Like who for instance?"

"Well, Nick, and that Kampelubbi gal from Red Oak?"

"How'd you find out about us? Emo Jim's?"

Isaac chuckles. "Yup, I get all my newspaper leads there. Even the pictures on the walls talk. The coffee may be too weak for young warriors like yourself, but the gossip is strong."

"Men my age should have some secrets from their mothers, don't you think?" says Hoppy. "Besides," he adds defensively, "the only reason she took the job in Dallas was so I could be close to the family, and Choctaw people. So, I've gotten close."

Isaac smiles. "I'm only checking in case your mother asks me about our weekends in Durant."

"*Imoshe,* why didn't you ever marry?"

"Did once. She died. TB got her. Met her at boarding school. When your grandmother and I packed up to go home, WaNima Jefferson, who had no family of her own, came with us. We married a week before I left for boot camp. She died while I was overseas and is buried in Poteau. I visit her grave now and then."

"I'm sorry. Mother never mentions WaNima, and well, it's just that…"

"What?"

"Nothing."

"Say what's on your mind."

"Well, it's just a feeling...but somehow, that seems all wrong."

Isaac guns the truck up a mountain road that twists and turns like a snake. His nephew is looking intently at him. "I'm sure some of the family has mentioned WaNima, you just weren't paying attention."

Hoppy shakes his head, no. Nick looks out the window of the truck, sensing that this is none of his business.

"The truth is, WaNima wasn't meant for me," says Isaac. "I shouldn't have married her, so when she died I said, '*Ataha.*' Means finished." Isaac pulls his cowboy hat down low on his forehead, as if protecting himself from a strong wind. "You see, it's like this: when you have *nan i hullo,* which means 'true love,' then traces of that one woman linger on you the rest of your life. Every other relationship is doomed."

"And your *nan i hullo* is—," Hoppy stops short. "Sorry Uncle, I was about to be disrespectful."

"Like I was saying," says Isaac, "when you find *nan i hullo,* make sure you marry her, and that's all I have to say about that."

They drive in silence the rest of the way until they reach the Talihina Way Retirement Center. Isaac parks his truck in the lot in front of the main house, an office where two Choctaw nurses live. The big purple and red neon signs proudly say that Talihina Way was built with Casino of the Sun money. Further down the path, there are rows of individual houses, situated on wooded lots, and lit up at night by large street lamps.

Hoppy seems dumbstruck. "This is a nursing home!"

"I thought we were going out in the deep woods to visit the spirits," quips Nick.

"Not exactly," answers Isaac. "Auda built this retirement center with casino money. Small cottages every so many feet, where old people can bring all their belongings and animals and live in peace. She worked hard making the Choctaw Centers a reality. We have three of them in the Nation. One in each district. McAlester worked hard for 'em, too. A blind hog finds an acorn every once in a while."

"What does that mean?" asks Hoppy.

"McAlester wasn't all bad," explains Isaac. "He turned bad. Greed got him. Say, where'd you expect Divine Sarah to live, in a shack somewhere, all by herself? That's not our way. Auda wanted these communities to be situated like our old towns once were. Little houses spaced not too far from each other, but far enough to keep down jealously. *Ooo-ee-e,*" says Isaac. "There is nothing more violent than a jealous Choctaw woman."

"Why is she called Divine Sarah? That's not Choctaw," Hoppy says, getting out of the truck.

"It's not her real name, either. She has lots of different names. Legend has it that when Teddy Roosevelt and his Rough Riders came through Oklahoma he met this wild-looking Indian gal standing outside his hotel in Bokchito. She was dressed in this long turkey-feather shawl and spouting Shakespeare, or so the story goes. Supposedly she said to him, 'To be or not to be, that is the question.' From that day forward she started calling herself Divine Sarah, the nickname Sarah Bernhardt used." Isaac winks. "I told you the Choctaws always liked the French best." Isaac closes his door quietly and they walk toward the small houses.

Hoppy looks skeptical. "*Jeez,* she must be about a bazillion years old."

"Who knows? The Rough Riders used to be the mascot for Bokchito's High School, before they changed to Mustangs. But Divine Sarah wasn't quoting Shakespeare. I think she must have said, '*Hatak nakni nuhullo ma Abi chi buna hoh-cho keyoh.*'"

"What does that mean?" asks Nick, pulling his long brown hair into a ponytail.

"Kill the white man?" replies Isaac, not even cracking a smile. "Or not."

They meander around the grounds trying not to step in the vegetable gardens growing beside the houses. Finally a tiny woman dressed in a blood-red evening gown and gold sequined shoes appears before them in the moonlight. She cackles with a lungy smoker's laugh, then greets them in Choctaw, "*Halito chi kanas achukma?*" Hello my friends, are you well?

"*Aiyobank keyu,*" responds Isaac. Not good.

She is nearly toothless, and puffs on a cigarette between two spidery fingers. "I knew it was you, Nitakechi," she wheezes, tonguing her words together. "I've been waiting centuries on you to come back."

"She looks like Yoda with hair," whispers Hoppy to Nick.

"Meet my green-haired nephew, Hopaii, and his friend, Nick. Hopaii's the one in the family with panache." Isaac scowls, embarrassed that Hoppy has spoken before he was spoken to.

"Oh, I know the short one," she retorts in a hoarse voice. "I heard his band, the Chocozombies, play last night. You were correct, prophet boy, that was me in the audience."

Isaac is not surprised; this is why he's come to a trickster. They can shake things up. He quickly pulls a pouch of tobacco out of his pocket and offers it to Divine Sarah, who accepts it, then pokes him in the chest with her cigarette holder.

"I know why you're here, Nitakechi," she says smiling, revealing white cotton gums. "Come inside and meet the rest of my clan. Bring along the Chocozombie, and the tall handsome artist, too. I love big men."

Nick smiles. As they follow her, Hoppy complains that he's not short. Isaac doesn't question anything she says, or why she keeps calling him by another name. Indians are always getting new names and, besides, Nitakechi is a name that belonged to one of his ancestors.

Divine Sarah strolls in front of them with all the stylish slothfulness of an aging diva. Her skin is the color of pecans. Inside, Isaac looks around the room and is amazed. The floor, tables, cabinet tops, and windowsills are completely obscured by a dozen dozing cats, five rabbits, seven raccoons, and a baby duckling. Countless birds of all kinds are perched on the tops of curtain rods. Isaac wonders why the floors aren't covered with feces.

He takes off his hat and smoothes his hair. The old woman giggles as if she's embarrassed at the mess. She pushes cat food cans, plastic beads, and buttons off her chairs to make room for them to sit down.

"Even in the old days we had nice cabins," she puffs. "Not as nice as these, but the people lived in either bark houses or green cane houses with roofs made of palmetto leaves. We were so cozy. Like living in a basket."

Hoppy and Nick make no attempt to sit. They seem wary of the strange-looking woman and her menagerie. Finally, Isaac says, *"Abenili,"* sit down. They quickly comply.

Divine Sarah positions herself on an overstuffed white Naugahyde chair, unmistakably shaped like a molar, now badly stained. She looks at the movie poster of *Last Tango in Paris* tacked on the wall and gestures toward it with her cigarette holder. "I was in that."

"Never saw it." Isaac smiles sheepishly, then to be polite he adds. "But I always wanted to."

"Would you like some peanuts?" asks Divine Sarah.

"No, thanks."

"C'mon, they're delicious. It's the salt that really gets to me. Porcupines will do almost anything for it," she says, pointing with her lips to the large object across the room.

Isaac is stunned. Sitting next to the wall is the four-foot-long silver peanut: Durant's Big Peanut.

"*Jesus Jones*, we've been looking all over for that!" shouts Nick.

"How did she manage to get that all the way out here?" asks Hoppy.

"Big Mother Porcupine can do almost anything," she says, proudly. "*How now, Horatio? You tremble and look pale*, well, as pale as an Indian can look. *Is not this something more than fantasy? What think you on't?*"

Divine Sarah lets out another lusty cackle. "O God, Horatio, we had such fun making *Hamlet*. Back then I was a big star, a goddess really. After I performed in Victor Hugo's *Hernani*, I was the queen of Paris. Victor was mad for me. *Life at the Theatre de l'Odeon* was magical and I was *etre cousu d'or*. Filthy rich. Sounds so much nicer in French, *oui?*"

Divine Sarah pauses for a moment. "*Pity me not, but lend thy serious hearing to what I shall unfold.*"

"*Speak, I am bound to hear,*" answers Hoppy.

"You know *Hamlet?*"

"My mother's an actress. I had to help her memorize her lines. But you know that, don't you."

The diva cackles, "Psychic Indians are such fun. C'mon, let's play. What else do you know?"

"We're in a lot of trouble," says Hoppy, slowly. "There is a war going on, but hardly any Choctaws know that it's a real war, except for me, and Uncle, and Nick."

"That's about to change," says Divine Sarah, in a matter-of-fact tone. "And your mother, Haya, she's become a great actress. Her performance opening night of *A Doll's House* was divine. Simply divine. Her talents will also help us win the war."

"But her name is Tema," says Hoppy.

"Details, details."

Isaac squints at Hoppy as if to say, no use trying to pin down tricksters and actresses. They never tell the whole truth. Hoppy seems to understand and lets it drop. Isaac fills his pipe with tobacco and pulls smoke into his lungs. He passes the pipe to Divine Sarah who exhales singing:

"*Tobacco I will smoke, bring me fire, I will dance.*"

Divine Sarah trills in a smoky voice. Her kohl-rimmed eyes swerve toward Hoppy. Abruptly, she stops singing and hands the pipe to him. "It clears the house of bad spirits. Smoke and song keep them out, but it won't stop them from lurking around. Last night in Dallas, I also saw a mean ᵐᵉ stalking Haya. A shape shifter. At first, it slithered around the room, then skulked like a big black dog walking on his back legs." She demonstrates by raising her arms and slowly strutting about like some stiff-legged creature, then returns to the tooth chair and flops down, as though exhausted. "Your mother sent it away. I knew she could do it, she's a powerful woman, a granddaughter of Shakbatina."

Hoppy looks as if he wants to ask a question about Shakbatina, but thinks better of it and remains quiet.

"I must know, who is after my family?" Isaac asks patiently.

"The spirits have come back to pick a fight, that's what I'm supposed to tell you. Didn't you see the prairie fire? Miles and miles of the countryside have burned. And who could forget the Doberman pinschers?"

"So that was you playing tricks on me, " says Isaac, with a smile in his voice.

"*Naturalle. C'est bon pour chiens!*" Divine Sarah's yawn radiates a warmth from her mouth that makes Isaac drowsy. He can barely keep his eyes open. The two young Choctaws slump over in their chairs. Someone is beating a drum far away, and Isaac follows it until he finds himself in an open field. It's sunrise and the sky is red and yellow. Warriors from three different towns are hunting together. They track the old fields belonging to the Alibamu, a people related to everyone on the hunt. Although Isaac is in the field, he can hear Divine Sarah's voice. It's as if he's in two places at once.

"It all started for me when a Red Fox boy shot a porcupine with a blow gun," laments Divine Sarah, her voice betraying her hatred. "Today we'd call him Redford McAlester, back then he was Red Shoes. So, Koi Chitto gave my body to Shakbatina, who cut the red sumac leaves and smoked in my honor. It was a grand ceremony for me in the full light of *Hashtali*. When she stitched my skin into those beautiful designs, I was so flattered that I promised I'd be her family's protector."

Dry raspy sounds come out of Divine Sarah's mouth and she coughs. "I've been waiting so long to tell you this," she says, "I'm all choked up." Regaining her voice, she begins again.

"Red Shoes' mother was a Chickasaw. His father was a Choctaw warrior from the Western District town of Couechitto. His mother sent him to Couechitto to live and learn how to be an interpreter. The Choctaws tattooed Red Shoes' face with the inter-tribal sign of friendship. He became a messenger for both tribes. What a perfect job for a covetous man! Think of Red Shoes like you would a postman. The postman knows where everyone lives. Maybe he gives the mail to the wrong person. Maybe he waits a few extra days before delivering it. Red Shoes rose to power by trading information for muskets—to the English, or the French, or his own. Clever man.

"Then something strange happened. In 1731 he turned on his mother's people. He murdered two Chickasaw men and sold their scalps to a French officer. This was a sign: he thought he could become a leader of warriors in the Choctaw towns. During the next seven years Red Shoes convinced the young Choctaw warriors in the western towns that he was *Imataha Chitto*, the greatest giver, the red leader who could unite the people against the foreigners, but in truth he was a bloodsucker."

Divine Sarah looks at the red-hot tip of her cigarette. She seems to disappear, as if she is killed by the life of her story. After a long pause her voice shatters the quiet like thunder. "RED SHOES WAS NOT *IMATAHA CHITTO!*"

The birds fly off the curtain rods, the raccoons jump off the tables, and the rabbits run for cover under her tooth chair. Hoppy and Nick remain sleeping, but Isaac is in both places, seeing all that is happening then and now.

"He couldn't unite anyone. All he did was cause problems. He was a man with two hearts. The first belonged to the Red Fox, the Chickasaws. The second, a puny one, was his Choctaw heart," she hisses. "Shakbatina's family became entangled with this ravenous man. He ran after Anoleta pretending to be Rudolph Valentino because he wanted her family's influence among the eastern Choctaws who controlled the rich bottom lands. If you controlled the land, you controlled all things the *Osano* craved. Anoleta loved Red Shoes. She brought him into Yanàbi Town and tried to make everyone accept him. He repaid her by causing her mother's death."

Divine Sarah takes a final drag of her cigarette and mashes it out. "Red Shoes started the war that continues even now, two hundred and fifty years later. I've come to tell you—what is in the past has not passed. The time has come, Nitakechi, for you to fulfill your destiny. No more waiting to make amends. Prophet boy here will do his part, too."

Isaac opens his eyes, he has returned to his one self. Divine Sarah's story spanned eons. He saw the time when the energy of a thousand created the Nanih Waiya. Rivers took flight, leaving mud and stone that marked its fragrance with life. Everywhere he looked he saw eyes practically identical to his staring back at him. Behind those eyes, he felt sure, were minds overcome by the same astonishment he felt. He saw himself, the most frightening Choctaw he'd ever seen. His eyes, like black grapes, gazed out of a thin angular face. His long hair hung to his waist and blended into the blackness as he stood silhouetted in the doorway of his cabin. His skin stretched tautly across the knife of his features. A hard belly, a muscular chest, proved he was an expert hunter with a bow and arrow.

A dark, pulsating energy flows between Isaac and his past. He was there when his sister Shakbatina exchanged her life for the life of Anoleta. She had sacrificed herself in order to buy the Choctaws more time. But before her death she had told him to find the *Imataha Chitto,* the greatest giver, and marry her. She made him promise to prepare her body in the Choctaw way for the long journey. He also witnessed the fatal mistake he had made that has plagued him ever since.

"So what happens now?" Isaac asks, forgetting that one does not ask direct questions of a trickster or an actress.

"See my new rabbit," exclaims Divine Sarah, ignoring his question. "Not really red, but this color is what Choctaws used to call red before they had crayons and red high-heeled shoes. Jean Baptiste came running up here and asked me if he could stay awhile. He's a beauty, but he has such a potty-mouth. Oh, can he cuss!"

Divine Sarah sings softly to the rabbit who has poked his head out from under her chair.

"Some old ladies chain, rabbit putting in the garden, can't come out, I bet you five dollars, can't come out."

Isaac listens to the wind circling the house. A gloomy sound comes from his throat. "But Choctaws have completely forgotten Red Shoes. It is the fate of the greedy."

"But they haven't forgotten Redford McAlester. Besides, that is the reason the *Osano* returns," warns Divine Sarah. "To continue consuming—it's his job."

Isaac looks over at his young companions and wonders what their children will remember of Choctaw history.

"Nitakechi, you better go, the house is on fire. Your family—I'm watching out for them, but sacrifice is coming. Do you understand?"

He nods yes and feels as if he's dying, but it's not him—it's the old woman dissolving into a sweet musk. Sitting in her place is a big porcupine with quills the size of feathers flaring out like a headdress. He jumps up, yanks Hoppy and Nick out of their chairs, and the three run willy-nilly out of her place. The door swings open and her voice booms behind them. *"Che pisa lauchi."* I'll see you.

When they reach the truck, Nick passes out next to the passenger door. When he comes to, Hoppy is splashing his face with warm coffee from his thermos.

"Whaddaya doin'?" asks Nick, in a weak voice. "You're getting my hair all sticky."

"You stroked out—I had to do something."

"I've never been chased by a big hulking porcupine before," he says. "She really got to me."

"C'mon," says Isaac. "We've got to get home. Divine Sarah said our house is on fire."

His nephew stomps the gas peddle to the floorboard of the truck and they race away. Isaac tries to remember everything Divine Sarah showed him. He ticks off some of the details of his past, but Hoppy and Nick keep asking him questions.

"Imoshe, the woman slammed us, didn't she?" yells his nephew over the roar of the truck engine.

"What?"

"Made us see stuff that had happened a long time ago."

"Yup."

Hoppy drives like a wild man; some of the curves he takes at fifty miles an hour, then he jams fourth gear into third and guns the pedal again. The truck whipsaws down the mountain roads back to Durant, where chaos resides. Off and on, Isaac grabs the dashboard. He takes comfort in what Divine Sarah said. "The boy will do his part."

"I saw a whole bunch of people sitting on white cane mats," shouts Hoppy, excitedly. "Others were on red mats. You and Grandmother were there. Man, are you guys Choctough!"

"What's that?" asks Isaac.

"Rugged."

"Good, I wouldn't want you to think we were wimps. What else?" asks Isaac.

"Everyone in my dream was trying to decide what to do about a bad guy named Red Shoes," says Nick.

"What do you think that means?" asks Hoppy.

"That councils talk about a problem openly, and they debate and debate until they reach consensus," explains Isaac. "A long time ago,

Choctaw councils believed that everyone had to agree but, more important, they discussed things openly in public."

"I understand," says Nick. "Today, at our tribal council meetings, McAlester is the only one allowed to speak."

"We've gotten away from our traditions," says Isaac. "It's as much my fault as the other elders my age. We should have banded together and put a stop to McAlester's corruption. But that's about to change, I'm back on the right path now, and I know others who will join with me. I'll tell you a story about the old days. The Choctaw councils met for nearly twenty years before deciding to move against Red Shoes. They waited until everyone agreed. When twenty-two Choctaw towns allied against Red Shoes, he was assassinated, on June 22, 1747, the longest day of the year. A very sacred day for the old-timers."

Isaac waits a long time for Nick and Hoppy to respond. It's a lot to consider: Big Mother Porcupine, Divine Sarah, Sarah Bernhardt, the French actress with her anecdotes of Victor Hugo and her visions of war. This is a trickster's story of what is coming.

Finally Hoppy replies, measuring his words, "Don't worry, *Imoshe*, we are learning from you, and no matter how much time we have left, I will do my part."

"Me too," says Nick.

When they reach the outskirts of Durant at four A.M., Isaac smells smoke. He worries that his sister's house is on fire. Revenge of the Peanut Growers' Club. But at the corner of Main Street, it's Bryan County Jail that's burning. He leaps out of the truck and hurries toward the smoldering building. Someone tackles him from behind. "My sister and niece are in there," he yells.

"No they're not," says a sheriff's deputy, pulling him off the ground. "Everyone got out safely hours ago, sir. Please go on home, this area is off-limits to the public. Too dangerous."

Isaac limps toward the truck. "Must have pulled a muscle," he says, but before he opens the door, he gets switched. Instead of stepping into the truck cab, he is standing in McAlester's office. The chief slumps in a chair, his boxer shorts wadded around his ankles. Auda is sprawled out, unconscious on the floor next to the dead chief, the gun beside her. Two men in suits are standing above her, arguing in Italian.

"You can stop playing tricks on me now, I know what to do," he yells at the two men. Just as the words leave his mouth, the door to his pickup opens and Hoppy is asking if his leg is okay.

In the distance he hears a throaty cackle. Divine Sarah laughing like hell.

A soft yellow light glows in the stomach of the Billy house.

Hoppy parks the truck on the street. As Isaac steps down he asks Nick to stay outside and watch for strangers. Hoppy was the first one out of the car, but Isaac insists that he go in first and his nephew agrees. Isaac walks inside, putting one foot quietly down, then the other, as if on a forest floor. At the door of the library, Isaac can make out the outlines of two shapes. His heart quickens and he draws his knife. He slips in ahead of his nephew, and when his eyes adjust he sees Susan and Auda sitting like drugged birds in the dark. He switches on the light and his sister looks up from her stupor.

"It's about time, old man," says Susan Billy, stirring from sleep. "I was afraid to turn on all the lights until my warriors arrived to protect me," she says, in a mocking tone.

Susan's long hair is pinned up in a bun. Gray wispy bangs lightly touch her forehead. Her clothes are simple: a high turtleneck, and loose-fitting pants, with Kleenex and hard candy stuffed in the pockets in case she encounters children on the streets. Lying across her lap is the porcupine sash. She looks down at it and lovingly strokes the quills.

"It's okay, Grandmother," says Hoppy, leaning down to kiss her. "Your warriors are late, but we made it in time for the battle."

Susan Billy stands up and hugs her grandson, then examines his green hair without making a comment.

"Yup, I was worried too," says Isaac. "Afraid you weren't going to make it home in time to cook us breakfast."

"I wouldn't miss trying out my new recipe. It's called chicken-fried Tonica. Supposed to be real tasty," she says, chuckling.

Isaac looks at Auda. Her eyes are open, unfocused; she doesn't see him. Her mouth is swollen and her long hair is badly matted with blood.

Just then, the front door opens, followed by the sound of running footsteps. Tema Billy enters the library, and she's breathing fast. "We've been looking all over for you two. The sheriff's men probably aren't far behind. How did you get out of jail?"

"Walked out," replies Susan, as she places the porcupine sash back inside the trunk. "Everyone was shouting and running around on account of the fire. The deputy seemed to forget us. When our cell opened, I walked us out of the building and on home. It was the strangest thing, as if we were invisible."

"Oh Mom, we've been so worried." Tema grabs her mother and holds her. Finally she bends down to kiss Auda on the cheek.

"Where is Adair?" asks Susan Billy.

"Bringing up the rear, Ma," answers Adair, who is followed by a tall slender man with braided hair and a briefcase. "We stopped to talk to the young man outside."

"That's Nick Carney, my friend," says Hoppy.

"Oh, he must be Martha Carney's boy. He's such a talented artist," says Susan. "Bring him inside, and both of you boys get something to eat."

Hoppy goes to get Nick, and Susan talks to her daughters. Isaac studies the Indian lawyer. He's seen many a good Indian sell himself to the *Inkilish okla* profession. Multitudes of them pedal "sovereignty" like liquor. To him, these paper warriors, men and women who've never handled a real weapon in their lives, have come forward only to collect five hundred years of back pay for themselves. Rarely, if ever, do they do anything for the people, and never for free. McAlester, another worthless plug, used to brag, "Even if we're wrong, we must fight to protect our sovereignty!"

Isaac turns his back on his sister and her girls, and the man they've hired. He reminds himself that they know what they're doing. He sighs.

Susan must sense what he's thinking because she stands up and walks over to Isaac, putting her hand on his shoulder. "Tomorrow, please get Auda to the doctor. I don't know what's wrong with her, but after I arrived at the jail, she suddenly went blank. The sheriff will probably be here any minute now. If I give myself up, maybe they'll leave Auda with you."

"I've spoken to Delores," says Isaac, dropping his voice low. "She and Dovie are coming."

Adair, who has been sitting quietly on the arm of the couch, finally takes charge. "Ma, Uncle Isaac, we're all here and we can help each other. Auda will see a doctor in the morning, and Mr. Battiste will work out your legal releases from the county jail," she says soothingly. "Mr. Battiste doesn't think the county technically has jurisdiction over the tribe."

Isaac studies Adair. She sure seems to be putting a lot of faith in a man she hardly knows.

Susan politely extends her hand to the lawyer. "I'm pleased to meet you, Mr. Battiste. Do you know Leota Battiste?"

"Yes, ma'am, she's my aunt."

"She and I used to sew star quilts at a women's sewing group in Tulsa, about a hundred years ago. So you're Alabama Conchatys. You know, our families are probably related if we go back far enough."

"That's what I've heard."

"Girls, please take Auda upstairs and put her to bed, I want to tell Mr. Battiste how I killed the chief, so when the sheriff comes, he'll know if he can help me."

Isaac listens without reacting. He doesn't believe for a second that his sister killed McAlester, because in his vision Auda was unconscious in the chief's office. And the two D'Amato brothers were standing over her.

He walks outside. Morning is coming and once again his family is together. The gate in Isaac's head has finally opened. The wind has blown away the smoke and soot caused by the prairie fire, and the Oklahoma skies are clearing. The world has a roof of clouds turning pink and yellow.

Isaac digs in his pocket and takes out a tiny gray stone no bigger than his thumb. It once belonged to his great-grandmother Nowatima. After he returned home from boarding school, he'd sit with her for hours in front of their fireplace. Night after night she would draw stories in his mind. He saw a hurricane so powerful that it made the Mississippi run backwards. At the river *Ahepatanichi,* he saw kettling birds of an unknown species dropping excrement on the heads of Spanish invaders. "What the *Hispano* didn't realize," smiled Nowatima, "was that magical excrement containing the seeds of potatoes had been dropped on them. So the invaders would unknowingly spread potatoes to starving people everywhere. A gift from our Seven Grandmothers." Isaac witnessed a war between the Natchez and the French that began over the slaughter of trumpeter swans. Nowatima said the French didn't know that they built their fort over a bird refuge, a place protected by the Natchez. When the Natchez leader, Stung Serpent, and his son brought a pair of mated swans to Chépart, the fort's commander, he threw them out of his house and shot the birds just to show how little he regarded their gift. This so enraged the Natchez that they killed Chépart and two hundred and fifty other Frenchmen. Then they planted the French heads on pine posts in the center of the fort. Food for the birds. Eventually the Choctaw helped the Natchez move in with the Ouachitas, who were living along the Red River. "You see," said Nowatima, "that is how the Choctaws saved the French, our allies. Otherwise the Natchez would surely have wiped them out. Now you know how a people in the swamp can slip into another name as easily as food slips inside your mouth. But the real truth of my stories is that nothing ever dies."

Isaac removes his bulky glasses and brushes a small tear away. Sunlight glints on his face like a mirror, the morning sky is bright blue.

Many years after Nowatima's death, he asked Auda to find out what the historians wrote about the Natchez war. She told him it happened in 1730, but that in addition to shooting the birds, the Frenchmen had called the swans worthless water fowl.

Hekano, he does not question Nowatima's stories. Her words were confident, rich with details. A long time ago—she would say. Isaac drifts into the world she made for him and the stone warms his hand.

5 | Prayers for the Mother

Durant, Oklahoma
Tuesday, September 24, 1991

Smoke.

It coils lazily toward the hole in the roof of the green cabin like a feathered serpent. From her bed Auda watches the smoke rise. Hours seem to pass before she walks across the dirt floor to the smoldering fire. It's then she realizes that this is not her bedroom in Durant. The walls are cane poles. Palmetto leaves thatch the roof.

She doesn't consider the enigma for long. A very strong desire, beyond understanding, makes her run outside toward the river where smoke hangs just above the water.

She sees a man. At first he looks unfamiliar, but she runs to greet him. Robust and solid, his tight brown skin is so lustrous he seems to shimmer. He picks her up. Her legs go around his waist and her arms lock around his neck. Lust drools out of her mouth and she murmurs his name, *Red Shoes*.

He looks at her. Lays her down on the ground, his long black hair falling around her face. She sees the zeal in his eyes. He wants to plunge in. They smile at each other.

"You're getting slippery, aren't you?" he coaxes.

Hearing his voice, her body absorbs him through a thousand open pores. She breathes like a horse running with an impatient rider, moans during orgasm, unable to say a word to the man who had once rubbed her painstakingly until he had deflowered her.

They fall asleep. Wake up.

Red Shoes whispers, "Here in the smoke with you, one more time."

She nods yes. "But first you must tell me what you know about the *Inkilish okla* and *Filanchi okla*. What is coming?"

He answers. "Pitiful as they are, they will one day crowd us out of our homelands. Also, everyone in the world will eat our foods—*Ahe, tanchi, tobi, isito, bapho,* but they will be called potatoes, corn, beans, squash, and peanut butter. Everything we have they will claim as theirs." He pauses. "For a time."

She asks. "*Baska* too?"

"Yes. They will be called casinos."

They stop talking. She pulls him to her.

He asks what she is doing.

"I'm looking at the tattoo on your face. Is that the same pattern we carve on our pottery bowls?

He smiles. "Yes, my father's *iksa,* the Choctaw warriors from the town of Couechitto, tattooed my face with the sign of truth and friendship. When I was a messenger I was instructed to deliver the exact feelings and words of our people."

She laughs. "Do you groan with pleasure when you tell people exactly how I feel?"

He grins a little mockingly. "Of course."

"I was sure of it." She laughs, then is silent. "But what if you lie?"

"Then I will be forgotten."

She takes his face between her hands. "What did you do?"

"You know."

She cries softly. "No, I don't know. My children are supposed to come from this marriage. My relatives will brag that I married the warrior Red Shoes, the *Imataha Chitto,* the greatest giver. Repeat my words exactly as I have said them. Say it," she demands. "Then it will come true."

Red Shoes does not speak but looks at her with longing. Smiles. And behind the smile she sees his despair. They both cry.

She kisses him. They hold each other, lost in the pain of knowing they cannot stop what is coming. She pulls him to her again, but he vanishes like a shadow in sunlight. Auda begins to whimper because she knows now that she is dreaming. She has no husband, no children. She sits on the edge of the bed. Tries to wake up, but hears gunshots, the ones that keep firing in her head. Black smoke fills the room. A sheriff's deputy charges through the door with a gun in his hand. Screams when he sees the dead man whose face and mouth she has covered with red lipstick kisses, like a consolation.

Enraged, she turns on the deputy. "Look at what is left of our people—a chin, a foot, a jawbone, and ten thousand feet of intestines hanging from the trees in Yanàbi Town. I demanded his head and got it," she says, not really sure what she means. She stays like that, riveted amid the din of ringing gunshots until she doesn't hear them anymore.

Auda rolls into the fetal position. She wants to stop the nightmare. Finally she cries herself awake. She knows she's awake because the photograph of Redford McAlester is still on her nightstand. She drops it into the trash can. He died on Sunday. They took him to the morgue. She told them that he had been nothing more than a common thief. That she could not stop what was coming.

Bitter tears run down the pinch of her black lashes. Her head is exploding. She's had headaches before, but nothing like this. She rushes to the bathroom sink and vomits water clear as rain. After standing beneath a warm shower, she feels more relaxed and returns to the sorrow of her bed.

The bedroom door creaks open and Adair comes in and sits next to her. A whole minute passes before she speaks. "I heard the water running." She gently pushes the wet hair off her forehead. "You're going to be all right."

Auda turns her face to the wall. Something cracks inside her. It's her voice. Noise comes out of this broken place. "I gave Redford McAlester everything. I didn't mean to."

"I know."

Silence.

"But just now, I was dreaming about Red Shoes." She turns back around. "You know the one I mean?"

Adair nods yes.

"It's the craziest thing, I know about him because of my research, but in my dream I was with him…" Auda puts her hand over her mouth to stop herself from speaking. After all, there are some things you shouldn't tell.

Her sister does not make a move to comfort her, nor does she act particularly surprised. "We've all been having weird dreams and hearing voices." Adair squares her shoulders. "You've got to get up. Help us, help you. The sheriff came at eight this morning and took Ma to jail."

"For what?"

"She confessed, again."

"Oh no, this is all wrong," says Auda, softly. "It won't help matters."

"Ma's telling whoever will listen that she shot the casino chief. It doesn't help matters that her gun was found at the murder scene. What else could the sheriff do but take her seriously?"

Suddenly a commotion erupts downstairs; an old man's voice reaches up to Auda's bedroom. He's speaking in Choctaw, saying that he does not accept things the way they are. Then they hear a door slam.

Adair shrugs. "It's been like this for the past four hours. Uncle Isaac, Hoppy, and a lawyer went to get Ma out of jail. The county transferred jurisdiction to the Choctaw Superior Court. Don't worry about bail money, I brought plenty of cash."

Auda drops her gaze. All the problems she's causing. Her sister seems to sense how she feels, but presses on.

"Aunt Delores called from the road. She and Dovie should be arriving any time now. The lawyer we hired is Alabama Conchatys. His name is Gore Battiste and he'll represent you, and Ma—if you agree. She said it's okay with her, if it's okay with you. He stayed up all night making notes about your case."

A truck pulls up in the driveway, the passenger door squeaks as if it needs oiling. Adair looks out the window. "More Indians. I think they're waking up," she says, lighting a cigarette. "The kitchen is overflowing with covered dishes. Some people have even brought money for Ma's defense. And yours, of course," she adds quickly.

While her sister talks, Auda examines her as a parent might. Weight same, fingernails smooth, a sign of good protein. Her clothes and hairdo, all retro, make Adair seem more exotic than ever. She's the daughter who can most easily pass for white if she wants to. Her light complexion helps people mistake her for French, Lebanese, Spanish, Mexican, or Italian. Adair smokes filterless French Gitanes and sometimes reeks of ash.

Auda understands; smoke is a screen you can retreat behind.

"Ma's worried because you were in shock, so I made appointments at the Choctaw clinic this afternoon with a doctor and a dentist."

Auda doesn't answer, she's stuck on the Gitanes. "Got any more on you?"

Adair gives her the pack and a lighter. "Ma's friends are organizing a gathering tonight at Blue Creek Grounds. I hope those old-timers don't want to start another civil war." She pauses. "About the lawyer…"

"What about him, anything I should know?"

Adair starts to speak, but merely shakes her head. "No, nothing I can think of. Ma's *pashofa* is on the stove. Come downstairs." Then pausing, she adds. "Funny thing, when the sheriff and his men arrived this morning, Ma offered them some soup before they handcuffed her. Then they asked us if we'd mind putting some of it in a Tupperware for them." Adair smirks a little. "And we did."

When her sister leaves, Auda puts her head in her hands. She tries to remember exactly what happened at the jail. She told her mother about the spirit of the Shell Shaker, then her mother confessed to killing the chief, then the rest is blank, until she woke up in her own bed. She feels so ashamed. They'd spent so much time arguing about Redford McAlester, and now her mother has traded places with her.

How did their feud begin? Perhaps at a feast her mother hosted, shortly after the election in 1983. They were having a venison roast, mashed potatoes, fried squash, and red beans. For dessert, sunflower cakes and her favorite, *bahpo*, a nut pudding made from peanuts. Several colleagues from Southeastern Oklahoma State University had been invited, along with tribal employees, and the neighbors. In front of everyone her mother suddenly turned on her. "Finish with that man," she had commanded. "McAlester is a *Osano*. End of story."

Susan Billy's fury had centered around an elderly Choctaw named Fred Tubby. It seems that same morning, the old Indian had asked McAlester to drill him a water well for his "punkins." Everyone around Durant knew that Fred cultivated large tracts of land for corn, beans, squash, and pumpkins, and that he gave away the produce to single Choctaw mothers.

"Fred comes to McAlester for a little help. Do you know what your chief told him?" ·

Auda shook her head.

"'This is not a welfare state, Mr. Tubby, we can't help you.'" Susan Billy then passed her a plate of fried squash, and left the feast. Auda was humiliated. Her mother had purposely prepared all the foods that Choctaws had eaten before contact with whites. She was trying to make a point. Even though McAlester knew Fred Tubby was growing Indian crops for Choctaw women, he still refused to help him. In essence, McAlester was starving his own people.

Later, her mother's comments became even more cruel. "Still the Casino Chief's whipping girl, huh?" Or, "How much money did he steal today?" Although she and her mother lived in the same house, they'd stopped speaking to each other, except when outsiders were present.

Over the past year, she'd felt abused by McAlester and abandoned by her mother.

It isn't her fault that she's not heroic like Susan Billy. Her mother is the seventh daughter of a seventh daughter. Powerful medicine. The story of the Billys is like the *begats* in the Bible. Auda can recite it from memory. There was Chunkashbili, shortened to Bili, later Billy, the family's last name. Bili is the mother of Marie. Marie gives birth to Noga sometime around 1779 in Louisiana, near Houma Town. Noga is the mother of Pisatuntema, and they have a farm near Yanàbi Town. Pisatuntema gives birth to Nowatima around 1825, in the same farmhouse. But after the Choctaws walk to Oklahoma in 1831, Yanàbi Town and the Indian farms are taken over by white people. Nowatima settles in Durant. Her daughter Laura marries George Billy. Callie, the daughter of Laura, comes along next. She marries John Miko in 1914. Callie Billy has six daughters by John, all stillborn. Susan, the seventh, arrives on September 22, 1921. Auda's great-great-grandmother, Nowatima, breathes into Susan the mysterious power of breath and mind, and she survives. Four years later Isaac is born, and the rest is history. Her mother marries Presley War Maker. Auda and her sisters have been raised in a house filled with ancestors, and their stories.

Auda removes a nappy white robe from her closet. She didn't ask for this. She's a firstborn, only without the offspring. Another criticism. She's the daughter who most resembles Susan Billy. Same eyes and hair, same height—five feet, two inches tall. Same brains, or so people assume. The eldest girl is supposed to take her mother's place as the head of the family, but she never wanted to. As a teenager she wanted to see the world, date men, be out of range of her mother's influence.

In 1969, when everyone was demonstrating against something, Auda was protesting too. The Billy house was a kind of Choctaw day care center for adults, and children, and stray animals. It was always jammed with Indians needing something and Auda didn't want to babysit. So she walked to the bus station, boarded a Greyhound for the two-hour trip to Oklahoma City, and never looked back. After a while, when the personal revolution wore thin, she started college. Later, in 1976, she entered graduate school, to correct the tribe's eighteenth-century record. This work would become her progeny—a history book.

Auda braids her long hair, then examines her broken front teeth in the mirror. She runs her tongue back and forth on the jagged edges. Strange feeling. She puts out her cigarette, pulls her robe belt tight, and descends the precarious stairs at the back of the house. When Nowatima built the house, she had the largest kitchen in Durant. Back then Billy women were well under five feet tall and the narrow wooden stairs were adequate. In 1991, they're better suited for the errands of children. She stands on the last stair and inhales. The whole room smells of corn. Fried corn fritters, corn soup, plates of cornbread, corncob salads.

In the corner of the kitchen a man sweeps up broken glass, the remains of his plate. Adair is holding a dustpan and Tema is talking on the phone. Standing silently on the stairs, Auda goes unnoticed. She decides the sweeper must be the Alabama Conchatys. He looks familiar. About forty—maybe older, it's hard to know with Indians. His brown hair hangs straight down around his shoulders, and he dresses like all the other Oklahoma Indian lawyers: Cowboy boots, starched jeans, white dress shirt, dark blue sports jacket. He seems comfortable with her sisters, as if he's family.

"Mother says she killed the chief," says Tema, into the telephone. "I know, of course she didn't. Thank you." Another long pause. "Yes, please do say prayers for the Mother, and for all of us. We appreciate that."

Tema hangs up. Seconds later, there is another ring. She repeats the conversation, nearly word for word, and listens patiently. "No, Auda's fingerprints weren't on the weapon, neither were Mother's. It's circumstantial evidence. Our lawyer thinks the case will be dismissed."

The lawyer carefully sweeps shards of glass toward Adair. "Have you seen today's paper?" he asks, softly. "There's another front-page story on Auda."

Adair nods and he corners her with the broom. Auda notices that, interestingly enough, Adair doesn't seem to mind.

Tema hangs up the phone and it immediately rings again. She answers, then smiles and takes the call in the other room. Phrases like, "you maniac," mixed with endearing, muffled giggles, float back into the kitchen. Auda knows the caller is her brother-in-law. Tema never cooed until him. She's always been a little envious of her youngest sister and Borden Beane. Who could have guessed that Tema would settle down with a man from England?

"Yes," says Tema, quickly dragging the phone back into the kitchen. "Good question. I'll ask our lawyer that ... I miss you, too. Break a leg tonight." Then she hangs up and walks over to her lawyer.

"Okay Battiste, I want to know something. Right after it happened, why was Auda taken to the county jail instead of the Choctaw Nation's jail?"

"Vernon Klinkenbaird, a sheriff's deputy, was the first to arrive on the scene," he says, matter-of-factly. "The sheriff knew he didn't have jurisdiction; I think he was trying to protect Auda from a "lone gunman" taking the law into his own hands." Her lawyer takes the dustpan from Adair and collects one last sliver of glass on the other side of the room.

At least he's thorough, thinks Auda.

"I went this morning and submitted our papers to Choctaw Superior Court; that's where this case will be heard—with the tribe. When your mother was released, she left with Isaac and Hoppy to run some errands. They'll be along any minute now," he says.

"Doesn't it strike you as odd that a local sheriff's deputy was there before the Choctaw cops?" asks Tema.

"Not particularly." Then he shakes his head. "I take that back. Everything I know about this case is off-kilter."

Tema continues probing. "What about Mother's confession?"

"Temporary insanity."

"Oh, Ma's not going to stand for that," says Adair, loudly.

Here it comes, thinks Auda. When they were little, Adair was the one most likely to throw a wild punch, usually at her sisters. Later at boys. She's never had any patience. For a Choctaw, she's hot-wired. Auda steps down into the kitchen; as the eldest, she should do something. But without warning her mother's voice roars out of her mouth, *"I killed Redford McAlester! I did it and I alone will stand trial for his murder!"* Everyone freezes. It isn't really her mother's voice, nor is it particularly loud, but she sounds so convincing, she can't believe it's her own self.

Neither can her sisters. From the look on their faces, they must be comparing the woman with the broken front teeth to the older sister of their childhood. The one who held their hands when they walked to school, or mopped the floor after they'd finished bathing. Growing up, Adair and Tema were almost twins. Only a year apart, they behaved like two wild ponies with skinny legs, so nervous they'd bite if she kissed them too much. But now that it's their turn to clean up her mess, she's as uncertain how to act as they are.

Her lawyer is the first to respond. "The Choctaw Superior Court has the last word on whether to accept your mother's confession or yours, Miss Billy. Whatever the case, if you want me to represent you, we need to talk now."

All at once, Auda feels shocky. Her head throbs. For an instant she's back on the floor of McAlester's office. Is there blood on her lips? She looks at her feet—bare. She has jettisoned her bloody red pumps by the side of his chair. A deputy yells. Then her blown-out teeth. Then nothing.

She blinks. She's no longer on the floor. It's Tuesday, she's standing in her mother's kitchen.

Look at what is left of our people! A chin, a foot, a jawbone, and ten thousand feet of intestines hanging in the trees of Yanàbi Town.

"Honey, I don't think you know what you're saying," Tema says gently, as she pulls out a chair for Auda.

"I said I did it."

"But after that?"

"That wasn't me."

Her lawyer is obviously uneasy, and her sisters glance at each other in the unspoken language they've shared since childhood. Auda usually knows what passes between them, but not this time.

"Don't do that," says Auda, sitting down. "I'm not crazy ...well, mostly not."

"We don't think you are. Remember I told you, we've all been hearing voices," says Adair, lowering her voice.

The lawyer drags out his leather-tooled briefcase and pretends he didn't hear that last remark.

"Eat something, please," coaxes Adair, "while you tell Gore what happened."

Auda looks at her lawyer. "My sister wants us to get acquainted."

He sits across from her and is very solicitous. "I don't know if you remember me Miss Billy, it's been about eight years."

She nods, trying to conceal that she doesn't remember him.

"I'm sorry we're meeting under these circumstances, but I've handled many criminal cases, and practiced in both tribal and state courts. Some of my cases have been ..."

She cuts him off. "If my mother and sisters think you're all right, Mr. Battiste, you're hired."

"Let's get to work then. With all the people coming in and out, we should really go to my office."

"Where's that?"

"Tulsa—about three hours from here," he says, smiling.

Good, he's trying to put her at ease. She wants to be at peace, to finally finish this. While he prepares to question her, she ticks off the places where they might have met. A tribal conference in D.C.? A National Congress of American Indians meeting?

"Mind if I use a recorder while I take notes?"

"Of course not," she says, lighting another one of Adair's strong cigarettes.

"Start at the beginning."

But before they can begin, a neighbor woman with two small children walks in through the back door of the kitchen. The woman doesn't raise an eyebrow at the sight of Auda calmly smoking cigarettes at the table. Like other Indians in the neighborhood, she knows all that has been said, and all that has happened so far in the Billy house. It's a belief Choctaws have—that almost everything in life is meant to be shared. Especially tragedy.

"I brought this for the Mother," she says, in Choctaw. The woman puts a plate of roast beef in front of them and abruptly leaves the same way she came in.

Tema and Adair join them at the table. Each takes a seat, one on either side of Battiste, which makes Auda feel as if she's appearing before a panel of judges. He rewinds the tape and searches her face for signs of something, perhaps growing insanity. "Ready?" he asks.

Auda slowly begins talking into the machine. She explains how she and Redford McAlester met, when she became Assistant Chief, what their original plans were in 1983 for revitalizing the Choctaw Nation. She's stalling. Preparing herself for the impact of what must come next.

"I want to know about you and McAlester," says Gore, his candid brown eyes looking directly into hers.

She waits a full minute before replying. The small cassette wheels of the recorder document her silence. Finally she speaks. "I loved the energy he put into things," she says. "It's funny...just now, I realize that I never saw him dance. Not at Green Corn, not at Stomp Dances, not ever."

Her lawyer doesn't respond, but continues looking at her.

"We were a popular Indian couple. We led a ceremonial life. Tribal dinners at home for local businessmen and state legislators. Elaborate banquets for senators in D.C. During our first two years in office we were continually in each other's company."

"What happened?"

"The casino."

"Go on."

"In 1988, after the National Indian Gaming Regulatory Act was passed, the Choctaw Nation built the Casino of the Sun. As you know, because we're a sovereign nation, there's no external oversight of the casino operations. Only three people—Red, Vico D'Amato, and Carl Tonica—were privy to the real set of books, not the phony ones they submit to the BIA. How much do you think the casino took in last year?"

Her lawyer's voice is impassive. "*The Daily Oklahoman* reported twelve, so I figure, fifteen million."

"Twenty million. But almost sixty million was deposited in our New York accounts. You figure it out, where did the money come from?"

Tema looks shocked, but Gore Battiste's expression remains placid.

"So, the tribe made more money than they reported. But with that much money, we could have paid off the original ten million to Shamrock and be shed of them," says Tema.

"Hardly," says Auda. "If you agree to always overpay, then you have a perpetual partner." For the first time she sees mistrust growing in her sister's eyes. She doesn't want Tema to think she agreed with McAlester's business dealings with Shamrock, so she tries to explain. "More than seventy percent of the casino income goes to pay our yearly contract fees to Shamrock Resorts. After the tribe pays Shamrock, and then pays the local bureaucrats to overlook all kinds of petty violations, we still have to pay tribal salaries, pay for the subsidized housing for the elderly, pay tribal health care costs, maintain the buildings, and operate our other tribal businesses on what little is left."

Auda's energy is growing. Her pace quickens and she realizes that she wants the whole world to know this story. "Look where the Casino of the Sun is situated! Durant is just one hour from Dallas, a city with thousands of people who want to gamble. More important, the casino is less than an hour from I-35. Retirees from across the upper Midwest can stop and gamble on their way south to Mexico, or to the Texas coast for the winter. With so much customer traffic, it looks like the casino could have taken in sixty million, but it didn't. We were set up to benefit the Mafia, not the Choctaw people."

Adair nods slowly. "There's a rumor going around among the securities brokers that the Feds are amassing evidence against a tribe and their New York bank for violating federal money laundering statutes. Our analysts follow that kind of thing because it impacts bank stocks. I've suspected ..."

Auda interrupts her. "Red was laundering money for the Genovese family. They're the ones who own Shamrock Resorts, which bankrolled the casino. Sure the tribe had issued some bonds to raise money, but the bulk came from Shamrock Resorts. In exchange, Red received a percentage, and some bonds. Over the past couple of months he'd been siphoning off more than his cut. Last week he took an extra large bite, two million. It set off bells and whistles all over New York. Shamrock is missing ten million, and the D'Amato brothers probably think that's the reason I shot him—for the money."

"What does all this mean, Auda?" asks Tema, sadly.

"It means, now that McAlester is dead, your sister could be tried as his accomplice *and* his murderer," says Gore. "But in federal criminal cases, the Feds must prove that the money being laundered is from an unlawful source, like drug trafficking, or that it's being used abroad in ways that violate international law." He continues writing.

Auda mashes out her cigarette. "I wasn't his accomplice, but I have an idea about what he was doing with the money." She pops a piece of meat in her mouth, and for a instant savors the taste until she realizes she can't chew normally.

"Is that why Tonica de-tribed us?" asks Tema, impatiently. "If you tell him where the ten million is, the Billys will be reinstated in the tribe?"

Adair sits up, stock straight, in her chair. At last she seems to grasp the situation. "No, Tema, kicking the Billy family out of the tribe is a public relations move to convince jurors that Auda stole the money. Don't you see, they want everyone to believe that the chief discovered what she was doing, so she murdered him. It's a perfect cover-up."

With difficulty, Auda swallows the partially-chewed meat, but nods to show she agrees.

Her attorney keeps writing, then suddenly stops. "What a neat and tidy story, Miss Billy, I'm only sorry that it's so full of holes."

They lock eyes. "I have Red's wire transfer reports hidden in my room," she says.

"Documents are only half-truths; you're an Indian historian Miss Billy, you know that."

Adair chimes in. "I've been doing a little data collecting myself ..."

Agitated, Gore waves her off. "Doesn't matter, Adair," he says. "She's not telling me anything I couldn't find out in a few weeks of investigating the case."

Auda throws him another bone, to hold him off as long as she can.

"Multiple sources of funds were wired to the Choctaw Nation's New York accounts and mixed in with our casino and other tribal business deposits. That disguises their origins. From New York, the monies were transferred to London and Swiss banks in the name of Shamrock Resorts. I traced conference calls to the tribe's 'relationship managers' in the banks in New York, London, and Zurich. I have proof."

He stares a hole through her.

"C'mon Miss Billy, why did you take your mother's pistol, load it, and shoot Redford McAlester in the head? A phone call to the FBI would have been a lot less messy."

He's baiting her, just like the lawyers on TV. She looks to her sisters for help. They're pouring all their love through their eyes, but they remain mute.

"Most likely Carl Tonica was also involved, so why didn't you shoot him too? So far, you've only given us reasons why McAlester should be in prison. He certainly didn't deserve to be shot with his briefs pulled down. Tell the truth, why did you kill the Chief of the Choctaw Nation? Say it!" he yells.

Auda slides her clenched fists down into the pockets of her robe and claws at the cotton lining. She utters a string of syllables that sound like a cry, mere redundancy. She can't think straight, so she concentrates on her mother's corn soup simmering on the stove, the red-and-white-checkered curtains above the kitchen sink, all things familiar, anything to delay the inevitable. But slowly and absolutely, she does what her lawyer asks. She abandons herself.

"Oh God, he raped you," says Tema, catching the shock of the news in her hands.

Auda can't bear to look at them. It doesn't help that they know, somehow it makes her feel worse. She sighs, remembering the long-dead woman inside her, the way she used to be. She folds her hands as if in prayer and lets the pain escape from her mouth. She leaves out nothing, it makes the story easier to tell. Then gradually she approaches Sunday morning when she walks into McAlester's office. "I really don't know what happened then. I went there intending to shoot him, but ... I can't see it."

Again the recorder collects silence.

Tema tries to light a cigarette, but Adair's lighter has quit. In frustration, she pulls the cigarette out of her mouth. "I don't even smoke," she says, wiping away her tears.

Gore picks up his pen again, but he doesn't write a thing. He seems to be measuring her words, then a look crosses his eyes, maybe pity; she can't read him, yet. "I'm sorry, but you had to tell us," he says, softly.

Auda covers her face with both hands. Her mouth aches. "I wish I was dead too," she whispers.

"*Shush!* Don't say that! Quick, take back the words!" urges Tema.

But Auda is again half-lost, sliding between past and present. "I must have…" she slowly nods yes, but whispers "no, I don't remember." She goes on speaking softly into the air, no longer caring who hears. "To me, Red was like a hummingbird. He could fly forward and backwards, or just hover above you for hours. He had incredible energy. Who else could have maneuvered the state legislators, the city bosses, the horse racing lobby, into negotiating a casino compact with the state of Oklahoma? Think of the long hours he spent, the hundreds of promises he had to make to develop a casino on their federal trust land in Oklahoma. But he was the one who had the vision and the drive to make it happen."

She breathes deeply. "No, in the beginning Red was not *Osano;* he was a hummingbird, a necessity of nature, impeccably beautiful, devouring all that is sweet in life to stay alive."

When Auda glances at Tema, she sees the chords of her sister's face are drawn into a tragic look of sorrow. She smiles, remembering Tema at five, who loved cucumber sandwiches, but only if she put them on gooey white bread.

"I don't think I could take back my words now, even if I wanted to," she says, sadly.

Gore turns off the recorder and goes to the sink. He drinks one glass of water, then fills the glass again, and drinks it too. When he comes back he seems propelled into action. He talks to her sisters, as if she's no longer present. "Once I get your mother's confession thrown out—"

Auda interrupts him, just to let him know who's in charge. "Don't you want to know what Red was doing with the other money?"

Gore slowly turns to her. His voice is low and terse. "So you do know where the ten million is."

"No, but I know what he did with his percentage."

"What percentage?"

"The payoff money he got from the Mafia. He was giving it to the I.R.A. to bomb the Brits."

For a moment, no one has the presence of mind to speak. Auda is astonished when Tema laughs.

"We've got to get you some help, honey."

"This has happened before."

"The Choctaws giving money to the Irish?" Tema asks. "I know that part, but the rest is too fantastic."

Auda gives them all a hard-eyed look. It is the look she usually reserves for her mother. "A man traveling under the name of James Joyce would pick up cashier's checks in pounds in London, then carry them to Zurich, convert them into Swiss francs and wire them to Belfast into an account called Chahta Legends. Why Belfast, I wondered. I started compiling newspaper clippings on I.R.A. activities. Times and dates of their latest bombings, little incidents that I could compare with the comings and goings of Joyce. I think that's why Red became involved with the Irish. He wanted to underwrite some of the I.R.A. bombings. The Feds must suspect as much, that's why they're investigating him and the tribe for violating money laundering statutes."

Silence holds until Adair throws up her hands, her voice now angry. "Our elderly have dire health care needs, we can't hire a competent surgeon for the Choctaw hospital in Talihina, and you're telling us that our *chief* funded the Irish Republican Army with money he stole from the corporate underworld? This sounds more like a B movie, and my God, Auda, if you knew…how could you live with yourself?"

"I've asked myself the same question every day," she says, wearily, knowing that at last they believe her. "But when I realized I knew how his mind worked, I followed his reasoning so I could stop him."

Auda fixes her gaze on her lawyer. He looks as exhausted as she feels. Eyes puffy, dark circles underneath, he's probably been up all night, but right now, she needs him to believe every word.

"Remember, our tribe gave money to the Irish in 1847 for famine relief. The Irish were starving because English bureaucrats withheld food from them. Red knows …" She corrects herself, "Red knew history. The English, who would become the ruling class of Americans, forced Indians to walk on the Trail of Tears, and they withheld food and supplies from them. Red appreciated historical ironies: Helping the I.R.A. get their revenge on the English was his own little joke."

"Do you have any proof of this?" he asks.

"Yes. I stole the wire transfer records, and remember, you do have a witness."

"Tonica."

She exhales and leans back in her chair, satisfied that Gore Battiste believes her story.

Gore immediately begins bending the ear of her sisters. He tells them they're going to have to hire more lawyers and one or two investigators. He says he will notify the Choctaw Superior Court, and the U.S. Attorney's office. They talk all around her, explain to each other what she already knows. It's then Auda remembers that the Alabama Conchatys were always the mediators between the warring tribes in the Southeast. More irony.

At this moment, there are several things she could ask her lawyer to do. Beg the court for mercy, plead insanity—not a far cry from the truth—or plead guilty. Before she decides, she climbs back into the past for one final visit.

The first day they meet. He is wearing a dark green shirt, the sleeves are rolled up and his Harvard tie is a bit askew. After his speech, she tries to pin him down. "If elected chief, how would you handle the tribe's yearly budget shortfall?" she asks.

He doesn't answer, but teases her in order to change the subject. "You know, I've been looking for woman like you all my life. Someone who will keep me on the straight and narrow path." This will be a pattern he repeats until the day she stops loving him and loves his dying.

She hears her sisters and Gore planning the strategy for her trial, as if she never confessed. Why continue the agony?

"If we can prove McAlester was laundering money and paying off a number of political cronies," he says, "we can offer alternative scenarios as to who else might have killed him. Since there were no powder burns on Auda's hands, and no gloves found at the scene, that might be enough to get the murder charge against her dropped."

"You will not do that," says Auda, quietly. She wipes the sleeve of her robe across her face. Whatever crazy expression there is rubs off. "I am responsible for what I did to the Chief of the Choctaw Nation. You will tell the court I am guilty, or you will not represent me. Do you understand?"

Her lawyer stands up and walks outside. Within minutes he comes back in, and reaches his hand across the table to shake on it. To Auda, it's a gesture as sacred as if they'd signed a treaty.

Just then, Hoppy walks briskly into the kitchen and kisses her gently on the cheek. "We're with you," he whispers, "and we've always been with you."

She wonders about his cryptic comment, but then sees the emerald green streaks in his hair and dismisses it as youthful drama. "Thank you, dear."

"Grandmother's home," he says, appealing to her heart. "She's outside on the lawn greeting the Choctaws who've come to pray for her. We just got through reciting the Lord's Prayer with a Choctaw preacher. He also read from the book of Psalms. *He leads me by the still waters...yea, though I walk through the valley of the shadow of death, I will fear no evil.* We repeated that last part four times, then a really old guy sang prayers for the Mother. I think the song was for Grandmother, but I didn't understand all the words."

Hoppy motions for her to get up. "C'mon outside, lots of friends are waiting. The old man is going to sing again." Her nephew proudly chants, *"Hatak okla hut okchaya bila hoh-illi bila."* The people are ever living, ever dying, ever alive.

Tema smiles proudly at Hoppy. "It's sort of a Choctaw double entendre, son. 'Prayers for the Mother' means Mother Earth."

6 | Koi Chitto, The Bone Picker

At the fork of the two roads, at the edge of the Blue Waters, Koi Chitto turns north along a timber wall. Black-headed parrots roost in the trees above his head as he continues walking toward Big Trace. Finally, when he reaches the southernmost end of the ancient trade route, he stops at a large watering hole and blows up a fire with the small piece of coal he carries. He lifts his pipe to salute the four directions. He is grateful for traveling so long without difficulty.

Koi Chitto sits and smokes quietly. In the distance he hears an alligator stalk him, ripping the swamp's underbrush as it approaches. It stops two yards in front of him and fixes its eyes on the fire.

Koi Chitto studies his guest. A young one, only five feet long, it must have a nest close by. He admires alligators. Like birds, they glide silently through black waters using river currents as drafts of wind. Perfect killers, alligators smother their victims in sand and water, saving them for rainy days—just as experienced hunters do. His people revere them so much they call one of their dances "Alligator Power."

On dry land the alligator is a different being altogether. Living tree trunks nesting in beds of mud, they surprise no one, except maybe the *Inkilish okla* and *Filanchi okla*, who are terrified of them. He motions and tries to distract the adolescent beast from the fire's light. It is useless. The fire has called it like a lover. Once hypnotized, an alligator will listen for hours to the crackling flames. What seductive stories fire must tell: the taste of burning wood, of palmetto leaves, the terror of rain. Fireflies carry those same stories, forming tiny constellations of stars in the arms of forests. Occasionally, a firefly overcome with emotion by the heat of its story will ignite and fall burning to the ground.

It's the same with people, thinks Koi Chitto. Too much fire in the belly and you die.

The old warrior walks away from his campfire and stands facing the darkness. He will give the alligator one more chance. Koi Chitto looks down at his feet. Phosphorescent molds shine underfoot on the dank leaves and he reaches down to touch them. He's been traveling alone for so long that he has become fascinated by minute things. The day after Shakbatina's body was placed on the burial scaffold, he left Yanàbi Town and headed south for the Blue Waters. During his three months of solitary wandering, he's visited many towns where distant cousins live.

He turns to look at his guest. Still captivated, it must obviously be a gift. He picks up his war club and walks toward it. It never moves or stirs, even when he bashes in its head. In his youth he killed and cleaned many alligators. It was good training for a warrior. The alligator has many purposes. The *tikilbi*, a stiff hide made from its skin, can be tied across a warrior's body as a shield against arrows and spears. The meat of the tail is a delicacy. He gives thanks to the animal's spirit before he lops its tail off and roasts the flesh.

As he sits watching the meat sizzle someone pokes him in the back. He whirls around. An old woman with a wizened bronze face stands before him. With her spiny fingers she gestures obscenely at him. He realizes she must be an animal spirit, and smiles sheepishly. He takes a small deerskin pouch filled with tobacco and passes it to her.

She accepts it and spits. "Old man, what are you doing?"

"Cooking."

"*Ai, ai, ai!* It's bone-picking time," she says, bobbing her head up and down like a porcupine. She opens her mouth wide, revealing cotton-white gums. Koi Chitto understands what she wants and blows smoke in her mouth. She fans the rest around her body. "*Ai, ai, ai,* you better get going to Yanàbi Town. Trouble is coming."

Koi Chitto agrees, and offers her a second pinch of tobacco and she snatches it. He takes the alligator meat off the fire and presents it to her. She refuses. "The alligator is for you—he must give you the strength to finish what you start. Use the river like an alligator and go fast, it's bone-picking time." Then the cranky animal spirit gives him a mean belly rub with needle-sharp fingers.

"Huh, stop that," snaps Koi Chitto.

"Go now," says the animal spirit.

Koi Chitto argues with the porcupine spirit. "It is not time for her ceremony. Only three moons have passed since my wife's death, three more must pass."

"*Aaaaaaghh!* You are wasting time. Get going!" she bullies. Smoke tendrils spun themselves around her and she goes up in fumes.

Koi Chitto is not shaken by her exit. Porcupine spirits are the nervous types, prone to fits. He picks up his tobacco pouch and pulls a ragged deer hide around his shoulders, but sleeps fitfully. Memories churn his dreams into nightmares. He sees Anoleta running toward her mother's cabin. When she pushes open the door she falls into the river. Her breath floats above the murky water like smoke. He runs to save her, but a feathered serpent stands up suddenly out of the water, bites him in the face, then flaps toward the sun. Koi Chitto puts his hand to his forehead. A drop or two of his blood hits the ground then swells into a river that whispers, *Anoleta is dead.*

Koi Chitto opens his eyes, the hot sun is already up. Exhausted, he drags himself to the river for a swim. Women from a nearby village are washing themselves. When they pass him sitting naked in the sun with angry red marks across his stomach, they point and gossip loudly. Silly women, he thinks. He will ignore them. He is a powerful warrior from the *Imoklasha*, war clan. He does not have time to explain things to women. But today, he will go north as fast as he can and heed Big Mother Porcupine's warning. Something is very wrong. He must reach Yanàbi Town, his daughters are in danger.

For three more days he tramps through the swamps until arriving at the village of his cousins, the Houmas. They believe they are part of the original people, descendants of the crawfish who had crawled up from the cave at Nanih Waiya to live in the sun. Their cabins reflect their beliefs. They are dome-shaped huts, fifteen feet high and supported from ground to roof by giant green cane poles. The Houmas adorn them with large round plates made of copper that signal to *Hashtali*.

An old woman who'd known Koi Chitto's father offers him sanctuary. When he tells her where he is going and why, she gives him a canoe. She says the Houmas are preparing for war. "We cannot stop what is coming," she says, sadly. "Many of our cousins have already moved west. They say they are going to visit their friends, the Caddos. Who knows if they'll return?"

Koi Chitto doesn't know what to say. He's a Choctaw warrior from Chickasawhay Town, the heart of a great and powerful nation. His town will never leave, nor avoid a fight. Finally the old woman offers her grandson to him. "Take my Grandson as your traveling companion. Trade my mulberry cloth to the *Inkilish okla* and *Filanchi okla*. Its whiteness has been made by our beloved Sun; if they wear it they will become hungry for peace. If they refuse, be sure that you trade for muskets and gun powder."

On his last night at the Houma village, Koi Chitto climbs into an enormous hammock that is laced between two trees. He stretches out on top of the white cloth as if he is floating on water. The white star road is bright in the heavens. He traces its path, and at the end of it is Shakbatina, like a firefly winging toward him. Everything carries him to her. Memories, their daughters, the aroma of sweet corn and wild plums. Tonight he wants to dream in complete wetness and feel her long damp hair tether his naked body to her.

Fragments of Shakbatina cling to him.

"Here, take this," she says, packing food for him to take on his journey to Chickasawhay Town for a council meeting. "For luck."

"What is it?"

"It's an alligator made from the pulp of mayhaw."

"Looks like a stick with four stick legs."

"Yes, bony like you. I see the resemblance now. That must be why I traded for it."

When they first met, Shakbatina was cultivating special healing plants and mining salt. She was trading them up and down the river for all sorts of things—calumets adorned with plumage of every color, red stones full of tobacco, and figures of dried fruit pulp in the shapes of men, deer, and alligators.

He was young and full of energy. He was already hunting for another Choctaw woman and her children who lived in Yashoo Town, and had once bragged that he was destined to make children in every town in the nation. But Shakbatina had other plans. In order to marry her he had to promise to hunt for only two families. "An *Imoklasha* can only provide so much if you are to meet your obligations protecting the Choctaw borderlands," she had said. He had agreed out of lust, but later realized the sense of it.

Koi Chitto raises his hands to touch Shakbatina, but grasps only air. He begins talking to the stars. If he doesn't reach home soon he will go mad.

At dawn he tastes something sweet. He opens his eyes. A small child has climbed into his hammock and put the flesh of a dried peach into his mouth. She chews another bite and pushes it between his lips. He smiles. Girl children are taught from infancy to be healers. He feigns sickness and begs for more. She giggles. It is a child's game. Soon the old woman's grandson appears. He explains that he is ready to go with Koi Chitto so he can trade with the Choctaws at Yanàbi Town. He picks up the little girl and takes her to a cabin not far away. When he returns they depart with enough supplies to last them a week.

Three days later Koi Chitto can smell Pearl River long before he sees it. Its rich liquid hangs in the air. The rustle of trees lining the banks make him hunger for home and he paddles faster. He and his companion make fifteen miles before they find nine moored canoes. They see no one, but the tracks are fresh. Koi Chitto and the Houma wait an hour, hearing nothing before they paddle another league. Soon they spot two women fishing on the bank. The women flee immediately, leaving behind a large basket containing a catfish, a man's foot, and a child's hand, all smoke dried.

Koi Chitto steals the fish and throws the rest in the water. Cannibals, the Attakapas. He hates them. If the Attakapas dare to encroach on Chickasawhay they'll be fed to the dogs. Minutes later, the two women reappear, with four men running along the shoreline after them. Koi Chitto is so enraged he stands up out of the canoe, and shows his penis to the cannibals onshore. "Eat this!" he shouts.

Stubby arrows barely miss the Houma, so Koi Chitto tries to make himself a bigger target. "Here, here, here," he screams, belligerently pointing at his chest. "Fetus eaters! You can't hit an *Imoklasha* warrior." He gives a loud war whoop as they paddle away.

In the distance, he and the Houma hear the violent screams of wild horses. The animals are running back and forth along the river bank. The two men hide their canoe and creep onshore to see what is wrong. Koi Chitto soon understands what the horses are running from. Burning carcasses smolder along the path to the village. A big splayfooted flea-sore dog hangs on a post thrusting a black tongue that won't retract. Koi Chitto thinks he sees a huge skeletal bird draped over a branch. Its dried wings flap wearily in the wind. He crouches low beneath the tree to inspect the thing. It isn't a bird, but a loosely-skinned human, badly charred.

All the canoes of the village are broken. Cut with very good axes. *Inkilish okla* axes. "They will not be satisfied until we're all dead," says the Houma, sadly.

"The *Inkilish okla* trade with anyone," replies Koi Chitto. "Even cannibals."

The two men paddle all night, wanting to get as far from the carnage as possible. The next day they carry their canoe and supplies over an embankment, only to find water that does not communicate with the river. It has long ago been damned up by beavers and is too brackish to drink. The Houma says he has made a wrong turn and they labor to retrace their path, carting the canoe with all their supplies back the way they came. The next day they cross over another embankment and find the river that will carry them closest to home.

Five more days pass until they reach the outskirts of Yanàbi Town. Koi Chitto and the Houma are greeted by runners who are returning from the surrounding towns of Kunshak, Abeka, Chickasawhay, Yowani, and Concha, all allied towns among the Choctaws. The runners tell Koi Chitto that they are gathering the people together for a bone-picking ceremony. As he walks into the village, Koi Chitto spots Nitakechi sitting in front of a cabin. At his feet is a basket of meat.

"I've been waiting for you," laughs Nitakechi. "I smelled your stench last night."

The two men greet each other with belly rubs and more insults.

"Miko Chitto and Alibamon Miko arrive today with many other representatives from their towns," Nitakechi says. "The horsefly is on his way here. Every day Red Shoes' mouth grows bigger. A truer *Osano* I've never known."

"It is time we make sure that he never hungers again," says Koi Chitto in voice that comes out of his gut. "In one of the towns I visited, I was told that Red Shoes said he would consider anyone his enemies who attacked the Chickasaws. He specifically mentioned the Red Fox village. I think he wants a war."

"That was before the *Inkilish okla* stopped trading with him," laughs Nitakechi. "Do not trouble yourself about the horsefly. I've heard that the *Intek Aliha* are cooking a special meal for him. That should cure his hunger pains. You should know that many men from the *Filanchi okla* are coming for the bone-picking ceremony, including Bienville and his Blackrobes. They will arrive tomorrow. Perhaps they will see Red Shoes before he is finished by the women."

The two men sit in silence. They pass the basket of meat back and forth between them. Nitakechi speaks carefully. "The eastern towns of the Choctaws are stirred up against the Chickasaws and their *Inkilish okla* supporters. Some of the warriors have brought Chickasaw scalps to sell to men of the *Filanchi okla*." He blushes and clears his throat. "Even some *Inholahta* men are speaking for war."

Koi Chitto understands. When a leader of a peace clan no longer argues against bloodshed, it means more than all the cries of warriors. He mulls this over before telling his story.

"I was told it was time to release Shakbatina's bones from her burial scaffold, but six moons have not passed. One more thing—in my dream," says Koi Chitto, "the river told me that Anoleta was dead. The signs of a coming disaster are everywhere."

Nitakechi listens carefully as Koi Chitto tells what he has seen. The description of the burning village and the cannibals who are on the move. Anoleta's strange death.

"I will tell the men in council what you have said," says Nitakechi. "Shakbatina has been coming into my dreams. She wants you to pick her bones, I am sure of her meaning now. You are a warrior, and her husband. Remember what she did on the day of her death, she sent a dual message. She painted her face for war, but dressed in white for peace, a very peculiar thing for an *Inholahta* woman to do."

"But a husband must not pick the bones of his wife," says Koi Chitto. "It's not right, even though I am from a different clan, this is not right. I fear the imbalance this will cause for our children's children."

Nitakechi agrees that this is very unusual, but he insists that Shakbatina must be released early, and that Koi Chitto must do it. "There is something else that relates to all this," he adds. "The war chief, Choucououlacta, has sworn to protect Anoleta, and her sisters, with his life. Anoleta has agreed to marry him. With Choucououlacta comes the support of ten more towns to be united with Yanàbi Town. That makes eleven. It should not be too much longer now."

Later that night, Koi Chitto jumps naked into the river. He feels nothing, it is the temperature of his skin. An alligator slips into the water beside him. A test. The river is not deep, he can walk or swim.

The alligator nonchalantly passes him by.

Koi Chitto crawls onto the bank, allowing the wind to dry him. It is a cool night and his purpose is sacrifice. He denies himself warmth, food, clothing, and shelter. The first night's ritual is for denial.

Throughout the next day Koi Chitto smokes the dreaming tobacco that will open his mind. He prepares black drink, a concoction that is used as an emetic. He vomits to purify himself. He smokes more of the tobacco and finally, when night comes, he collapses on the floor of his sweat tent. He stares into the small fire in the middle of the tent. Intoxicated at last, Koi Chitto climbs into a river of memories of his life with Shakbatina. Their first night together he is entirely wedded to her body. After caressing him she rubs him down with bear grease. Time races by. A newly delivered baby cries softly at Shakbatina's breast. One daughter is followed by two more. A little girl comes toward him galloping along the green-belted banks of the river and shouting, "Father, hold me."

In the fire he sees Shakbatina's death coming into focus. He watches the vision unfold again. He cradles her head on his lap. Blood oozes from her eyes and nose as she struggles for air. At that moment he loves her so much that he spits a drop of saliva into her mouth thinking it will save her. Foolish, he knows.

"You see me," he screams, "I know you do. Wait for me!"

Koi Chitto puts a hand over his eyes, hoping to stop the vision. The Red Fox man hits her two times, just to make sure. Anoleta sucks in her breath and runs toward her mother shrieking, *"Alleh, alleh, alleh."* He rocks them both in his arms. The dead woman and her daughter. He knows Anoleta is innocent of killing anyone so he whispers for her to wait until after the bone-picking ceremony. "Then we will take our revenge for your mother's death."

Koi Chitto rolls away from the fire and sits up. Everyone at Yanàbi Town understood his wife's double message. Make peace now, but make war when the time is right.

He takes another drag from his pipe. He's supposed to remember that his ritual is for renewal. Not sadness. He sings a love song and prepares his claw-like nails, grown purposefully long since Shakbatina's death. He smokes and refills his pipe. He repeats the cycle until he feels completely spent. Finally, the thing he seeks comes to him. He enters the *na tohbi*, something white. As always, when it first arrives he is terrified, yet seduced by it. And through his terror he knows he is participating in a life mystery. On the evening of the second day Koi Chitto slips into unconsciousness. Through his ritual he will become his people's sacrament. The purpose of the second night is indulgence in the sublime.

On the third night, Koi Chitto emerges from the sweat, much thinner. He has not eaten in three days. He speaks to no one. He smears bear grease on himself. He feels invigorated knowing that he has succeeded in his purification ceremony. While no two ceremonies are alike, no two purifications are alike, only the knower knows when the experience is complete. Koi Chitto has seen his future in the seductive hallucinations of the tobacco and black drink. He will one day be reunited with Shakbatina. Their children's children will survive, but not without many hardships. The purpose of his ceremony tonight will be rebirth.

Koi Chitto heads to Shakbatina's burial scaffold dressed only in a string cloth. There are hundreds of people gathered for the ceremonies. Many others have died. Shakbatina is not the only one whose bones will be picked clean on this night when the Sun sleeps longer than any night of the year. He climbs the burial scaffold. He listens to the drums; his clansmen have been beating them all day. Their purpose is to wake the dead. Under the influence of black drink he can hear the internal drumming of the plants and trees. He can hear the collective prayers of the people and, if he concentrates, he hears the thoughts of a single person. The combined noise is maddening, yet all-consuming. His people learned to hear the internal drumming of the plant world eons ago. No one knows when this special communication began, only that it exists and the ancestors used it as a tool of survival. The humming and vibrations of the trees and tall corn plants are a soothing comfort to the people. When the musical sounds of the plants changed to frantic drumming during the dry season, the people helped the plants by imitating plant rhythms on their drums. This helped bring rains. In return the plants gave themselves willingly to the people as a gift.

Koi Chitto examines his wife's decayed body. She remains steadfast at her post, just as her relatives had placed her, like a warrior watching over the people. He rakes the leaves that have blown over her, leans down and touches the fragments of her hair. Shakbatina's small jawbone and teeth lie surrendering to the sun, like gleaming pearls. Her skin has been turned inside out by some sharp-beaked, flesh-eating birds. What is left has dried to the bone and resembles snake skin.

Koi Chitto believes, as all Choctaws believe, that the spirit is related to the body as perfume is to the rose. Shakbatina's smell is erotic. Over time her exposed bones have taken on that stark, delicate beauty the Choctaws regard as *Chunkash Ishi Achukma*. The good bliss.

Three months before, Nitakechi had prepared her body in the *Inholahta* way. For *Inholahta*, the preparation ceremony is as ritualized as the bone-picking ceremony. Her body was rolled in every direction. The flesh directly above both her thighs had been sliced away in half-moon shapes in order for the blood and body fluids to run out of the buttocks, because the blood of a dead animal gravitates to the lowest point of the body if an exit is provided. They also pierced her stomach and bladder in order for the bloating gasses to escape in the wind. This was to announce to the animal world that a woman of the people was coming.

Shakbatina's head had been turned east so that she would greet the rising sun each morning while she too waited for the day of her rebirth. Her umbilical cord and medicine bag had been tied around her neck as part of the ceremonial incubation. The umbilical cord of a peacemaker is their first toy; with them before birth, it accompanies them into death.

Koi Chitto looks over his wife's things. A corn hamper made of swampcane lies beside her. Inside is a small basket with an opening shaped like a mouth. He picks up the basket and opens it. Hiding in a dense nest of fluff and turkey feathers are Shakbatina's ear spools, the turtle shells she tied around her ankles and wore to the dances, and her black and white porcupine sash. He remembers how she looked with it strapped around her, proudly singing her death song. After tonight, his daughters will retrieve these things from the scaffold.

The drums grow louder. They seem in rhythm with Koi Chitto's heartbeat, and he drops the basket. At last, the roar of forest, the constant drumming, and he begins to chant to the crowd gathered below her scaffold.

"I am the Bone Picker, dancer of death, transformer of life, the one who brings sex, the one who brings rebirth. You must have death to have life. The people live by killing, by stripping the flesh from the animal corpse. The people live by dying. That which dies is reborn."

A shrill moan comes from the belly of Koi Chitto. He dances faster, and rolls his eyes back in his head. He is again at the center of *na tohbi*. The drums vibrate his body and the scaffold shakes as if it will break apart, then it stops. He sees his wife dancing toward him, and he shouts. "Shakbatina is coming. She is here!"

She looks like she did so many years ago. Her skin is vibrant brown and she is half-naked. Her calf-length hair glistens in the moonlight. She comes very close, puts her hands on his penis. He puts his hands around her hands and together they stroke him, until he ejaculates on her body and screams, "Flesh of my flesh, I will be with you always. Flesh of my flesh, I will return with you always. Until the nothingness becomes everything. Until everything becomes nothing. I am the Bone Picker, dancer of death, transformer of life, the one who brings sex, the one who brings rebirth."

Shakbatina's spirit dances around the platform and Koi Chitto can hear her talking to him. "Dance with me, my husband, this is the dance of life and rebirth. This is my body. Pull away my remaining flesh. I charge you to get inside me. Release me now, so I may watch over our people. Dance the dance that releases me."

She smiles and entreats him to touch her corpse and tear the remaining flesh from her bones. "*Hatak holitopa*, beloved man, release me and dance the dance of life and death. *Che pisa lauchi*. I will see you."

Hearing her promise that she will return, Koi Chitto gathers his courage and tears Shakbatina's skull and spinal column from the rest of her bones. He holds them in both his hands high above his head and salutes the four directions. He believes when he finishes this spirit dance, and Shakbatina's bones are painted and placed in the box, he will not see her again for a long time. Until then he lets her fading scent engulf him. He closes his eyes. They are together, dancing the dance, both knowing that this is the ecstasy of life and rebirth.

7 | Penance

DURANT, OKLAHOMA
TUESDAY, SEPTEMBER 24, 1991

N ow Auda remembers. It happened in the twinkling of her mother's eye. The moment Susan Billy stepped inside her jail cell, the world that had separated them vanished. With one look her mother forgave her everything. For using her family to get Redford McAlester elected Chief of the Choctaw Nation. For the gambling business that had, with the stroke of a pen, mortgaged a thousand years of Choctaw sovereignty—in one night. As her mother speaks to the crowd in front of the house, their unspoken affection hangs in the air. Auda feels it around her, warm as a goose down comforter.

"My beloved family is here with me," says Susan Billy. "Adair from New Orleans, Tema from Dallas, her son Hopaii, who will be attending art school in France later this fall, and, of course, my brother, Isaac Billy. I want you to know that we've all made great mistakes in the past, siding with the wrong people and such. I know I have. But the Billys are going to survive this, and I promise you it will come out that my girl Auda is innocent of all charges!"

Auda winces.

There is a flurry of looks. Adair and Tema, and Gore Battiste, each want the other to say that Auda has confessed to murdering Chief McAlester. But no one dares.

Outside, Auda and her mother stand side by side. Susan Billy in a royal blue suit she usually reserves for tribal receptions, Auda in a white frumpy bathrobe. They pray with the Choctaw Baptist minister, the Choctaw Presbyterian minister, the Choctaw Methodist minister, and

108 | SHELL SHAKER

the many Choctaw elders. They shake hands with their neighbors and their neighbors' children, and all their supporters who've never believed that Susan Billy had anything to do with the murder. Now they've heard her say Auda didn't do it either.

Her mother makes another short speech. "Anyone who believes that there's no power on earth who'll return Choctaw's land to Choctaws except the casino Mafia, I have news for you. We're going to take back our tribe, our lands, and kick out the gangsters. Just wait and see."

There is a clamor of applause. Shouts of "Amen" and "that's right, Mrs. Billy" reverberate around the yard. Auda looks at her mother. For a woman whose aging body is shaped like a peanut, her mother stands extremely erect and self-assured. She's rallying the Choctaw tribal elders and the young people, a dangerous combination. Auda slips her hand inside her mother's. Susan Billy's gaze is now fixed on her. Her eyes say it all; at last they are of one mind. Forgiveness.

When the people begin to disperse, Auda excuses herself and heads inside to change into a dress. Gore follows her, but seems apprehensive as they enter the house.

"I need to see your evidence," he says.

"I haven't forgotten. Come upstairs with me."

He peruses her bookshelves while she looks under her bed, then in her closet. She rummages through the manila file folders on her desk, but the phone logs and bank statements she'd stolen from Tonica's office are gone. A wave of anger washes over Auda. Someone has been going through her things. What else is missing, she wonders?

"Not here," he says, nonchalantly.

"Someone must have taken them," she says, trying to control the fire in her voice. Auda waits for a reaction from her lawyer, but he merely shrugs, and turns his attention to a picture on the wall. Why the hell is he looking at her photograph? It's from 1960, an enlargement of her and her sisters swimming with their aunts, Delores and Dovie, in the "Love Lake." Their horse pond. Beads of water glisten on the sisters' faces and hair. Their cheeks are pressed together. Tema's and Adair's braids hang like black arrows down their small chests, but hers are long and scraggly. She is nine years old and her front teeth are missing. Thirty-one years later, some things are exactly the same, she thinks, running her tongue over her broken teeth.

Suddenly he exclaims, "That's Delores and Dovie Love; they're famous! There's lots of articles on them at the Oklahoma Historical

Society."

"Yes, they're my aunts. Not blood relations, but Indian-way aunts."

Gore smiles. "I have some of those, too."

"Every summer when we were kids, we spent a couple of weeks with them. Before I got ...sidetracked," she says, her voice softening, "my next book was going to be a biography of the Love Sisters."

"They're twins, right?"

"No, a duet, eleven months apart in age. Delores is the eldest, but Dovie is the boss."

"Kind of like Adair and Tema," he remarks casually, "although Adair is definitely the bossy one."

"How do you know so much about us?" she says, going through her dresser drawers to see if anything else missing.

He keeps his eyes on the photograph while he talks. "Adair told me. We've met before, but you don't remember, do you?"

Auda sits down on the edge of her bed. "No, I'm sorry. Where was that?"

"The Oklahoma Historical Society lecture, right after your book *The Eighteenth-Century Choctaws* came out. I worked there while I was in law school. Adair and I had dinner...after your lecture."

She studies his face. "Of course," she says, turning red. "I'm still so embarrassed about that. Never give whiskey to an Indian."

"You weren't much trouble. I enjoyed watching some of the Society's benefactors squirm."

"So have you and Adair stayed in touch? She's never mentioned you—, I mean, do you ever see each other?"

"No," he says, turning away to look at other mementos on her walls. "We exchanged business cards, had a couple of drinks after we helped you to bed, that's all." Auda can tell he's withholding something. She could have kicked herself for getting drunk that night. When she woke up, she had a terrible hangover. By the time she got dressed, her sister was already downstairs in the hotel's restaurant looking through the newspaper ads. Adair had said she'd decided to buy a house in Oklahoma City, a "getaway place," but she never did. Auda had never thought twice about Adair's impulse. Until now.

As he brushes the dust off her photograph, she notes that he isn't wearing a wedding band. They make eye contact and Auda raises her eyebrows. Now it's his turn to squirm, she thinks.

"No, really," he says, putting his hand in his jeans' pocket. "I never heard from her until she called and asked me to represent you. I just remember being impressed that Adair flew all the way from New Orleans to hear your lecture. You two must be very close."

Gore's last remark disarms her. What a kind thing to say after all he's heard today. His casual manner, and the tone in his voice, eases her anger at discovering her evidence has been stolen.

"Yes, we are close," she says, a little ashamed that she's always felt closer to Tema. "What else do you know about our family?"

"Um, lemme see. Well, I know a lot about your aunts," he says. "In 1924, Delores and Dovie Love ran away from boarding school. They got jobs at the Miller Brothers' 101 Ranch that sprawled over 110,000 acres of Ponca Indian land. At the turn of the century, Colonel George Washington Miller had turned the 101 into the most diversified ranching operation in the world. It had housing for employees, schools, stores, a meat packing plant, a tannery, experimental breeding barns where they crossbred buffaloes with Brahmans. Much later, after its heyday, Al Capone tried to convert the 101 into a colony for immigrant Italian families."

"That sounds memorized."

"I was the archivist at the Historical Society. They wanted me to collect materials for a book about Oklahoma Indians, Al Capone, and the 101 Ranch."

"What stopped you?"

"Law school. After that, I started my own practice. Now, criminal cases like yours take all my time."

"Indians and Italians," she says bitterly, "seems like you can't escape your destiny."

He looks at her black velvet painting of Elvis and frowns. "Hey, were you going to mention Delores' affair with Ronald Colman in your book? I've heard it began in 1937 while they were filming *Lost Horizon*."

"I was going to devote an entire chapter to it."

He turns and grins at her. "Delores has denied it in print."

"Yes, but she's Choctaw. We always deny having affairs with foreigners."

"I see," he says, still grinning. Then he leans against the wall. "But think of all the things that Delores and Dovie have done. They toured the country in *The 101 Real Wild West and Great Far East Combined*. They even met Al Capp, who was a struggling artist at that time. His sketches of Dovie..."

"...became the inspiration for the Indian femme fatale in his comic strip *Li'l Abner*," says Auda, finishing his sentence. "I know, I know, ... you've really got a crush on them."

They both laugh. Auda puts a hand over her mouth to hide her front teeth.

"Have you ever met them?"

He shakes his head no.

"Today's your lucky day," she says. "They'll be here soon, but I hope you're not disappointed; they're sort of eccentric—not your traditional little ol' Indian ladies."

Gore seems puzzled. "I just admire them, that's all. They represent a generation of Oklahoma Indians who became trick riders, screenwriters, Hollywood actors, newspaper reporters, dancers on Broadway, and famous poets. They proved to us—our generation—that we could still be tribal people, and make it in the white world."

"I don't agree," she says, feeling her muscles tense.

"Why not?"

"Somebody's got to stay home. Maintain the land, maintain the community. If we all move away and do our own thing, who is left to be the tribe?"

"Are you're saying that if Indians learn to play the piano, they can't be tribal any longer?" he asks. "I thought that kind of colonial attitude only belonged to white historians and anthropologists."

Now Gore's beginning to sound a little like McAlester, who used to say, "Tribes can do anything they can get away with." It was his justification for everything. When he saw the effect his words had on her, he used them like a stick to beat her.

She stands up to face her lawyer. "You're misinterpreting my words. Individual Indians can do whatever they want, but not without a price. We, the Choctaw people, are the assets of our tribe—not the buildings, not the HUD houses, not our tribal bank accounts. Chances are, though, if all the Indians are off doing their own thing, tribalism will die."

"We're damned if we're progressive, and damned if we're not, is that it?" he asks, suddenly sounding irritated.

"I don't have all the answers," she says, "but I've seen what happens when a tribal leader is accountable to the Feds, and to a large corporation, but not to his own people. What's worse is that I know I'm responsible for what has happened here."

"Not entirely," he says.

Auda waits for Gore to say more, but he doesn't. It occurs to her that most Indians in Oklahoma, including him, don't consider the details of their tribal history as she and Red did. Though there was a difference. She wrote about Choctaw history as a way to correct the misinformation about the tribe, Red saw their history as a means to an end. Perhaps it was the disease that finally consumed them both.

She continues, trying to control her emotions. "Red's excuse for everything he did was based on America's treatment of Indians. 'America,' he would say, 'has grown out of the mouths of ravenous white people … our lands, our foods, our bodies have been the hosts the whites fed on, until we're nearly all dead, so we should be able to get even.'"

"So we're absolved by history?" he says, flatly.

"That's what he meant." She then speaks very slowly. "Don't misunderstand, I'm proud of both my sisters—an actress and a Wall Street broker. I'm proud of all the Indians who are musicians, filmmakers, lawyers, and scientists. I want Indians to do whatever they are capable of. But it's foolish to believe that tribes, and tribalism, don't suffer as a result."

"I see your point," says Gore, shifting his weight, looking uncomfortable. "It sounds as if you and McAlester always disagreed about tribal politics."

"No, not always. Especially in the beginning when we shared so many common goals. Red was a very complex man. He always had money for drunks and anyone down on their luck. Every time we went to D.C., he'd listen to the sob stories of street people sleeping on the heating vents. You know the ones I mean?"

"Yes."

"He'd reach into his pocket and give away all the cash he had on him, which infuriated me, 'cause he could turn down his own people, but give to strangers. Did you know that he picked stray dogs off the streets and took them to the house-up, the cabin we shared outside of Talihina? He must have a dozen dogs living out there." Auda gasps, "Oh my God! His dogs, they haven't been fed since …" She suddenly puts her hands over her face and weeps uncontrollably. For so long she'd wept without letting anyone see her tears. Wept without letting her mother, or Uncle Isaac, know how tormented she was. And now she breaks down in front of her lawyer.

Gore sits her down on the bed and holds her while she cries herself out. Finally he says, "We'll get someone to feed the dogs. Probably some of McAlester's friends have taken care of them."

"I don't know if anyone knows about his dogs… or maybe Hector does," she says, pulling a tissue out of her robe pocket. "You know, Red and Hector had been friends since Dartmouth. That's how he got his connections with their organization. Hector and Vico are related to the Genoveses. When I found out, I accused Red of all kinds of horrible things. We never spoke again, until last Saturday, when he ordered me into his office and..." Auda stops, then takes a deep breath and steadies herself.

"If you two didn't speak, how did you handle tribal business?"

"Through typed memos. Hector called our memos the paper wars."

Gore nods slowly to himself. "So there's a substantial paper trail between you two?"

She says yes.

He looks at her very intensely. "I need to know the truth about the documents you had stashed here."

"You don't believe I ever had any evidence?" she asks.

He hedges, glances around the room, but finally admits that he doesn't.

"I made copies."

"Where are they?"

"I mailed duplicates to Tema's agent in New York. Call and ask her to open the package marked 'Hold until Christmas.' Times, dates, bank routing numbers, it's all there."

Now it's his turn to be embarrassed, and he stands up. "Isaac told me the BIA boys were here, probably they took whatever you had collected. I'm sorry, I do want to believe you... it's just that criminal lawyers are used to being lied to."

"Why are you helping me, especially now that you know what I've done?" she asks.

He doesn't hesitate. "Last year, Oklahoma reported that the total revenues of the wagering facilities in the state—that's casinos, bingo, and horse racing—were three-quarters of a billion dollars. It was only a matter of time until international gangs, or the corporate Mafia, found their way onto Indian land by loaning start-up money for casinos. These are the new Indian wars, Auda. Redford McAlester was the first casualty. It's time Indian lawyers weigh in on the side of Indian people, not just their tribal governments."

"I'm as guilty as Red."

"Hardly," he says. "I'm not absolving you of his murder—but you tried to stop him from going into business with Shamrock Resorts. You tried to stop him from selling tribal sovereignty to the highest bidder. Whether you realize it or not, you've become a warrior for your own people." Gore looks at her thoughtfully. "We've all been on the side of someone who has reduced us to desperation."

As she listens, she feels he might be talking about himself, too. Then again, it might be wishful thinking on her part to imagine that someone else in the world could empathize with what she's done: killed the man she once loved.

"What do I do now?"

"Tell the story, see what happens."

"Tonight at Blue Creek Grounds," she replies. "I will tell everyone what happened to me, to Red, and to the tribal government."

"It's a beginning," he says, softly.

A half hour later Auda comes downstairs wearing a blue denim dress. Gore is still awake, sitting in the library making notes on a yellow legal pad.

"I'll be leaving soon for the clinic. Anything you need?"

He puts his pen down. "Having a doctor's report on you will be good for our case, no matter what your plea is," he says, returning to his notepad.

"I thought you were going to nap." She leans over to see what he's writing. The word "quirky" appears at the top of the page.

"I drank another gallon of coffee, so I thought I'd jot down some notes on the Billys. Never know when they will come in handy. At trial. A sensational bestseller."

"You're punchy. There's nothing unusual about the Billys."

"Besides the obvious?"

She blushes. "Except for me, a confessed murderer, we're a normal, happy-go-lucky Indian family."

"Your sisters hear voices. They both swear that spirits are chasing them all over the country. Tema claims she was attacked onstage the other night in Dallas. Do you know where Adair is right now?"

Auda shakes her head no.

"She's in the kitchen cutting up the local paper. Adair collects two things. Money and newspaper clippings of the macabre. She's very excited, she just found a report of a jogger in Canada who'd been torn, limb from limb, by a bear."

"Like I said, a normal Indian family."

"There's more."

"Tell me."

"Hoppy says he and Isaac visited Sarah Bernhardt last night. You know, the French actress who's been dead since 1923. Apparently, Sarah Bernhardt has been living at the Choctaw nursing home in Talihina. She's not really a human being, but a porcupine spirit who claims she's fighting an evil war chief named Red Shoes, come back in the form of Redford McAlester. A spirit killed him, not you."

"Red Shoes was assassinated in 1748, and lately, I've had weird dreams about him."

"Of course you have, and that's why 'quirky' is scrawled on the top of this pad," he says, gesturing with his pen. "Did I mention that Sarah Bernhardt, the porcupine, claims she stole Durant's Big Peanut?"

"And what is the government doing about it," she says, playing along. Privately though, she wonders if the porcupine spirit, or whoever Hoppy and her uncle talked to, is telling the truth.

"Then there's your mother and uncle who are completely off the Indian Richter scale."

"You said it, I didn't." She grins.

At that moment, Isaac walks in and announces that the Check-off Sisters have finally arrived. He looks at his watch. "Typical! Two-thirty in the afternoon, what took them so long?"

Gore turns to Auda, mouths "quirky," and the three of them head out the door to welcome the Love Sisters.

A 1963 red Ford convertible is parked next to the oak tree in the middle of the back yard, about four feet left of the Billys' driveway.

"Sorry," shouts Dovie Love from behind the wheel, as she pulls off her glasses. "I'm not used to these new-fangled pedals."

The white cloth top of the Ford has been duct-taped in so many places it looks like a star quilt. Ambling from the car are Auda's two elderly aunts in stylish black dresses. Clearly they've come for a funeral. Gore dutifully runs to help them. He picks up their suitcases, and hands the large plastic bottle of green liquid to Isaac who reluctantly takes it, but mutters under his breath.

For as long as Auda can remember, her uncle has called Delores and Dovie Love by a variety of names: Loveless Sisters, Unlovable Sisters, and, when he's in a bad mood, The Check-off Sisters. The latter, he claims, is because of their tiresome habit of listing all the bad things that have happened to them. Their father killed by a stray bullet in a hunting accident. The unexpected death of their mother. A brother murdered, and a younger sister who drank herself to death.

Auda has always ignored her uncle's remarks. Delores and Dovie Love are hardly maudlin. Just the opposite. She senses there's always been some kind of weird thing between Isaac and Delores, but no one will say what it is. Not even her mother.

She watches as her aunts float toward her like a pair of avenging eagles protecting their nest. Although fragile and in their eighties, they've maintained graceful figures. "Not too round, not too thin" is Dovie's motto. Auda thinks they could easily pass for women fifteen years younger. Delores is beautiful, even at her age. She has soulful brown eyes and wears tiny granny glasses. She threads her long gray hair into a single braid and pins it up at the back of her head. She has radiant brown skin, with only a few wrinkles around her mouth and eyes. In many ways, Dovie is the opposite. She's a bit wiry, with large hazel eyes, and she never wears her glasses in public. Too vain. Since her Hollywood years, Dovie's worn her hair cut short, and dyes it soft black. Delores occasionally uses a cane in winter when her arthritis is acting up. But Dovie is still pretty spry, claiming that her agility is because she's Poteau's yoga master, although Delores disputes this.

Auda can just imagine how they looked when they were billing themselves as "The Love Maidens of The Five Civilized Tribes." How their long black hair must have whipped in the wind as they rode bareback on Paint ponies, parading their history in skimpy loincloths. At their ranch house in Poteau is a large poster-sized print of them with Will Rogers on the set of *Life Begins at Forty.* Delores had a small speaking part in the movie. In the photograph, all three Oklahoma Indians are wearing cowboy get-ups with shiny new boots and cowboy hats; they look as though they've attained the most American of ideals—wealth and fame. But, as they all would learn in the coming years, it came at a high price.

Her mother rushes out of the house toward her aunts. "Mr. Battiste, if you'll put their suitcases in the downstairs bedroom, the one with the two beds, I'd be so grateful."

Susan Billy takes the large plastic bottle of green liquid from Isaac and lifts it high in the air. "Maybe we all ought to start drinking this stuff, right away!" Isaac just shakes his head and enters the house alone.

Delores and Dovie never travel without a supply of their homemade herbal teas, which they insist cure everything from cellulite to cancer.

Her mother hugs Delores for the longest time, then Dovie, then fairly shouts toward the heavens, "I'm so glad you made it!" She is genuinely exhilarated and keeps repeating "so glad," "so happy," "thought you'd never get here."

Her mother is not the emotional type, as she's proven over the past few days, and the outbursts startle Auda. Susan Billy has always been more like a military strategist. After she was told that her husband had suddenly died from a brain aneurysm, probably the result of an old childhood injury, she sat very quietly in the library looking at old photos of him. Later, she walked upstairs and screamed into a feather pillow. The next morning she buried the pillow and all but one photo of him in the backyard, took a job as a grocery clerk, and went on to raise Auda, her two sisters, and many other Choctaw children whose parents were down on their luck, in jail, or dead. For most of Auda's life, her mother had behaved like a soldier on duty.

Delores hugs Susan tightly. Then she turns to Auda and says in a soothing voice, "Everything is going to be all right...but honey, you look just like a vampire with those two little spikes for front teeth."

"What took you so long?" asks Auda, putting her hand over her mouth.

"We left Poteau right after we got Isaac's call," she says, wiping perspiration from her forehead, "but the car broke down. I told Dovie we needed to get the oil checked, but she wouldn't stop until we'd burned up the engine. We had to spend two nights in Talihina while the car was being fixed." Delores pauses, looking around the neighborhood. "Say, this whole town looks like our car engine. Charred."

"Don't listen to her. Wasn't the oil at all," protests Dovie, waving impatiently at her sister. She faces Auda and stands tall, as if preparing to deliver her lines on a movie set. "My girl, I have some important news for you about Redford McAlester."

"What is it?" asks Auda, holding her breath.

"We did his chart, and then we looked at his transiting planets. Last Saturday, when all this happened, Pluto was squaring his Pluto."

Auda doesn't know whether to laugh or cry, and she can't help but notice the bewildered look on Gore's face. She suspects he's making a mental note to add her aunts to his list of quirky Indians he's met at the Billy house.

"Auntie, I have no idea what that means."

"Listen," says Dovie, conspiratorially. "McAlester was destined to die—badly. I should have read his chart a long time ago. I guess I'm getting old, 'cause I never considered it until now. Were you aware that he was born on Hitler's birthday when you got involved with him?"

Auda swallows a grin. But then she realizes that this is Dovie's way of absolving her of any wrongdoing. "No, I didn't know that."

Anxiety melts away from Dovie's face, and she hugs Auda. "There, there, my girl, I was sure you didn't know. None of this is your fault. I think your lawyer should present my evidence in court. We'll call it the astrology defense. They do it all the time in Hollywood."

Gore waits a beat, then reaches out his hand to introduce himself. "Miss Dovie, Miss Delores, my name is Gore Battiste. I'll be representing Auda. I've read so much about you over the years, it's truly an honor to meet you both."

Dovie steps close to him so she can get a good look. She eyes him suspiciously, then glances at Susan, as if to ask, have you checked him out. "I don't imagine you carry around your exact time of birth, do you?" she asks.

"Oh for Pete's sake, Dovie!" says Delores, shaking his hand. "Nice to meet you, Mr. Battiste. Please excuse my sister, she's on a new kick. You'll just have to ignore her. Are you related to Leota Battiste?"

"She's his aunt," says her mother, quickly coming to Gore's defense. "We're practically related…you know… Indian-way."

Everyone nods their heads solemnly.

"I bet we have met before, only you were too little to remember," says Delores, politely. Then she adds, "Of course…you must be Velma French's boy! I guess I should say Velma Battiste, after all this time."

Gore smiles patiently. It's obvious to Auda that he's been through this Indian ritual before. Everyone knows that relationships in the Indian world are based on kinship and ardent familiarity, which often results in more kin.

"Susie, did you know that Velma is distantly related to the Choctaw Wesleys at Clayton?"

"Yes," replies her mother, "and Gore's father was Henri Battiste, a schoolteacher at Tulsa. Poor thing, Henri was an only child."

Auda notices that Gore is a little uncomfortable at the mention of his father, but her aunt quickly comes to his rescue.

"I know your family well," says Delores, looking kindly at him.

However, Dovie still doesn't seem completely satisfied with what she's heard. She looks Gore up and down, then folds her arms confidently and asks, "Are you a Leo?"

He laughs out loud. "Get out of town! How'd you know?"

"The hair," says Dovie. "Leos take a lot of pride in their hair. Now take McAlester and his Mafia brothers. Not a Leo among them."

"Miss Dovie," interrupts Gore, as graciously as he can. "Just what do you know about McAlester and the Mafia?"

"Plenty," says Dovie, wiping her thin brown face with a black lace handkerchief. "Ever been to the Casino of the Sun? Check it out. Oh sure, some Choctaws sweep the floors there for ten dollars an hour. But the ones who make the big money are the dealers, and they're all named Lucky Luciano or Vito Corleone."

Delores chuckles softly. "Vito Corleone was a movie character."

"Whatever. The Mafia and our newly-demised casino chief, McAlester, were blood brothers. Blood suckers, more like it," quips Dovie. "He might have fooled us for a while, but he couldn't hide his dirty business forever, not from the Choctaw people. Did you know he was giving money to the Irish Republican Army?"

"I hadn't heard that," says Gore, innocently. "Can you fill me in, Miss Dovie?"

"Stick with us, honey, we're in the know."

Delores continues to laugh good-naturedly at her sister. "Every time we'd hear about McAlester's shenanigans—that is, before we learned he was dead—Dovie would hyperventilate."

"Well, he's finished now," says Dovie, curtly. "Some of the elders want Delores to lead the singing at his funeral. They want her to do the old-timey pole planting at the graveside. I think she should. Even a *Osano Chitto* deserves a proper Choctaw funeral. What do you think, Susie?"

Susan turns to Auda. Another silent message passes between them. They both know that Choctaws are deeply reverent about the dead. And forgiving. A traditional funeral would bring the community together so they could begin the healing process. Her mother speaks slowly. "Making peace with the dead is something we must do."

Then she asks Delores and Dovie for their help. "I'm going with Auda to the Choctaw Health Clinic. She was in shock and I want to talk to the doctor. We need to take a lot of food to Blue Creek Grounds tonight. Tema and Adair are in the kitchen cooking up a storm. Will you take charge of the fixings until I get back?"

Delores smiles and tenderly pats her cheek. "Susie, don't fret about the meal. That's why we're here, for bone-picking and chicken frying."

Rain hangs in the air, but refuses to fall.

Auda stands in the middle of the backyard and surveys the sky before she leaves for the clinic. She decides to search the yard once more for her rabbit. Jean Baptiste has been missing for two days, since the morning of McAlester's murder. At his advanced age he's too feeble to outrun the neighborhood dogs, so she believes he must be dead.

She adopted the small French Angora ten years ago when she was writing her dissertation on eighteenth-century Choctaws. She decided she needed a pet. Not a dog she'd have to walk, or a cat she'd have to shoo out of her bed. Remembering that her father had kept rabbits, she adopted one from a shelter and named him after the Frenchman whose history was completely intertwined with her tribe's. She'd become totally fascinated with Jean Baptiste Le Moyne Sieur de Bienville when she was researching Choctaw history. She somehow felt as though she knew Bienville, or had firsthand knowledge of his relationship with the Choctaws. However she dismissed this as a curse of her profession. Many historians talked about developing psychic communications with those they researched. After their work was finished, though, they often realized that their "channeling" had been a result of having read too much into what little they'd found out. Nevertheless, as she pored over the French documents, certain episodes that dealt with her tribe and Bienville felt more like memories than mere historical events.

From the beginning of Bienville's tenure in Louisiana, he allied himself with Choctaws and, on occasion, he had Choctaw women living in his house. In 1701, the Choctaws were at war with all the nations to their north and east, and had six thousand warriors in the field. The next year, Bienville traded muskets to the Choctaws so they could fight the English and Chickasaws. He asked for their political and military support and most towns complied. In return, Bienville frequently lived with Choctaws along the Pearl River, and learned to speak their language fluently. After serving under a string of political appointees from France, he was finally named governor general of the colony in 1718. However, six years later he was recalled to Paris and fired. Amazingly, at age fifty-three, Bienville triumphantly returned to Louisiana in 1733 for a second chance. He ruled as governor for nine more years, then was dismissed after his failure in the wars against the Chickasaws. Bienville returned to France at his own expense in 1742. Strangely though, especially for a Frenchman, he never married.

Auda knew that Bienville must have been adopted by one of the

Choctaw warrior societies, because he had Choctaw women living in his houses. Someone had claimed him as theirs. But who? Finally she discovered that he'd been tattooed on the arm, a sign that he'd been made a member of one of the eastern district towns. But she was never able to discover what the symbol was. She liked to imagine that it was a *chukfi*, rabbit, one of the trickster animals in Choctaw wisdom tales. *Chukfi* is a cunning adversary, the ultimate survivor, and in the rabbit world, the female rules.

Auda gingerly searches her mother's iris beds, trying not to destroy them. Then something catches her eye—the entrance to the dilapidated root cellar at the back of the house. Jean Baptiste might have gone in there. She opens the heavy wooden door and walks down the sod steps, hoping she'll find him happily living underground.

She feels the cool ground around her, as if from a distance. She watches the world whirling away, moving through her, whispering the past. She's a young girl holding her mother's hand in front of their cabin made of cut canes. There is a river nearby. A man is speaking in Choctaw, but his accent is funny, almost childlike. It's Jean Baptiste Sieur de Bienville and her mother is asking why he must leave. "Because," he says, his stare as cool as a snake's, "I openly despise the Chickasaws, the Natchez, and Chitimaches—all your enemies—so now I must defend myself to my chief. But someday, Shakbatina, I will return to you and your daughters. Not the pull of Paris, nor the tether of kings, can keep me from you." Even then she detects something incomplete. Bienville is not telling the whole truth. She wonders if her mother also sees through him, as she does.

Fine dust makes Auda sneeze. It breaks the shock. The woman she'd found in the diaries of the French priest in 1738, and again in 1747, was her ancestor. Until now, she'd only considered the woman's name—the same as her ancestor's—a coincidence, but at this moment, she believes the impossible. That she is the young girl in her vision, standing beside her mother, Shakbatina.

Auda's eyes adjust to the half-light in the cellar. She runs her fingers over the sod. Clusters of spiders' eggs occupy the pockmarks in the dirt walls. Round bloodless bodies, centuries old. From now on, her world will always be marked by the seconds just before the gunshot. She's living on borrowed time. She wipes her face with the tail of her denim dress. Her rabbit is dead, and only now does she realize that her mother's heroism is for her.

Midafternoon, Auda, her mother, Hoppy, and Isaac leave for the Choctaw Health Clinic. Isaac is driving. Immediately behind them is an ill-sorted procession of neighborhood vehicles. A white 1967 Chevy Impala. Behind the Impala, a motley 1981 Buick LeSabre with a missing headlight and caved-in passenger door. The last car in line is in mint condition, a yellow 1979 Volkswagon Beetle. Each of the drivers are Choctaw friends of Hoppy. However, it isn't long before three police cars and a Bryan County sheriff's vehicle begin forcing the supporters' cars off the road. Finally, Isaac's is the lone car driving along Elm Street, until Durant's Big Peanutmobile streaks by them, heading in the opposite direction as fast as a 1976 Delta 88 with peanut wings can possibly go. One of the two remaining patrol cars whirls around and chases the Peanutmobile.

"Nick Carney to the rescue!" shouts Hoppy.

Auda turns around to watch what happens. "I hope they don't shoot him."

"Isaac, those boys are going to get hurt!" says Susan Billy. "Why did you let them come along?"

Her uncle doesn't answer, and it's clear to Auda that something terrible is about to happen. When Isaac stops in front of the clinic, her fears come true. Two policemen jump out of the patrol car, and drag Isaac out of the car. They arrest him for reckless driving. Hoppy bounds out of the passenger's side, and one of the cops pulls his revolver.

"Get back or I'll shoot!"

Hoppy puts both hands on his head.

Isaac yells as he's being shoved into the patrol car, "Stay with the women, stay with the women!"

"Don't worry *Imoshe*, we'll get you out!" shouts Hoppy.

The cop holding the gun orders Auda and her mother out of the backseat, then he jumps in their car and speeds away. She and her mother close ranks around Hoppy and face the angry crowd at the clinic. What Auda wants to know is how everyone knew she was coming to get her front teeth capped? High school kids dressed in pseudo-military fatigues, Durant store owners, stray dogs, and preachers all gawk, trusting that something ugly will happen. A dozen or so white men, supporters of Tonica, hold up red and white placards painted with the words *MIKO TUBBY*. All the Choctaws in the street will read them as *CHIEF KILLER*. Suddenly a white man with a handgun rushes toward them. Hoppy charges the man and they tumble onto the pavement; the revolver slides a few feet away. Two Choctaw guards run out of the building, grab the loose gun, and pull the man off Hoppy. Her nephew's forehead is badly cut, and blood streams down his face.

The double doors of the emergency entrance fly open and her cousin Buster Jones, a physician's assistant, hustles the three of them inside. The guards take the attacker to a Choctaw paddy wagon nearby.

Instantly the mob shouts the war cry.

"*Miko Tubby!*"

"*Miko Tubby!*"

"*Miko Tubby!*"

"*Miko Tubby!*"

Auda spins around abruptly. Looks defiantly at the sea of faces through the glass doors. "Has the whole town gone mad?" she yells.

"Come away from there!" shouts Buster. "Tonica's men have the people all torn up." Her cousin glares incredulously at her, as if she should know why people are behaving like this. "Aunt Susan, are you all right?" he asks, shifting his gaze from Auda to her mother.

"I'm fine, Buster, but Hoppy needs stitches."

"Don't worry about me, Grandmother," he says, wiping the blood with his shirt sleeve.

Buster looks out the glass doors. "The police are scattering the crowd. C'mon Hoppy, I'll sew you up myself."

"Make this quick, I've gotta get my uncle out of jail!"

"Auda," asks Buster, "can you go by yourself to the dentist's office while Aunt Susan calls a lawyer?"

"I'm not going now, there's no way—,"

"Don't you see what's happening?" he snaps. "This whole thing was a set-up. The local police wouldn't have arrested Uncle Isaac without some reason, like maybe an anonymous phone call saying 'crazy old Isaac Billy is going to bomb the Choctaw clinic.' Something like that. Think of what's transpired, Auda. The prairie fire, McAlester's murder, the county jail burning down—it's not much of a stretch to believe the Billys are capable of bombing a tribal health clinic. You've gotta go about your normal business here and prove them wrong. Let the men finish the war that Tonica has started!"

"Buster's right, Auda," says her mother. "I'll call Gore and Adair to come and get us. You go on with your appointment. Let's show the police, the tribe, and the whole town that they've made a mistake."

Auda agrees, and hugs her mother and her nephew. "Don't worry,

Mother. We're going to be okay. We're Billys, after all," she says, winking at Hoppy. She walks toward the dental wing of the clinic. Before she's three steps away, she hears Buster tell Hoppy, his voice filled with love, "Aunt Susan practically raised me and my sister after our mother died. When I only had one pair of hand-me-down jeans, she brought me my first new pair of Levis. I'll do anything for her."

She realizes now that no matter how many dirt roads she and McAlester paved, no matter how many gas stations and subdivisions they built for the elderly with the casino money, it could never compete with the simple act of giving away a pair of jeans. Why had it taken her so long to see it?

A middle-aged woman greets Auda at the dentist's reception counter. A curtain of brittle hair falls over one eye as she scrutinizes Auda. Auda reminds herself that after what she's done, she has to get used to being stared at.

"I think the dentist is expecting me," she says, noting that there are no other patients in the waiting room. "I'm Auda Billy."

The woman doesn't answer her directly, but chatters away with her chin propped on the tall counter, as if her head is separate from the rest of her body. A mouth with no trunk. She talks about the rain that is predicted. Her new car. Her vacation in Bermuda; she leaves tomorrow. "I've been working for this all my life," she says.

"My appointment is for 3:30, has it been canceled?"

"Of course not," says the dental hygienist. "We've been expecting you all afternoon, Miss Billy, but the dentist is at the pharmacy. Something about a medication problem. He'll be right back."

Auda thinks there's something foul about the woman. Perhaps it's the lingering effects of the crowd scene. Suddenly, she recalls last summer's Green Corn Dance. People were aghast to see Carl Tonica with the bottle blonde in a lime-green evening gown at a Green Corn Dance. He sent his wife and daughter to Ireland for the summer, and brought Vergie Reagan instead of his family. He must have forgotten to mention that it was not an evening gown affair.

As Auda enters the examining room, the bright fingers of the sun cut through the plastic blinds. The hygienist jerks the curtains across the window to block the light.

"Sit in the chair," she commands.

Auda has sensed that something is wrong, but hasn't wanted to show it. Finally, in the small room, she realizes what it is. The woman has a pewey smell. Like someone who hasn't washed up from sex. Carl Tonica, she moans.

"Isn't this a marvelous room?" coos the woman. "I love the off-white walls. Carl said it is the most modern dental facility in Indian Country. Marvelous, marvelous, marvelous."

"I'm glad you like it," says Auda, coldly. "I'm the one who approved the building plans for the clinic, even down to the color of the walls."

The woman puts on a white mask and asks Auda to open wide. "Yes, I've heard we have you to thank for all this." She picks up an explorer, a dental tool that looks like a miniature sickle, and pushes Auda's lips away from her broken teeth. "We need to take some X-rays and impressions." She laughs, it's more of a snigger. "Probably we can fit temporary caps on your front teeth this afternoon so you won't look so much like Bela Lugosi," she says. Then she digs hard into Auda's gum and cuts a deep gash with the needle-sharp point of the explorer.

Auda grabs at the thing embedded in her mouth. It feels so icy hot that tears run down her cheeks. Where is the dentist? Buster? As she tries to pull it out, the masked woman quickly jabs her in the arm with a needle. Auda attempts to stand up, but a hammering pain batters her chest. She loses her balance and dollops onto the floor like dough. The woman lifts her up into the chair and stares intently into her eyes. Removes the bloody tool from Auda's hand. Waits patiently. Finally glides away like an apparition.

Auda's chest grows tighter. She's breathing underwater. The pain crushes her and she feels sad and abandoned. She sees the river, the shimmering water. She wants to lie down. Her father is standing beside the river bank. He yells, "Anoleta, go back." Presently a gar breaks the surface and flashes green and red, then flies into the air.

A spasm shakes her body. Something red comes out of her mouth. Auda throws her head back; she's running beside the river faster than she's ever run before. Smoke coils lazily above her cabin. The green cane door wiggles as she pushes it open and she's aware of the filling of her lungs. She slips off her red shoes, curls on the floor beside the chief's chair. She kisses him... *Hah!*... there is blood on her lips. Red was right, dying is like dozing.

8 | A Road of Stars

A noleta is marooned in her sleep. Trapped in a white room with white cane mats on the windows, she can see herself sleeping, sitting up, wearing her mother's white deerskin dress. But whose cabin is this? Where is the hole in the roof for the smoke to escape? Maybe she has accidentally slipped into *na tobhi,* the something white. But *na tobhi* is where aging warriors go for their visions. It is not a place for women.

All at once the spirit of a woman enters the room. She has a white mask over her nose and mouth. The woman approaches Anoleta cautiously, then forces her mouth open.

Anoleta screams and a grasshopper-like arm pulls out her teeth. Blood gushes from her mouth. She feels the pain. She wants to ask the woman if she is *Filanchi okla* or *Inkilish okla,* but is catapulted across the night sky onto *fichik tohbi hina,* the white star road. When she looks down at the ground she sees her body strapped on a wooden frame, glowing like fire.

"I'm being tortured," she screams. Her words echo all the way to *Fichik Issi,* the Deer Star, who agrees with her.

"Look at what is left of you. A chin, a foot, a jawbone, and ten thousand feet of intestines hanging in the trees," he says, turning his antlers so he can watch her body wither on the frame. "You can stop what is coming," he says, clearing off on a vapor.

"Alleh, alleh, alleh, Chishke apela..." Mother help me. Anoleta wakes up with a start, and indeed she is wearing her mother's white deerskin dress, but standing over her is Red Shoes, his naked torso painted for

war. He holds a war club in one hand, a heavy killing tool made from a cypress tree, with the skeletal head of a gar lashed to its top.

"Get out! Am I to be your next victim?" she shouts with such ferocity that Red Shoes backs out of her cabin.

She leaps up and chases him after him, yelling, "Wait! How can you show your face to me after what you did?"

He stands partially hidden among the oak trees, a few feet from her cabin.

"I heard you scream. Are your dreams so terrible?"

"That's not what I asked."

"I have nothing to hide," he says. "I came to the bone-picking ceremony to honor your mother, along with the others who have died in the past months. Now I am gathering many warriors to fight against our *Inkilish okla* enemies with Bienville. At last I will be able to prove that I had nothing to do with your mother's death."

He steps toward her with a calm face, presenting an image of goodwill. She's heard that he's fallen into debauchery, but he looks as good as ever. Straight-backed, tall, and muscular. Self-confident. She pulls her knife from its sheath and holds it taut against his belly. "All you have ever proven is that you will fight in the pay of anyone who gives you muskets."

He neither flinches nor moves; rather, he uses his height to peer down at her like a bird inspecting carrion. "That is true, but it is part of my plan. I believe if our warriors have enough muskets and powder we can rid ourselves of both the *Filanchi okla* and *Inkilish okla*."

Anoleta hesitates, the knife feels heavy. Right now she should slice him open before anyone can intercede. Working efficiently she could hang his intestines in the trees, watch them quiver in the wind as they grow cold outside his bloodless body. Instead she cuts him, a scratch really. It could have been an accident, though he knows it isn't. She wants his blood on her mother's dress and she makes a big show of wiping the knife on it, then she walks away and nonchalantly begins to hack off small sprigs of an oak tree for kindling. She looks up at *Fichik Issi*, the Deer Star. If only Red Shoes would drive out the foreigners. That is what they promised each other. Push the *Filanchi okla* and the *Inkilish okla* out of their region. Once she believed he would do it, but now she knows that was never his intention. Already, warriors of Yanàbi Town worship their muskets as if they were children, and he continually fills their heads with dreams that there are more where those came from.

"Where are my sisters?" she asks, across the darkness.

"I don't know, probably singing with your relatives at the dance grounds. I was only interested in seeing you," he says, examining the wound she has given him.

She looks at him again, quickly. She must find out what he is going to do, but she doesn't want him to think she's overly concerned.

"Come inside," she commands.

"Some of the men say that you are going to take Choucououlacta for your husband."

"Yes," she says, placing the kindling over red coals to keep them from dying. She wants her cabin to glow with warmth.

"When?"

"Tomorrow."

"Do you want him very much?"

"Very much."

"You're sure he'll be a good husband?"

"Better than you."

"What is it about him you want?"

"He will fight against the Inkilish okla. He also hates the Red Fox for killing my mother. And Choucououlacta does not have any other wives."

"My wife from the Red Fox village is dead. Someone cut out her heart, remember?"

"It wasn't me, or any of my family, who killed your Chickasaw wife."

"You knew it was my mother's wish that I marry her. I could not disobey my mother," he says.

"Nor can I!" she says, bluntly. "I am no longer your wife. I renounced you. The words were spoken a long time ago, and you heard them. Now get out."

"Then I would like us to be married again," he whispers, pitifully.

Silence.

"Why? So we can make each other suffer like before?"

"Yes, but it was good pain. The kind that made us cry out for each other."

"Maybe this pain will finally kill us," she says, looking at him with all her strength.

"It is you who I have protected with my life," he says. "I had a dream. We are very old and living together. Our children and families are all around us."

His voice lingers in her head, and Anoleta wants to hold it there forever. The night pulsates with songs, the call of insects and tree frogs. Smoke coils around them. The scent of memory, erotic, makes her drop to her knees. She shakes her head no, and cries softly. Says she can't keep from crying for what is going to happen.

Red Shoes sits down on the cane mat next to her, gives her hand a squeeze, buries his face in her breasts. "I'm wanting you again. You will never know how much."

She says he shouldn't say that.

He promises never again.

She runs her fingers across his tattooed face. Gives him her mouth and tastes what he is saying. Then she says it to him, the same way.

When Anoleta opens her eyes, Red Shoes is gone. She must have fallen asleep for a few moments, long enough for him to slip away. He had promised her that they would share a meal together before he left to fight the *Inkilish okla*. She searches her cabin. His travel bundle is still beside her bed; he will return to her before leaving.

She quickly puts on her mother's dress, then begins to pull dried plants out of her baskets to make this special meal. She has learned how to brew healing plants into medicines. It is a skill that women of *Intek Aliha* learned. But this will be the first time she has used her knowledge to kill rather than cure. After the brew is made she pours it over some meat, then goes out to find Red Shoes.

In the center of the grounds, she finds a Blackrobe making a ceremony for the men in his group.

Hoc est corpus. Sanctus, sanctus, sanctus. She remembers some of the foreign words, but they are empty to her now. She has seen the performances of Blackrobes before, when she and her mother visited Bienville's house. The *Filanchi's* speech always sounds sweet and wet, like a mouthful of peaches, but she will never admit to liking it.

Anoleta looks at the older Blackrobe and imagines that he's a giant opposum; his skin is so pale, and his brown eyes never seem to blink, even in sunlight. Poor thing, he's so pitiful looking. How his Mother must have suffered when the other children taunted him. The younger Blackrobe, the one with hair on his face, isn't as ugly. He has kind eyes. But she must remember—they are all the same—*Filanchi okla* only come to beg for land, food, and anything else they can carry off.

"*Ad Majorem Dei Gloriam. Alvarez De Paz, Luis de la Puente, Antoine le Gaudier ... Compañia de Jesus.*"

When will his words end? As a child she was taught to never inter-
rupt the speeches of elders because it was ill-mannered. However these
men are not elders, they are foreigners.

"*Auferatur hic abusus de medio vestrum...*"

Now the younger Blackrobe is all stirred up, his eyebrows continually arch as he talks to the men. Anoleta stifles a smile, a swarm of flies
thwarts his speech causing him to stop and shoo them away. Why don't
Blackrobes wash themselves daily in the river like her people do? It
would keep them from smelling so badly.

"*...deus faber.*"

The men of *Filanchi okla* smile and exchange glances, as if they agree
with what the young Blackrobe is saying. Finally, when he puts something in one of their mouths, Anoleta decides that she no longer wants
the foreigners to hold ceremonies in her presence. She is tired of having
them around, tired of their dirty faces, and she blames all of them for her
mother's death. She steps forward and stares at the men defiantly. If they
were Choctaw warriors, she knows how they would react. They would
leave. Warriors will not stay around when women want them to leave.
But since these are men of the *Filanchi okla,* she does not know what to
expect.

For a while the three Blackrobes do not move. Finally one of them
calls her by name and begins speaking in her language.

"Anoleta, I tell you again most solemnly, if you do not eat of the flesh
of the Son of Man and drink His blood you will not have life in you.
Anyone who does eat my flesh and drink my blood has eternal life, and
I shall raise him up on that day. For my flesh is real food, my blood is real
drink. He who eats my flesh and drinks my blood lives in me and I live
in him!"

When she walks closer to him, he backs up, as if he thinks she might
stab him.

"Anoleta, if you let Father Renoir instruct you, you too will have life
everlasting. Please let us teach you about the one true God. He is your
God also but you must believe in life everlasting."

By this time Haya has arrived, and stands next to her. Other Choctaw
women walk closer to hear what is being said. She can tell that the three
Blackrobes of the *Filanchi okla* are afraid. They are unaccustomed to having
Choctaw women stare at them, so she speaks softly and slowly, as if they
are children. She hopes the foreigners can comprehend what she is saying.

"Did you not see my mother, the one called Shakbatina, raised up from the scaffold this very night? Did you know my mother's flesh was food? Her blood was drink? Alive, we use the animals. The animal is consumed. In death, the people are consumed by the animals." Pointing to herself she says, "We are life everlasting. *Filanchi okla,* we will pick your bones after you are gone." Then she repeats the expression Father Baudouin used. "Life everlasting, we are it!"

She turns to walk proudly through the crowd, and passes the temporary shelters made of palmetto leaves and brush for the men of the *Filanchi okla.* As she looks back, she sees Haya grab the cup from the Blackrobe's hands and greedily swallow its contents. Then her sister tosses the cup into the air and runs away.

Haya giggles loudly as she enters the cabin.

"Why did you drink from the *Filanchi*'s cup? I told you not to do that," says Anoleta, trying to look stern.

"I love it. It makes me dizzy and I like it. I want this *bah-andi,*" says Haya, trying to pronounce the foreign word. "Why do you waste your time on the Blackrobes? They didn't understand what you were saying. Some of the elders say the Blackrobes are cannibals because they speak of eating the bones and drinking the blood of their honored dead in their ceremonies. But when we tested them, they ate food. If it's true they pray to die, perhaps we should give Red Shoes to the Blackrobes. They might pray him into death and save us the trouble."

"No. I promised our mother that I would finish Red Shoes."

"Where is he now?" asks Haya.

"At the stickball field. He'll come soon."

"Will you still take Choucououlacta for your husband?"

"Yes."

"Neshoba told me that the young Blackrobe, the one with all the hair on his face, has passion for her. She smelled it on his body," says Haya, casually.

"Does Neshoba want him very much?"

"She didn't say." Haya pulls a small strand of blue glass beads from her leather pouch. "Look at what the one with sore feet gave me. I love his presents."

"How did you get that?"

"I took him. His body is covered with soft, tiny white hairs. He feels like a baby duck. He is not a cannibal."

"You live four paws up," says Anoleta, "always wanting men."

"So do you. I saw Red Shoes leave your cabin."

Anoleta puts a hand over Haya's mouth. "And he will come here again tonight, but I tell you, it is not what you think. I will end his life and keep my promise!" Then she spits to show she is putting her words in the ground.

Just then a man from the *Filanchi okla* enters her cabin. He carries a large bundle wrapped in white deerskin. He greets her and her sister in their language, but his pronunciation is babyish. Anoleta recognizes his accent at once.

The man places a small cane mat on the ground and sits down in front of her fire. Then he takes a red stone pipe and a long wooden stem out of his bundle. He attaches them, and fills the pipe with tobacco. He offers it first to Anoleta because she is the oldest. She politely takes it from him, and after taking a few puffs she passes it to Haya, who does the same. Once they finish smoking, the man begins to talk casually with them, as if he is family.

"So, you no longer recognize me," says Bienville sadly, taking off his cloak and rolling up the sleeve of his shirt. "After visiting my house when you were children, you have forgotten your old friend, no? Was it not I who you once called Uncle? Was it not I who held you on my lap and fed you from my own plate? So this is how you repay your relative. You insult the priest I have provided for you? Why did you talk with Father Michel Baudouin like he was a cursed thing? Is this the result of your mother's teachings? I do not think so."

He shoves an exposed forearm to Anoleta. His tattoo is the same design as her uncle Nitakechi's. "I have carried your family's symbol halfway around the world. I knew your mother well. Shakbatina was my dearest friend and I will speak of her. I don't think she would like the way you are conducting yourself," he says, at last making eye contact with her.

Bienville waits for Anoleta to respond. When she doesn't speak, he sighs deeply. "Ah yes. It is a sad situation that I have returned to. *Faire la bouche en coeur, no?*"

Anoleta doesn't understand the last phrase, so she cannot acknowledge it. She no longer comprehends his language. Once she had known a few of his words and phrases. She and her mother stayed in his house every spring when they were collecting the trade goods he owed them. On one occasion Bienville pulled a small bird out of his shirt and presented it to her. Before she had a firm grip on the bird's tiny legs, it flew away. She couldn't tell if he let it go on purpose, so the next day she retaliated by putting a green snake around his neck that crawled down the front of his shirt. He laughed and said, "good snake, go home." Her mother scowled and sent her away. There was a strong bond between Bienville and her mother. Anoleta never understood it. What had her mother seen in him? He could never measure up to her father, Koi Chitto, nor her uncle Nitakechi. When her uncle adopted Bienville into his *iksa*, he found a cousin willing to marry him, but Bienville declined, saying that since he could not have the woman he wanted, he would have none at all. Anoleta refused to believe he loved her mother as he had proclaimed to her uncle. She believed their commitment to each other was based on an exchange of trade goods, nothing more. Anoleta had to admit though, her mother had treated Bienville like a pet. Strangely enough, he seemed to like it. She had always teased him, saying when he first arrived he was like a baby, only able to express himself with cries of wonder, mad leaps, or with objects he took from his bundle. Anoleta may have been jealous of him when she was a child, but the main reason she'd grown to hate Bienville was that he'd constantly spoken to her mother against Red Shoes. "That savage will one day kill you all. He's a traitor!" Now Bienville had come to smoke with her tonight just to shame her into admitting he'd been right.

Finally Haya speaks up and smiles. "Hello Uncle, how is your life? Are you well?" Then she turns to Anoleta. "He speaks our language perfectly, doesn't he? Better than even me."

"Yes," smiles Anoleta, pleased that her youngest sister is complimenting Bienville's language ability, practicing her diplomacy skills. Quite necessary, because Haya will one day be trading goods between the towns in their region.

"Tell me," continues Anoleta, "have you smoked with my mother's brother, Nitakechi, and our father, Koi Chitto?"

"Of course," he answers, his eyes mocking her. "After all, we are family."

Haya fetches water and offers them both a drink from her gourd. They oblige her because it is the proper thing to do. Then there is more silence.

Haya tries again to make conversation. "Uncle, I understand that you went far away when you left us."

Anoleta and Bienville smile ironically at each other, amused by Haya's remarks. Now they seem almost friends. He takes up Haya's polite tone in his reply.

"I never wanted to leave here, but my chief ordered me to return to Paris, a town that exists across the sea."

"So you cannot live where you want?"

Bienville laughs. "I'm afraid not."

"We live where we want," says Anoleta, haughtily.

"For a time," answers Bienville. "But once your husband Red Shoes bargains away your towns to the *Inkilish okla* you will have nowhere to go. He is ruthless and resourceful. Only three months ago, he said in open council that anyone who attacked the Chickasaws were his enemies."

No one speaks for a long while.

Bienville takes a deep breath and begins putting away his pipe and tobacco, gently folding a piece of cloth around them.

"Red Shoes is no longer my husband, you should know that. I will soon marry Choucououlacta."

"A good leader, Choucououlacta," says Bienville. "I approve." Again he looks at her, but says nothing more until he stands up. "You are in great danger. Red Shoes will not go to war against the *Inkilish*-supported Chickasaw towns as he did two years ago at the battle of Akia. Besides, I know what happened, I was there. Although I arrived too late to save your mother's friend Pierre D'Artagurette, I was able to bury his charred remains after the Chickasaws burned him at the stake. No, Red Shoes went, not to help the *Filanchi okla,* nor to help the warriors from your town. He was there for the Red Fox, his true allies. Had it not been for your leader Miko Chitto, my men would have been left on the battlefield to die by his deeds. For no matter what Red Shoes is telling you, he conspires to kill us all. The man is a demon. I believe he would slice you in two if it meant he could profit from each half."

Suddenly Anoleta is fighting off tears. "No, Red Shoes will never harm Yanàbi Town. I will prevent this."

"We shall see."

Anoleta realizes she's said too much. Bienville must not even suspect that within a few hours she will keep her promise to Shakbatina.

At last, Haya breaks the silence. Her final attempt at small talk with Bienville. "The reason we still love Red Shoes is because he doesn't know that he has become corrupted. He'll never believe that, even if someday he causes us all to die."

Bienville looks warmly at Haya. He seems to examine her feature by feature, as though he is memorizing her. Trying to understand what she is made of. Then he reaches out and touches her lightly on the cheek.

"Why did you look at her like that?" asks Anoleta.

Bienville searches for a word. He can't find it, the word escapes him, and that's what he finally says to Anoleta as he walks out of their lives. That the word must not exist in her language.

9 | Borrowed Time

A no ma Chahta sia hoke oke. Call me Shakbatina. For six generations I have waited, marking time, daughter by daughter, before splitting my spirit in half, as the great warrior Tuscalusa did before me.

While I waited, bustle-skirted ladies blossomed into flappers. Flappers grew into hippies, with the symbols of American Indians sewn on their jeans. I have witnessed the panic of 1907, the second confiscation of Choctaw lands. Statehood for Oklahoma. The giddy 20s. The desperate dustbowl years. The crash of '29, and two World Wars. But I am skipping parts and jumping ahead. I do not want to do this, because gradually we become indivisible from our memories. I want to remember it all.

In 1831, throngs of ragged children, my descendants' children, were forced out of Mississippi. Walking west with their stomachs in their hands, they were compelled to beg for food and water. I endured the songs they sang for the dead. There was no one left who could tell them the stories of how their grandmothers had once turned themselves into beautiful birds in order to fly to safety. There was no one who could conduct a proper funeral. No one to pick their bones, afterward. Imagine my agony.

But their sweet remains, their flesh and blood, seared stories into the land that kept account of such things. Mother Earth would exact a price. Twenty-nine years later, the white people who pushed my children out of their homelands were driven insane. Witness the destruction of their Civil War and the decades of waste and ruin that ensued. Plantation children were turned into homeless beggars who would one day birth the Ku Klux Klan. Today, their descendants drive by the Nanih Waiya, our beloved Mother Mound, with their car windows rolled up for asylum trying to drown out the ghostly screams of Choctaw children who were walked to death on the road to the new promised land. But they cannot. Now they have seen what happens when Earth and spirit and story are reunited, and we pull stars down from the sky and cause a fifty-mile prairie fire.

Hah, I wonder who will recognize me?

Carl Tonica groans and doubles over his desk at the Casino of the Sun. He has a glass stomach. It breaks every so often. He pops a chewable tablet in his mouth and waits for the pain to subside. He thinks the doctors at the Choctaw Health Clinic purposefully ignore his stomach complaints. They tell him it's his bad diet. Too much pork and cheap beer. But he argues with them. Tells them that he's a slight man of only 165 pounds. That he does not eat pork or drink beer to excess. But the doctors don't listen and he knows why. Like so many other Choctaws, they're against him. Next week though, after he's found the money and put things in order, Tonica vows he's going to make an appointment with a white doctor in Oklahoma City. Someone unconnected with the tribe, who he can trust.

After the pain in his stomach eases, Carl Tonica picks up the telephone and calls Washington D.C. He checks his watch. 3:45 P.M.; 4:45, Washington time. He should be able to catch the FBI agent who's in charge of McAlester's murder investigation before he goes home for the day. Those nine-to-five-boys in D.C. really have it made, what with paid federal holidays, health care benefits, and juicy retirement funds. He wishes he'd applied for a government job years ago. It would have saved him about a million stomachaches.

Tonica waits while the secretary tries to locate the agent; he figures the guy is probably on the can reading a magazine. When the agent picks up the phone, he makes a lot of excuses about why the investigation into McAlester's murder is going so slowly. Tonica listens and finally loses his temper.

"The real killer is free again on the streets of Durant," he shouts into the phone. "I don't care if the U.S. Attorney isn't interested in this case. Hell man, her mother didn't do it, it was Auda Billy. The FBI's gotta place her in their protective custody until a trial can be set. For Christ's sake,

Auda Billy assassinated the Chief of the Choctaw Nation!"

Tonica has learned to do his bullying over the phone. He's never had McAlester's balls. He has trouble presenting a poker face. In the past two television interviews he can practically see his own mouth twitching as he lies for the camera. He secretly curses McAlester every time he has to speak to reporters.

He half-listens as the bureaucrat tells his story. "There are problems in Washington." "Budget restraints." "Congressional hearings on tribal misuse of funds." "Congressional hearings on BIA misuse of funds."

Tonica cleans his fingernails while the man continues a litany of complaints about Indians. Anytime he's on the phone to Washington he tries to catch up on personal hygiene, knowing the government's list of excuses can take a long time. He replies with the appropriate "Uh-huhs," and wishes this were over. For months before McAlester was murdered, he tried to warn the chief that the Mafia was closing in. That McAlester was fucking around with people who carried guns and calculators in the same briefcase.

From the time construction began on the Casino of the Sun, McAlester was going drastically over budget. The tribe had awarded construction bids to some of Southeastern Oklahoma's wisest good ol' boys. Concerning the cost overruns, they'd agreed to split the kickbacks equally: Indians fifty percent, white boys fifty percent. Tonica smiles to himself. Some Indian men play golf, some Indian men—such as himself —run around on their wives, but not Red. To him, making deals was the big orgasm. In the case of the building project, McAlester just connected the construction foot bone to the casino backbone and wound up siphoning money from Shamrock Resorts right from the get-go.

At first, Vico D'Amato had tried to groom McAlester for bigger things in their organization, they'd grown to be such close friends. But D'Amato didn't understand who was conning who. Maybe he did toward the end. Perhaps that was why he sent for his younger brother Hector, to help him corral McAlester; but the chief had an instinct about people. When he felt the Italians squeezing him, he switched alliances to the Irish. Brought in James Joyce.

Tonica remembers the day tribal members were invited to Ireland to commemorate the "Long Walk" made during the Irish Potato Famine of 1847. McAlester was ecstatic. He said he could now solve all his problems. "It's too poetic for words—at last I'll be able to keep the money, and my promise to Auda," he had said.

Tonica questioned McAlester about what he'd had meant that day, but he never got a straight answer. The chief liked to talk in riddles, especially in front of Joyce, an Irishman who loved to fracture the English language with his thick Irish brogue.

McAlester's whole life was an enigma. Every Tuesday and Wednesday, he would go on the road lobbying other Oklahoma tribes to support the casino compacts. He said the 1990s would be remembered as the heyday of the gaming business. "Huge fortunes can be made. Many strands of history and international commerce are coming together in Southeastern Oklahoma, but only for a short while, and only for those who act now." But then on Sundays, McAlester would be in church telling the minister and the congregation that he was against gambling—that it was the tribal council who had voted for the casino.

Crimony, the man was a shameless hustler, sighs Tonica, as he puts away his fingernail clippers. He tried to tell McAlester that the Italians could smell embezzlement. But the chief had called him a "Sissy Mary." Told him to put a wet towel on his face and help him "skim the cream off the top of the milk." Sometimes he'd just laugh. "Carl, it's small potatoes to them. Quit worrying; you're getting your cut."

McAlester doesn't have to worry anymore, thinks Tonica. His troubles were over the minute that Auda Billy put a bullet in his brain. He'd told Red she was stealing the tribe's bank documents. McAlester said not to worry, that he could prove he was still in control. Even made a bet with Hector. McAlester should have realized long ago that Auda Billy was the one deal he'd made that went sour.

At last, Tonica's ready to get off the telephone, and interrupts the federal government. "What if one of these redneck Indians takes the law into his hands and kills Auda Billy?" he asks. "Remember what happened to Lee Harvey Oswald?"

Just as he gets a rise out of the FBI agent, he hears a voice calling his name.

Carl Tonica, do you hear? Do you understand? I am a descendent of Grandmother of Birds. Time flows out of my beak with a sound that can pierce the most foolish plan.

At first, the voice seems to be coming from inside his office, but then he looks outside and sees a feeble old woman walking up and down the sidewalk in front of the Casino of the Sun. The enormous golden disk revolving atop the casino puts her in the shade, and he can't tell who she is. Then the old woman raises a homemade sign high in the air that horrifies him. It reads: *I know where McAlester hid the ten million.*

Tonica stares at the sign, then the old woman. He's sure he's seen her before, but can't quite remember where. She has bushy gray hair that blends into the nappy shawl wrapped around her shoulders. The large sign she carries might as well be a rifle in his belly.

There's an expectant pause on the other end of the phone and Tonica realizes he's lost track of what he's saying. "Listen, you're in D.C. while I'm here in the trenches in Durant, Oklahoma. It's all our tribal police can do to keep the peace. I'm telling you, the Choctaw people are out for blood. They might kill Auda Billy if you don't act quickly. We're in a state of war."

The agent reminds him that the wheels of justice take a long time. "Uh-huh," says Tonica, breaking into a sweat. By now several women from the Choctaw Daycare Center have come outside to read the sign. The old woman's voice thunders across the parking lot as if she's speaking into a microphone. She says Chief McAlester stole millions from the Mafia and gave it to the Irish Republican Army to kill Englishmen for crimes they committed against the Choctaw two hundred and fifty years ago. She says McAlester's shame is a disgrace Tonica must publicly acknowledge.

Carl Tonica, do you hear? Do you understand? I did not come back to be Grandmother to a tribe of entertainers at the Casino of the Sun. I am here to stop you from offending anyone else with your face or your tongue.

Another busload of tourists from Dallas arrives at the casino. Most people push past the old woman and ignore her sign. Tonica isn't worried about the white people who frequent the casino. He knows they would rather eat their children than miss an opportunity to gamble. Besides, whites want to believe that Indians get rich off casinos. It relieves their guilt for stealing all the Indians' land.

Tonica realizes he's out of "Uh-huhs" and takes the offensive. "If something happens to Auda Billy before she reaches trial, I'm holding the FBI responsible," he says, slamming the phone down. He paces back and forth in his office. The next call he makes to Washington, he can say, "I warned you... Auda Billy has been murdered." He claps his hands together. "One problem solved, one to go." Tonica expels stomach gas running down the hall to Vic D'Amato's office. Both D'Amato brothers have telephones stuck in their ears, and he's grateful they haven't seen the woman outside.

"Is it the old man in New York?" he asks, steadying himself, so as not to raise their suspicions.

Vico nods his head.

Tonica goes stoic. He's not about to let the Italian know he's scared shitless, and he interrupts him again.

"Have you heard whether she's dead yet?"

"*She*, who?" says the elder D'Amato, covering the phone with his hand.

He knows he's being taunted. D'Amato just wants to hear him speak her name aloud. To see if there's a twinge of guilt that will someday grow into a fully-developed memory with a voice. He's heard the Italian's theory on "free speech" at some of their late-night conferences. "Who knows what a voice can do? Sing? Tell stories? Implicate us in past wrongs? Why wait for such a talent to develop?"

"Auda Billy, is she dead yet?" he deadpans.

"Shouldn't be too long," says Hector. "Your girlfriend, Nancy Reagan, or whatever the hell her name is, said she was going to load her up with enough insulin to kill ten little Indians." Hector mumbles something in Italian and hangs up the phone. "You've got two more days, Tonica. Find the money McAlester stole from us, or we start leaking your own little investment schemes to the FBI. We know all about the cash Red had been putting in your greedy little fists. Do we understand one another?"

Tonica holds his head as high as possible. He can't let Hector or Vico think he's hiding anything. "McAlester didn't cram ten million up his ass. It's around here somewhere. What about his cabin outside of Talihina where he and Auda used to shack up? Why don't you look for the money, instead of making threats to me? I want to find it as badly as you do, and I never stole money from the mob!"

Vico bores a hole into him with his stare. "I liked Red," he says quietly. "I never trusted him, but I liked him. He had a kind of style that inspired us to think beyond the Choctaw's casino." Almost absent-mindedly the elder D'Amato drags an index finger across his gray shirt collar. "But you," he adds, "I don't like. You're a pretender. And not even a good opportunist. If I thought for one infinitesimal moment that you had our money, your wife would be finding pieces of you nailed all over this building. You understand?"

Tonica smiles with his mouth only, as if he's just been told a bad joke. "There's an old lady waiting for me outside who says she knows where McAlester hid the money. When I come back I'll have your ten million."

He walks confidently out of the room. Tonica believes he has shown them who's in charge.

The wind outside is warm at first, full of voices. A strange tickling sensation makes Tonica feel helpless. As he draws near the old woman he realizes he hasn't the slightest notion of what to do. What he feels, he can no longer translate into words. The face, which he doesn't recognize, yawns as it turns on him. It is then he believes she could make *Hashtali* open if she wanted. He sees her loose hair hanging like silk around her head. Her body, though very old, is straight and still. At last she stretches out both hands to greet him.

"I am Shakbatina. I know when it is time to return to the earth that I have lived to protect. Come with me."

Carl Tonica says good-bye to the Casino of the Sun, and to the flock of birds waving to him from the sky. He steps into the street and is only vaguely aware that he is already dead.

Many hours later, a janitor at the Casino of the Sun, who just happened to be outside around 4:30 P.M., tearfully told the Choctaw police and the D'Amato brothers that there wasn't no old lady waiting around to talk to Tonica. That Tonica must not have seen the eighteen-wheeler pulling into the parking lot; he didn't even look surprised when it hit him.

10 | Funerals By Delores

Delores' hands are like two shovels kneading bread dough into mounds of stone. As she stands at the kitchen table, she scoops and re-scoops the white clumps of flour in the bowl. She's oblivious to what she's doing. With her mind she tells Isaac that they should have been together this past half-century. If only she had understood his stubborn nature earlier. She could have gone to him when he returned home from World War II. Today he looked tired. More fragile. As always he acknowledged her, but then he walked away without speaking.

Absentmindedly, she wipes her sticky hands across her black organdy dress, then she plunges them back into the flour mixture. He wants to speak with her alone, she knows it. The night he called on the phone to tell her what had happened, they spoke only in Choctaw. As he related the details of McAlester's murder, Auda's jailing, and Susan's confession, his tone grew softer and more serene. Finally he said, his voice choked with intimacy, *"Ohoyo aiyala."* Woman, come at last.

"Oke," she had answered.

"Chekusi fehna." Hurry.

"Ia lish." I will.

She could just see him turning the small gray stone he carried over and over in his hand. There was a long silence. Neither knew how to continue so she whispered, *Wi hi yo ha-na-we, wi hi yo ha-na-we,* words from an old song of communal encouragement that the Choctaws sang on the Trail of Tears. They both cried, but he was the first one to hang up. In that gesture she saw everything. He loved her as before, but was still unable to forgive her for sending him away nearly fifty years ago.

When she and Dovie had arrived at the Billy house, she understood that he could not show the feelings that he'd kept hidden for long, so Susan had expressed them for him. "So glad," "so happy," "thought you'd never get here." They were Susan's words, but Isaac's feelings.

"*Hah!*" says Delores aloud. "You have to understand a lot of codes to be Choctaw." She looks down at herself, amazed that her black dress is completely wet with nervous sweat and clumps of sticky dough.

"What Auntie?" asks Tema, scooping more Crisco into a frying pan.

Delores wipes her dress with a wet cup towel. "We're all Code Talkers."

"*Yummak osh alhpesa,*" says Dovie, nodding in agreement.

"How so, Aunt Delores?" asks Adair, mashing the potatoes in a bowl so they can take it to Blue Creek Grounds for tonight's feast.

"Because everything that is important to Choctaws, or all Indians for that matter, is not written down. We have to live the life to know the ways, and so much goes unspoken," says Delores, turning her attention to the bowl. "Maybe I should add more grease?"

"You're overworking the dough," says Dovie, authoritatively, "you should let me do that before you kill the yeast."

"*Wishia cha...* you flour the chicken parts," quips Delores, "I'll make the bread."

Dovie puts her hands on her hips. "Delores is a Gemini, they can't concentrate long enough to become really good cooks."

Tema and Adair both giggle. They've always laughed when she and Dovie argue. As Dovie continues bossing her, Delores has an overwhelming feeling of sadness. She will miss Dovie terribly. She doesn't understand why she feels they'll soon be parted. Perhaps it's the anticipation of what will happen between her and Isaac. Perhaps it's the coming funeral she must conduct, regardless her nerves are raw as open sores. Her eyes tear up as she remembers the first time she came to the Billy house fifty-two years ago. It was the beginning of her new life—helping to conduct traditional funerals for Choctaws.

The year was 1939 and Delores was young, only twenty-nine, although by the standards of the day, a spinster. Her mother had just died and the funeral was her first experience with laying out the dead, with singing the soothing words that would coax an unyielding body into its transformation to dust. A year later her brother Orvil was killed, and she washed and dressed his body, as she had with her mother. A few terrible years later she would do the same for her youngest sister, Lola. For over a half-century, she's prepared Choctaws for their journey to the spirit world. Unlike the years she spent riding bareback in Wild West shows, or acting in the talkies, Delores believes her role as a modern *foni miko*, bone picker, is the only useful thing she's ever done. But McAlester's funeral is different. Her niece, the cause of his death.

She and Dovie once met Redford McAlester and his mother, Minnie. It was sometime in the late 6os at a summer tent revival outside of Rush Springs, Oklahoma. A friend had invited them to hear a young Choctaw named Red McAlester witness on the miracles of the Lord. The young man had finished his sermon by saying he would be entering the Baptist seminary in Fort Worth, Texas. Many years later, when McAlester was running for chief, neither she nor Dovie brought up his brush with the Baptists. It didn't seem proper. Lots of people change horses in mid-stream. She had. But who would have guessed that McAlester started out wanting to be a preacher? She wonders if Auda knows the whole story. Delores sighs deeply and silently prays for guidance. She's never buried a chief, or anyone, accused of rape and other despicable crimes against the Choctaw people.

She picks up the bowl of dough and examines the mess she's making. Water might help. She adds a tablespoon or two and continues knead-ing. Suddenly there is a gust of wind, a hint that someone has entered the room. A clock strikes four. A voice calls from afar. Footsteps, barely audible, touch the floor. There is a spirit. A loving compassion circles the room. She leans toward the apparition and opens her sticky palms as if receiving a gift. She stays that way for a moment, honoring the one who has given her the essential knowledge of how to properly bury the dead.

November, 22, 1939—her own dear mother had died the day before. She drove the hundred miles from the Love Ranch to Durant in order to find the Billy matriarch, the one who could sing the ancient songs for a proper Choctaw funeral. Her sister Dovie had stayed behind at their ranch to greet the people coming to pay their last respects. The drive took all day. Back then, the dirt roads were narrow and went through forests and dozens of tiny communities of three or four families. In 1939, Southeastern Oklahoma was a patchwork of Indian towns. When night-fall came she pulled up in front of the Billy house. For a moment she stood motionless in the yard. As she gathered her courage, so did the wind until it was swirling all around, demanding that she pay attention.

She turned her face to the dark sky, meager black clouds were flying above. A storm was coming.

She walked onto the front porch, but before she could knock, Susan Billy opened the door. She was fresh out of boarding school. Eighteen. Her long black hair streamed down her back. Susan smiled and ushered Delores into the library where a sweet thin voice was calling in Choctaw, "Hurry up, woman, you're the one I've been waiting for. I am the great-great-granddaughter of *Chunkashbili,* Heart Wounder, and she was the granddaughter of Shakbatina whose name doesn't mean 'Wildcat' like people say. Her name means Survivor!"

The old woman looked as fragile as the wings of a butterfly. She had rounded shoulders. Faded eyes. Only a few snags of teeth. A black scarf was tied around her thinning white hair. She wore a yellow skirt that stopped just above her tiny ankles. The blouse was also sun yellow, with long puffy sleeves. Both were trimmed in blue rickrack that formed four zigzag rows around the edges of the skirt and sleeves. The old woman was sitting in the rocking chair holding in her hand a tiny gray stone with holes in it, like a skull. Delores would later learn from Isaac that the stone held the essence of two powerful Ancestors. It was as necessary to the old woman's comfort as a roaring fire.

"Tell me what to sing when your mother dies," Delores blurted out.

The old woman lit up with happiness. No one had asked her this in years. She rocked gently back and forth in her chair, indicating that she would tell Delores what she knew.

"I keep hearing the words you spoke and the songs you sang at Conehatta Annie's funeral," said Delores.

She continued rocking. "You were no bigger than a flea when she passed away. That was so long ago, why do you remember my words?"

Delores hesitated. She was afraid her formal Choctaw was a little rusty, so she spoke to the woman as if she were a relative. "My mother, Elizabeth Love, treated you with extreme respect. She told me that you were very wise in these matters. Now I must bury my mother, and I would like to sing the honor songs that will send her on the journey."

The old woman shook her head, kept shaking it all the while Delores spoke, as if marking time. "We said good-bye to Pearl River in Mississippi. The agent was able to do very little to alleviate the suffering of those who were going to walk the hundreds of miles from Bogue Chitto, Conehatta, Pearl River, Red Water, Standing Pine, and Bogue Homa to our new home in Indian Territory. That was before our people made the whites change the name to Oklahoma, home of red people. Some laid down on the roads to die. They were resigned. As we passed them by they gave away their shoes. We were surrounded day and night by our enemies. It was very unsanitary as to our personage. No way to make a toilet. We all had fevers. Millions of flies ate from our flesh. They left many scars on my body."

The old woman's eyes stared vaguely ahead. She raised her left arm. "See for yourself. I have been a good host."

Delores struggled to understand the old woman's Choctaw. She used different words than those Delores used. The accent was strange. Perhaps she had reverted to the dialect of her childhood. Susan Billy quickly rolled up the sleeve of her grandmother's blouse, treating her with such tenderness that Delores was ashamed she'd wanted to see the scars. The woman was called Nowatima, "She who walks and gives," and, by her own reckoning, she was one hundred and fourteen years old. Delores examined the diligent arm. The upper muscle looked as if it belonged to a tireless farm hand, sinewy, but wrinkled. Lower down on the forearm there were cross-hatched scars where larvae had once wriggled through the skin. Delores believed the scars must have been screwworms that had burrowed into the woman's flesh. Like Indians, the insect was supposed to have been eradicated by the 1930s.

"Heavy-booted soldiers feasted on bread and meat," said Nowatima. "When they ran out of government rations the soldiers ate their own horses. On occasion, I myself principally ate dirt. There were exceptions when we came on a friendly town. People gave what they could. But not many did. We carried everything our families owned in baskets, and I learned all the songs because we sang day and night for our dead. Babies' stomachs, right before the end, swelled like bread dough. My mother, Pisatuntema, my brothers and sisters, aging warriors, beloved friends, were all left behind on the trail. I'm the only one from my family who made it. Conehatta Annie was another one who made it. She was my friend. That's why you remember the words I spoke for her. They were sacred. You will never forget them."

A heavy silence fell inside the library of the Billy house. But outside the wind roared and the oak trees shed their leaves like tears as Nowatima told the story of her walk on the Trail of Tears.

Finally Susan Billy spoke. "*Pokni* needs sleep now." Before Delores could excuse herself, she was stopped by the old woman's reply.

"First, I will teach our guest what she came to learn. *Alla tek,* you sleep for me." Susan smiled, but never left her grandmother's side.

It was morning before Nowatima stopped singing the funeral songs. Sometimes she hesitated, rocked in her chair as if she were listening to something only she could hear. Then she'd begin again, softly chanting to herself, *Wi hi yo ha-na-we, wi hi yo ha-na-we,* which would grow into another song for the dead. Before the old woman was led off to bed by Susan, she grasped Delores' hands. "You will sing good now that I have taught you. You are the one we've been waiting for," she said sweetly.

Delores remembers how frantic she and Dovie were when they received the telegram that said their mother was dying. At the time they were living in Santa Monica, California, and car travel in 1939 was not what it is today. Gasoline could be scarce in the small towns. The steering wheel of their Ford was big and tiresome and their front tires often went flat due to thin inner tubes. So it seemed only fitting that a blistering wind whipped the Ford the last hundred miles to Poteau, as if to remind her that she'd been a disobedient daughter. That she'd stayed away too long.

It was true. She had run away. First from boarding school. Then from her family—all except Dovie. She'd run to European colognes and beaver coats, to cafes where cinematic men with thin mustaches repeatedly said, "Delightful," and "Darling." In Hollywood, she'd grown into the double-faced woman in the black and white films. Spoke slivers of dialogue in gushes of euphoria, or tenderness. The other her.

In Oklahoma, she was Elizabeth Love's oldest girl. The one responsible for laying out her mother's body.

Delores didn't want the formaldehyde embalming solution for her mother so she bathed her in a mixture of baking soda and lavender water. The dried husk of her mother's body became smooth again. Looked almost born. She dressed her mother in a blue silk suit and placed her hands around a small bouquet of roses. Dovie put Indian head nickels on Elizabeth Love's eyes, and tucked sprigs of sage and pinches of sweet snuff in her suit pockets. The room smelled of childhood memories and Indian tobacco.

When she was done, Delores threw out the basin of bath water and watched it soak into the yard. Everything changed for Delores in that instant. The water which held the essence of Elizabeth Love was returned to the Earth as it should be. Minutes later, Delores pulled her Hollywood studio contract out of her briefcase and set fire to it. No more

Westerns. No more cowboys and Indians. She wasn't going back to California. She was going to stay in Oklahoma and hold a traditional funeral for her mother. When she asked some of the neighbors what songs to sing, what words to say for a proper Choctaw funeral, she was told to go to Durant because the Billy matriarch would know. That's when she remembered Conehatta Annie's funeral—and that moment would mark the beginning of Delores' service work to the Choctaws.

Her two sisters and her brother Orvil put up six poles around their mother's grave. Then they hung vine hoops on top of each pole, and colored streamers of cloth to signify that a burial had just taken place. Delores fasted all day before she began the funeral cry, just as Nowatima had instructed. She made the cry, then sang four songs that Nowatima had taught her. Many elderly cousins said it was the most heartfelt ceremony they had ever attended. Afterwards, Choctaws from other towns began asking her to sing at their relatives' funerals. Delores realized she didn't know enough, so she returned weekly to the Billy house to sit with Nowatima. She continued learning the old songs and, without realizing it, she started a revival of Choctaw music and traditions. Many other women began coming to Nowatima to learn traditional songs and rituals. The number of Choctaw singers grew. When Nowatima died in 1941, there were twenty-two singers who sang traditional songs at her funeral.

That same year, she and Dovie hired Isaac to work on their 360-acre ranch outside of Poteau. He was sixteen at the time, too young to go to war. He began working full-time and built them a one-room funeral parlor on the ranch.

Trouble began at Love's Funeral Parlor when Dovie decided to build an additional room. She wanted to open an herbal tea shop and teach tai chi, something she'd learned from a Chinese boyfriend during the filming of *Lost Horizon*. Grinding herbs and reading tea leaves were both habits Dovie had picked up from him, and she thought she could make a little extra money this way. However, a local Baptist preacher, always on the lookout for contraband, spread the rumor that Dovie Love was *Isht aholla*, a witch, and that her teas were love potions of the devil. He even got one Indian playboy to confess to being bewitched by Dovie after drinking one of her elixirs. Most folks knew this was just a feeble alibi. The man's wife had caught him, again, with another woman. But there were those who became cautious of the Love sisters after that.

Then there was the murder. An accident really. It happened one night when an old lady from Yanush was sitting up with the dead. She was notorious for falling asleep on the job. Everyone knew this. Around midnight, three Choctaw boys slipped in and removed the body of the dead man. One of them climbed into the wooden casket. When he raised up and shouted "Hello!" the old lady woke up, screamed, and caved in his skull with her cane.

Delores had to conduct two funerals that week. The whole town of Poteau turned out to view the two Choctaws lying side by side. The teenager, killed by his own joke, and the old man, dead of natural causes. The Yanush woman was promptly exonerated in an investigation by the county sheriff. He said there was nothing to be done about the deceased teen and labeled the cause of death "An Act of God."

Afterwards, Delores decided to go underground with her funeral ceremonies, and Dovie would only sell her herbal teas to friends. Their services were reserved for those they could trust. They began hanging strips of red cloth along the barbed-wire fences of the southeastern roads to signal that one of their all-night sing-alongs or a private funeral was happening until the public forgot about love potions and the songs for the dead.

4:30 arrives. The kitchen of the Billy house is hot and liquid. Steam rising from the frying chickens covers the walls with droplets of a greasy elixir only Southerners appreciate. Delores comes out of her reverie and puts a cup towel over the bowl of dough. She washes her sticky hands and sits down. Her feet and legs ache.

Dovie makes a show of putting away the last of the chicken wings on a platter to cool before she takes a piece for herself.

Tema puts her arms around Dovie and hugs her. "How are you doing Auntie? Getting tired?"

"I can't complain," says Dovie whimsically. "Did I tell you I located Atlantis?"

Tema doesn't look surprised, which slightly annoys Delores.

"Oh yes. It's not where everyone thinks," says Dovie.

"Where is it?"

"Off the coast of Texas."

'Imagine that," says Tema. "I would have thought nearer to the Caribbean."

"C'mon you two," interrupts Delores. "Enough."

"But Aunt Delores, sometimes foreign ideas are closer to Choctaw ways than you think," says Tema. "When I performed in *The Conference of the Birds,* I realized how much the Sufis are like Choctaws. I'll give you an example. Sufis believe that there is only one God, and all things emanate from that energy. Mankind's distinctions between good and evil have no meaning in Sufism because the two are connected to the unity that is God. The poetry we spoke in the play was about destroying the self, and the importance of experiencing overwhelming love for the collective. I had the role of the hoopoe," she says, stepping away from Dovie to deliver her lines.

Besotted fool, suppose you get this gold for which you drool—what could you do but guard it night and day while life itself—unnoticed—slips away? The love of gold and jewels is blasphemy; our faith is wrecked by such idolatry. To love gold is to be an infidel, an idol-worshipper who merits hell. On Judgment Day the miser's secret greed stares from his face for everyone to read.

"Oh, my girl," says Delores, standing up to hug her. "Isn't she talented?" she says to Dovie.

Her sister is quietly wiping her eyes with her black lace handkerchief, and nodding her head yes. Delores reaches out to Dovie and embraces them both.

Tema excuses herself to grab a Kleenex. "The play reinforced my Choctaw beliefs," she says, sniffling. "Women are the essence of Mother Earth. We create life and, during Green Corn, we shake shells to reconnect with all living things. The Sufi poetry reminded me that survival of the collective is what is important. The Sufis must be Choctaws at heart, don't you think? Everything is everything, *nana moma.*"

Dovie smiles. "*Yummak osh alhpesa. Yummak osh alhpesa.* That is it. That is it, my girl."

"Speaking of the collective," says Delores, "what happened to Adair?"

Tema grins mischievously. "You must have been lost in thought when she and Gore ducked out, otherwise you would have noticed the code talking going on."

They all giggle.

"Actually, what I meant to say," continues Tema, "is that Adair went to show Battiste to his room, and we haven't seen her since."

Dovie laughs conspiratorially. "Did you see how he looks at Adair when he thinks no one's watching?"

"Ladies, please," says Delores, giving her sister the eye.

Dovie turns to Tema. "Wanna sing our song, it'll make us all feel better."

"Sure."

"Still remember the words?"

"Of course."

'Mid the wild and woolly prairies lived an Indian maid
Arrah Wanna, Queen of fairies of her tribe
Each night came an Irish laddie with a wedding ring
He would sit outside her tent and with his bagpipes loudly sing
Arrah Wanna on my honor.

"You remember!"

"How could I forget? Every summer you made me practice it on the piano until I could play it in my sleep."

"You said you wanted to learn our theme song," says Dovie, carefully choosing a perfectly crisp wing to pull apart and devour.

"I was afraid you wouldn't let me watch Saturday morning cartoons if I didn't."

"Now you're pulling my leg."

"A little," says Tema, glancing first at Delores, then Dovie. "But I loved looking at all those old pictures of you two when you were in Hollywood. You're the reason I decided to become an actress. I wish you could have seen my dance as Nora Helmer. I imagined I was a bird."

Delores eyes float in tears. Tema was the daughter she never had. She tries to imagine an Indian playing Nora Helmer, soaring above the audience like a giant eagle during the Tarantella scene. She's so proud. Of course, she adores Adair and Auda, but Tema is special.

Delores smiles weakly. She can't shake the feeling that something terrible is going to happen.

Tema continues singing.

I'll be kind and true
we can love and bill and coo
in a wigwam built of shamrocks green,
we'll make those red men smile
when you're Misses Barney-heap-much-Carney
from Killarney's Isle.

"Did you or Delores choose that song because of the money the Choctaws sent to Ireland in 1847?" asks Tema.

"Naw," says Dovie, picking up another chicken wing. "Joe Miller picked out that song for us. We didn't know anything about that. The first time I heard about the Choctaw saving the Irish was sometime in the mid-seventies. Isn't that right, Delores?"

"Sounds right," she replies, deciding to hammer the dough again.

Tema picks up the skillet and pours the excess grease into a tin can. "Terrible lyrics, though. Why would red men smile if Indian women married white men?"

"Glad to be rid of us!" laughs Dovie.

"Then why does Uncle Isaac give me that pinched look, like his undershorts are too tight, every time I mention Borden's name?" asks Tema.

"Ignore him," says Dovie, "Isaac has a thing about the English."

"Why?"

"Who knows," snorts her sister.

"Because he was jealous of Delores and Ronald Colman?"

"How did you know about that?" asks Dovie.

"Once I overheard him telling Mother that he hated sissy English actors with thin mustaches, and all their films, so I put two and two together."

Delores is more than a little irked to hear her sister and favorite niece blather away as if she wasn't there. It does no good to chide Dovie for gossiping—sometimes it has the opposite effect.

"Isaac was just a teenager when he came to work for us," says Dovie. "Of course, by Indian standards of the day he was considered a grown-up."

"It's funny to think of my uncle that way. A boy with a crush."

"We were all young once," says Dovie, smoothing the pleats of her black dress. "Besides, it was boarding school that messed him up."

Delores hates it when Dovie brings up the subject of Indian boarding school. She's tried most of her life not to think about it. Though at times—it's impossible to say when or why—she will remember a child's muffled night sobs, the smell of urine in her bed, a teacher's taunting sing-song.

Delores is a dirty bird, she's wet her pants again.

Ahah achi, aholabi. No, liar. Okay, okay, it's time to speak English, just don't call me that. It wasn't true, she hadn't wet the bed, but the teacher wouldn't listen. For a second night in a row Delores had curled herself around the little Ponca girl, trying to give warmth to the dying child. If only her mother had been there. Elizabeth Love would know how to cure the girl's hacking coughs. She could set broken legs and pull bad teeth. Once when Delores had a bellyache her mother built a hot fire in the oven and heated a stove lid. When it was red hot, she wrapped it up in a blanket and put it on Delores' stomach. It not only cured her belly, but branded her. A week later she was still walking stooped over to keep her shirt from touching her burned skin.

But her mother wasn't there to cure the Ponca girl; all Delores could think to do was keep her warm. She'd only fallen asleep for a moment, or so she thought. When she woke up she was soaked from the waist down. The bed was stone cold and the girl's face was yellowish-gray, swollen and contorted—her black eyebrows and night shift were all that Delores recognized. She felt the girl's chest. Still. Her forehead and small hands were cold, and her eyes, half-closed, looked down inside herself.

Later, after the girl's funeral, Delores began to bleed, and it was Dovie who knew what to do. *Run, Delores, run, I don't want you to die too. Hurry, you're bleeding. We gotta get outta here, you shouldn't have tried to save her. I'll carry you if you can't run. You okay, Delores? Answer me.*

Dovie practically dragged her all the way across the blowing wheat fields, toward the main road which led north or south, away from the school. A thrashing Oklahoma wind caused bits of wheat shaft to sting their faces like needles and they had trouble seeing. They leaned forward, trying to offer as little resistance as possible, but it was all they could do to fight their way against the golden dust. Dovie, just thirteen at the time, was determined to save Delores, so she pulled her along screaming, *I'm the Miko, leader, now. You have to do what I say. Come on Delores, run.*

From then on, Delores would forever acquiesce to Dovie. It was her sister who'd proven she knew what was best for them, who'd shown she was a thousand times more courageous than Delores ever could be. A few days later the cook at the 101 Ranch, where they had taken refuge, told them it was natural for a girl to bleed when she got her period. No one at school had bothered to educate them on becoming women. Her mother should have been the one to explain what to do with menstrual blood. Because they were Indian girls consigned to a government school, a stranger showed her how to wad a piece of used clothing inside her panties. Delores felt humiliated. It was then she spoke the words she would later regret: "I don't want to be Indian anymore."

"Speaking of boarding school," says Tema earnestly, "I've heard the story from Mother—of how you two got away, but I'd love to hear you tell it." Delores realizes her niece isn't asking one of those talk show host questions like, "how did it feel to be abused?" But today, she isn't up to telling the story.

Tema looks from Dovie to Delores. Finally, Dovie turns away for a second, as if rehearsing her lines, then she speaks softly, "Nothin' to it, really. We just hitched a ride on a cattle truck. When he stopped at the 101 Ranch we got out. Chilocco Indian School wasn't more than an hour or so north of the ranch. Think of it today. Two kids running away from school to join a Wild West show. It doesn't seem real to me anymore, kind of like a movie script."

"You're leaving out parts," says Tema, "and that still doesn't explain why Uncle Isaac hates Borden."

"Isaac doesn't hate anyone!" says Delores, shocked at her own fervor. Lowering her voice, she adds, "It's just that he holds a grudge for what the English did to the Choctaws, that's all."

Tema runs her fingers through her short punky hair. She looks at Delores, trying to gauge how much to say about what she's been told. "Okay, maybe we're still pissed off at the English—I just don't want my family to be mean to the Englishman I sleep with."

"My girl," says Dovie soothingly, taking up where Delores left off. "No one in your family dislikes Borden. Haven't we always fed him, opened our homes to him? Be assured we are all for you and Hoppy living with Borden,—and I know I've told you the story of our escape. Afterwards, Delores sent word to our mother that we had found jobs on the 101. The school never came looking for us, and the rest, as they say, is history."

Tema's tone softens. "There's a lot more to it and you know it. How will Auda write your biography if you two withhold the juicy stuff? Was Uncle Isaac one of the reasons you stayed in Oklahoma?"

Dovie looks thoughtful before answering. Now it's all going to come out, thinks Delores. Finally, no more shadows, or hidden pasts. When her sister begins speaking again, it is with firm determination.

"If you want to know private things about your uncle, ask him. All I can say is that Isaac came to work for us shortly after his grandmother died. After he left boarding school he wanted nothing more to do with whites, or Indians who were subservient to whites. One day after he'd been working for us a while—he must have been around seventeen—he threw a fit like a wild animal. He'd found some pictures of Delores with one of her actor boyfriends and then went through the house and ripped up our Wild West costumes, and cursed Delores for being a floozy. I wasn't home at the time—if I had been, I'd have knocked the stuffing out of him! Imagine him tearing up our costumes. He quit us right then and there. A month or so later he finally came around with his tail between his legs, but only to say good-bye. He'd lied about his age, joined the army, and married WaNima Jefferson, in that order."

"Did he love WaNima?" asks Tema.

"Why do you think he would he marry her if he didn't?" asks Dovie.

"I don't know? Rebound. Obligation. Guilt."

"Tema," says Delores sternly, "have some respect for the dead."

"Sorry."

"WaNima, poor thing," says Dovie, pausing. "For years she'd followed Isaac around like a puppy. She died before he came back from the war, but like Delores says, at least he's honored her memory by staying single."

Tema realizes her questions have made Delores tense. She doesn't mean to be so disrespectful. She smiles at her aunt, "I bet Ronald Colman thought he was in heaven to be with Delores Love. Auntie, you were such a sex kitten back then."

"Back then?" says Delores, relaxing a little. "Waddaya mean, back then!"

"*Huh,* green teas can't fix our wrinkly old bodies," laughs Dovie.

"No comment," says Delores, shaking her finger at her sister. "And, you know perfectly well that Isaac loved WaNima."

"And two dozen other women in Bryan County." Dovie winks at Tema. "That'll get her going."

Delores picks up her bowl of dough. It is time she shapes it into dinner rolls. She hears Dovie telling more stories of their years in Hollywood, but she's no longer able to make sense of what is being said. Faintly uttered words reach her as if through a keyhole. *Ohoyo Omishke A numpa tillofashih ish hakloh. Attention woman, listen to my remarks. It is time for you to return to your homeland. You must bury the dead chief there.*

Delores decides that her imagination is playing tricks. Now the words split into two, three, four languages, and more. She hears many voices, everything that is said, and she is aware that she understands them all.

Ohoyo Omishke A numpa tillofashih ish hakloh. Attention woman, listen to my remarks. The gravediggers are wrong. Not all the ancient burial mounds

*were stuffed with beloved leaders. Some contain bad people who were given
everything in death that they had coveted in life. Shell beads, copper, axes,
knives, pottery bowls, baskets, animal skins, blankets. There were times
when good people followed the bad ones into the spirit world to care for
them. Like the parent of a spoiled child, they were there to give things to the
bad ones. Make them comfortable so that they would not want to leave their
resting place and harass the living. But when the mounds were opened by
grave diggers, these flawed spirits escaped like flesh-eating flies. They passed
through many changes. Always becoming predatory. Put your dead chief in
a mound so he will be protected from escaping again. Give him everything
in death he wanted in life. That way he will never leave it again.*

Delores doesn't understand. She can feel herself vanishing. She seizes
the bowl of pastry and holds on. It's hot in her hands. The clumps of
dough glow red like the coals of a fire. The heat blinds her, but she clings
to the bowl anyway. At last her fingers let go and she is pulled away as
soundlessly as a shadow.

She sees herself as she was at thirteen, but things are somehow
topsy-turvy. At thirteen she would have been at boarding school, yet she
is entering her family's old farmhouse. The windowpanes are still intact,
so are the curtains, the dishes. Even the skeleton key hangs on the hook
her father fashioned from a mule's shoe. Delores lingers among her family relics. In the center of the room is a rosewood dining table that
belonged to Elizabeth Love. It's covered with a fine layer of silt.

Her mother was very particular with the Queen Anne table. She
never let it get dusty because she feared the Oklahoma grit. Said it would
destroy the original look of the wood. The table was the only piece of
furniture her family bought new. They ordered it from a Sears Roebuck
catalogue. It was their first attempt at buying colonial. When it arrived,
her mother and father, her brother Orvil, her grandparents, Dovie, and
Lola piled into a borrowed truck and hauled it home from the train station in Fort Smith, Arkansas.

Each summer, home from boarding school, they all took turns pol-
ishing the table. They applied a variety of homemade remedies to keep
the finish looking like new. Her father even used his handkerchief and
his all-purpose oil to shine the table he called *"Nam pisa."* Something
special.

Delores fingers the edge of the table. She thinks of her mother,
Elizabeth Love, trying to decipher the care instructions aloud in English,

her face twisted with concern as if she were in charge of a baby.

Honoring her mother's teachings, Delores uses the hem of her black dress to wipe the surface clean, but the dust has turned into layers of dirt. She grabs handfuls of Earth but the more she scrapes off the more there is. She begins filling basket after basket and still the Earth grows higher and spreads like a lake of mud.

Soon relatives appear out of shadows to help the young girl. Memories dressed in thick bear skins with ice in their hair. Thoughts with gorgets made of mastodon toes around their necks. Voices with long black braids and flint hoes give rise to ancient arguments on how best to move the Earth.

Not to be outdone, the grandparents of tribes part the clouds with their blow guns and assist the digging crews. Finally a grandmother, always the one with big ideas, calls her grandson. When the famous warrior arrives, he is driving a giant yellow Caterpillar with four wheels the size of houses. Together with a thousand hands they help the warrior open Mother Earth's beautiful body. Slowly and lovingly Mother Earth turns herself inside out and a gigantic platform mound emerges out of the ground. When this sacred ovulation rises to meet the Sun, a private blush sweeps over Mother Earth and becomes grass. A gift.

Thoughts, Voices, and Grandparents plant corn on top of the sacred mound and hundreds of years come into view in the dance of Green Corn and tomorrows. Delores marvels at creation and wants to remain forever with her ancestors, but a dust devil the color of a panther wobbles in the wind toward her. It's time to go. Blurry trees and blurry people float in front of her as she's carried in the paws of the panther across the sky.

From above, the Nanih Waiya looks like an emerald city, so lustrous it shimmers. Now she realizes why she was brought here. Why didn't she understand in the first place?

While the moon shone down upon them Arrah Wanna sighed,
Some great race must call you Big Chief, then I'll be your bride.

Delores is returned to the kitchen as if she never left. Tema is still singing. Adair must have grown tired of flirting with Gore Battiste because she's standing at the stove sipping a taste of Dovie's recipe.

"How is it?"

"Wonderful. What did you put in it?" asks Adair.

"Whiskey."

"I never thought of putting whiskey in chicken dumplings."

"It's a remarkable ingredient," says Dovie. "It takes on the flavor of anything you cook with it."

Dovie offers her a taste. "Don't look so pious, Delores, you know we've always made chicken dumplings with whiskey."

"Come quick, this dough has turned to mud," says Delores, breathlessly.

"I told you before, the yeast won't rise if you overwork it."

Delores raises her hands in the air and reveals black sticky fingers.

Her sister shrieks, sucks in a gulp of air. "Where did that mud come from?"

"Mississippi."

"How did it get in there?"

"I was taken up into a whirlwind and our ancestors told me to put our dead chief in a mound near the Nanih Waiya."

"But I watched you mix up the dough," says Tema, examining the bowl of mud.

Dovie stands with her arms folded. Finally, she says, "I've seen this kind of thing before."

Adair eyes Dovie strangely, but turns to Delores. "What does this mean?"

"I'm not sure," answers Delores. She tells them everything that happened in her vision. "I think it means we've got to bury McAlester in the soil of Mississippi, close to our Mother Mound. We can protect him by giving him everything he ever wanted, and placate his troubled spirit."

Adair is flabbergasted. "Redford McAlester raped my sister and committed a hundred other crimes against Choctaw people. Why should we want to make him happy, or protect him?"

"So he'll never return."

They stare numbly at her, then peer down at the mud which is beginning to percolate like a pot of coffee on a hot stove.

"I'm using the word 'protect' the way the old-timers used the word. If we protect him he can't harm our people," she says. "If we don't take him to Mississippi, something awful is going to happen, I just know it."

"You mean more awful than the murder and mayhem that's already erupted in Choctaw Country?" Adair says, in a sarcastic voice.

Tema shoots her sister a hard look. "I'm sorry Auntie, Adair isn't intentionally disrespectful, it's just that—how can we take McAlester's body to Mississippi, unless we steal his coffin? It's a great risk."

"You'll see; no one will notice," says Delores.

She can see that they are skeptical, so she scoots the bowl across the table and urges her nieces and sister to touch it. "The whole Nanih Waiya area represents the cradle of the Choctawan civilization. A long time ago people came from all directions to settle there. It takes a sacred space like that to heal a troubled spirit."

Tema raises her hands up in the air to expose the sticky goo. "But Auntie, your vision started in your family's farmhouse on top of a Queen Anne table, what does that mean?"

"I don't know," she answers, impatiently. "I'm not Moses with the clay tablets, just an old lady with a bowl of mud."

"*Shu-u-sh,*" says Dovie, pushing her muddy palms out in front of her. "I'm encouraging my body's chi, or vital energy flow. This is all very unsettling. I need to get in harmony with my surroundings."

Delores watches her eighty-year-old sister step in slow motion to the basic movements of tai chi. First she lifts one leg, then the other. She mistrusts Dovie's wacky practices. Sometimes she's into tai chi, sometimes it's astrology, then for no apparent reason she'll return to the ways of their ancestors and act as though she barely speaks English. Perhaps Dovie is the best actress in the family, after all.

"Everyone breathe deeply," instructs Dovie. "Wait, I've got it! Adair's sleek bob just reminded me."

"What?" snaps Delores.

"Just now, I was thinking about Louise Brooks."

"Dovie, does this have anything to do with what's going on here?" asks Delores.

Her sister continues unperturbed. "Of course it does. Remember when we first met Louise?" She turns to Tema and Adair, "We didn't know her well enough to call her 'Lulu' like some of her friends. It must have been 1928, still a jazzy time for us. We'd moved to Santa Monica the year before and were having a high ol' time. Louise was from Kansas, not far from Chilocco Indian School. Anyway, we all wore too much rouge and ruby lipstick to this party. Seems like the three of us were running away from wheat, cattle, and cowboys, 'cept Delores and I ended up making movies about it."

Dovie puts her muddy hands together as if she about to pray. "The whole thing went to my head. Went to Delores' head, too."

"No, it didn't."

"Did too," says Dovie. "Anyway, we never saw Louise again because she went to Germany to make that film *Pandora's Box*. Adair's hairdo reminded me that Delores and I and Louise shared something in common. We believed having enough money could save us from our troubled pasts."

Adair chimes in. "I see what you mean. The dining table represents consumerism. The things the English and the French taught the Indians: to love foreign things above all else. Auntie, you're describing internalized colonialism. If you think foreigners' things, ideas, and religions are better than what your own culture has, then you're internally colonized. Then you don't care about your own things, culture, or land. In Delores' vision, one Indian can't do anything alone, but needs the help of ancestors and young people to build the future."

"That was a high definition event," says Dovie, matter-of-factly. "Not your run-of-the-mill vision."

Delores could kiss Dovie. She gives her a hug, and accidentally smears mud on her cheek. When she tries to wash it off, both her palms and Dovie's cheek are stained. Tema and Adair do the same, and realize that their palms have become stained dark brown.

"Look at the mud!" cries Tema, "It's spilling out of the bowl!"

Delores and Tema begin scraping it up into a trash can when they hear a Jeep screech to a halt in the driveway. Within seconds Hoppy and a young Indian woman burst in the kitchen door.

"Why haven't you been answering the phone? We've been calling and calling," says Hoppy, out of breath.

"There's nothing wrong with the phone," snaps Adair. "What's happened?"

"Uncle Isaac's been taken to jail. Gore needs to help me post bail," he stops short, measuring his tone more carefully, "and Aunt Auda's in a coma."

No one moves or says a word. At last, Adair propels herself into action. "Gore's upstairs asleep." Turning to the young woman beside Hoppy, she says, "First bedroom on the right." Then to her nephew, "Tell us everything that happened."

Hoppy looks at the growing pile of mud. He looks at Adair's hands. Curiosity, rage, amazement all filter across his young face. "The official report is that a dental hygienist named Vergie Reagan accidentally gave Aunt Auda an injection of insulin, but Grandmother doesn't believe that. Neither do I. We don't trust the hospital administration, so Auda's on her way home in an ambulance with Grandmother. Grandmother's Chevy was impounded by the police, so finally I had to call my girlfriend, Kelly Kampellubbi, to come and get me."

Tema raises her eyebrows at Hoppy's news, but a hot disbelieving outrage seizes Delores. "Why is Isaac in jail?"

"On the way to the clinic," says Hoppy, controlling his anger, "the cops pulled everyone off the road until we were the only car left. We made it to the clinic, but the police arrested Uncle Isaac for reckless driving. I wanna find out how they knew *exactly* what time to expect us. Someone must have tipped them off."

"It was me. I told them," Tema says, in a voice filled with remorse. "A man called from the clinic and asked what time he could expect Auda ... so I told him."

"Oh, Tema, how could you fall for that? Do Indian docs ever call to find out what time their patients will arrive?" asks Adair.

"I'm so sorry, I didn't think."

"It's no one's fault, we know why this is happening," says Delores. She gently touches Hoppy's forehead. "How did you get this?"

"A man ran out of the crowd toward Grandmother and Auda. I jumped him, but he clobbered me. Now I realize it was only an act to divide us, to get Auda alone."

"It's Redford McAlester's spirit," says Delores solemnly. "Every hour that he remains above ground, things are going to get worse."

Just then Gore walks into the kitchen, his eyes drowsy and half-asleep. He asks for a gallon of coffee. "Where's the guy with the Peanutmobile?" he asks, yawning. "C'mon Adair, Hoppy, let's ride in a car that'll piss off the cops."

The Billy house braces for a siege. The walls thump, the windows snap shut, and the floors creak loudly as furniture is moved around in preparation for Auda's return. Outside, a dozen or so Choctaws stand guard against an ambush by D'Amato's hired thugs. When the ambulance arrives Auda is wheeled into a downstairs bedroom, and Susan remains by her side. After the equipment is set up, Buster Jones comes out of the room and explains to Delores what happened. "There's a wound inside Auda's mouth," he says quietly. "It looks like the Reagan woman cut Auda's gum to catch her off guard, then shot her up with insulin. A dose like that mimics a heart attack—shortness of breath, dizziness, sweating, nausea, and fainting. It took us a while to diagnose what was wrong. No one knows where Vergie Reagan is. The tribal police are hunting for her, but my guess is that she's long gone." Buster looks around the living room to see who is listening. "It doesn't look good, Auntie. If Auda does comes out of the coma, no one can say what shape she'll be in."

Dovie leans on Delores for comfort. They take time to pull themselves together, then, holding hands, they enter the makeshift hospital room with its bleeping machines monitoring Auda's blood pressure and heart rate. Susan is bent over with her forehead on the edge of the hospital bed. She seems to be praying. Tema is moistening Auda's lips with a cotton swab.

Auda has a sickly death pallor. Her rubbery neck seems unattached to her body and her eyes, half-open, ticktock from side to side like one of those plastic wall clocks shaped like a cat's face. A ventilator tube down her throat pumps her chest up and down, swelling, sucking, then repeats the cycle. For a moment, Delores sees the little Ponca girl at boarding school, lying in a pool of her own urine. She blinks; it's Auda, again.

Delores makes a silent vow, her niece is not going to die like that. She grabs Susan Billy's hands, rigid as rocks. Susan seems to draw Delores into her, turning her over and over in her mind. Finally she says, "Yes, Delores, it is what you must do, but you and Isaac must go together."

"Susie, how did you know?"

Susan holds up her brown stained hands and answers mysteriously, "These are the mud of the Nanih Waiya."

Back in the kitchen, there are a dozen or so young Choctaws gathered around the growing mud mound. They seem unperturbed by its percolating action and are instead devouring the chicken, mashed potatoes, and other assorted dishes, while watching it grow across the kitchen floor.

"Ever seen the old movie *The Blob?*" asks Kelly, wiping her mouth with a napkin. "It looked just like this."

"I think we should move the bowl and mud outside," says Delores. "It's going to cover the floor soon."

As the teenagers begin taking the mud outside, a report of Tonica's death airs on the 11 o'clock news in the next room. According to a reporter, the Acting Chief of the Choctaw Nation, Carl Tonica, died from injuries sustained when an eighteen-wheeler hit him as he was crossing the street. So far, Tonica's death is being considered a freak accident; the truck driver hasn't even been charged with accidental manslaughter. The reporter reads a list of sorry events that have occurred in the Choctaw Nation since September 22. Two dead chiefs in three days. Rumors of missing casino money. Former Assistant Chief, Auda Billy, in a coma. The reporter goes on to say that charges are expected to be filed against the Choctaw Nation and their New York bank for violating federal money-laundering statutes: "The Federal Bureau of Investigation announced this evening that they are sending teams of agents to Durant to begin a full-scale inquiry into the murders and the tribal mismanagement of funds," he says. When the film clip comes on the screen of an unconscious Auda Billy being carried out of the Choctaw clinic, Delores turns off the set.

Everyone in the house falls silent. Slowly Dovie steps between the teenagers, adults, and children seated on the floor of the living room. "Looks like Tonica got himself absentmindedly killed," she says. Dovie holds up her brown-stained hands to the crowd. "We've got a sign from our ancestors. I think we'd better do what they ask."

A young boy sits with his back against the wall. He is focused on Delores. He has dark brown skin, a round face, his straight coal-black hair hangs like a bowl on his head. He doesn't move, as though nailed in place waiting for instructions. Finally he speaks. "Tell us what to do, Aunt Delores."

"Take the chief and the mud to Mississippi to be buried in a mound." There is a long pause before the boy replies.

"Okay, we'll do it."

The boy reminds Delores of why the people will survive. Because he will try with all his strength.

When Hoppy, Gore, and Adair return with Isaac, the four of them head straight for Auda's room. After a few minutes Isaac emerges to speak to the people on behalf of the family.

"We've decided to take action," he says. "My friend Gore Battiste and my niece Adair are going to New York City to gather evidence to show that it is the D'Amato brothers, Redford McAlester, and Carl Tonica who are the ones guilty of laundering dirty money. We think this is the best way to clear our tribe and get the FBI out of Choctaw business." Isaac pauses. "My sister Susan and the docs are keeping a careful watch over Auda, so I've been asked to take McAlester back to Mississippi to be buried. I'll be calling on our Mississippi Choctaw relatives to help us find a spot not far from the Nanih Waiya. Anyone from here who wants to come along, let me know."

There is a show of brown-stained hands. He smiles and tells them to be ready to leave first thing tomorrow morning.

Isaac is accommodating when Delores asks him to speak with her alone in the library. She brings along two cups of coffee and puts them on the table, then closes the door behind her for privacy. They sit on the sofa. She knows Isaac has already forgiven her.

She tells him about her vision and all the things she saw that relate to Redford McAlester. "All we know is that we do not know. We know nothing about what happens when a man makes a decision to try and control everything that is beyond his control. Now he has died for it, and he will have to beg pardon in the afterlife for what he's done to the Choctaws. But I must have a good heart to bury him, to be able to say the words that will soothe his troubled spirit."

Isaac takes the stone from his pocket. "Auda took a beating as the assistant chief, I can see that now. And she did it to atone for something that happened long ago. I think I know why, but I don't have all the answers. One thing is certain—by tomorrow afternoon, Durant will be crawling with federal agents."

"We better leave early then. After we bury McAlester, the healing can begin. Somehow I know it will reunite the two Choctaw communities: the ones in Oklahoma with the ones in Mississippi. We've been separated too long," she says, sadly. "Each of us has only half a heart until we're rejoined."

"Are you talking about the Choctaws, or us?"

"Both."

Isaac places the tiny stone in her hand and continues speaking quietly. "The first day I returned from overseas, I don't know why I didn't come to you. I was afraid that you'd turn me down again," he says. "Then I decided if I had lots of women following me around you'd be jealous and come after me."

"I wanted to, but I couldn't."

He tells her that he's been angry with her for making them live apart. For all the lost years, but that he loves her as before. He says from now on, they will be together. "I will never forsake you."

"I remember the first time you said that."

"And I never have."

He closes his eyes and Delores senses that he's stretched out in a basin of memories. The fall of 1942. The day he came back to the Love Ranch just to say good-bye.

She read the documents he'd shoved in her hands.

"When will you go?"

"I leave tomorrow for Tulsa. Then on to boot camp."

They sat across the room from each other in her living room. In neutral corners. They didn't look at each other. Couldn't look at each other. She thought that after a moment it would be too painful and he'd run away, but he didn't. He sat perfectly still.

Finally she spoke up. "So you married WaNima. I'm glad for you. I want you to be happy."

"*Aholabi.* " Liar.

Delores winced. "I am speaking the truth," she cried. "It has to be this way. I'm not jealous, really I'm not. I'm just very, very sad."

"It's sad, that's all. No point in crying. This is not one of your funerals. No one has died. This is about our life, the one we could have made together, not your list of reasons why we couldn't be married. My age. Your age. Our fifteen years."

She didn't answered. She was defenseless. She thought of how Isaac looked the first day he arrived at the ranch. Growing up in an Indian boarding school had marked him. The small desks and tiny oblong beds. His shadow crammed inside angry muscles and bone. He had held the gray stone that had belonged to Nowatima as he'd asked for the job. He had no money. What had charmed her about Isaac was what remained inside of him. Choctaw things. The language. Childhood memories. Animated stories of their most heroic and ancient towns. He could lead her to the edge of them, two hundred and fifty years ago in Mississippi, and draw the battle scenes from the lullabies of Choctaw children.

Although she was fifteen years older, they had made a good couple. Teacher and student, they switched roles easily. He worked the ranch and together they had doctored horses, lanced leg wounds, pulled foals from the wombs of mares. They'd also danced around the fire during Green Corn. He sang the ancient warrior songs and she followed him. A Shell Shaker and her warrior.

The blue-green smell of summer paraded over their first time together. He was barely seventeen. They had rolled around in the pasture like horses at play. When they were both full they moved indoors.

What she still remembered of that day were his blue overalls on her bed, like another body. Mingling her blood with his. Hoping Dovie would not find them melded together, bent over a chair, making love.

Isaac had pushed the wild strawberries in her mouth with his tongue, and then kissed her until she swallowed. No white man had ever done that. Choctaws call it *pishechi*. Baby feeding. All summer they'd seemed to live "over there," across the century from their families. Hidden from Dovie and Susan, and the gossip mongers of Poteau, who would say she was too old and worldly for the Billy boy. And it was true, she'd been with many men, while he'd only been with her.

"No, you're right. A Choctaw man needs a woman who can make children. I'm thirty-two, you're seventeen. By the time the war is over, I might be too old to have any. Then one day you'll come home and tell me you want a younger woman. I couldn't stand that. At least this way you will leave me now."

"I will never forsake you."

"How can you say that now that you are a married man?" she asked.

"Because you know it's true."

Isaac opens his eyes and quickly takes off his glasses to brush away a tear. When he puts them back on, she smiles and gingerly places the stone in his palm and curls his fingers around it.

"This should go to Hoppy: it holds the Billy family together."

He nods and slides it back in his pocket. "But it's your history too."

"I know."

"This is my favorite place in the whole world," he says softly, looking around the room.

"Mine too. This is where we first met the day I came to visit Nowatima. I don't have to tell you what it means to me to be sitting next to you again. Tell me a story," she urges.

"A long time ago a lonely frog fell in love with the Sun." Isaac pauses, then raises his voice playfully. "I have been telling you stories for years—I hope your big ol' Indian ears have been singed off!"

She laughs. "On occasions, I've heard your fiery words floating through my windows."

"I've cursed you, that much is true, but I've always sent along words of affection, sometimes when I was in the tub, sometimes on the road in my truck. Over the years I've kept you informed of what's been happening to me. What the cows thought of the coastal hay I once bought by mistake. The color of my latest Choctaw warrior shirt."

He sighs. "How much I still want you. What we've missed Delores, what we've both missed."

She leans over and touches his chest. "Hardly anyone recognizes the most important events of their life at the time they happen. So I'm telling you now, this is our moment. Oh, there will be more time, Isaac, but it's short."

His gaze matches hers, he is aiming himself into her. For the first time in nearly fifty years there isn't any pain in his eyes, she knows. There is only hunger.

"In that case," he says, clearing his throat, "maybe you should try asking me a straight question."

"Marry me tonight. I want you to marry me," she says bluntly. "I'm eighty-one, and you're sixty-six, I know it's my turn to ask—"

"*Ia lish, Ohoyo.*"

She puts her hand to his brown face, her fingers caress the flesh of his cheek. "With Auda in such bad shape, it may seem selfish to some, but we'll make it up to her for being away for a few hours," she says tenderly.

"*Okay,*" says Isaac, thoughtfully. "Delores, I also know what is coming."

She rests her head on his shoulder. "For years, I had this recurring dream … I never told anyone, not even Dovie. It is a long time ago. We are ourselves, but different. You are a monthly visitor to my town and we marry. I become pregnant, then I die. Somehow, I watch as you place a blue necklace of glass beads around my neck so I'll remember. Then I am dancing beside you in a dress made of *fichik hika,* shooting stars—you know, the little stars who sacrifice themselves when they fly to the ground to unite Earth and sky."

He holds her closer, as if trying to protect her from what will come. "I've had that dream too," he whispers. "I knew we'd be going together to Mississippi. You are *Imataha Chitto,* the prophesied leader who will reunite our two tribes."

Delores decides not to consider what he's just said. She doesn't want to worry about the future. She wants it to be like this always. They continue sitting together and look at each other like lovers at a reunion, happy in each other's company. She sips the inky black coffee, which puckers her mouth. Then Isaac kisses her gently.

11 | Black Time

HASH KOINCHUSH
HEART OF THE PANTHER
JUNE 21, 1747

I have carried the severed heads of the three *Filanchi okla* for months. Rot so strong, our unwashed bodies, and the putrefying carcasses we haul of our own felled *iksa* brothers cause the air around us to thicken with flies.

As expected, an emissary from the nearby village arrives at our temporary camp. Her long shadow tells time. This will be a drawn-out day. She has a fierce appearance mixed with wild sorrow. She stares at us for a moment then makes a step forward. If my *iksa* brother, Imataha Pouscouche, hasn't been here with the *Inkilish okla* trade goods we are done for. They will surely turn us away, we cannot bargain for their support with empty baskets.

A knot of warriors appears from behind the canebrake to support their emissary. A gaunt man with half an arm gone begins talking. The woman continues looking straight ahead, but seems to be agreeing with him.

I am bitterly offended. People once thought I was the *Imataha Chitto*, the greatest war leader, and they would sing my praises as I walked into the councils of the Natchez, Alibamu, Chahtas, Talapoosas, and Abihkas. Now I must hide myself among my warriors like a starving dog.

The one-arm leader moves with grotesque jerks. "*Wishia cha,*" he keeps repeating. He wants us to clear out. No pack trains have been through here, we are not welcome. There is no food. Their corn was burned last month by a town of warriors on the side of the *Filanchi okla*.

He says they await their new trading partners, the people from Yanàbi Town, who will provide them with corn and beans in exchange for information. They desire peace.

I can see the cage of his ribs moving in and out. His mouth is wide open; it gives him an eerie ravenous appearance, as if he wants to swallow our camp. He says Yanàbi Town people will not like it if we are here when they arrive. He must be shouting, but his voice is weak and I cannot clearly hear all he is saying. He falls back suddenly, a helper catches him.

Above, a black smoke cloud dents the blue sky, but I do not see the fire. The sunlight is thin; unripened peaches fall from the trees and break my concentration. A bad sign. I will not wait for another. Stinking of excrement and sweat, I step through the crowd to address the speaker.

"Only the hands of a killer do not tire," I say. "Here are the killed by me." I toss the three *Filanchi okla* heads at his feet. "Old friends," I say. "Your new friends." I pause and let my actions tell the story of what kind of warrior I am. They must see that I will not hesitate to make the path run red with their puny blood.

"That one," I say, "sliced at me with his bayonet, but he missed. I knocked off his head with my war club, the one I had chiseled from a cypress tree when I was but a child." Pointing to the second head with my lips, I explain how I caught my enemy unaware, then axed his shoulders and neck. "His blood," I say, "moved slowly across the land like the branch of a river. He staggered with his hanging head then wheeled to the ground. The third head I hacked off quickly, but it lay in the mud for many days. A crow had dug out *Filanchi's* eyes and was yanking at a fat neck vein with its beak when I returned, saving me the trouble. I transformed *Filanchi* into something useful: food for birds," I say, my voice full of irony. "After all, do not our traditions teach us that alive we are the consumers, in death we are the consumed? We are life everlasting," I say, earnestly touching my chest as I have seen Blackrobes do. "To be consumed by our relative the crow, it is a good end, *huh?*"

The one-arm leader is deliciously flawed, an egg of a man. Breakable, I mean. I relish his anguish too much, until the woman emissary begins chanting:

"Red Shoes, do you hear, do you understand? Do not forget the dead are helping the living. The villages who have supported you, the Couechitto, the Nushkobo, and the West Abeka, will be totally destroyed after your head is broken. You are a dead man. The words have been spoken and attach themselves to

you like leaves on trees. Blood, a gorget you wear. Red Shoes, you are the walking dead."

Just then the wind, an agent of the emissary's voice, sends out her words. They buzz around the trees, dress in the forest, and come out a spirit, Shakbatina. Her spirit dances across the sky. She wears a list of wounds. Her deerskin dress is bloodied at the neck and hem. Smoke rises from her turtle shells and forms a black cloud that she holds in her palms before flicking it upward to *Hashtali*. She touches the porcupine sash tied around her waist and says it will someday tell the story of what happened to me, too. I am not consoled.

"Give it up," she says, floating above my head. "The time has come for you to sacrifice yourself, as I once did."

"I will not," I say. "The *Inkilish okla* already do my bidding. Soon the *Filanchi okla* will work only for me. Anoleta, my heart, will return when she realizes I was not the cause of your death. Together she and I will drive out the *Inkilish okla* and *Filanchi okla*. I am *Imataha Chitto*, the greatest leader since Tuscalusa."

Only the hands of a killer do not tire. The wind echoes my words back to me.

"Painful," says the spirit of Shakbatina. "Greed has conquered you."

Something reaches out of the gloom and grabs the lower part of my jaw, pulling my head to the east, toward the future. I yelp and mill my arms until the thing goes away. I have no idea what it is. A lie. I am in the clutches of a vision. Whirling across oblivion, I take comfort in knowing that for ten years after my death, I am all my warriors speak of. All *Filanchi okla* will speak of. Most important, the month in which I am killed will forever be known as *Luak Mosholi*, Fire Extinguished. It will be rubbed out of the seasons, blotted out of memory as too horrific.

"But," I ask, my heart full of remorse, "what of the story of my death?"

Silence.

"Since there is no reply," I say, "I will tell you now."

"We leave the village that will not host us. My warriors and I travel fast, downriver ten leagues, and make camp on a stubble plain outside of the Alibamu Conchatys village, supporters of the *Filanchi okla*. My men meet up with Red Fox warriors who have pledged to trade only with the *Inkilish okla*. All are quite exhausted. In the morning we will plunder their storehouses and distribute *Filanchi okla* muskets to our *iksa*. Throughout the night we lie quietly on the dew-laden ground to wait for daylight. Black grasshoppers couple in frenzies. Even they sense that time is short. They cover our bodies as the chill of the swamp penetrates our bones. We do not dare swat them or make a fire which might alert the village. The moon and stars are hidden from us by clouds, in league with my enemies, no doubt.

"An hour after dawn the village still rests in slumber under a blanket of white smoke. It is then we rouse ourselves and advance toward the Alibamu Conchatys. My feet crunch as I walk slowly over the bodies of the mated. There are tall heaps of cane we hide in as we creep toward the village. A child is the first to spot us; he runs a few steps, then stands still and cries out in a tone of astonishing strength, 'Don't hit me, Uncle.'

"I fling myself at the boy to quiet him, stumble kneeling in the grass. My suddenness frightens him and he throws up in my arms, then tries to scream, but instead drops in a heap of blood rushing over his little body from my knife that has killed him. I look into the child's eyes as they go dead; hardened flat. I think they probably look the same as mine. Seconds ago he was alive, now he is among the killed by me. My corruption complete, I regret it all, but know there is more.

"I lay him gently in the grass. I cannot help but remember that this is the same Alibamu Conchatys village that judged the dispute between my people and Yanàbi Town nine years ago. I lost both wives that year— the Red Fox woman by my own hands and Anoleta, payment for the Red Fox wife. An irony I have had to live with. I raise my shirt and examine the scar Anoleta gave me. My fingers need to touch what she has touched. I yearn for what has not been between us. How she sneered at me for running away the night I was told she intended to poison me. She kept her word and married Choucououlacta. I finally had him killed in the month of *Hash Bissa,* but I was told they made a child, a girl called *Chunkashbili,* Heart Wounder. I believe Anoleta named her for me. With that in mind I rush headlong toward the Alibamu Conchatys, cutting down women, men, children, the youngest of warriors, even the village animals. It is glorious."

The wind talks back. *See Red Shoes with his tattooed face half fried off. His life will be forgotten.*

"But my story is not finished," I argue. "I will caress the inevitable coming to life in front of me. My head on a pole branches like the red leaves of autumn pruned too late to heal. On the longest day of the year when the eye of the Sun finally closes, an assassin will set fire to my body, then remove my head. Then nothing, not even breath, can come between Anoleta and me in a place where the net of air and earth have been rearranged for this purpose. It is she and Haya who will track me down on the road to Couechitto. After the slaughter at the Alibamu Conchatys, after the hundreds dead, I decide I *do* want to sacrifice myself. I will help in my own death, but when heat rising from the fire makes me vomit the last bit of moisture out of me, I don't want to end. Red smoke sizzles on my tongue. A hot tingling runs over the top of my head, I am being roasted alive. Flesh oozes down my cheek, tears of light run down my face. I am no longer one who is here, yet I am here. A chorus of frogs, deep voices, announces my departure, and I understand, there will be no birds coming for me. Everything around me is moving away, unsteady. I am raining down on the ground, dissolving in a blood clot of sadness. In my last solemn moments I pray for a reflection, a shape that will defy the astounded dead. I will not be a stone without eyes. I will not live where no one sees me or knows my name. *I will return,* I sing. *I will return,* I sing. *I will return.*"

You are raving, says the wind.

"Huh! A road does come for me. There is a whistling sound, searing. A meat-whistling that shrivels everything."

ON THE ROAD TO ALIBAMU CONCHATYS
JUNE 21, 1747

Nitakechi and a young warrior squat by a rack of deer meat on a spit in front of his temporary shelter. Neshoba, his niece, walks toward them. She puts on a somber face for the boy.

"The Blackrobe is very well, Uncle, he does not carry the sickness." Neshoba turns her back to the boy and winks at Nitakechi. "Good gamble." Then she walks away toward a cluster of other temporary shelters.

"Huh! Pay up. You lose. I win," shouts Nitakechi as he fingers a haunch of meat.

"You old shit," laughs the boy. "You have fleshed this hen. Here, take my knife. I have nothing else to gamble."

"I told you the Blackrobe was not sick, just scratching with his feather brush. He calls it *ecrire.* It's like body tattooing, or like the drawings we make on our deer hides. Each drawing means something. *Filanchi okla* doesn't understand our meanings. We don't understand his *ecrire.* You know what I think, *Filanchi okla* must *ecrire* every day because he cannot remember anything. He does not know where he is so he scratches to remember where he has been. It makes me sad, but I must say it, the Blackrobes are simple-minded. I tried to tell you, but you would not hear of it. This is a lesson, young one. Listen more closely to your elders." Nitakechi reaches for the knife, but the boy stops him.

"Yes, take my knife. The one I traded fifty deerskins for. The weapon that has killed many men. The knife that has skinned one thousand deer. It is yours, Uncle. Be proud when you draw it in battle, and remember that it once served a brave warrior."

Nitakechi examines the metal blade a second time. He smiles. "A thousand deer? Really?"

"Yes, it is good to gamble with such a knife," the boy says arrogantly, brushing the twigs from his leggings. Suddenly, though, he grabs his chest and falls on the ground, face first.

Nitakechi watches the boy playfully act out his death scene. Was he ever so young and bold, he wonders.

"*Hekano,* I am finished," says the boy, rolling over on his back. "I am now impoverished. This night you have sincerely fleshed this innocent hen."

Nitakechi picks up the knife and throws it in a pile of things next to the fire. He laughs and decides to teach the boy how to speak the language of Tuscalusa, the old code, *Mabila.* Just the insults at first. Eventually, he makes another bet in old code. This time he loses his black horse to the boy who belly laughs until he farts.

"Let's go find my niece, Neshoba," says Nitakechi, standing up with as much dignity as he can muster. "I'll walk. You ride."

"Uncle, I have heard that more than twenty of our towns voted to kill Red Shoes. Tomorrow when we arrive at the Alibamu Conchatys council, will you recommend me to be the assassin?"

Nitakechi thinks for a long time before speaking. He's horrified that a boy from the *Inholahta* is considering murder. Times are changing too fast. "How old are you?" he asks.

"Eighteen winters."

"What are you called?"

"Hopaii Iskitini," answers the boy. Little Prophet.

"Hopaii Iskitini, an *Inholahta* warrior holds the traditions of our clan in his heart. We are the ones who do not make the path run red with blood. A prophet-in-training, an *Inholahta,* should know this."

No sooner have the words left Nitakechi's mouth than Koi Chitto hurries toward him with a grave face. "A runner has just come. Voices in the wind told the elders of the *Conchas* that Red Shoes and his Red Fox warriors, and the *Inkilish okla*, intend to lay siege to the Alibamu Conchatys."

His oldest friend tells him the war clans are preparing to break camp and fight in the pay of their cousins. "We have a covenant to support one another. Choucououlacta's *iksa* is also on the move. They bring ten towns of warriors. Together we will fight at the beard of our enemy. We are too old to miss this battle, will you come?"

Nitakechi looks down at his trembling hands. He puts them behind his back so as not to reveal his secret—that he wants to use his hands to squeeze Red Shoes by the throat until *nuklamolli*, he strangles him. He keeps his voice low when he responds. "I am ready, but first you must promise to let me try and speak with the *Osano*. Perhaps I can stop the bloodshed."

The boy jumps off the horse and offers him the rope. Nitakechi waves them away. "From here on out," he says, "I do not want my feet to leave the ground ... prematurely."

The three of them walk to the center of camp. Warriors are already taking turns striking the post in the ceremony that allows them to tell of their past heroisms in battle. It energizes them for what is coming. Nitachechi stands by as his relatives paint their faces with streaks of vermilion meant to resemble lightning bolts. Warriors believe they are the storm that blows across land. All his life, he's had to fight the urge to grab a club and make *tushka panya*. By this time tomorrow he will have given into it.

When the Swiss soldier approaches, Father Renoir ignores him and continues writing feverishly. He must finish his account of the past nine years before he leaves it behind for those who will want to read it.

"Father, I have bad news," says Jean-Marie Critches.

"A moment please," says Renoir.

... we traveled long hours, savage style, for eight days until reaching the place they call Yanàbi Town. Four nights ago hundreds of the Chahtas, from twenty other villages, arrived and built fires and shelters close to the site where the ceremony was to take place so they could participate in the ritual singing for a headwoman, some kind of honored woman among her people.

Many other savages were scaffolded here including those who had died of old age or disease. While not knowing their ways, I observed more than three bone pickers among the villagers.

Before sunrise three days ago the Chahta assembled in small circles of twenty or thirty mourners, kneeling around drums of hollowed-out cypress and stretched skins. The beaters used wooden rods to make the drums sound dichotic, and the clatter of wood was sometimes earsplitting. Both men and women then placed blankets over their heads and cried and sang with ten or twelve voices tracking each other in diaphonic tones, sustaining a timbre a hundred times more powerful than the choirs of Notre Dame. I was hypnotized. Such feelings of loneliness I have never known before. It was terribly mournful, almost romantic, like the intermittent howling of mated wolves. I think I've learned the specific cries for the dead. Seated within proximity of the singers were pipe-smoking savages, harping to one another, their strident voices ripping through my very soul. For no matter what Father Baudouin says, the Chahta language is incredibly foreign, spit out of the mouth one syllable at a time.

Then there are the camp noises: barking dogs and clanging pony-bells on the horses and the high-pitched glee of the savage children. Child's play is not what one thinks of when one watches their games. Their games imitate all aspects of savage life. Hunting. Killing. Making war. Gambling. Giving birth, the savage child's version of playing house. I observed a tiny girl perhaps four or five, pretending to be in labor. She was lying on her back, propped up by two young companions who were softly encouraging her in the delivery. The girl's legs were spread apart and she moaned and grunted as if this thing were happening to her. A truer imitation I have never seen. Another child was playing the role of a doctor, waving a kind of feather fan over her. Two other small girls were helping pull the imaginary baby out from the child's legs. I watched in awe, thinking how at their young ages, they had probably all witnessed many such births. Extraordinary. All this childishness going on while in the background their parents sang for the dead.

Two more days and nights we waited. The wailing and hoarse quavering continued, straining against our ears, ringing in unison with a thousand different sounds of the night forest.

Father Baudouin and I were huddled together for hours, sometimes roused at midnight by savages who shoved clay pots of food in our faces that we were forced to eat. Father Baudouin says it is considered a grave insult to refuse their food. Sometimes we were overlooked entirely.

Winter solstice came, 22 of December, 1738. At sunset, an old bone picker known as Koi Chitto, meaning Big Panther, finally climbed the scaffold and began to pick the bones of his dead wife, the headwoman called Shakbatina, whose remains have been left out in the open since September. This is the same woman who gave her life to avert a war between the Chicachas and Chahta when her daughter, Anoleta, was accused of murdering a Red Fox woman. All sorts of animals, birds mostly, have already destroyed Shakbatina's corpse. What remained, the bone picker himself pulled apart and cleaned and painted. He is the father of Neshoba, the woman who has helped me understand their ways.

"Excuse me, Father, but your writing must wait," says the soldier. "A messenger from the *Conchas* just arrived. He is near collapse, but informs us that the devil Red Shoes…"

Father Renoir raises his hand to silence the Swiss soldier. He's already been told. It is the reason he has come to a decision about his future.

"Did the Concha say anything else?"

"I interrogated him myself, Father. He said a messenger brought the words to him. He was very much distressed by the news of warfare between the Chicachas and Chahta tribes."

"Jean-Marie, if you will be so kind as to wait for one moment, I will explain."

… Once the ritual was over many of the Chahtas carried fire in baskets to each other to signal the beginning of the feast which is continuing as I write. If I am correct, the Chahtas worship, among other things, Hashtali, whose eye is the Sun, and Miko Luak, fire. When the ceremony was completed, they set pine fires and burnt cedar incense all around us. Whiffs of burnt honey drift in the air and mix with the aroma of roasted nuts, herbs, cooked meats, and their special tobacco.

I am convinced now that Chahtas pay more respect to their dead than any other race. To them the bones of their relatives are holy. Proof that they existed in the past as they will exist forever. They are extraordinary people, so beautiful with their long flowing hair, I can hardly believe that it is my destiny to live among them. But it is, thus I go to seek my future with a woman called Neshoba. Her name means "She-wolf," or Protector. To find love, the temperatures of one's skin changes throughout the day, like a blush.

Renoir marks out the last paragraph, making sure it is illegible. No use in leaving behind evidence that will disgrace his father in Quebec. It's better if his father thinks he was killed still honoring the Society of Jesus. He begins again, this time writing hastily, as if these are daily entries.

· *Chicachas were barricaded in their fort at Octibea, 10 of September, 1737. The people of the Red Fox and the Yanàbi people were at the heart of this conflict.*

· *Our Chahta chiefs appear to be stirred up against the Chicachas more than ever. They often bring scalps—but considering what it costs the French in war expenses, how long can we pay the price...? 1746*

· *Critches has informed me today, 22 of June, 1747, of the death of the Chief of the Alibamu Conchatys who thought himself stronger than the brandy which killed him. All the chiefs, fearing that they will not get brandy, have fallen into debauchery. Deprived of this drink, the chiefs and warriors will surely kill each other to the last man, woman, and child.*

Red Shoes and his English trader Elsley are involved in this chicanery. His iksa brother, Imataha Pouscouche, brings another pack train with English brandy and muskets into the region, but our allies say he has not arrived yet. Since the savages never drink before night for fear of the sun's rays, I expect the rampage to begin shortly after dark. Because the summer solstice is upon us, perhaps I will be able to reach them before nightfall and stop the madness. The battle field will be...? I am taking Neshoba, the daughter of the headwoman Shakbatina, as my guide. Neshoba has taught me well the language, she still knows the country better than most Frenchmen. God grant me safe passage.

Renoir carefully rolls his book and pen in his blanket, and gives the journal to Jean-Marie. "I am not going with you. I leave with the *Chahta* woman. We will take the children and the infirm to safety. In case something happens to me, if I am killed, I want you to deliver this to Father Baudouin. Tell him my written words are true."

He slings his bedroll over his shoulder and bids farewell to Jean-Marie. He has no way of knowing if his countrymen will be able to pass on his documents, his lies to history and the French Province of Louisiana. He reasons that it is best for France and the Church not to know that the greed of their faith is causing the demise of Indian tribes. Even though he is leaving his religion, he cannot bring himself to speak ill of it. Besides, why would anyone believe that Indians degenerate over brandy more so than other races? Drink is the common debauchery of all people. This will just be remembered as another war with the godless English, and the Indians.

Renoir's senses burn as he walks across the humid black Earth to find Neshoba. Tonight he is taking the trip that will surely kill him, at least in the eyes of the Society of Jesus. Images of his beloved whirl around him. She converted him to her ways, that much is true. He will move into her house. Become her man. Learn her ways. He can almost feel her opening herself up to him again. The taste of her breasts, her two little scoops of wheat, and the luxuriant abundance between her legs. When they embrace she whispers, "Inki Cheets, Inki Cheets." *Inki* for father, *Cheets* for Jesuit, the Chahtas having no *J*. He thinks the Chahta are enchanting people—the way they talk, the way they believe everything is related to them. He doesn't know if it is possible but he intends to *faire peau neuve*, try and grow new skin and believe as they do.

Renoir recalls his Paris of poets and the poor. His vows to St. Ignatius. Why had he been sent here? To serve God, the only answer he was given. He will pray for amnesty, but he knows his God is asleep. Has been for centuries. He looks up at the sky. Flakes of stars are burning away as pink daylight approaches. Rain is coming, he smells it. Self-absorbed, he nearly slips in the dew-covered fields close to the boat. Neshoba sees him and laughs at his clumsiness. She motions that he must hurry. Her *caju*, flatboat, is full of bundles and supplies that she will trade up and down the river. She is surrounded by black-haired children holding onto her like a sail in the wind. Bili, her niece, is his favorite. A chubby little child, she has the most graceful of strides. He will teach her to read and write; maybe in the future she will call him *"mon Père."* Who knows? He steps onto the *caju*. Silently Neshoba pushes them away from shore. Renoir studies her broad, exquisite face, her full lips that pout for no reason. Surely he has died and gone to heaven.

"Yes, death, please," he repeats in her language.

Neshoba stares suspicioiusly. "Why do you pray to die?"

Dawn.

Anoleta, along with two hundred warriors, has been walking most of the night. She struggles to cross a log with her burden basket strapped across her forehead. It's fully loaded with powder horns, several pounds of corn, water skins, and two hatchets. One is for her, the other is for Haya. If necessary, they will wield them against their enemies.

Mud clings to her toes and she falls on the slippery bark, but gets up unharmed. She straightens her load and looks around. There is a line of swamp, about two leagues long, that must be endured in order to reach the Alibamu Conchatys. Through a steaming curtain of hot rain the swamp looks more like a massive green wall than anything else. Impenetrable, with brackish water canals, this swamp might once have communicated with the sea.

Along the route, the arteries of runny mud clot like dying blood. Many warriors she passes sit silently on the wet ground waiting for the rain to cease. Others have covered themselves in the sticky black goo and are dozing like *shukata*, opossums, in the mosquito-laden trees along the edge of the bayou. They are almost invisible. After her failure with Red Shoes nine years ago there was no more talk of the *Intek Aliha* finishing him. No one believed he would return to her. They were right. People no longer speak about Red Shoes to her, it's as if he never happened—but he did, and he caused the death of her mother. She has never given up hope of fulfilling her promise to Shakbatina.

She heaves her basket atop a giant broken cypress knee, now a stump, and sits at its base. This is the kind of swamp her mother and father were most at home in. They loved watching panthers loll in the arms of cypress trees; they didn't mind cutting through spider webs the size of her cabin. When she was little, they'd take a *caju* up and down the *Atchafalaya*, Long River, trading everything from beehives to bear oil to alligator hides. Sometimes they'd be gone for a month or more. When they'd return, Shakbatina would press tiny river pearls into her hands and tell her to save them for a necklace to wear on her wedding day. Over the years Anoleta saved enough pearls for several necklaces, but she never used them. It's just as well. If she returns she will give them all to Chunkashbili, Heart Wounder, "Bili," as she calls her seven-year-old daughter.

Her sister, Neshoba, was the first to touch Bili when she was born. Neshoba put her hands on Bili's head as Anoleta pushed out. At that juncture, Anoleta and her daughter glided above two worlds: their ancestors' and their future. Anoleta could not stay there at the center but for a moment. Her body closed when Bili took her first breath. How the baby shone, glistening with the thick liquid syrup her body had fed her. With her arms and legs folded together like baby hawk wings in an eggshell, Anoleta knew what to call her daughter. "You wounded my heart with your beauty," she whispers drowsily, hoping the wind carries her words to Bili's ears. "Neshoba will keep you safe in case I never return. But, my girl, do not forget me."

At the edge of sleep, Anoleta's vision shifts. She turns and looks behind her. Floating above the river like an immense crane is her mother, Shakbatina. "You are my firstborn!" her spirit says sternly. "I was the first to see your tiny brown face. I folded and unfolded your wrappings until your human breathing was normal. With your mouth full of my milk you were perfect. Fat. Your belly was warm lying against mine. Fingernails and toes were good and strong. You snatched a strand of my hair. I put the liquid corn in your mouth and you were the first to dance beside me. You quieted my hungry womb—for a time; Neshoba and Haya came next, but there will be others after you. Bili is the mother of Marie, born at Wolf Creek Parrish, a place named for your sister, Neshoba. Marie is the mother of Noga, born near Houma Town. Noga is the mother of Pisatuntema, born in Yanàbi Town. Pisatuntema is the mother of Nowatima, born in the strange time called 1825, also in Yanàbi Town. Nowatima will build a great house where many Bilis will live. Do not fear. Seize my nipple, daughter, take my milk, family boils out of me into you!"

Anoleta is suddenly awakened as a hand covers her drooling mouth. It is her father's. He points with his lips to the yellow torches coming along in the swamp wall. In dawn's twilight, little foxes, usually silent and regal, bark that death is approaching. The camp holds its breath as the torches bob up and down, but do not stop. They must be *Inkilish okla,* no one else would announce themselves like that, especially when warriors all across the region are on foot.

After the torches are out of sight her father says, "Forty times before I believed we should move against our enemies; I hope we are not too late."

Anoleta wipes the saliva from her mouth and looks at him with tears in her eyes. "Mother was talking to me just now, but I couldn't understand all her words. She's angry; I feel it. She said something about Bili's daughters."

"She shouted at me too," shrugs Koi Chitto, "she was just there." Her father points to the mist above the river. "It's because she does not know yet how to help us; she is still learning to be a spirit, and patience has never been her friend. I fear your uncle and I improperly read the signs. Your mother needed more time on the scaffold before her bone-picking ceremony released her into the spirit world. Trouble is coming and she cannot stop it."

Anoleta studies her father's face. Does he mean she cannot help Bili's children? However she does not have a chance to ask. They are on the move again. It's hot, the trees are tall mute witnesses to their struggle. The whole world looks like a fatal green vision. Now the men walk deliberately in front of the women to protect them in case of ambush. The longest day of the year is fully awake. Anoleta hears collective breathing, as if they are the lungs of the swamp, she feels the sweat trickling over them, as though they are one body.

Suddenly, a runner from the Alibamu Conchatys appears out of a palmetto bush, as if a rare progeny of foliage. He says in a terrified voice that the *Inkilish okla* and Red Fox attacked his people as soon as it was light. She watches her uncle question the man, then advise the warriors of Yanàbi Town. As a respected elder he calmly helps them decide what to do. The men finally agree to send two runners, Hopaii Iskitini and Tatoulimataha, on a scouting mission.

In minutes they regroup and their pace quickens. Many eat dried peaches or corn from their pouches while they walk. Anything to keep going. Rain passes them like a wanderer. The clouds are replaced by an angry red eye of fire that will not close for hours. Anoleta is hot, hotter than she's ever felt. The swamp air becomes more and more stifling, thick with deadly life. The youngest of the warriors, *hatak imatahali,* collapse. The war party must wait for them to recover. The swamp is salty, so she and other women hike up and down the path giving their fresh water to the thirsty young men. When at last she and her sister, panting like tired animals, sit down to rest, Haya asks, "Do you still intend to finish Red Shoes?"

"You dare speak of him to me!" hisses Anoleta. "I know it was you who warned Red Shoes of the poison I had prepared in the meat. Why did you betray me?"

Haya's face blanches and swells. The scar on her cheek, a birthmark, rises like a red welt. It's not the oppressive heat that causes this, but her shame. Haya nervously presses a forefinger against a sharp edge of her burden basket until it splits her skin. She pays for her betrayal as blood oozes down her finger. Her eyes plead for understanding.

"I thought," says Haya, pitifully, "if he knew that his own people wished for his death, then he would change back into the warrior we had loved. I was very wrong, please forgive me."

Anoleta suffers a strange sensation of pain, as though the fissure is hers, not her sister's. The truth went from Haya's finger into the basket, and into her. It said they were the same. Red Shoes, as he was in the beginning, was a worthy memory. When Anoleta married him Haya was a little girl, but he treated her sister like their baby, even carried her on his shoulders around Yanàbi Town.

Anoleta sighs. They both loved what he had been. Before she can say forgiving words to her sister, Nitakechi interrupts her.

"Come, quickly, the Alibamu Conchatys village is just beyond and our warriors want to strike now. You two must carry the powder horns." Then he stops. "But if things go badly, you must run, and don't stop to look back," he says. *"Ohoyo omishke a numpa tillofashih ish hakloh!"*

"Yes, Uncle, we are paying attention," answers Anoleta. "We will do as you ask."

They follow closely behind him. The sky turns charcoal. The cornfields are black. Scrawny deer graze in burnt fields. Here and there, perched in the arms of charred trees, swamp chickens nap. However, in the far distance a shadow creeps toward them. As the phantom gets closer it begins to run, like a horse at full gallop. It's Tatoulimataha, and when he stops before her uncle, he faints. His diluted pupils stare dumbly, white dikes of salt flank the sweat canals lining his skin. Anoleta goes to work kneading back spasms that curl him into a fetal position. Suddenly his legs cramp—visible pulsations under the skin knot the calf of the left leg and the thigh of the right. The boy yells as he comes to consciousness. "I have a message," he finally says, wheezing through the pain. "The head of the coiling snake will be here before dark. Do not strike without them."

"It's Choucououlacta's *iksa*," says her uncle. "They must not be far away."

Anoleta continues to rub the boy's legs. She gives him small amounts of water to sip so he will not choke. Nitakechi finally asks him what happened to Hopaii Iskitini.

"We were being followed, he told me to run ahead with the message," says Tatoulimataha, gritting his teeth. "He disappeared."

Twilight comes. Koi Chitto watches as the head of the snake slowly slithers toward him—two hundred warriors in all. He sees many old friends and they exchange greetings and information: It is known the *Inkilish okla* have placed a cannon atop the ridge, and they will surely use it. At least one hundred more Red Fox warriors have arrived and taken refuge inside the rampart surrounding the village. The occasional shots that he hears are those of the Red Fox, drunk on death.

Koi Chitto decides there is enough light left to take a few seasoned warriors and advance to the outside of the rampart. They will search for their enemy's weaknesses. Nitakechi goes with him. Within minutes they encounter a few Alibamu Conchatys hiding amongst the burnt cane not far from a fallen wall. Three old men, a blind grandmother, and six ragged children tell terrible stories of how their enemies, led by Red Shoes, massacred their families. But the worst story they tell is of the women of the Pacana Village who were loyal to their relatives, the Alibamu Conchatys, and the *Filanchi okla*.

"They are in a bad way," says one elder, whose eye is bleeding from the blows he received from their enemies. "The women were taken over there," he says pointing in the direction of the fort's rampart.

Nitakechi stands like a ghost among men as he hears of the Pacana massacre. His senses are intact, he smells the burning fires, he hears the sounds of the swamp not far away, but he feels killed by the story. The Pacana woman he calls *tekchi*, wife, must be dead. He turns away from the warriors standing beside him. He does not trust himself not to sing his death cry and alert their enemies.

Until Shakbatina had insisted, shortly before her death, Nitakechi never intended to marry, nor make children. He was content to watch out for his nieces. Even then he dawdled another seven winters before finding the woman who had for years troubled his dreams. Shakbatina had said the true *Imataha Chitto* was most likely a woman, and when he found her living in Pacana Village, they married. Mantema, as she was called, was supposed to be safe with her relatives in Pacana. He never imagined that the war with Red Shoes would spread this quickly.

Nitakechi draws his knife; he intends to use it on Red Shoes.

Koi Chitto puts his hand on Nitakechi's shoulder. "My brother," he says softly, "let me go and see what has happened. I know Mantema— she is young and has most likely escaped."

"No, I will scout ahead, you follow," says Nitakechi, turning to face Koi Chitto.

"We are not in council, we are at war!" says Koi Chitto sternly. "You must take the stragglers to your nieces. These people are in need of food and water. And it is not proper for an old peacemaker to order a powerful warrior from the *Imoklasha*, war clan!"

The two men stand nose to nose. Nitakechi considers what he should do. He has not lived an insolent life, but how much more can he endure?

Briefly, he visualizes breaking Red Shoes' head with an ax, then slicing it away from his body with his knife. This would put an end to the misery the renegade has caused. But he sees how warriors from Yanàbi Town eye him. They expect for him to help their injured allies first, before he takes any action.

"Don't be long," he says, "This old peacemaker will not be far behind!"

Koi Chitto and the other warriors depart to scout the fort. They cross a small stream where the gar and sunfish are floating atop the water. A volley must have exploded there. Koi Chitto takes care to warn his warriors that a cannon is already pointed in their direction. He approaches the rampart first and sees something large and red on a log, but he can't make it out. He draws nearer; it's the body of a young woman nailed there by an *Inkilish okla* bayonet. The handle sticks up hideously into the air from between her naked legs. Her eyes are fixed on the bayonet. It is Mantema, she had been pregnant. About her are other women, perhaps twenty in all, variously killed, their sex staring out in an obscene manner. It is a sight of madness. The women gave up their lives so the few Alibamu Conchatys could escape. A fire ignites inside Koi Chitto's belly, growing hotter by the minute. To see men killed in battle is one thing, but to see these women horribly tortured is another. The warriors around him burst out in *tushka panya*—their cries, near hysterical laughter, alert their enemies.

Koi Chitto forgets himself and screams, "*Imoklashas* will cut off the head of Red Shoes and all his allies!"

Across the sky, orange and blue fire explodes, so beautiful he watches what will surely kill him, but it does not. The cannon sounds are muffled, though, as if shot through a blanket; perhaps his ears are blown off. He moans, and then slowly heads toward a downed tree. He sits there for a while shivering, looks at the Red Fox village then back at his shoulder that has been nearly torn off.

After some minutes, Koi Chitto stands up very slowly, holding his war club in his one good hand. Bending low to miss the volleys and swaying as if he will fall, he runs straight toward the enemy. It's a long run down a slope, and the Red Fox cease firing. He knows they will stop long enough for him to sing his death song.

He stands tall in front of them, crying for the ancestors, then for his beloved Shakbatina, then for all those who have fallen around him. When he finishes, all their muskets fire together and Koi Chitto, riddled through and through, feels himself flying across the sky like an eagle on route to his mate. From aloft, he watches a Red Fox warrior chant in his honor before taking his head, then it is paraded high in the air.

Anoleta's eyesight is strong. From the hill where she is camped she sees what she does not want to see. Her father's mutilation. Then her uncle, in a fit of rage, tears his shirt off, grabs a hatchet and runs like a madman shouting to the warriors on one side, then on the other side, "I will take his place," he says screaming, "if you want to see an old peace-maker at work, follow me!"

The Yanàbi Town warriors and Choucououlacta's *iksa* scramble after Nitakechi to attack the Red Fox and *Inkilish okla*. They stretch out and hit their enemy from the left and the right. When they have them in a close mass, they begin to squeeze, cutting them to pieces with terrifying speed. This is the first time Anoleta understands why her people use the symbol of the coiling and uncoiling snake.

Within moments two dozen *Filanchi okla* soldiers, led by the trusted friend of Bienville, Jean-Marie Critches, arrive. They head toward the *Inkilish okla* cannon like a swimming alligator. When attacked, they halt, take cover, and fire again. There is no haste, no hesitation, and eventually they take out *Inklish okla* manning the cannon.

At last everything becomes clear to her: the burned grass, the dark sky, the complete serenity she feels in knowing what to do. Picking up a knife and her hatchet, Anoleta follows the warriors to scout for enemies who are too weak to run. They will be her prey. Once enraged, women are the fieriest killers of all, cutting out beating hearts, skinning the heads of wounded enemies, leaving them to die slowly. The night marks time with the sounds of tearing flesh and screaming men. For an Indian woman at war, there is no tender mercy. Many of the enemies have dropped dead in their tracks before Anoleta reaches them, but her hands continue to find pleasure in their tasks; they do not tire. Today she has witnessed her father, and many beloved relatives, killed. All this because she failed nine years ago.

As she picks her way through the fallen men, she discovers one of her own, Hopaii Iskitini, the boy her uncle had called "nephew." The boy screams when he sees her. His thigh has been shattered by a volley, the soil around him is wet with blood. In the fashion of war he has been fur-ther tormented. A bayonet was hammered through his shoulder, pin-ning him for the insects. Yet, even so, he is still fully conscious.

"Who did this?" she asks.

He drops his eyes. "Red Shoes and his *Inkilish* trader. They got away, they got away," he cries. "West."

It is very dark now, with a wind bearing great gusts from the gulf. In the salty night air, occasional flashes of musket volleys can be seen twinkling like fireflies. The boy utters one more phrase before he expires. "I saw your uncle hanged in a tree with his stomach still in his hands. A flock of birds surrounds him."

Anoleta has entered the place of blood revenge. She heads back to their temporary camp where Haya has been caring for the Alibamu Conchatys survivors. She picks up her burden basket and orders Haya not to follow her. Her words have little effect. Haya says together they can find him. And she is right. Within an hour they locate the tracks of a pack train heading toward Red Shoes' stronghold, the western town of Couechitto. The country toward Couechitto is elevated, covered with hills. Anoleta and Haya struggle each step of the way, sometimes taking turns pulling each other along. She worries that when she does find Red Shoes, she will be too feeble to kill him. Several more hours pass before they smell the smoke from an immense fire. Anoleta tastes ashes in the breeze. She and her sister hide, then sneak close enough to see who is there.

Red Shoes is sitting before the fire, as if he expects them. Next to him sits his *Inkilish* trader. Red Shoes throws off his deerskin shirt and examines the wound on his stomach. In moments, he raises his voice in song. When he begins to dance, Anoleta and Haya walk slowly into camp. No one says a word as Anoleta approaches him. Just then she has an odd thought. She wants Jean Baptiste Bienville to know that she is the one who finished *Imataha Chitto*.

Red Shoes studies her face, but does not read her deceit. His eyes say, "There have been no years between us." Then the warrior cries to *Miko Luak* as they dance. Haya follows them. Around and around they go, and without warning, Haya bolts and, using both hands, she pushes Red Shoes into the flames.

12 | Suspended Animation

Talihina,
Rocky Road

N ight has come. Rain falls in the center of Talihina, the tiny Choctaw town in Southeastern Oklahoma. The blacktop road shines like a mirror as Auda drives her Jeep up Bengal Mountain. The taillights of Red's Mercedes seem to leave the road and Auda is convinced she's following a flying car. It's probably an eye trick, but she feels headed for the sky.

On previous trips to their house on top of Bengal Mountain, she and Red have usually taken one car. They pack fancy meats and breads, imported cheeses, several bottles of wine, and the expensive pears she orders by mail. Yet for some reason they're driving separate vehicles tonight. She can't remember packing any food or clothes, not even a toothbrush, but she dismisses this.

Red's taillights disappear and she guns her Jeep, trying to catch up with him. When she reaches the top of the mountain his car is already parked under the carport. She runs across the driveway to avoid getting wet, and as soon as she steps onto the front porch the rain stops. Red is sitting there casually in a rocking chair. But where are all his mongrel dogs? Usually they run to greet her; something must have happened. He looks as if he's been waiting a long while. There is a cooler next to his chair, filled with beer.

He offers her one and she takes the bottle from his hand. She doesn't say a word. His eyes, like black stones, follow her every movement. She drinks. She had not planned to come to this place; she had not planned to find him again, but after all the years—and hundreds still to come—

how could she possibly resist. His slender body swells like a grub then returns to normal. Another illusion.

"You're too tense. Do you want another?"

"No," she says. "I don't."

He scans the sky as he fingers the frayed cuff of his white linen shirt. "The clouds are so dense we can't see a thing."

Auda is fascinated by the sight of the whirling mist above her head. She forgets Red for a moment and stares into the blackness. The air is heavy with water.

"What do you want to know?" he asks, standing up to rub her neck and shoulders.

Auda doesn't want to tell him, so she's slow to answer. Finally she asks him for the names of the Choctaws he bought off in order to sell the casino project to the rest of the tribal council.

"Nitakechi, Koi Chitto, and of course, Choucououlacta. Sooner or later they all came around to my way of thinking!"

She smiles, knowing that he's lying and walks inside the cabin.

Red follows her. He seems intrigued by his own answer. He says he doesn't know those men, that he'd once heard their names in ceremonies at the Nanih Waiya. "But I don't really know anything for sure. Wait a minute," he says slowly, "I did know those men. It was at my instigation that the warriors had stained the roads red, and that Nitakechi and Koi Chitto were killed." Then he begins to weep.

"Much later, the council went along with the casino deal. Like you, they wanted to believe me," he says, his voice choking with sobs. "Why can't you understand? I did it to make our tribe strong again—like we were in the old days."

She studies his face, sees that the back of his head is caked with blood, but is not disturbed at this. In fact, she thinks this is the way it ought to be.

"What about your trips to Ireland?"

"Poetic justice."

"Explain."

"I met James Joyce in a pub in Belfast. He said something like, the Choctaws and the Irish have a common enemy—the English. We both want revenge. It was a marriage made in history," he says, wiping tears off his face.

"Then what happened?"

"I concentrated on what I wanted. Revenge for what the English did to you, and for the disease they brought our people. After all Elsley, the *Inkilish* trader, betrayed us both. He was the one sitting next to me in front of the fire, remember?"

"No."

"Elsley got what was coming to him. His head was broken with an ax four months later by warriors from Yanàbi Town. So now you know. When I'd read about a building in London exploding or an English train derailing, I'd think 'that's Choctaw revenge, too.' Eventually I began stealing money for us. Look, I can prove I'm telling the truth."

Red takes her to a large barrel of dog food. He hauls a large black nylon bag out it. It's stuffed with cash.

"Nine million—the other million I already handed off to Joyce. My last hurrah. Stealing from the Mafia ... it's kind of mythical, isn't it? I always knew I'd be caught and killed. You'll make good use of the money, won't you?"

She stares at him in disbelief.

"You said yourself that we'd never make enough money from smoke shops and truck stops to buy the Nanih Waiya from the state of Mississippi."

She can't say that he's wrong. "I once had hope," she says. Then she walks outside and into darkness.

The car—they're off again. The earth and air and space are rearranged for this purpose. At last they can tell the whole story, beginning with the hunger of the *Hispano Osano*. He looks straight into her eyes. "I'll tell you all of it. What difference can it make now? People thought all I cared about was power."

She nods yes.

"Sometimes you did too, didn't you?"

"After a while, I knew it was true," she says.

"When Carl discovered you were stealing wire transfer reports and other documents, he told Hector." Red continues solemnly, "The D'Amato brothers wanted you dead, but I couldn't let that happen. I told them I'd handle you. To prove it, I made a bet. If you wore the Italian dress to work, it would mean I was in control, and Hector had to leave you alone. If not..."

She waits for her rage to return, but feels nothing. "You lost," she says, dryly. "Look where we are now."

They both laugh a little too much.

Auda searches the sky through the car window. Eyes practically identical to hers stare back at them. Perhaps they're stars, yet when she blinks, they dissolve. There is only her and Red floating on a black ribbon. She takes all this as normal, but she doesn't know why. She can't wait until they get to Mississippi. They'll sleep on top of the mound at the Nanih Waiya. "The sky will be clear and bright there," she says, "and I know we'll at last be happy."

"You wore the dress I gave you, after all?"

Auda scrutinizes her clothes. She's wearing the red dress, but her high heels are splattered with dried blood.

"I put it on for you." She laughs at the absurdity. He laughs too, the same way.

"Still, the dress really suits you," he says. "It's amazing how good you look in it—it's as though it was made for you."

"Where's your Harvard tie, the one you always wear? What's happened to it?"

Red laughs again. "I don't know about the tie. I seem to have lost it along with everything else."

Now they're both in hysterics looking around in the car for his things.

They stop laughing abruptly when they see the large black nylon bag in the backseat of the car full of blood money. The mood becomes sad, and they both know the truth of what has happened. The tribe split, land all burned up, her body violated like the land, his shot clean through. And who could forget the blood revenge that began in 1747?

Auda and Red stare ahead at the road. Their sorrow rises and falls, congealing into an artificial cloud that engulfs them. They drive in blackness. The inside of the car has the coolness of a cave. There is no sun. Not here, but there are little paths jutting off in all directions.

13 | The Nanih Waiya

Mississippi
Thursday, September 26, 1991

In the waning Sun of autumn, fantastic shadows fall from the branches of sycamore trees and watch as seven vehicles from Oklahoma, of varying sizes and models, pull up and park in front of the Nanih Waiya. "Finally," says the one to the others.

The black earth of the mound is soft and open from recent rains, like the pores of skin. Above, although hidden by the sun's rays, *Fichik Issi* shakes his head, making the air taste sweet from the dust of his antlers, and he shouts joyously to his friends around the universe. "Ah hah, look at what's left, a chin, a foot, and so much more!"

Isaac Billy gets out of his truck, limping from sitting so long. His khaki pants rustle with each step he takes around the mound. Like an old-time warrior acknowledging the perimeter, as if the Nanih Waiya still had a perimeter, Isaac offers a silent prayer of thanks for their journey. When he feels it's safe for the others to get out of their cars he calls out in a loud voice, *"Falamut."* As the word leaves his mouth, the ghosts of red children begin playing *toli*, and the wind laughs, and streamers of ancient songs rise from the ground and dance.

Delores slides off her loafers before getting out of the truck. Rather than take the wooden steps to the flat summit of the Nanih Waiya, she slowly walks up the east side of the mound using her cane. She feels the wet grass between her toes and is elated. In a few hours it will be twilight; the skies will be clear, and the air still warm, as she sings the funeral songs that will put McAlester's spirit at peace.

Once on top of the mound, Delores searches the nearby forest for signs of animal life. She lifts her nose toward the Pearl River and inhales, shedding all her anxiety and fears. This is truly a sacred place. Bringing the chief's body to Mississippi for burial was the right decision, although risky. When Nick Carney demanded that "his Uncle Red" be loaded into a U-Haul trailer, the Durant funeral home didn't resist or ask a single question. But she and Isaac were still worried. They constantly looked in the rearview mirror for McAlester's supporters or the D'Amato brothers, or both. So far, they've seen no one.

From her vantage point, Delores can see the load of mud they hauled that began as flour, water, and a little lard. The spectacle of it percolating in Isaac's truck bed and the stains on her hands nearly make her swoon. The other six cars in their Okie caravan are stuffed with McAlester's clothes, ties, shoes, golf clubs, magazines, a computer, and an office copier. Of course, the most outrageous sight is the Big Peanut-mobile. Hoppy, Kelly, and Nick used the 1976 Delta 88 to pull the trailer with McAlester's coffin and a large black nylon bag found at McAlester's house. Hoppy said an old man discovered the bag hidden inside a huge barrel of Purina Dog Chow. "Poor guy, he didn't know what to do so he brought it to us."

They all believed the bag was stuffed with the money McAlester stole from the Mob. But, like the old man said, "As long as no one don't open it, or touch it, it's likely they won't become *Osano*."

He spoke the truth. It was an old lesson, never touch what evil has touched. They took a vote and agreed to bury the money with McAlester. Delores laughs aloud. In a hundred years or so, when archaeologists stumble upon McAlester's skeletal remains, they'll find gifts from Xerox and Microsoft, along with millions of dollars buried next to him. His gravesite will confirm the long-held theory that Indians so deeply revere their leaders that they bury them with precious gifts.

She sits down on the ground and smoothes the wrinkles in her dress. For a moment she toys with a thread hanging from the hem. She considers leaving it, but then yanks it out. No, there will be no more loose ends, nothing left undone. Looking skyward she squints as two blue herons fly toward her. They pass overhead and land on the banks of the creek. She tries to imagine what they see as they fly: the Pearl River nearby, small perch they wish to feast on, the Nanih Waiya as it once was. Everyone knows it was rimmed with an earthen rampart. Eighteen wooden lookout posts were built at various intervals so the young men could watch for approaching visitors coming to trade their goods. She tries to remember a story about this, but can't focus. She'd rather enjoy the Sun and think about her nine-hour trip to Mississippi sitting beside Isaac.

In the distance, a line of cars approaches the mound. Delores watches as Isaac and the other Oklahoma Choctaws gather below to greet the convoy. She hoists herself up with her cane and walks back down the side of the mound to join him. They are a couple now: she should be there. She smiles. The things she is rediscovering about him in such a short time.

The cars rattle on. Isaac and Delores greet the people. She asks if he knows everyone and he shakes his head no. Eventually, a man wearing khaki clothes similar to Isaac's approaches them. His gimme cap says "Chahta" across the front, and he greets Isaac in Choctaw. His name is Earl Billy, a distant cousin, and she hears them say they haven't had a long visit in some twenty years. They talk among themselves. Isaac then motions for Hoppy and his friends to come so he can introduce them to the elder Choctaws who've just arrived. When he comes back to her, Earl is still with him.

"Meet the wife," he says proudly to Earl. "We married yesterday after a fifty-year courtship."

Earl looks at Delores oddly, then Isaac.

"We wanted to be sure, that's all," says Delores solemnly.

Earl nods his head. "Yes, I've heard that the Oklahoma Choctaws have developed some strange customs," he says, winking.

The three of them laugh while Delores and Earl shake hands. They begin the familiar Indian ritual of "who is related to whom?" After a while, Earl brings up Redford McAlester and the arrangements they've made.

"We're going into a swampy area," he says. "We had to use a backhoe to dig such a large hole. We're going to put your chief and his things in the ground, cover it up with the mud you're hauling, then let Mother Nature takes it from there. We'll hold the ceremony back here. Maybe McAlester will stay put that way."

She nods in approval.

"They say you have to have a sign," he says, looking toward the Pearl River. "It can be a snake, a bear, maybe the little people, but something will put you in touch with the spirits. They say that you can tell when a boy is young if he's going to be a spiritual leader. He usually goes into the woods all alone. He may go out and stay all night. Sometimes he will walk in his sleep, and that's when it happens. That's when he receives the gift."

Earl looks down at his hands, rubs his eyes and shakes his head sadly, as if he is reliving the moment when McAlester was shot. "I have it on good authority," he says, "that that is what happened to Redford McAlester. He received the sign and was supposed to be a healer. But for whatever reason—we don't know what happened—he rejected it."

He takes a breath. "So on this day the Chahta people who've been split apart by circumstances beyond us—we've come back together to put this man's spirit at peace." He turns to Delores. "Would you like to meet some of the women now?"

She doesn't have to answer; Earl reads her thoughts and walks her where the women are standing. She looks back at Isaac. At last he's relaxed. They've come to finish what they started long ago, nothing will stop them. He knows it, too.

Delores begins shaking hands with the women from Zwolle, Louisiana; Homa, Louisiana; Lexington, Texas; and Mobile, Alabama. After a while, they decide to walk together around the sacred mound.

"We were told as kids," Delores says, "that before the Choctaws left Mississippi, they came here and grabbed a little bit of the Nanih Waiya to take with them on the long walk."

"Then again," says Edith LaHarve of Pearl River, Mississippi, her voice filled with irony, "there are those of us who never left."

"*Yummak osh alhpesa*," says Delores, hanging her head in shame. She can't believe she's said such a callous thing, as if the only true Choctaws went to Oklahoma. She came here to help reunite people, and now she's spoken out of turn. Many Choctaws stayed and fought for their rights, and in 1918, the Mississippi Band of Choctaws was officially recognized by the federal government.

Edith LaHarve walks over to her. "We've been separated for so long, it's hard for us to remember that we once thought of ourselves as one body with different parts, but with one heart. However we always believed this day would come." She holds out her brown-stained hands to Delores. "We've been to the truck bed," she says tearfully.

"*At chi hullo li*," says Delores, holding out her hands to Edith. "I care for you."

"*At chi hullo li*," replies Edith.

Then all the women begin chanting:
At chi hullo li

At chi hullo li
At chi hullo li
At chi hullo li

Delores slows down her breathing as she's done a hundred times before in preparation for singing the songs for the dead. But her gaze shifts and she sees the afternoon sunlight dancing around them, as if birthing new life. She exhales, pushing all herself out of her body and, in this moment, she feels a miraculous beginning as she and the other Chahta women of the Southeast join hands and sing.

14 | Road of Darkness

The room is a bed of wind.

In one instant Auda's lungs are filled with the delicious rush of sunrise; swelling like a sail she floats high above it all. Her feet, eyes, and her faces are everywhere, leaving a warm imprint in the air. She is amazed at how effortlessly she glides through the cocoon of white sheets that protect her trapped body.

But in the next second she is hollow—herself pushed out through a fissure—and she goes down, down, down into the blackness through a sound. He is still with her. She hears breathing. His and hers. Their rhythms are in sync. Dressed in his best suit, his Harvard tie neatly knotted around his neck, he drives along an endless road. Something has brought them together. Now she remembers. Blood. He wraps himself in her light and shadow. She doesn't mind.

Finally he says in a low voice, "I had a dream. We are ancient and still living together. Our children and families are all around us."

Auda looks at him. "It's an old preoccupation that penetrates our emptiness."

Once again she is thrust up into the open air and the light. Suddenly her cousin, Buster, is next to the bed listening to her heart with a stethoscope. Her mother sits beside her stranded body. Her head is bowed. Auda can't see her mother's face clearly, but hears her prayers:

Presley War Maker, we need your help. Please come.

Auda looks up through the windshield. It's misting rain. She hears a group of women speaking softly in Choctaw, calling on her father's spirit to save her. Auda pictures her father in her mind, but instead sees a sky of umbrellas black as birds. They open and close their wire wings. Auda stretches out her arms to fly and emerges in a garden of green corn where a paunchy deer grazes. He nods his antlers in her direction, as if to say, isn't this fun?

She is living in a town fat with food. In the cool underneath of the cane trees, women from the *Intek Aliha* cut the palmetto leaves for the new cabin that is being built. Hers. Beyond, alligators nap in the swamp. She is so happy running along the river bank to meet her father, yet when she blinks she's falling into the churning waters. A feathered serpent stands up out of the water next to her, preventing her father from pulling her out of the water, then it flaps toward the sun. She sees a drop of her blood hit the ground, then swell into a river. Now she remembers what happened.

Her first failure to kill Red Shoes was in Yanàbi Town, the night after her mother's bone-picking ceremony. When Red Shoes returned to her cabin he was mad as a snake. He did not stop to eat the poisoned meat she had prepared for him, nor did he even pause to look at her. He brought two men with him who waited outside and talked with Haya, her younger sister. She can still see Red Shoes' bodyguards. They shouldn't be there. Three more of his warriors grow out of the path to Yanàbi Town and stand beside her. Frightened, she reaches her hands out to push away the past, but nothing happens.

He is again driving the car too damn fast.

"I can't believe you are here. What was I saying?" he asks.

"You were telling me how our history could have been different."

"The Choctaws," he says, his words as warm as breath, "had been major trading partners in the Southeast for centuries. But you knew that."

She nods. His shadow fades and a warrior's muscular body comes into focus. It's the Red Shoes she remembers, the greatest war leader, the enemy of her enemies, the astute, the ruthless, the savage.

"I made my first bold trade for weapons and other goods with the *Inkilish* in 1729. That success convinced me I could unite the Chickasaws and the Choctaws against the foreigners."

"But as a result," she says, her mind sliding across old news, "you played an important role in the mass killings of the Western Choctaws and the Eastern Choctaws for nearly two decades. Your death managed to turn our homelands into one of the most terrifying places on earth."

"It was my dream to have all the advantages the foreigners brought into our nations without surrendering to their rules. It was the same with the casino business."

"I see."

"No, you don't see. It's just the trappings of time that have changed. Whether it was Bienville and the *Filanchi,* or the D'Amato brothers and the Italians, it's just the trappings of time that have changed for Choctaws."

"But Bienville was like a member of our family. We had to support him," she argues.

He smiles. "You're forgetting, the Choctaws adopted me, too. The only difference between you and me is that I've killed *for* you."

She is silent for a long while, then gasps. "You murdered your wife from the Red Fox village!"

"She intended to destroy you. She had cut your hair and was going to give it to a *isht ahollo* to make witch medicine," he says nonchalantly. "And she would have found a way to use it on you, if you survived the alligators. I once told you I had protected you with my life—now you know what I meant."

Auda sits in silence, remembering a struggle that began so long ago. Here they are shedding skins, becoming a reflection of what they once were. She sees it all happening again. She catches up with Red Shoes on the road to Couechitto with his *Inkilish* friend. She bides her time. Another mistake. They dance around the fire until Haya pushes him in. When he crawls out of the flames, she circles his kneeling body. Rubs her fingers over his face, his thighs, his head. She bends to see what he sees. He slaps at her with what is left of him. She stands him up and embraces his charred flesh. They are a two-headed animal staggering in the darkness. A sense of oblivion is in the air, in the fire. He whispers to try and save her, "Look, behind you." Too late. A volley careens through the air and shatters her jaw. Her teeth scatter across the ground. Blood rushes from her nose and mouth. She falls. Another shot hits Haya in the chest. She watches her sister die. She thinks, in an instant nothing will remain of me, but it does. The last thing she sees is Elsley standing above her before he pulls out an ax and splits her in two.

"I wanted revenge for your death, too," Red says sadly. He shifts nervously in the front seat of the car; his fingers clutch the wheel, steering them along the crooked road.

Red reaches over to hold her hand. "Do you remember when I asked you to round up all the prominent Choctaws for the opening of the Casino of the Sun? You asked, in that smart-alecky voice of yours, 'But the place is crawling with Mafia, won't the elders be in danger?' I laughed and said, 'Of course not, they only kill each other.'"

He turns to her and smiles, his eyes as black as the road ahead. "What I should have said is that it's also true for Choctaws." Auda knows that he's relating what no one else will ever see—their last time together. She had walked in and begged him to make love. He pushed his pants down before he saw the gun. In the split second that followed, he had merely shrugged and said, "dying will be like dozing."

Red begins to change. She watches as he transforms himself back into the sophisticated big-time Indian politician she remembers. He is magnanimous as he continues talking about his criminal dealings. "You know Citisavings Bank came up with a whole new strategy for me. Kind of makes you wonder about the J. P. Morgans of the world, doesn't it."

His body puffs up to match his demeanor. "I can hear the bells of the slot machines from here, the jingle-jangle of the coins in the pockets of hungry tourists. There is still a parade of eager white people who only want to spend their money at the Casino of the Sun. What a reversal of fortune, huh?"

"How do you do it?" she asks.

"What?"

"Make me love you one moment, and love your dying the next."

He seems genuinely crushed by her words. "There are 90,000 Oklahoma Choctaws who will benefit from my hard work," he says softly. "The tribe could use my extra nine million...that is, if the Feds don't find it first."

Auda smiles, recovering some of her old power. "You're desperate. You don't know how desperate, but I will know it for you."

She turns away and suggests they shut their eyes as he drives.

He laughs. "Why not?"

She suddenly remembers what Bienville had once told her: That Red Shoes would never be far from her enemies.

"It's strange how attractive I still find you—considering everything," he says.

She opens her eyes and looks at him.

"I think I like it here," he says, earnestly.

She lets her shoes fall off her feet, and leans back in her seat. "This is an awful story," she says, as the car dissolves along a blood clot of darkness.

15 | Heart of the Panther

A dair is sitting on her living room couch when gangsters break down her front door and pump her body full of bullets. As the shots hit their mark, she gives a little *"oh-oh"* which wakes her up in time to see Warren Beatty get it the same way in the in-flight movie, *Bugsy*.

But it's not the gunfire she hears in the earphones, it's her father's voice: Pichahli, *remember what I told you. You are the true hunter in the family.*

She jerks the earphones off. Gore Battiste is seated next to her in the aisle seat, typing furiously on his laptop. She looks out the small oval window of the jet; thin stringy clouds whirl by. All is quiet in the first-class cabin. Was it really her father's voice? It's been a long time—she was only nine when he died—perhaps she's mistaken. No one ever called her *Pichahli* except her father. She wishes she had a cigarette. She doesn't feel like much of a hunter.

"Indians aren't capitalists—we can't buy anything. Haven't you read the history books? We must trade for what we want," says Gore aloud, chuckling as he types.

"What?"

"I was typing some notes for the trial."

"Speaking of history—" she says, pausing.

"Was I?" he asks.

"Why haven't you ever mentioned—well, the last time we saw each other?"

He grins at her with that crooked little smile that makes her want to smack him, then make love to him. The problem is, he knows it.

"I've been waiting for you to bring it up," he says, mischievously. "Considering the circumstances, wouldn't it have been a little cheesy to say, 'Hey Adair, how've you been since the last time I saw you naked?'"

She raises her fist, he raises his eyebrows. "You never called, I just want to know why," she says.

"A couple of reasons. Our timing was off. I was living in law school and you in New Orleans. After all, you're the six-figure-a-year girl," he says, closing his laptop.

"Ah, here it comes, the hostility because I'm successful."

"Don't be ridiculous. I want the mother of my children to be a six-figure-a-year girl, except you'll have to stop smoking like a chimney when you get pregnant."

She must look stunned because he laughs loudly, then kisses her. "Nice," he says, softly.

"What are you saying?"

He looks serious, and clears his throat for a speech. "The real reason I never called you was that I got married shortly after we met. We were in law school together, but it didn't work out."

Adair is thoughtful. She hates prying into people's pasts, yet she can't help but ask, "Why didn't it work out, can you tell me?"

"We were of different faiths—if you can believe that matters in this day and age. It became a very big deal the longer we were together."

"How long have you been divorced?"

"Annulled, you mean."

"Catholic?"

"She was, I wasn't, and if there were children..."

"I see... So what about us?" asks Adair.

"Over the past three days, it's clear that we're crazy about each other. Your whole family thinks we're perfectly matched. Everyone's quizzed me about how we met, when, where. I had to tell them something—that you once put the moves on me, but I outmaneuvered you. However," he says, grinning from ear to ear, "now that you've changed your hair and dress like a man, I'm having a much tougher time."

She punches him in the stomach.

"Stop hitting me." He laughs and grabs her fists. "Even your mother said, 'Welcome to the family, son.' *Jeez*, you Billys are really brazen when you want something. Did you put her up to that?"

"No, I did not!" Adair feels her face turning a shade redder.

"According to Aunt Dovie, you're not seriously involved with anyone else. I'm disease free, I have a steady law practice, and I want to make lots of little Indians with you. I'm asking you to marry me."

Somehow she'd known he'd married another woman. Now that he's free, she can't believe she's hedging. Adair looks away from Gore's face, intense and vulnerable. How can she be so happy while her family is being put through hell?

"Marry me, Adair."

Silence.

He must be reading her mind because his demeanor changes. "C'mon, Miss Billy, marry me, please," he whispers, then kisses her brown-stained palms. "According to my uncle, who taught me this, even the meanest of Indian women after hearing a sincere marriage proposal will offer her tender weapons in exchange for a warrior's true heart."

Her eyes fill with tears.

"C'mon, Miss Billy, it's a good exchange between very old, very dependable trading partners. This is the way it's been done for a thousand years. The Alabama Conchatys want what the Chahtas have. Trade hearts with me. Say yes."

"Yes," she says.

"Then we have a treaty. I'll bring the wampum belts," he says, caressing her cheek.

Once they check into their hotel room, Adair makes love with Gore. When she thinks he is soundly asleep, she gets up and paces the room. At two A.M. she's still awake, writing a priority list. First, retrieve the package from Tema's agent. Second, find James Joyce. Third, hire her hacker friend to download the tribe's computer bank files. All this will cost a fortune—perhaps all the money she has stashed away. She calls the answering service for Tema's agent and leaves a message. She'll pick up the package before noon tomorrow.

Gore gets up and stumbles to the couch. "It's two-thirty woman, what are you doing?" he asks, yawning. "Come to bed, why are you knocking yourself out this way?"

She's quiet for a moment. "It's just that Ma has never depended on me for anything truly important. She's always known that I'd be all right, so she kinda ignores me," she says, shrugging. "Auda's the oldest, Tema's the baby."

"I promise never to ignore you," he says tenderly.

She smiles. "I want to show my family that I'm worthy too. Understand?"

He nods yes. "You need sleep. Tomorrow I'll call a friend of mine in D.C. who can help us. She works in the Attorney General's office and is very aware of the problems that Redford McAlester was creating for the tribe. Besides, we've gotta get some help tracking down this James Joyce character."

Adair wakes up at five, a force of habit. She drags on her robe and heads to the bathroom. Gore is still sleeping. When she comes out of the bathroom, she sees a huge panther lolling on the sofa of their hotel room. The panther has a thick tan coat; its body completely spans the three-cushion sofa. The brown markings across its cheeks remind her of her father's facial scars, the ones he got in World War II when he fought hand-to-hand with a German soldier.

"Dad," she says, staring into the panther's fiery eyes, "is that you?"

Adair sits on the chair facing the couch and then falls into a deep sleep at the sound of her father's voice.

Do you want to live with the Alibamu Conchatys?

Yes.

This is good news. They're admirable people, I have always trusted them.

Will Auda get well?

Things are not always how they seem, Pichahli. *Don't worry I am watching over my girls.*

How do I find James Joyce?

He'll be waiting for you at a restaurant called Harry's at Hanover Square in New York City. But you must hurry, he leaves town soon, and you will not be able to track him.

What does that mean?

That his time is up.

Dad, I miss you.

Go back to sleep, my girl, you need your rest.

Gore sounds panicky as he shakes her. "Adair, wake up, what are you doing on the floor?"

"My father's spirit was here," she says sleepily.

"I should put on some clothes."

"Don't be silly, he came as a panther. He didn't have on any clothes, either."

"Does this happen often?" Gore asks nervously, pulling on his pants.

"Almost never."

He looks from the sofa to the bed. "That's good to know."

"What time is it?" asks Adair, sitting up.

"Nine forty-five."

"He told me where I can find this guy, Joyce. He'll be at—"

The phone rings. They both look at it, as if it were a foreign object. When Adair picks up the receiver, it's Tema's agent. She has the package for her. Also, a man with a thick Irish accent named James Joyce has been trying to contact Tema. Won't leave a number; says he's leaving town today. Adair says she'll take care of it and hangs up. "I'm worried that Joyce is going to leave town before we get to him. He's been trying to reach Tema."

"We just have to go on what your father's given us," Gore says, pulling her into the bathroom. "Clearly, Joyce wants to connect—though that puzzles me."

Before they leave, Adair tries to call her mother's house, but no one answers. "Someone should be there," she says. Then she remembers. The phone lines were jammed once before when Isaac had been arrested.

Harry's at Hanover Square is a famous Wall Street haunt. Adair knows it well from her regular trips to New York. Every Monday through Friday afternoon, brokers, traders, sales assistants, fund managers, and recently graduated M.B.A.s line up to drink dinner there.

When she and Gore arrive, they're escorted to a small table. Two cold glasses of beer are placed before them. Sinking into a fissured leather chair, Adair sees a man in a tan overcoat approaching her. He carries a glass of beer and a copy of the *Times*.

James Joyce looks like he could be the twin of Willie Nelson. Same dark eyes, ruddy complexion, deep wrinkles for laugh lines. Strange how people choose one profession over another. A country western singer versus an explosives expert, or an assassin for the I.R.A. "You're a Billy alright." He sets his glass down, pulls a large manila envelope from between the folds of the *Times* and tosses it on the table. Then he sits.

"Nobody listens to me," he says. "It was bound to happen. True, our operations are kaput; we knew it wouldn't last long, opinions within the ranks were always at variance. Everyone's quarreling. How shrill, how harsh—the barbs wound the likes of us all. Tragedy about Chief, isn't it? Poor bastard, getting it that way in the head. I've seen worse—he'd seen worse, to hear 'em tell it. Immortal role, chief. It can't be easy. Dissenting voices to contend with, hurling curses at one another, profiles-in-courage types dealing you a Mickey Finn. Who knows who's doin' what, to whom? Palms raised toward the Sun in prayer, or pressed together in front of the Virgin Mary—it doesn't mean a thing, I grant you. Oh, don't look at me so skeptically. One religious gesture you're in, another you're out."

He inhales the last of his beer. "The way Chief would stride back and forth, take to the open air in Belfast, he was a right one, he was. He stood firm on his history, never let it be forgotten. 'Who owns the past? What are we quarreling about?' he would ask me. 'Whose land is it?' I would answer. 'Where is the goddamn sovereignty?' And to that I'd reply. 'Whose property is to be held, won back, shared with the bloody crown? Oh, Queens, be damned!'"

He flags a waiter for his check. "Plutocratic terrorists, that's what we all are, now. That's where most of the money went, you see, not where Chief wanted it to go. Hoped it would go. But I've done what he asked. You can have what you're after, it's all here. But why are we talking about the end of the world? Plenty of plans left in my dreams. Chief was a hilarious, unique creation, but he wasn't commanding enough, was he? He would say, tomorrow I'll get back to saving the trees. We enjoyed him too much," says James Joyce, folding the newspaper under his arm.

Adair hasn't understood a word. She glances over at Gore, who, by now, has tipped his beer glass toward Joyce, as if he were toasting him.

"Then why don't you just cut off their feet?" asks Gore, downing his own beer.

"The whole lot is going to be stinking dead," replies Joyce, carefully rubbing the back of his neck. "That's what independence will do for us, look what it's done for Indians. Ah, well—a change of climate might help, a shift in the currents, that is if she comes out of it, right as rain, so to speak. She was good for metaphors. Her perseverance unraveled every stitch of his sweater. No, we're all dying and that's that. It's the trend—"

"Stop!" shouts Adair, putting her hand up. She looks at James Joyce, then over at Gore who seems surprised that she's upset. "Mr. Joyce, please, no more incoherent sentences. I never could get through *Finnegans Wake*."

Joyce says nothing, but he smiles innocently in Adair's direction. He sits quietly at the table. When she can stand it no longer, she tries a more direct approach.

"Mr. Joyce, Auda's in a coma. Red is dead."

"Queer business, isn't it," he quips.

"But what I want to know, are you going to tell us what happened to the money McAlester gave the I.R.A., why you got involved with him in the first place, and why you left a message with Tema's agent? And ..."

Gore interrupts her. "Honey, he just told us why, and this envelope contains the evidence we're after."

With that, James Joyce stands up, nods politely in Gore's direction and walks out of the restaurant.

"You're letting him get away!"

Gore reaches for the envelope on the table. "Boy, for a woman who just said she spoke to her dead father the panther, you certainly fall apart when the conversation is amongst the living."

He looks inside the envelope and passes it to her. "It's the wire transfer reports from the bank. I can't be sure, but it looks as if the balances are zero. At least it proves Auda's story."

"Why did Joyce give us these documents?"

"You heard him."

"I didn't understand a word. And how come you're such an expert on James Joyce all of a sudden?"

"I'm not. But I'm an expert on legalese. Reading between the lines, understanding what is said and what is implied. As you know, James Joyce, the famous author, was trained in Jesuit schools where he received an excellent grounding in religious doctrines, the basis of Judeo-Christian beliefs, hence English law, and hence—the basis of American law."

"So."

"Obviously the man who just left here chose that name for a reason. Speaking in a stream of consciousness might be helpful if you're a bag-man, or...whatever it is that he does for the I.R.A."

"I see," says Adair, thoughtfully. "What else did you understand that I missed?"

"He liked McAlester. He saw similarities between the problems of Northern Ireland and the British, and American Indians and the federal government. As a result, the I.R.A. and McAlester had history in common. Most of the money that McAlester paid them didn't go toward killing other people, but to the I.R.A. bureaucracy. That's why Joyce is angry with his own organization. That's why he turned over evidence. That's why he's going to disappear."

"Boy, you *were* reading between the lines."

"Writing between the lines, Adair. You can read it all in my brief *before* we go to trial."

Tema can't remember what day it is, or whether the Sun is coming up or going down. She's been in the makeshift hospital room since they brought Auda home. She won't leave Auda, somehow feels responsible for what has happened. She's always felt a debt to her sister, but can't explain why. There have been times over the years when she would wake up believing she knew why. But like the color of running water, she can't name it. In Tema's dreams there is a road of fire, the glint of an ax. Immobility. Nothing.

The past few days have been an emotional roller coaster ride. She misses Borden, more than she thought possible. Before Hoppy left for Mississippi with Delores and Isaac, he said he didn't want to go to school in Paris. He said he wanted to stay in Durant and help Isaac work the ranch. One reason is Kelly Kampelubbi—she knows her son well enough to know that—but that's not all of it. She decides to call Borden—surely he'll have some advice—but when she picks up the phone in Auda's room, there's no dial tone.

The house suddenly creaks. It tells Tema a stranger has just entered uninvited. The oak floors upstairs pop. Someone has just walked across them. It can't be family or friends. Buster's gone to the hospital to get more medical supplies. Her mother and Aunt Dovie are at the grocery store. Tema's had a premonition that someone might break in, but she's shrugged it off. The house groans again. She draws her Swiss Army knife out of her boot, opens the door of Auda's room and looks up to the second floor landing. Someone is there, but she can't see a thing. She listens. Another move. For a brief instant fear grips her and she can't control her breathing. Every breath cuts her chest. Someone takes another step. Then another.

To calm her breathing, she whispers the lines from *The Conference of the Birds.* "Come out—I see you peer and pry; you know my treasure's home and you must die." She knows she's going to have to leave Auda and attack whoever is up there. She looks over at her sister, then checks the machines. They're working fine. She decides to go up the front stairs and then come down the kitchen stairs at the back of the house. Perhaps she can draw whoever it is into one of the bedrooms then lock the door behind them.

She remembers a story her mother once told her. To clear a path, Choctaw warriors once had to remove autumn leaves one by one, with their toes, in order to make a surprise attack on an enemy village. She makes herself into such a warrior. Taking off her boots, she slides across the wooden floors. Her own heart is beating so loudly that she will later say she never heard the pounding on the front door. All she will say is that she saw a stranger starting down the back stairs. He held a gun in his hand. She bolted and knocked him down the narrow kitchen stairs. The fall broke his neck, and within minutes he was dead.

When the policeman asks her how Hector D'Amato got the claw marks all over his face, she will shake her head and say, "I don't know." It's not the whole truth. Just as she pushed the invader, she saw a large panther leap out of a wall of the Billy house and attack him. Together the panther and the Italian rolled over and over, all the way to the bottom.

16 | Absolution

One more curve in the road and Auda Billy is sitting in a car that has come to a stop. Redford McAlester is next to her in the driver's seat. Standing in the middle of the road a hundred feet away are her Uncle Isaac and Aunt Delores. They hold hands like lovers.

All roads should be this black, all headlights so dazzling. They walk out of obscurity toward the high beams and stand before her. Behind them seven women are shaking shells and dancing. As Isaac and Delores draw nearer, the shell shakers form a circle around them. All space and air vibrates as the women transform themselves into multicolored beaks and wings that take flight. Voices arise from the throats of birds. The sound penetrates Auda and her body glows white hot, filled with absolution. The birds circle above the car before they disappear, leaving Auda to confront the dead chief.

"Where did they come from?" he asks curtly.

"Look at me," she says.

He refuses.

She leans toward him and whispers, "We are going to be separated forever. You thought I'd forgotten."

He cries. Seeing him makes her cry too. She moves so close that she can hear the sound of his breaking bones. He grasps at what he is losing, the life that is leaving him, the memories that are turning to stone. He says quickly, as if it has just occurred to him, "You're making this up."

She shakes her head no.

"I want to know how you would have finished me that winter night in Yanàbi Town," he says, pitifully.

"Like a true enemy," she answers, "I would have killed you with cruelty. First poison, then I would have severed your head from your body while you still breathed. Next I would have posted it on a white pine of peace in the center of town and sung to you in the full light of *Hashtali*." Auda's voice trails off.

"I see."

"Wait," she says. "There's more."

He listens.

"After your death, I would have covered myself with white chalk, sung my own death song, and slipped out of my body into *na tohbi*. At one time I wanted to be with you forever, to have our bones buried together in a nameless mound where no one would ever disturb us, but this was not to be."

He is totally still. "Naturally, when we met, it was the same for me," he says, his expression suddenly tender. "Go back and take up where I left off. You could still run the casino, just use the money for good."

She looks at him and feels herself divide. Part of her watches him with the utter sadness of knowing the one you love is gone forever; her other self feels completely free. "If only you could have been…"

"Truly," he says, putting his fingers over her mouth to stop her speaking. Redford McAlester then squares his shoulders, his warrior body returns. He grasps her fingertips, kissing them one by one. "I'll never leave this place, I promise. After all, my fortune is here," he says, motioning toward the black nylon bag in the back seat.

For a while longer they remain like this, linked by icy hands. At last she moves. "I must go back and stand trial for what I've done," and the man she has simultaneously loved and murdered goes all out for her. He blows her a small kiss and unlocks the most hidden passageways of his heart. In an extraordinary moment the car door opens and Redford McAlester pushes her out into the road where she is met by Isaac and Delores.

Her uncle hugs her as if she were a child and gives her the stone that once belonged to Grandmother of Birds. "Delores and I will take over from here. Be sure to feed GeorgeBush for me."

Auda pretends to be strong for her uncle. She can only guess that he and Delores must have been killed by one of the D'Amato brothers.

Isaac reads her mind. "This is what was meant to happen," he says, helping Delores into the car. "Someone must remain with the chief and help him to stay put. It's not so bad. Delores and I will be together and this is what we've wanted all along," he says, locking himself inside the car.

But Auda doesn't want her aunt and uncle to be condemned to a future of obscurity and isolation with Redford McAlester. She strides alongside the car with her palms pressed against the window until he hits the gas and the car peels away.

The wind is warm at first. Auda's senses return and she smells corn soup and coffee.

Auda, do you hear, do you understand, wake up.

Her mother's voice sounds far away. When she opens her eyes Dovie's hands seem to flutter over her face like tiny birds pecking, patting, blotting. Tema is very calm, she doesn't even flinch as Auda tries to pull the tube out of her mouth. *"Chiske apela,...* Mother help me," are the words she tries to speak before falling asleep.

During the next three weeks Auda receives many visitors. Buster Jones and the doctors marvel at the fact she is alive. They claim it's a miracle that she hasn't suffered too many ill effects from the coma. Her sore throat, caused by the ventilator tube, takes the longest time to heal.

Eventually her mother and Aunt Dovie tell her what she already knows. Delores and Isaac were shot sometime after McAlester's funeral near the Nanih Waiya. They were the last to leave his burial site, and apparently Vico D'Amato caught up with them. The FBI is searching for him, but Gore thinks his body will roll out of the swamp one of these days. Just when is anyone's guess.

When Auda regains the use of the muscles in her hand, she writes out a confession. On the day Tema and Borden wheel her into the Choctaw Superior Court at Tuskahoma, Judge Aaron stares dispassionately at her.

Auda turns around and scans the benches behind her. It seems the entire Choctaw Nation is looking over her shoulders. The small courtroom is packed with Indians, reporters, agents from the BIA office, a lawyer from the Attorney General's office in D.C., and, of course, seventy young warriors Hoppy has gathered from Southeastern Oklahoma, Mississippi, Louisiana, and Alabama. All her family is present except Susan Billy. She catches Hoppy's eye before speaking. He points to the warriors, then mouths the words, "Just in case there are complications."

Auda walks to the witness box and, before the judge and all the people in the courtroom, she reads her confession:

> At nine A.M. on September 22, 1991, I went to Redford McAlester's office to shoot him with my mother's gun. Although I can't remember exactly what happened, I know I must have done it. Afterwards, I covered his face with kisses, then I let the gun fall to the floor. This is all I remember.
> Auda Billy
> October 17, 1991

As she is reading the date, her mother enters the courthouse escorting a tiny old woman. Susan Billy is wearing her best blue suit, with the porcupine sash tied over the shoulder. The old woman wears a traditional Choctaw red dress. It has a very full skirt, with a white apron, and she has a white head piece with long ribbons that stream down her back. Auda thinks the two elder women look ridiculous as they walk slowly toward her and Judge Aaron. After her mother and Gore Battiste have a short conference with the judge, Auda is asked to step out of the witness box. The older woman then takes her place.

Her name is Sarah Bernhardt, she says. In the beginning her testimony is prompted by Gore. But after she gets going, Sarah Bernhardt talks easily without hesitation. The old woman tells the court that she's a volunteer switchboard operator for the tribe and that she works weekends. Auda scrutinizes Sarah Bernhardt. She can't remember ever having laid eyes on her before, although she realizes she's forgotten a lot of things. They tell her this is normal after a coma, and someday part of her memory may come back.

Sarah Bernhardt's testimony before Judge Aaron is everything a theatrical performance should be. It rocks the audience with surprise and is full of emotion without seeming rehearsed. Auda puts her head in her hands and listens to a tearful Bernhardt explain what happened on the day of the McAlester's murder.

"I was fixin' to go home—I can't work long hours, like I used to, but them, them gunshots scared me so bad, Your Honor, I nearly wet my panties."

There's a lot of chuckling and tittering among the audience. Judge Aaron bangs his gavel. "*Chuloso!*" he says, looking sternly at the courtroom audience.

Bernhardt says that curiosity got the best of her after she heard the shots fired, and she peeped in the side door of the chief's office. "Standing there like a demon, above poor unconscious Auda, was Hector the Harpoon," she says, her voice shaking. "He had a gun in his hand."

"Was McAlester dead?" asks the tribe's prosecutor.

"He seemed to be," answers Bernhardt.

"Then you can't say for sure whether Auda Billy shot him, or Hector the Harpoon shot him," quips the tribe's prosecutor.

Auda looks up when she hears a flaw in Bernhardt's testimony. Maybe there's hope for the truth to come out, after all?

"No sir, I can't," says the old woman, "except Mr. Harpoon says on the tape I brought with me, that he's going to splatter Chief's brains all over the state of Oklahoma if Chief don't return the money he stole from Hector's Italian family back east."

The courtroom erupts. The judge pounds his gavel and screams quiet again.

Sarah Bernhardt continues stringing her audience along, threading her story together into a pattern. "Chief had been shot, and them two men talked in a language I can't understand, Your Honor. Anyway, I watched 'em rub their fingerprints off the gun and drop it beside our girl...I mean, Miss Auda Billy."

The tribe's prosecutor leans over to Gore Battiste and begins talking. Both men shake their heads conspiratorially. Auda can't believe this is happening.

Bernhardt then tells the judge that she ran back to the switchboard and called the county sheriff's office. "A deputy was the first on the scene, and ever since then I've been living in desperate fear for my life," she cries. "I'm so ashamed that I didn't come forward until now."

Gore Battiste interrupts Bernhardt's testimony by saying he's received a file from the FBI proving that Hector D'Amato's alias was "Hector the Harpoon."

"Hector was a member of the Genovese crime family," continues Gore, "and, as the court has also learned, Hector and Vico D'Amato were brothers. We can further prove that Hector met Redford McAlester at Dartmouth, Your Honor. The Mob seems to have been involved with McAlester since the 1970s."

The judge politely accepts her lawyer's evidence. Then Gore replays the tape cassette Sarah Bernhardt brought with her. The date recorded at the beginning of the tape is September 21, 1991. Hector D'Amato can be heard talking to an unidentified voice, saying exactly what Sarah Bernhardt says he said.

The old woman weeps loudly on the witness stand as the tape is being played and replayed. Susan Billy rescues Sarah with a box of Kleenex and a nappy gray shawl.

Auda studies the judge. It's all over. The expression on his face says everything. Her lawyer has won her case without having to put up much of a defense. She listens as Battiste summarizes the events.

"We've heard Hector D'Amato say he's going to kill Chief McAlester for stealing the Mob's money. On September 22, he does this. On September 24, Auda Billy is shot up with insulin at the Choctaw Health Clinic by a cohort of Vico D'Amato's. Miss Billy nearly dies, and her assailant, Vergie Reagan, is still at large. September 26, Hector D'Amato breaks into the Billy home, apparently to finish what Vergie started. Tema Billy kills him in self-defense. On this same day in another state, Isaac Billy and Delores Love are shot and killed. The FBI believes that Vico D'Amato, thinking Mr. Billy and Ms. Love were running away with the Mob's money, is the assassin. Currently Vico D'Amato is still at large. On September 26, in New York City, Adair Billy and I obtain a set of documents from James Joyce, not his real name. These bank records prove that McAlester was siphoning off money from Shamrock Resorts and funneling it to the I.R.A."

Judge Aaron interrupts Gore.

"Mr. Battiste, if you had all this evidence, why did you allow Miss Billy to perjure herself by saying she'd killed Redford McAlester?"

"I made a promise to Ms. Billy when I took her case," says Gore. "I didn't have all the facts at the time, but I still had to keep my word to let her tell the story her way."

The judge scratches his head. He says he's throwing out Auda's written confession. "All I can say is that your client is suffering from the effects of the coma. She must have gone to the tribal headquarters intending to shoot the chief, but Hector D'Amato beat her to it. I'm not excusing intent, but it's obvious she's innocent of murder."

Judge Aaron cites more evidence. "Her fingerprints were not on the weapon used to kill Redford McAlester. Nor were there any powder burns on her hands at the time of her arrest. Because of Hector D'Amato's obvious motive for killing Redford McAlester, because of his knowledge of the Billy home and its contents, and now, because a witness has come forward who saw Hector with Mrs. Susan Billy's gun in his hand, the Choctaw court finds Hector D'Amato guilty of murdering Redford McAlester, Seventh Chief of the Choctaw Nation."

Sarah Bernhardt grins widely and stands up to leave the witness box.

However, Judge Aaron orders her to sit down while he gives her a tongue lashing for not coming forward earlier. "You have nothing to fear from this tribal court," he says sternly.

"Yes sir, I deserve your anger, but go easy on me, I'm just a poor old worn-out porcupine."

"What's that?" he asks, cocking his ear.

"*Pokni,*" says Bernhardt. "I meant to say *Pokni.* Grandmother, Your Honor."

"You're dismissed, little Grandmother, the court thanks you."

With that, Gore stands. "I ask the court, in light of this new evidence, to drop all charges against my client, Auda Billy."

"Any objections from the tribe's prosecutor?" asks the judge.

"None, Your Honor. But we reserve the right to recall Auda Billy in other criminal matters relating to Redford McAlester, as well as in our investigation of the murders of Delores Love and Isaac Billy." The tribal prosecutor pauses, pulling out another file. "And in the case of Vergie Reagan, a hygienist who allegedly injected Ms. Billy with insulin."

"That's agreeable," says Gore.

"Motion granted, Mr. Battiste."

With that, Auda loses her chance to convince anyone that she was a murderer. Neither her sisters nor her lawyer believe her any longer. She feels defeated. She asks Tema and Borden to drive her home, especially since her mother and Sarah Bernhardt are nowhere to be found.

Over the next few days she lies in bed trying to put her life in order. What will she do? Where will she go? When Gore brings her more papers to sign, he begins filling in the details of what is happening at the federal level.

"The FBI shut down Shamrock Resorts. They're still investigating, but McAlester's accounts at Citisavings Bank Corporation were part of a very complex money laundering scheme in the United States, Ireland, England, and the Cayman Islands. Citisavings Bank officials had ignored some of their own safeguards against the laundering of illicit funds. They'd moved millions from McAlester's accounts and never asked for standard information on his financial background, and made virtually no effort to verify the source of his money. Even when Citisavings finally warned the Feds of McAlester's suspicious transactions, the bank failed to tell the government about the network of foreign 'shell accounts' they had set up to shield McAlester's money."

"That's interesting," she says, flatly.

"Auda, you can't stay in bed forever."

She pulls her face into a blank mask. "Why not?"

"Your family needs you, and the Choctaws need a leader who knows how to fight and how to compromise."

"Clichés."

"It's the truth. You said you wanted to help the tribe; that doesn't always mean you get what you want."

"Are you saying you understand why I didn't expose McAlester to the Feds?"

"I'm not saying that, it's just something that James Joyce said."

"What?"

Gore imitates an Irish accent. "She's good for metaphors. Her perseverance unraveled every stitch of his sweater.'"

"Meaning?"

"That you were determined to finish McAlester's story."

It is her turn to be surprised. "Perfect, the only person who understood us both was an incoherent, melancholic agent for the Irish Republican Army."

"Look, many tribal and BIA officials are coming forward to testify before the Choctaw Superior Court about what they know about McAlester's deals," he says. "You should be proud; their testimonies will mean the end of their careers. Early retirement—or worse."

Auda swings her legs out of bed and sits up. "Why haven't you told me about the investigation into my uncle and aunt's murders?" she asks. "That's all I really care about. Catching Vico D'Amato!"

"The FBI believes Vico D'Amato is already dead. But they're hunting him. They've traced his movements through credit cards and phone logs to Philadelphia, Mississippi, shortly before Isaac and Delores were killed. D'Amato probably asked Delores and Isaac where the ten million was and when they couldn't—or didn't—tell him, he shot them. D'Amato became too visible. By the time the FBI finds him, he'll be nothing but bones."

"You believe that?"

"Absolutely. Right now I'm much more worried about Hoppy. These past three weeks have been hardest on him. He blames himself for Isaac's and Delores' deaths. After the Choctaws buried McAlester, he'd offered to stay with Isaac and Delores at the mound, but Isaac told him to head back to Oklahoma.

"I know what happened, then."

"How do you know?"

"I just know, that's all."

"Tell me."

"Isaac and Delores stayed at the mound to look for something."

"What was that?" asks Gore.

"Their destiny. When the police found them, they'd both been shot in Uncle's truck. Their heads were facing east," she says.

"That's right."

"Toward the Nanih Waiya."

"Yes," he says.

She doesn't answer, but expects him to figure it out.

An October wind blows through Durant, cooling things off. Auda smells fall, which always makes her feel more serene. She gets up out of her bed and resolves to go out into the world again. Touch the things she hasn't touched in a while. Her oak desk at the Choctaw Nation, her project files, the unopened mail she's left. It is time to pack up her things and bring them home.

After she dresses, she walks down the narrow kitchen stairs, setting her feet in the familiar grooves worn there by the many women who've lived in the house before her. When she reaches the kitchen, the rest of her family are seated around the table playing cards. Tema has a long cigar jammed into the side of her mouth like Arnold Schwarzenegger. Gore holds his cigar between his thumb and forefinger as if it were a baton.

"Cuban, *huh?*" asks Tema. "Adair, you wanna try a puff?"

"I quit," says Adair, grudgingly.

"Hand it to me, darling," says Borden, shuffling the deck of cards. "You don't even smoke Tema, you'll be sick."

"Borden?" asks Auda, "I thought you'd returned to Dallas. What about *A Doll's House?*"

"Didn't you hear?"

Auda shakes her head no.

"The theater sacked me—sacked us both, actually."

"I'm sorry."

"Don't be. It gave me a chance to come to Durant, save my wife from the Mafia, and then, of course, attend an Indian trial. Imagine that, an actor from England in a Choctaw Indian Court!"

"Auda, didn't I tell you the whole story?" asks Tema.

"I don't think so," she says.

"The day Hector the Harpoon broke in, Borden and the cops were hammering on the front door, as I was fighting for my life—and yours—on the stairs."

"She's always upstaging me," he says, smiling.

Auda genuinely likes her brother-in-law. She walks over and gives him a hug. "I'm in your debt, Tema." Then to Adair, "I'm also indebted to you. Which reminds me, when are you two getting married?"

"We're off to the Bahamas to spend some of Gore's money," laughs Adair. "Or I should say, our money."

"Speaking of traveling, Auda," says Borden. "You must come to London and see Tema and me in *The Taming of the Shrew*. Our agent called today—the director wants us both."

"That's wonderful news," she says. Then, turning to her mother, "We could go together, couldn't we!"

"I'd like that," replies Susan Billy.

"Where is Hoppy?" asks Auda. "I have something that may cheer him up."

"Gone with Dovie and Kelly to feed GeorgeBush," says Adair.

"What do you have, my girl?" Susan Billy walks across the room and puts an arm around Auda's waist.

"It's Uncle Isaac's good luck stone," she says. "He gave it to me to give to Hoppy."

Auda watches her mother finger the gray stone. Since Delores' and Isaac's murders, her mother is more withdrawn. Her hair looks almost completely gray now.

"Yes, it's always belonged to a powerful leader," says Susan Billy. "I think Hoppy should have it." Her mother walks into the library and returns with the porcupine sash and two burden baskets filled with loose shells. She wraps the sash around Auda's waist, and divides the turtle shells among her other daughters.

"These are very old: the leather twine that once held the shells together snapped a long time ago, before Nowatima carried them with her from Mississippi to Oklahoma. All we have left are the shells. The porcupine sash and the shells once belonged to a descendent of Grandmother of Birds. If we're lucky, maybe they'll survive another generation or two. Who knows?"

Auda examines the loose shells, feeling the curved edges of the turtle's mantle. All around her are the family she loves. Despite the sorrow they've suffered the Billys seem once again full of hope.

"Thank you Mother, these mean a lot to us," says Auda.

Susan Billy then turns to Tema and Adair. "These burden baskets belonged to two of our ancestors, Haya and Anoleta. You've probably heard me tell the stories about them. They used these baskets to carry supplies when we fought the Chickasaws in 1747. The baskets were their legacy and I want you each to have one. I know you will cherish them as I have."

Auda kisses Adair on the cheek, then Tema. Each of her sisters stifles tears. Her mother pulls out tissues from her skirt pocket and hands them to her daughters.

"Over the years," Susan says, "I've cried a million tears. I feel like I was crying in the womb. Maybe I was crying for all my sisters who were stillborn before me, I don't know. Nowatima said I was born crying. She said she knew I was going to make it because my tears were healing the deep wounds that I came into this world with. Somehow they have—and although I'm mourning the loss of my dear brother and Delores, I am through with tears."

And then her mother's voice, low as though filtered through cotton says, "I want you to know how proud I am of you all, and for the way you came together as a family. You girls are my true essence."

The house is suddenly warm as wool, and alive with the ghosts of aunts and uncles, and future relatives. Auda feels renewed as she walks upstairs to put away the porcupine sash that once belonged to Shakbatina. As she stands in front of her mirror, she sees some other woman's face staring back at her, radiant and bright with anticipation. Someone she's never seen before.

17 | The Shell Shaker

Now I must tell you what really happened. Since I had acquired the knowledge of splitting myself in two, I must be the one to tell the story of *Itilauichi*, who came back to Choctaw Country when day and night were in perfect balance, and Indians had all the luck.

My story is an enormous undertaking. Hundreds of years in the making until past and present collide into a single moment. Auda did hold the gun in her hands, gently, as if it were inlaid with jewels. It was then that I slipped my hands in front of her hands, and together we struck a pose. The day was hers, all hers, but it was my day, too.

Nuklibishakachi, my breath is warm with passion; we Choctaws are *hatak okla hut okchaya bilia hoh illi bilia.* Life everlasting.

Hekano, I am finished talking.

Author Note

Shell Shaker is fiction and the portraits of all the characters appearing in it are fictional, as are some of the events and journeys. Still, some of the characters who appear in the novel are based on historical figures, such as Red Shoes, Bienville, Choucououlacta, Stung Serpent, and Chépart, and many of the areas described-such as Yanàbi Town and Ahepatanichi River-existed.

Primary documents were important in my research: *Mississippi Provincial Archives, French Dominion,* vols. I-III (Press of the Mississippi Department of Archives and History), *Mississippi Provincial Archives, French Dominion,* vols. IV and V (Louisiana State University Press), the Smithsonian's National Anthropological Archives, Cyrus Byington's papers, and the papers and recordings of Frances Densmore.

Secondary documents I consulted were Richard White's *The Roots of Dependency;* Patricia Galloway's *Choctaw Genesis; The Hernando de Soto Expedition,* edited by Patricia Galloway; *Iberville's Gulf Journals,* translated by Richebourg Gaillard McWilliams; and *Journal of Paul du Ru, (February 1, May 8, 1700) Missionary Priest to Louisiana,* translated from a manuscript in The Newberry Library with an introduction and notes by Ruth Lapham Butler. In creating the character of Red Shoes, I relied on Richard White's article "Red Shoes: Warrior and Diplomat," Joe Wilkins' article "Outposts of Empire: The Founding of Fort Tombecbé' and de Bienville's Chickasaw Expedition of 1736," and I used statements by Alibamon Mingo about Red Shoes' birthright to conclude that Red Shoes' mother was not Choctaw. For the character of Jean Baptiste Le Moyne Sieur de Bienville, I relied on Grace King's biography by the same name.

Some liberties have been taken with the Choctaw language in the novel. I use the verb *Itilauichi,* meaning "to even," as a noun for "Autumnal Equinox." After studying the historical Choctaw calendar names in Byington's dictionary and in his papers at the Smithsonian, as well as Henry S. Halbert's articles on the Choctaw language and culture, I reasoned that there may have been phrases used by early eighteenth-century Choctaws for the equinoxes that have fallen out of use. Important events for Choctawan people seem to have taken place around the autumnal and vernal equinoxes, and the summer and winter solstices. For example, on June 21 or 22, 1847 (depending on whose report you read), after twenty-two Choctaw towns united, Red Shoes was assassinated when the Sun went down.

Another story concerns the meeting between Hernando de Soto and Choctaw leader Tuscalusa. Documents tell us that on September 17, 1540, the Spaniards reached Talisi and found it evacuated, but with rich supplies that had been left behind. One explanation is that the towns-people had left for their yearly ceremonies. At Talisi, a runner, accompanied by a man assumed to be one of Tuscalusa's sons, finally came with a message from Tuscalusa. De Soto sent them back to Tuscalusa to gather more information. The Spaniards, meanwhile, stayed in Talisi until September 25, after the Autumnal Equinox, when Tuscalusa finally appeared with supplies, food, carriers, and women for de Soto. I suggest the reason for Tuscalusa's delay was that he was collecting warriors at a ceremonial gathering who would help attack de Soto at Mabila on October 18. Planning attacks on enemies during times of ceremonial gatherings was commonplace in the Southeast. Some two centuries later, in March, 1731, Red Shoes used the same strategy as Tuscalusa. He traveled to a community gathering, telling the French allies he was attending a stickball game. Once there, he assembled a group of warriors and made an attack on his enemies.

The word *Osano,* used in the novel to mean "horsefly" or "blood-sucker" comes from a song by Choctaw Sidney Wesley, recorded by ethnomusicologist Frances Densmore about January 1933.

According to Densmore, Wesley was the oldest among the Choctaws living around the seven old towns in Mississippi. Wesley's Choctaw name, *Lapin tabe se ihoke,* translates "Kills It Himself." Two recordings of the War Song were made, one containing the phrase "Hispano head man I am looking for," the other, "Folance head man I am looking for." Wesley substituted *Folance* (French) for the reference to the Hispano (Spaniards). Densmore says that Wesley did not know the meaning of either word, but sang the song as he had learned it as a young boy. She also notes that the song has more verses, each defying the head man of a tribe of Indians designated as *Osano.* The tribe could not be identified, but one of Wesley's Choctaw translators said that *Osano* was given to mean "horsefly," a term of contempt. *Osano* is pronounced WAH-sano. There are other Choctaw words for "horsefly," such as *olano.* For more information concerning the Choctaw language see *A Dictionary of the Choctaw Language* by Cyrus Byington.

My translation and spelling of the word *Ahepatanichi* comes from several sources. The *Ahepatanichi* River (designated by Delisle, Carte des Envirns du Missisipi par G. de I'lsle Geographe, 1701), has a variety of spellings. Scholars have suggested it is the Black Warrior River where de Soto and Tuscalusa met. I used _Ahepatanichi_, because I believe it was called that by the _Ahe pata Okla_ people, the Choctaws once belonging to the eastern district of the Nation in Mississippi. The name derived from a place where many wild potatoes grew. _Pata_ means "spread out" in Choctaw. Indeed, modern Choctaws around Daisy, Oklahoma, refer to the mountains in Southeastern Oklahoma as the "Potato Hills." _Tanichi_, part of the root of _Ahepatanichi_, means "to raise, to cause to rise; to raise to life from the grave." For those interested in maps pertaining to the Choctaw, I suggest Galloway's chapter in _Choctaw Genesis_ (1995, 205-263).

Concerning the factions of the Choctaws, I have tried to remain faithful to the divisions present in the eighteenth century. The western and the eastern factions supported, at various times, different European allies. Even after removal, Choctaws continued to refer to themselves by three distinct regions. What is most interesting to me in the eighteenth century is that towns within these regions seem to have practiced slightly different, but related, ceremonies. Some towns had shell shakers, some towns had gourd dancers, and in some towns dancers used eagle feather fans. I believe that much more research and investigation into eighteenth-century Choctaw history will reveal a diversity of practices, and I urge more Choctaws to investigate the documents and their family histories to write their stories.

In the case of the Seven Grandmothers in the novel, I have used the story of the seven venerable women from "Story of the Treaty of Dancing Rabbit" by H.S. Halbert (_Mississippi Historical Society_, vol. VI).

A final note about location: Yanàbi Town was located in modern Kemper County, Mississippi, not far from the Sucarnoochee River to the west. Yanàbi Town was part of the eastern factions, loyal to the French. The Nanih Waiya is located north and west of Yanàbi Town. For more information about Choctaw towns, see John Howard Blitz's _Archaeological Report on Choctaw Indians of Mississippi_ (1985).

Before writing fiction, plays, and scholarly essays, **LeAnne Howe** worked in Oklahoma as a waitress, and in a factory making the stems for plastic champagne glasses. She has worked on Wall Street for a securities investment firm, she has been a journalist. Most recently she has taught at Carleton College, Grinnell College, Sinte Gleska University on Rosebud Sioux Reservation, and at Wake Forest University. Ms. Howe is an enrolled member of the Choctaw Nation of Oklahoma.

AUNT LUTE BOOKS is a multicultural women's press that has been committed to publishing high quality, culturally diverse literature since 1982. In 1990, the Aunt Lute Foundation was formed as a non-profit corporation to publish and distribute books that reflect the complex truths of women's lives and the possibilities for personal and social change. We seek work that explores the specificities of the very different histories from which we come, and that examines the intersections between the borders we all inhabit.

Please write, phone or e-mail (books@auntlute.com) us if you would like us to send you a free catalog of our other books or if you wish to be on our mailing list for future titles. You may buy books directly from us by phoning in a credit card order or mailing a check with the catalog order form.

Please visit our website at www.auntlute.com.

Aunt Lute Books
P.O. Box 410687
San Francisco, CA 94141
415 826 1300

This book would not have been possible without the kind contributions of the Aunt Lute Founding Friends:

Anonymous Donor
Anonymous Donor
Rusty Barcelo
Marian Bremer
Marta Drury
Diane Goldstein

Diana Harris
Phoebe Robins Hunter
Diane Mosbacher, M.D., Ph.D.
William Preston, Jr.
Elise Rymer Turner